TEA SET AND MATCH
TEA PRINCESS CHRONICLES BOOK 2
CASEY BLAIR

TEA SET AND MATCH
Tea Princess Chronicles: Book 2

Copyright © 2022 Casey Blair,
All rights reserved.

No part of this edition may be reproduced, distributed, transmitted, or used in any manner whatsoever without permission in writing from the author, except in the case of brief quotations in a book review. For permission requests, email Casey.L.Blair@gmail.com.

This book is a work of fiction. Names, characters, places, and events are either the product of the author's imagination or are used fictitiously. Any resemblance to actual persons, living or dead, events, or locales is entirely coincidental.

Cover design by Hampton Lamoureux of TS95 Studios, 2021.
Author photograph by Mariah Bush, 2013.

Ebook ISBN: 9798985110128.
Paperback ISBN: 9798985110135.

www.caseyblair.com

CHAPTER 1

I STAND ALONE IN the dingy common space of my new apartment, ready to leave for the tea shop if for no other reason than I can perhaps feel more settled there.

"I'm heading out," I venture toward Risteri's door.

It's a compromise we've reached in the last few days. I don't like announcing my comings and goings, because it makes me feel beholden in my own home. I've had more than enough of that.

But I like less how Risteri, who has had to pay such attention to the presence of others in her home to sneak around her father's plotting for years, watches me so closely.

So I've agreed to verbalize my movements, and she's agreed to make an effort to not scrutinize every one of them.

Her habits of secrecy are deeply entrenched, though, so these announcements are one-sided and more often than not leave me speaking to an inanimate piece of wood.

A clatter sounds from the kitchen, reminding me I am not, in truth, alone in the apartment, despite Risteri's absence.

I sigh and turn to see what mischief my tea spirit familiar has managed this time.

Our apartment is small, so I'm able to cross quickly enough to catch the next plate Yorani bats off the counter with her tail.

Caring for Yorani takes its own adjustments.

The tiny blue dragon bounces on the counter, delighted—with my attention or her success in breaking another plate, I'm not certain.

It's not that we aren't neat, but I'll have to remind Risteri that leaving anything delicate out where Yorani can access it—which is everywhere, because she is small and devious and *can fly*—will soon see us with no dishes left.

No sooner do I set the rescued dish back atop the pile than Yorani's tail swipes out again. Because of course now this is a game.

I pick up the whole stack and open cupboards—only barely, because Yorani is following me and huffing annoyed whorls of smoke over my shoulder—until I find one that can accommodate the dishes. I've not yet managed to block Yorani effectively from entering the cupboards to wreak havoc, so instead I secure her under one arm while I shepherd the dishes to safety.

By the time she wiggles out of my hold, I've succeeded.

She flies in front of my face and puffs smoke into my eyes.

"No, little one." I crouch to gather the ceramic pieces off the ground. "We do not break things for fun."

Unfortunately, what exactly tea spirits can safely do for fun remains a mystery.

The Te Muraka tried gifting her with a lovely set of colorful marbles. Yorani proceeded to systematically break them in unique ways: using one to shatter a window, cracking open another, melting a third.

Given how the marbles were forged Sa Nikuran was particularly impressed by the last, which fortunately meant she wasn't offended by the rampant destruction.

"Let's at least get you a change of scenery." I snag Yorani out of the air by one foot as she flies circles around my head, and wish my motivation was solely for her sake.

Holding onto Yorani, I gather my tea kit from the common area. Although there's a bedroom each for both Risteri and me, the apartment's increased number of walls was its key selling point, and the principle there still discomfits me.

I've been assured the existence of such walls makes it one of the nicest apartments in the neighborhood we moved into. We stayed near the Gaellani night market by her family estate, mostly out of fondness for and a semblance of familiarity with the community, as neither of us has lived on our own before.

But we also hope my presence—even on the outskirts, as we don't wish to force ourselves upon the Gaellani or worsen their space constraints—might serve as a form of pressure to the council.

I will know as near to firsthand as possible how the council's decisions impact the community's everyday lives, and perhaps pressure from a tea master will help improve conditions that should long since have been addressed.

And yet, while I understand the apartment is comparatively spacious, inside I feel—unreasonable though I know it is—boxed in.

I'm sure it will feel cozy once I've adjusted. Risteri and I only moved in about a week ago.

I still find our setup mildly distressing when I think about it too hard.

I would have preferred to take my time, filling my space carefully with pieces that speak to me, and us, and deliberately make this a home.

But life did not allow for such deliberation: we needed to move immediately. So our apartment is full of cheap furniture we hope to replace as we do find time and funds, as well as gifts passed along from acquaintances, a mismatch of clashing patterns and incomplete sets and adaptations to tide us through.

In a way, that in and of itself makes it a home: a product of our reality, a reality we both chose and strove toward, as well as a product of our community. I am humbled by our community's generosity, by their excitement to welcome us by helping us set up however they could.

I remind myself of that, when I feel less content, because I don't deserve to be.

Humbled, too, to be able to have the freedom to even try to make my own way. The spirits blessed me with a path to be myself, complete with opportunities to be of service, people I want to deepen connections with.

Settling in, feeling comfortable with my space here, will come if I step back and give myself time. To listen, to reflect.

Surely.

"Miyara!" Lorwyn snaps as soon as I enter the back. "I'm not allowed to set this spirits-cursed mage on fire, and since it's your fault I'm saddled with him you owe me."

"I'm not going to set him on fire either," I say without particular concern. She's greeted me with some variation of this every day since her magecraft training began.

"And it's you who owes me," Ostario tells Lorwyn. "Specifically, you owe a stable version of the spell I assigned you to master."

"I'm working on it," Lorwyn growls, absently intercepting Yorani when she heads straight for the restored tea pet and pointing her instead at a pile of sticks—probably what Lorwyn's supposed to be using for the spell. I'm overcome with envy at how effortless redirecting Yorani is for her. "I'm not exactly overflowing with free time."

"I never told you this would be easy," Ostario says. "I just told you to make it work."

Lorwyn scowls, and as she tosses her hair with the motion I notice how messy it is, when she always looks so put-together.

And then that she's wearing the same clothes as yesterday.

"Did you sleep here last night?" I ask.

"More like half the night," she grumps. "I need more tea. Will you collect your tea spirit before she jumps in the kettle again?"

I sigh, but it's not Lorwyn's job to dragon-sit Yorani. "That's the third night this week." I steel myself for Yorani's ire when I interrupt her enthusiastic gouging into the sticks.

Perhaps I should find a pile of sticks to bring back to the apartment, but Yorani will probably consider them boring if she thinks I can bear their destruction with equanimity.

"Well, I couldn't do anything useful at home without interference, and it's not like anyone would be here," Lorwyn says.

Ostario says, "You're going to need to learn how to maintain focus and control in chaotic environments. The best way to do that is from the beginning."

Lorwyn rolls her eyes. "Have you ever shared a bedroom with five younger sisters? No? That's what I thought."

Yorani darts out of reach as I go to grab her. I close my eyes briefly. "I admit practicing among chaos seems like a worry for a time when you're both more certain of her control."

Mildly, Ostario says, "I'm certain it's none of your business."

I flush, and bow. He's right.

Lorwyn sighs, somehow managing to get a hold of Yorani and passing her to me without even trying. "Honestly though, it's actually worse than usual, even for my family, what with all the people moving into town."

"You mean the Te Muraka?" I wince as Yorani scrambles onto my shoulder, her claws digging in with so little finesse I suspect she's poking me on purpose.

"No, lots of foreigners, actually," Lorwyn says.

"Really?"

"There's some kind of event maybe? I haven't exactly had time to pay attention." She glares at Ostario.

I'd noticed the increased traffic, but it hadn't occurred to me it wouldn't be related to the Te Muraka—tourists coming to gawk, bureaucrats coming to work on their transition.

My sisters.

Ostario says, "Miyara, if you wouldn't mind, my apprentice and I should continue this lesson privately."

I bow once more, shallowly due to Yorani's perch, and take my leave.

The chaos that sisters will bring is for another time. Spirits be thanked, today my greatest challenge will be to be content with my place here.

I perform the tea ceremony for a customer for the first time since the dramatic events of recent days, and I revel in it.

This, at least, feels right. Using my skills, and the position I earned, to serve my community. To be working toward something sure.

I'll face tests in the future. But for now, this is one piece of my life that has fallen into place.

It helps that, thankfully, Yorani seems content to sit quietly for this: she's curled up on the cushion I've placed in the corner for her.

So I lose myself in the movements of the ceremony, in the catharsis of drawing forth the parts of myself and building the bridge the customer needs today. I look up at the customer as I pour, although their attention has focused on the cups.

Which means I'm the only one who sees the steam rise out of the teapot as I pour.

I'm the only one who sees the strange wispy animal shape it forms, just for an instant, before it shimmers away.

Did that truly just happen?

I blink and glance down. The steam floating out of the dragon teapot looks utterly normal now, but it occurs to me this is the first time I've made tea with it since I made Yorani.

She's not looking either, having apparently settled in for a nap.

I turn my attention back to the customer, to serving them, and wonder what I just saw and what it means—or whether I imagined it entirely.

When the customer and I emerge—Yorani, to my surprise, is content for the moment to continue napping—I discover Tea Master Karekin waiting.

I bow.

But when I straighten and see his careful expression, my chest tightens in sudden warning.

Something has happened.

"Tea Master Karekin, it is my honor as always. How may I serve you today?"

"Would you join me?" He gestures at the empty seat at his table. "We have matters to discuss."

My heart rate accelerates. "Of course. Please give me just a moment to check on the shop."

He nods assent, and I do a quick round of the front, trying not to panic before I have any information, but that in itself worries me.

I know how fast change can happen. I've proven it, these past weeks.

But how did something change fast enough I had no inkling it was coming?

Meristo is on shift today, so at least I don't have to worry about leaving the front in his care. I let him know I'll be meeting with the tea master, offer up a silent prayer to the spirits, and return to the table with a tea tray.

As I busy myself with serving, I say, "I admit I didn't expect to see you again quite so soon. How have you been?"

Karekin snorts. "Busy and put-upon, as you might expect. I've been fielding a lot of questions from our colleagues, and I have news for you."

I hoped doing something with my hands would help calm my thoughts, but this is not the case. I set down the teapot.

"I notice you don't specify whether the news is good or bad," I say.

A smile flickers across his face. "Indeed. But I'm sure you can guess the subject."

I take a bracing sip of tea. "My mastery is provisional. You told me to expect further evaluation at a later date, but I'd assumed it would be a somewhat later one."

"So had I," Karekin says. "But our colleagues think it best to expedite the matter."

I study him. "Is this because of Yorani?"

"In part," he says. "A tea spirit hasn't been seen in generations. The sooner we can induct you completely into the tea guild, the better, and that requires more than a provisional mastery. We guard a great deal of knowledge, and as you've brought some of it to the forefront of public consciousness, my colleagues wish to be sure there is no question of you."

"Because I was a princess," I say softly, "and the tea guild must be known as impartial even if that information becomes public knowledge, too."

"I wish I could reassure you that isn't part of it," Karekin says frankly. I grip my teacup tightly, able to focus on his next words only because I know he has never cared about my history. "But it's possible your background may come out one day, and it will behoove you to have demonstrated beyond a shadow of a doubt that there can be no question in the *public's* eye that you have earned your position. Given your dramatic ascension into our ranks, there will be challenges to the validity of your appointment and the neutrality of the tea guild's judgment. It is not to anyone's advantage to allow that to fester."

He's right.

But at the same time, this is also a rationalization, and as I meet his eyes silently, I see we both know it.

The tea guild has centuries of an unassailable reputation for clear judgment. They could choose to stand behind me and affirm my appointment without putting me through further testing, without making me prove to them or anyone else, again, that I belong.

That is not what they have chosen.

I sip my tea again, letting that understanding pass through me and the emotions it causes with it, and when I speak again my voice is carefully even.

"I take it," I say, "a testing opportunity the tea guild deems satisfactory has presented itself."

Karekin's eyes narrow, noting my word choice. He has referred to "our colleagues," because he wishes me to feel as though this is part of service to a common cause.

I will call them "the tea guild," separate and impersonal, because that is how they are treating me.

And Karekin makes a choice with his next words as he says, "We have."

Not *they*.

I may have his respect, but he will not treat me as a tea master in truth until the rest of the guild does.

Perhaps I should have expected that, but I did not.

The degree to which that stings, though. That does not surprise me in the slightest.

Saiyana did always say my trust in people would hurt me. As a tea master, I thought I could demonstrate the opposite.

Perhaps I am not a tea master in truth after all.

Perhaps my place here *is* assailable.

This time, when I pick up my teacup, I raise my walls the way I learned long ago, disciplining my movements into smoothness.

Tea Master Karekin will see no more of myself than I wish him to, now.

I ignore the note of regret in his expression. I could manufacture such an expression if I thought it would help my cause, and so can he. His regret does not change that he is standing by what he has chosen. "Tell me about the test."

And this I say not as a supplicant.

Karekin nods thoughtfully. "Are you familiar with the Top Tea Specialist Tournament?"

I blink. "I've read profiles of the winners, though I don't know much about the actual competition."

"Then let me summarize the salient points briefly," Karekin says. "The competition is an international, annual event ostensibly to determine the best tea specialist from among the continental nations."

"The Isle of Nakrab is not invited to participate?"

"The Isle of Nakrab has disdained the very suggestion of participation," Karekin says, "though they are free to change that position at any time. Throughout the history of the tournament, the tea guild has also been invited to participate, and has declined to."

Ah. "Until now."

"Until now," Karekin agrees. "The guild typically offers an exhibition during the tournament or a private consultation to the winner to acknowledge this gesture, so as not to appear aloof to the many people who hold it in high esteem. But since the tournament's foundation, the organizers have always reserved a spot for a tea master in the finals in the hope we will one day take them up on it. For the first time, the guild has decided to."

The tournament organizers are clever, then—if the tea guild did offer to compete, not only would the tournament earn incredible publicity, it would be in a position to judge the tea guild's worth, positioning the almighty tea guild as supplicants, their reputation subject to subjective challenge. Which is of course why the organizers could safely assume they'd never have to make arrangements to accommodate the tea guild and could instead use the courtesy of their relationship to wrangle legitimacy out of them.

But apparently the organizers are willing to make good on their offer after all.

"Have you already entered me in this tournament?" I ask.

Karekin shakes his head. "Not yet, no. With your agreement, we will. But we did arrange for the tournament finals to be held here in Sayorsen. Although you won't have the sponsorship resources of the other contestants, the tournament experience, or the time to mentally prepare, the only new environment you'll have to adapt to is the tournament itself."

I let out a breath.

He's not trying to make me leave. At least there's that.

Under the circumstances I wonder if I would have left my place in this community for the sake of my place among the tea masters.

For the first time, they're at odds, and that in turn makes me wonder if it will be the last time.

And although Tea Master Karekin may not be wholly behind me, he's not abandoned me entirely either. That is something, though *what*, I'm not sure.

"That was very thoughtful of you," I say. "If I refuse to join the tournament, what will the tea guild owe the tournament?"

"The tea guild's commitments under that circumstance are not your concern, and I think it best you not have the option to consider them in making your choice," Karekin says.

"I am not inclined to feel especially gracious toward the guild at the moment," I say blandly.

He inclines his head, not disputing my interpretation of how this is playing out. "But you are gracious by nature, so nevertheless I will keep this to myself."

I narrow my eyes. "So all the people who've been arriving in Sayorsen, then, are here for the tournament?"

"Spectators, officials, and the people who make up the tea specialists' teams, yes. If you agree to participate, you'll be facing the final three contestants in a series of challenges that will test your tea mastery in the public eye, where anyone and everyone can judge for themselves whether you merit the name of master. Do you understand the terms of the test?"

Oh, I understand enough.

I understand this is, at its core, a very common reality, and yet I find that makes it no less infuriating to face.

I understand I found a place for myself. I worked for it. And despite that, it can be taken away from me—by the people who could have supported me, who instead expect me to represent them but will dismiss who I am in the service of their goals.

Like my family. But that contest, at least, is still in my future.

Because if I want to keep my place, I will have to fight for it.

"To clarify," I say, "will I be representing the tea guild in this tournament?"

Karekin tilts his hand this way and that as if to say, *yes and no.* "You will be representing yourself as a nominee by the tea guild," he says carefully.

I look him in the eyes. "Which is to say, the tea guild won't claim me as their representative unless I win."

"Ah. Let me state explicitly perhaps the most important point. If you win, the tea guild will publicly claim you as a tea master. If you lose, your provisional mastery will be revoked."

"And if I refuse to compete?" I know the answer, but I want him to have to tell it to me honestly.

"Also then," Karekin confirms, his nose wrinkling in distaste.

Even if the reaction is feigned, I do feel better for seeing it on him.

"I dislike how you have maneuvered this, Master Karekin."

"As do I," he says. "Nevertheless, these are the terms of the test. Do you accept this challenge?"

I am worried.

But I'm surprised that I am also angry, and the latter, at the moment, outweighs the former.

Nevertheless, I know how I will choose.

"I do, if you'll answer one question," I say.

His eyebrows lift. "Oh?"

"You didn't bother to negotiate a consequence for the tea guild in case I refused the challenge," I say, "did you."

Karekin smiles faintly. "No. I knew you would not give up so easily."

I nod. "And I will not."

And with that, I am committed.

I have one chance to fight to keep the place I have made, the life I am making—every part of it.

One tournament will decide my course.

CHAPTER 2

DESPITE MY RUSH TO get to the tea shop that morning, I'm gone the instant my shift ends, carrying Yorani until she grumpily perches on my shoulder.

One thing I've learned these last weeks is I can't truly serve others by negating myself. I need time separate from service to re-center, but I don't really have that time. I'm due to meet Deniel this evening: we've planned to make something of a celebration of, at last, introducing Yorani to Talsion.

We hoped treats might help kindly dispose them toward each other. I've already acquired Talsu's gift: imported fish snacks. Thiano was so amused I'd ask him for such a thing he charged me a reasonable rate.

If I could have predicted what Yorani's mood would be like today, though, we'd be headed back to my apartment instead. Yorani spent the afternoon trying my patience, and I've seen no reason to believe she'll tire of it soon. But Deniel is taking the time to cook for me, and I will be attempting dessert. So we will try, despite the ominous portent of Yorani's tail whipping against my neck in a steady rhythm.

I head to the same Gaellani night market Risteri introduced me to weeks ago for ingredients, overwhelmed by the prospect of trying something so new, today, in front of Deniel, *for* him. It's not that he'll mind if it doesn't work—I will. And he'll be happy to help, but we are trying to contribute equally to this evening's planning and he is already hosting while I am bringing a vexed tea spirit and all my worries.

I take a deep breath, closing my eyes for a moment and blocking everything but Yorani's tail smacking my neck.

Thwap. Thwap. Thwap. Thwap thwap thwap thwap—

"Spirits, Yorani, what is it?" I open my eyes. But she's not looking at me, her attention caught by something in the distance. I try to follow her gaze, but instead my attention is caught by something.

Or rather, someone.

Ashen hair quickly ducks away into the crowd. Not hiding, exactly, but—blending.

A skill I know well.

I'm also somehow certain they were watching me.

I continue deeper into the market, hoping this isn't a mistake, wishing, unexpectedly, Entero were guarding me once again. There's still been no word from him.

After another minute, I'm sure this girl—most likely; Gaellani boys typically don't wear their hair long—is following me. She looks around the age of ten, perhaps a bit older.

I try to keep a covert eye on her as I move through the market, where no one appears to even see her.

Except Yorani, who tries to take flight off my shoulder.

I snag her foot. "No, little one. Not just yet."

I pause at a kiosk, making myself clearly available, wondering if the girl will approach.

I pick up a jar full of something cream-colored and ask the shopkeeper what it is.

"Sweet bean filling," she says.

"Like for stuffed honey pancakes?" I ask, and inspiration strikes. Perhaps given my lack of focus tonight I can attempt a simpler dessert, but still something new. "Do you know how hard they are to make?"

The woman smiles and launches into an explanation of how it's done, and when I move on it's with a different shopping list than I came with.

The weight of the evening suddenly feels less heavy. Perhaps what I need is a distraction, not time alone with my thoughts to brood. Yorani has calmed down, too, as if waiting to see what I'll do with the girl who is still shadowing us, hunching a bit into her worn clothes as the temperature drops.

I don't know why this girl is following me in the cold yet won't approach. If she weren't Gaellani I'd be more concerned. But the people who might have reason to concern themselves with my activities either don't associate with Gaellani or wouldn't rely on children.

Untrained children, at any rate. I imagine Entero started his work young.

So I won't force this girl into a confrontation. Instead I stop at another kiosk selling steaming beverages and pay for a cup of warm milk with honey.

I shake my head when the shopkeeper goes to pour and describe the girl to him. "If she passes this way, please give it to her," I say, bowing before I take my leave.

※

When Deniel opens his door, the frazzled state of his hair tells me his day has not likely gone a great deal better than mine.

But his expression brightens immediately upon seeing me, and that goes a long way toward improving mine.

"Yorani, it's a pleasure to see you again," Deniel says, bowing toward my shoulder.

Yorani chirps at him, accepting this as her due, and we head inside.

I am trying to set my bags down gracefully when Yorani's claws dig into my shoulder. I freeze, not sure whether dropping the bags will startle her into something rash or if I'm going to need both hands free to restrain her.

"Easy," Deniel murmurs, bending down to pick up Talsu, whose fur seems fluffier than usual. "Talsion, this is Yorani, a tea spirit in Miyara's care. Yorani, this is Talsion, a cat who deigns to visit my home on a regular basis."

Yorani and Talsu lean toward each other hesitantly, sniffing.

Then Yorani abruptly stands up on her hind legs, startling Talsu, who hisses and reflexively bats out with his paw.

I take a quick step backwards, pulling Yorani out of range with me, as Deniel quickly carries Talsu across the room, murmuring softly.

But Talsu squirms enough that Deniel releases the cat, setting him down on the floor where he immediately takes a couple steps back toward me and Yorani.

Who immediately launches off my shoulder.

I do drop the bags then, heedlessly, sending Talsion shooting away with the suddenness so I can yank Yorani back.

Yorani breathes smoke in my face, thrashing.

"Miyara, Talsion is fine," Deniel says, as the cat pokes his tiny furry head around the edge of the sofa, watching Yorani's wings beat frantically.

I sigh, drawing Yorani closer to me with both hands. She tilts her head back and opens her mouth, and I see the light of a spark in the back of her throat.

"Talsu is important, and I will be very unhappy if you upset him," I say. "Please be careful. Do you understand?"

I have no idea if Yorani understands anything I say, let alone the concept of "careful." But the spark dies, and she huffs smoke at me once more. She's stopped struggling.

I feel, strangely, as though she's just rolled her eyes at me.

I let her go.

Yorani immediately flutters to the ground, and she and Talsion take each other's measure from across the room, approaching and circling slowly.

Deniel motions for me to stay back, and I follow his lead, keeping a watchful eye as the two get closer and closer. They sniff each other, heads in constant motion.

Then Yorani darts in quickly, and Talsu, not missing a beat, whaps her on the nose.

But either Talsion didn't use his claws or they don't affect Yorani's scales, because my familiar only looks startled, blinking.

Talsion eyes her for another few seconds before turning primly and sauntering away.

Yorani glances back at me, as if unsure. I smile and nod, hoping this is helpful and not encouraging something dire.

My baby dragon turns and waddles after the cat, chirping.

"We should keep an eye on them," Deniel says, "but I think that went as well as we could expect."

I will take his word for it. "What about the treats?"

"Let's save them," Deniel says. "I think they'll be more useful as a nice break or reward later."

"In that case, I'll—oh," I say, finally noticing the result of my sudden dropping of the bags.

Namely, that a bag of flour has split, spreading white powder across the floor.

"I hope you didn't need all that flour," Deniel says, amused.

I sigh, spotting a dribble of liquid. "Or the eggs. I'm sorry, I'll clean it up."

"I'm not worried about it. Why don't I get the stuff and you get the floor? I'll watch the little monsters."

His lips brush my cheek before he bends down into my mess.

Before my face finishes flaming, I hie myself to the closet where he stores cleaning supplies.

When I return, Deniel asks from the kitchen, "Did you change your mind about what to make tonight?"

"Yes," I admit. "Today... it's a long story. I wasn't feeling up to the other recipe. How did the ingredients fare?"

"The flour looks worse than it is, but how many eggs did you need?"

"Two."

"Okay, I have enough for us both then."

I glance up from wiping up the flour. "Did you change your recipe, too?"

Deniel runs a hand through his hair distractedly. "I'm sorry. I meant to do something elaborate tonight, but... I overreached, if I'm being honest. I don't think I'll have time for something like that for a while at the rate I'm going, so I have stuff for noodle bowls—why are you looking at me like that?"

"You still had flour on your hands."

He blinks, looks down at his hands. Closes his eyes. "My hair is full of flour now, isn't it?"

I cross to him and kiss him on the cheek, smiling as Deniel swallows. "A little. You have some on your face, too." I hesitate only a moment—I can still hardly believe I no longer need to restrain the urge to touch Deniel casually.

But I wipe the flour off with one of my towels and pause there, my hand on his cheek, our faces close.

My heart thumps. Touch is not the only new thing between us.

He kisses me slowly, and I melt into him.

Until the sound of chirping makes me tense and draw back.

Talsu is sitting on the small table in front of the couch, and Yorani flies up to join him.

Talsu's ears flick; his tail swishes. With one mighty bound he lands on the top of the couch and starts washing his face, as if to say, *Such prowess is nothing to a cat like me.*

"He's not running away," Deniel says, amused. "I think this is more like he's challenging a tea spirit to a duel."

"That's... good?"

Yorani starts to lift off; stops.

Then she hops.

And hops again, higher, and higher.

"Can the table take that," I murmur.

"We'll find out."

Then with a mighty bounce, Yorani launches herself to the top of the couch too. Though she has to scrabble a bit at the end to keep from slipping.

Talsu eyes Yorani for a moment, then seems to decide either this effort is acceptable or at least merits consideration, and settles on the top of the couch as Yorani wiggles happily.

"Should we preemptively rescue your books?" I ask, gesturing at his tall bookcase. "There aren't many surfaces higher than the couch, are there?"

"There's the roof," Deniel says dryly. "And don't worry, I'm pretty sure Talsu won't let anything happen to his favorite story books."

"It's the law tomes I'm worried about," I say. "I know his opinion on those."

Deniel's expression tightens, but he shakes his head and asks, "Why does Yorani's chirping make you tense? I thought that was a happy sound."

"It is," I say, "but what she considers grounds for happiness is not always in line with what I do. She chirps every time she breaks something."

"Ah," Deniel says, wrapping his arms around me from behind and resting his chin on my shoulder. "I'm sure letting her follow a cat around will definitely not teach her any troubling behaviors."

I lean back into him, reveling in his warmth, in him. "Why did you look unhappy to be reminded about your law books?"

Deniel huffs out a breath that tickles my ear, making me tingle. "You never miss anything. Why don't I get started on dinner while we talk?"

"I suppose that means I have to move," I say regretfully.

"Mm."

I feel him pause.

He kisses the hollow of my throat.

Warmth suffuses me, and I stand utterly still as my heartbeat thunders, not daring to move.

He kisses a line up my jawline, then gently turns me to face him and kisses me again on the mouth.

Everything else has gone wrong today, but this, here, with him, is still right. Better than.

When we finally pull back for air, Deniel's eyes are bright, and his smile looks as earnest as mine feels.

After staring at him besottedly for an eternity, I finally duck my head and take a step back. "We'll never get to eat if you keep that up."

"That would be tragic," he agrees in a soft voice that makes me shiver slightly. I mock-glare, and he laughs in delight.

"Since your recipe may not be totally beyond my ken after all, can I help?" I ask.

"Yes, let's absolutely work closely together in front of heat sources, there is definitely no way that will go wrong." He grins. "As long as I get to help with your dessert, too."

We make space for each other in the kitchen easily, as if we've been doing this all our lives and not once in a while over weeks. The ease of this on its own relaxes me.

Until Deniel asks, "So what happened with you today?"

I sigh. "Aside from the challenges of a baby dragon I don't know enough to care for properly? Too much, unfortunately. Which I will tell you, but only after you. I always end up unloading my worries on you right away."

It's Deniel's turn to sigh. "Yes. Because I am far happier to try to ease your burdens than I am to dwell on mine, which are insignificant in comparison."

"Not to me," I say.

TEA SET AND MATCH

He nods. "I use starter sauces for the noodle broth. It's more expensive, but so much less time consuming everyo[ne] when cooking at home. Don't let anyone wealthy tell you rea[dymade] cooking is the same as from scratch, because those are the people with all the time in the world to waste."

I'd never thought of it like that. "And you don't have that time."

"No." Deniel pours carefully. "I was already busy with making art and running my business. Adding in council work..."

"It's not just the work," I say. "It's learning the work. I know you've been going to council meetings for years, but—"

"Right, I'm used to looking at things from the other side. I don't know all their processes. Which some members of the council are only too happy to remind me at any opportunity."

My fingers clench on the vegetables I'm holding. "Are they."

Deniel waves this off. "I expected this, honestly. I'm Gaellani, and I was forced on them."

"I expected better," I say, my voice cold.

"The problem isn't really their attitude," he says. "It's that they're not wrong."

I frown. "What do you mean? You've probably attended more council meetings than they have. You know the troubles facing the Sayorseni and the Gaellani in particular, you've studied law—"

"All that is meaningless if I can't demonstrate how it's useful," Deniel says. "I want to believe I can get there, but that doesn't help me now." He laughs, but it's an empty sound. "And I don't know enough law. That's actually part of the problem. I've read a lot of theory, but I have no experience in practice. I can sometimes tell enough to know when I really ought to look up the details on something they're trying to slip past me, but not always, and I don't have *time* to stop every time. In theory there are city employees who could assist me, but I don't even know what, or who, to ask. And every time I ask questions I look that much more incompetent."

I pass him the vegetables I've chopped while he takes a breath. "I doubt that's it."

Deniel shakes his head. "You don't see how they act."

"No, I don't dispute they're disparaging you, though I wish it were otherwise. They may not embrace change as wholeheartedly as I had hoped. Until recently, they've been comfortable in their positions. Your taking this work seriously, and trying, and learning, is more than most of them have had to do, or are willing to do. Seeing you do so will be threatening to them, because they can sense if they don't knock you down now you're going to surpass them and they won't be able to."

Deniel is silent for a moment. "I'm worried you have too much faith in what I can do."

I still. "Would you have preferred if I hadn't made the council accept you?"

"No," he says, though he sounds hesitant enough that my heart aches. "No, I want this, but I fear I'm... outclassed."

"Never that," I say.

"You know what I mean," Deniel says. "Even if you're right, it unfortunately doesn't help me with all I don't know *now*."

"Can I help?" I ask. "I realize you can't give me all the specifics, but I may be able to help save you time researching the histories of some laws, or at least refer you to sources. Treat me like a consultant and send me questions via messenger."

"If I make a habit of that, I'll be seen as your puppet among the council," he says. "Coming to you whenever I need help won't help me in the long run."

"But it may help you now," I say. "I do see your point, but maybe after dinner we can talk about a few of the laws you had questions about?"

"Hmm," he says. "I'll take you up on that, but perhaps you don't know what I mean. It *is* a class thing. Because it's not just the information I don't know; it's the social cues. It's how to make people take me seriously so we can do the work that matters. I learned to present what Istals with money expect to see from a high-end artisan, but it's not the same. You've been steeped in learning that since you were born, so perhaps you don't realize it's not something everyone can navigate so easily."

"Oh no," I say, "it is certainly a skill." I've seen enough varying adroitness in it at court I can never pretend it's irrelevant. "But you're right, it's one I was expected to become adept at so young and that I took to naturally, that it may be... difficult for me to be helpful in that regard."

And I should have anticipated this, and arranged for something. A tutor, perhaps? But who could I possibly call on, or trust with that?

"Not to mention, you learned as a princess," Deniel adds. "I'll never be able to interact with these people the way nobles do, because they'll never see me as one of them. From what I understand I might have learned some tactics if I'd been able to actually attend law school. But I couldn't. So every time it's not just the council business on paper I have to learn, it's this whole invisible world behind it I have no access to. Does that make sense?"

"They won't see your merit if you don't have a reputation they respect, and you can't get that reputation if you can't demonstrate your merit," I say.

"*Yes*," he says, blowing out a breath that's half frustration, half relief that I understand inasmuch as I can. "That's it exactly. Pass me the eggs?"

We focus on cooking for a few minutes.

Then Deniel adds suddenly, "I don't expect you to solve this for me. In case I gave that impression."

"You didn't," I say, hesitating, then add, "though I do feel like this is my fault and I should be able to help regardless."

Deniel shakes his head. "I don't want to rely on you for this. I need to be able to stand on my own feet."

"That's not the same as not being able to accept help," I say, "as you have pointed out to *me* often enough these past weeks."

He flashes a grin. "I suppose I have. And I newly understand how frustrating it must have been to listen to me."

"Oh, so you're the only one who gets to chide me about not wanting to depend on others? I hardly think I can agree to that."

Deniel snorts. "Allow me to still feel badly that I had hoped to overwhelm you with a beautifully crafted dinner and instead I've had to resort to noodle bowls, because I couldn't summon the time or energy to cope with the task that should've been a gift."

"So in the midst of everything you still made sure you'd be able to feed me, and instead of your original plan you've taught me how to cook yet another dish I'm unfamiliar with. Or to put it another way, you've offered your knowledge and given me a safe opportunity to practice with it so I can stand on my own more confidently."

He looks at me sidelong. "I see what you did there."

"I cannot change what you feel," I say, "but nor can I accept your justifications for feeling badly about this."

Deniel rolls his eyes, but it's with a smile. "You underestimate yourself. You can change what I feel, at least for a little while. Thank you."

"You're welcome." I follow him to the table, each of us carrying bowls and utensils.

"Now let's talk about your day," he says.

I hesitate. "May I offer one more thought, that was once given to me?"

Deniel pauses. "By whom?"

"I can't discuss the details," I explain. "It was part of my dedication ceremony."

His gaze sharpens. "The one where you chose to abandon being a princess."

"Yes," I agree, "and probably I shouldn't even say this much about it, but I don't think the spirits wish for wise counsel to be hoarded."

"I think they will forgive you," Deniel agrees, bowing slightly, "and I'm honored you would share it with me."

"There will always be work for those who know how to listen," I quote. "It's not just what people say. It's how they say it, and what they leave out. It's the sound of silence, the speed of reaction, the force behind their words."

"I don't know how *you* listen, only that you do. You listen when you make art, and you hear the heart of what matters when we speak. While it is true I engage with you sincerely, if you can argue me to a standstill, as you have in the past, I do not have any doubts you'll be able to learn to cope with the councilors. I don't mean it will be easy, just that my faith in you is not borne out of my bias towards you, but from your actions."

I meet Deniel's eyes, and we are both silent for a moment.

Finally, he bows. "Thank you. For your faith, and your words. I will endeavor to be worthy of them."

"You already are," I say.

He ducks his head. "The person who told you that," he says. "Do you think they knew what you needed to do?"

I take a bite of my noodle bowl, savoring it. As always, even under stress his work is incredible. "Specifically, I'm not so sure," I say. "In fact, I suspect she may have had something else in mind. But she knew I needed something different than the options I considered available to me."

"What do you think it was?" he asks.

"Well, I don't think she knew I'd leave Miteran, or Entero would've found me faster."

Deniel pauses with his food almost to his mouth. "We're talking about the dowager queen?"

I sigh. So much for respecting the sanctity of the ceremony and my knowing how to carefully weigh words.

Or maybe it's that I want him to share this with me.

"Yes," I say. "I don't think tea mastery is what my grandmother had in mind for me."

Then I wince, and Deniel says, "I gather something happened."

"To put it mildly," I say, and launch into the explanation as we eat.

It takes enough telling that we finish eating and move back to the kitchen to start experimenting with dessert.

Deniel has to help show me how to flip the honey pancakes, and he takes advantage of the opportunity by standing close behind me, his hands covering mine.

Holding very still, I ask, "Is this how your parents taught you to flip pancakes?"

Deniel huffs a laugh against my hair. "Sort of. But there are some key—" he kisses my temple "—differences."

My first attempts to flip the pancakes result in a not insignificant amount of pancake batter outside of the pan.

"With results like that," I say, my cheeks still warm, "perhaps I should try more teasing and less baking."

He laughs, but I do finally manage a few passable pancakes mostly on my own.

I overstuff the first honey pancakes too full of sweet bean filling, and it glomps onto the ground as I try to squeeze the edges together.

Yorani zooms past, licking it off the ground and giving me a very pleased-with-herself look before darting off again.

Gazing after her I notice the string.

"What in the world...?"

"I believe your tea spirit has stolen Talsu's ball of yarn," Deniel says. "I'm not sure which of them to hold responsible for how it's strung across the room."

Leaning over the kitchen counter, Talsu bats at the string on the ground as Yorani flies around, carrying the ball that is its source.

Then Talsu's paw has trapped it so securely that Yorani can't get any further without breaking the string—and she doesn't.

She lands on the ground and grabs at the string herself until Talsion releases his hold to pounce anew.

"*Yarn*," I breathe. "Do you think she'd play with it without Talsion?"

"One way to find out," Deniel says. "That is—or was—my only yarn ball here, but the night market will still be going when you head out."

Yarn. I close my eyes. A toy humans and cats alike enjoy playing with, and one that's not destructive—at least not usually.

No wonder she's been so frustrated.

I haven't been listening well.

"Can I try making a pancake? I have an idea," Deniel says.

"By all means," I say. "I wanted to try making another kind of filling, if you'll make some space there."

He scoots over, and I pull out the supplies I think I'll need.

"Are you worried about whether you'll win this tournament?" Deniel asks. "I know the competition is fierce, and you'll be starting in the finals."

"I've hardly had time to worry about it," I say. "But yes. I don't know what I'm getting into, and everyone else will have more experience. Normally that wouldn't faze me, but I feel as though I've been... out of sorts? Unsettled. I worry it will affect my ability to meet this challenge."

"It's natural not to feel settled." He frowns over the batter and adjusts it with the spatula.

"I know," I say as I work, "but I should be doing better by Yorani, and you, and Lorwyn and Risteri and spirits, *Entero*, whom I've still not heard a word from. If I can't do this much—"

"You're comparing yourself to an impossible ideal no person ever meets, no matter how they seem," Deniel says. "I know you're still relatively new at being on your own, so please, please take my word for it. You're doing far better at everything than anyone could have expected, even if they knew you."

"But what if it's not enough," I say quietly. "Spirits, I've been trying to care for Yorani and couldn't manage to think of *yarn*."

"No one else did, either. Miyara, you've hardly had a chance to breathe."

"And now I don't get one," I say. "Oh, I know that must sound silly—"

"It doesn't."

"I just wanted to try to settle," I say, distressed to realize I'm tearing up as I say it. "I wanted to be able to try."

Deniel doesn't say anything to that, just stops what he's doing and draws me into a hug. I bury my face in his shoulder and take a deep breath.

Then he swears and lets go suddenly. "I'm sorry. This dragon may have had a little too much fire exposure."

I peer over his shoulder. "Spirits, are you making dragon-shaped pancakes with the batter? And—is that a cat? With whiskers?" I gape at him. "Deniel! You are showing me up again."

He grins, unrepentant. "I couldn't show off my skills with dinner, so I thought I'd give this a try. You should see what my mom can do, though."

I nod. "Yes, I'm quite certain I will never, ever be able to bake in front of her."

He laughs. "And what are you making?"

"Tea-flavored custard," I say. "I hope." I dip a spoon in to taste, but before I can Deniel intercepts the spoon. He holds onto my wrist, eyes sparkling as I feed him the custard, and I suddenly feel very warm once again.

"You've succeeded," he says. "For someone with no cooking experience, your ingenuity with flavor is remarkable. For what it's worth, I think you'll be able to meet the challenge ahead of you. You have everything you need."

"But so will they," I say. "And I don't know the rules of the contest yet."

"Then it's too soon to worry," he says, "though I realize that won't stop you."

I smile. "Instead all I'll have to worry about is—well, hello, little ones," I say to the two faces who've arrived together on the counter.

"I think perhaps it may be time for treats if we're to have any of our own," Deniel says.

We each pull out our treats—and do a double take.

Thiano provided me a jar of magically preserved marbles of fish, imported from the Istal coast, for Talsion.

Deniel has an identical one for Yorani.

"No wonder Thiano was so amused," I say. "I suppose I don't get points for originality after all."

Deniel shakes his head, smiling, and tosses two marbles from his jar into the air.

Cat and baby dragon alike gleefully leap to catch them and devour them in instants.

"The results of our execution, on the other hand, cannot be contested," Deniel says.

I lean my head against his shoulder and take a breath. We're not where we need to be, but perhaps we'll be able to figure out how to get there.

CHAPTER 3

I ARRIVE AT TALMERI'S early for a shop meeting. Since the tea guild won't sponsor me, Talmeri has agreed to take on that responsibility, in name at least if not in actual finances. Tea Master Karekin arranged things with her—his willingness to deal with her on my behalf is unexpectedly heartening—so she'll be explaining how the tournament works.

Lorwyn is, as usual, already in the back when I arrive, though she pauses at my entrance. "What is that smell?"

"You don't want to know," I say.

She turns toward me frowning, trying to identify it. "I mean, it's not a *bad* smell, exactly—"

"Do you truly wish me to tell you about spirit poop?"

Lorwyn hesitates. "Actually, yes, I think I do. Really?"

I sigh, patting the baby dragon curled contentedly around my neck. "Yorani ate some magecraft-preserved treats last night, which she was very fond of, but apparently her system processes them... uniquely."

"At least it processes them at all," Lorwyn notes.

"I have yet to find anything she can't eat," I say, "which is good and bad. I've had an epidemic of spirit poop on my hands all morning."

"Now you know what having baby sisters is like," Lorwyn says.

"I do have one of those," I remind her. "Or I did. While it's true I wasn't responsible for her care, I'm reasonably certain this is not the same."

She shrugs. "There's more overlap than you'd expect. So, any idea what the surprise meeting this morning is about?"

I look at her sharply. "Talmeri didn't tell you?"

Lorwyn's eyes narrow. "Tell me what?"

I insert myself between her and the door to the front. She needs to hear this from me, and not in front of an audience.

"Remember how you mentioned yesterday all the people suddenly in town?" I ask. "The event they're here for is a competition to determine the top tea specialist from among the remaining continental nations."

Lorwyn scoffs. "Oh, so Talmeri thinks we can capitalize on this? Great."

"Not exactly," I say. "The tea guild challenged me to compete in the finals. If I win, I'll be inducted into the tea guild in truth."

Lorwyn blinks slowly, and then a scowl gradually darkens her expression.

"What," she says crisply.

"Had I refused, they would have revoked my tea mastery for good," I clarify.

"Oh, I understood the first time. You just accepted an ultimatum like that?"

"I am displeased," I snap, and her eyebrows lift in surprise at my tone. "But I'm not yet in a position to negotiate. I intend to change that, but I will need help."

"Will you," Lorwyn says, her own tone decidedly cool. "How unexpected. I take it I'm to play a role."

"If you don't want to, when we walk in there I will make sure Talmeri doesn't give you any trouble," I say.

"I can fight my own battles."

"And you have others on your hands already. I will defend your choice, whatever it is. But—"

"But of course you have some compelling reason why this is actually in my best interests," she says flatly.

I open my mouth, shut it. "Sort of," I admit, "but..." I bite my lip.

"But?" she prompts.

I sigh. "I didn't want to lead with this, because it's selfish. But mainly I really don't want to do this by myself, and I'm also not sure I'll win without your help. But if you're not willing to, of course I'll try."

"You'll try regardless," Lorwyn says, and to my surprise the edge has gone out of her voice. "And you're right, I know enough about this silly tournament to agree you need me. So what have you come up with that's in it for me?"

I frown at her. "*That's* what you needed to hear?"

"Look, you don't feed me spirit poop, I won't feed it to you. I know how important tea mastery is to you. But I do want to know what could possibly be in this for me, because I really don't have time for something this ridiculous."

"I know," I say. "I'm sorry. I know Ostario doesn't want me involved, but can I help at all with the magecraft training like you helped me with tea mastery?"

"Maybe," Lorwyn grunts, which tells me how badly she thinks it's going. "So?"

"You don't want to work for the state," I say, "but you've already been outed as a witch, which means the state would afford you protection. I think if you compete in this tournament as my partner, or at least visibly, it'll help you make your own reputation. You can establish yourself as a tea specialist so that if you want, not only will you be able to leave Talmeri's one day, you'll have other options without state support."

Lorwyn crosses her arms. "You mean compete openly as a witch."

"You don't have to," I say, "but if you want to establish your reputation, yes. I think you'd have to be open about that for it to matter."

Lorwyn nods. "Yeah, that sounds like a terrible idea. I'll think about it."

I'm not entirely certain how to take that. "So does that mean...?"

"Yes, of course I'm with you, and yes, I maintain I should have left you sopping in the darkness all those weeks ago. Let's go."

"There are three contestants Miyara will be competing against in the finals," Talmeri explains. "You'll face them in three different contests."

"What sort?" I ask, trying not to worry that Yorani has scampered off toward the tea counter, where there is all manner of trouble for her to get into.

"We won't know the specifics in advance, but you'll learn what the first one is later this afternoon," Talmeri says. "I'll write the time and place of that meeting down for you later. But what I do know—"

Someone bangs on the door.

Talmeri frowns. "How odd. Our hours are listed right on the door. The 'closed' sign is out, isn't it?"

"Yes," I agree, standing. "Shall I see what's so urgent?"

"No, no, I'll take care of it," Talmeri says, shooting to her feet with alacrity.

I exchange an amused glance with Lorwyn; Talmeri is so beside herself with excitement about the marketing opportunities this tournament presents she's being uncharacteristically considerate of us.

My amusement evaporates when I hear the person at the door announce coldly, "I am Princess Saiyana of Istalam, and I'm here to speak to Miyara."

Talmeri bows as low as I've seen, backing up out of the way while remaining bent over.

Frozen in place, I exchange a very different glance at Lorwyn.

Her expression asks, *Are you okay?*

I manage to nod, a minute jerk of a movement, though my whole body feels like it's gone rigid like ice that can shatter at any moment. *I'll be okay.*

Her expression twists; she knows that's not an answer. But she lets me get away with it so she, too, can drop into a deep bow.

I've never seen Lorwyn bow like this. It looks wrong on her.

Especially since I know that from her, the bow does not indicate respect. She's only bowing to prevent trouble from falling on her or her family. And not from someone like Kustio, but from my own sister.

I dislike this immensely.

"Well," Saiyana says, looking me up and down. "Here you are."

I incline my head to my sister without bowing. I am still provisionally part of the tea guild, and that means I do not answer to her.

Her eyes narrow.

"Grace Talmeri," I say, "would you excuse us for a few minutes? I believe the princess may have questions for me about recent events in Sayorsen."

"Is that what you believe," Saiyana says.

"I'm not sure why else you would approach me in such a way, your Highness," I say.

At my use of her title, Saiyana's expression turns disgusted. "Yes, leave us. I see this may take a few minutes."

"Of course, your Highness," Talmeri bows again. She doesn't even bother to gather her things, just edges out the door, shaking.

"Was that really necessary?" I ask.

"It was your idea," Saiyana says.

"And you know perfectly well," I say, "I'm referring to your high-handedness. Your Highness."

"Would you have had me tell her why I'm really here?" she asks sweetly. "Yes, that's what I thought you were implying. This one can leave too."

Saiyana wouldn't have said something like that except to get a rise out of me, but I let her have the reaction. "*This one* has a name," I say. "She also already knows who I am. Was."

"*Really*," Saiyana says, looking her over. "Then you must be the witch."

I see Lorwyn's frame seize—with tension at least, and likely fear and anger besides—and I pass through shock at my sister straight into fury in an instant.

Enough.

"Lorwyn, please rise," I say. "No one who behaves this badly merits deference of any kind."

"Thank you, I'd like nothing better than to be brought into the middle of your fight," Lorwyn drawls at me as she straightens. Spirits be thanked, her spirit isn't broken—and even more, she's trusting me to handle this.

I cannot let her down. Not now; not in this.

I draw in a breath, focusing, as Lorwyn continues, "For someone who was a princess until only very recently, you have a very loose grasp on observing forms."

"For someone who has spent the bulk of my life observing them," I say, "I find I have little patience when the gestures are empty."

"You think you can turn your back on everything you were given and disrespect it to my face?" Saiyana demands. "Yes, tell your poor little friend here to go before I remember the part of the story where she knew there was a warrant out for you and didn't turn you in. Or perhaps the part where we both know perfectly well she's an unregistered witch and should be brought up on charges."

Lorwyn goes still, and I step between them, right into my sister's space, forcing her to fall back a step.

"How dare you," I say in a low voice. "How dare you threaten her like that, even implicitly. And a 'letter of the law' argument no less, from you, on a law I know perfectly well you despise? You're angry with me. Don't take it out on her."

"I will do what I please, and how dare you attempt to threaten me," she growls, stepping back in so our faces are separated only by breaths of space.

"Yes, what a fine reflection of your commitment to service it is to abuse your station to intimidate someone you should be helping," I snap. "What a pinnacle of grace you are, a paragon we should all aspire to no doubt! What *can* have inspired me to leave supposed royal *service*, it is quite a mystery."

Saiyana's jaw clenches.

"For the record, I'm not intimidated," Lorwyn says behind me. Her voice is carefully controlled, and I know she's keeping it together as much to convince herself as anything. "And you can stop trying to block her view of me. If I were going to be brought up on charges it would've happened by now."

Saiyana snorts, but takes a step back. "You clearly don't understand bureaucracy."

"I do," I say coldly. "Intimidation was still the intent behind my sister's words, even if it failed, and it was uncalled for. You should know I am not so easily manipulated, Saiyana."

"Should I?" she asks.

"If you thought so, you'd never have suggested I follow in your footsteps."

"A suggestion you rejected in the most dramatic fashion possible without ever discussing with me why! What should I know about my sister who would turn her back on all her responsibilities and abandon everything with no explanation?"

She's right that I never told her how badly I didn't want the life she'd laid out for me, and I understand she must see my departure as a betrayal—of her trust, and our relationship.

Once upon a time, I would have attempted to mollify her, and part of me wants to, because I don't want her to be upset. But I'm surprised that instinct isn't stronger.

I'm no longer that Miyara.

"Which responsibilities did I abandon, precisely?" I ask.

She's incredulous; outraged. "You need to ask?"

"Yes, I do," I say. "I made the only possible choice to be able to serve people meaningfully, and I wonder which responsibilities you think trump that."

"You call this meaningful?" Saiyana waves her hand around. "You run a common shop! You're playing around with tea when you should be working on behalf of your *family* to do the work that—"

To my surprise, and Saiyana's, Lorwyn interrupts. "Uh, like negotiating a peace treaty in one sitting at a first meeting and exposing a nobleman's criminal enterprise, saving an entire city and all of Islalam's refugees in the process? Within weeks of leaving her royal life behind? Pretty sure Miyara's got you there, Princess."

I blink at Lorwyn. I'm glad to hear her sounding more like my irreverent friend, but a little surprised to hear her put my role in those terms.

I don't know why I doubted she would have my back in the tea tournament. I evidently have a lot to learn about friendship.

Saiyana makes a sound of disgust. "I'm sure you think so. I'm sure she'll keep being able to pull such coups out of her teapot, too, so staying here is definitely worth her while. And do you realize how much cleanup work Miyara created with that treaty, let alone how much of a nightmare this is on the investigative side?" She glares at me. "If you'd done this properly—"

"I'd have done nothing at all," I say. "Because I wouldn't have been here, as you weren't. As *no one* was holding Kustio accountable, and no one would have known the extent of what was amiss until it was too late. I regret the workload I have dumped on you, but I won't apologize for it."

Her expression tightens. "We'll see about that."

The door from the back slams open. "Ah, Lorwyn, there you are," Ostario says, and Saiyana freezes.

Lorwyn spins around. "I locked that door."

"Yes, and I'm a high-level mage," Ostario reminds her patiently, as though she's forgotten. "A lock is not beyond my abilities. Is everything all right in here?"

"How long have you been listening on the other side of the door?" Saiyana demands.

"Long enough," he says with a long look.

Saiyana flushes in simultaneous anger and embarrassment.

"I thought the door blocked sound," I say to Lorwyn.

She shrugs. "He's also a witch. I'm not sure why I even bothered asking, honestly."

"Because you want to know how I did it," Ostario says. "And I'll happily show you once you've mastered your current set of spells."

Lorwyn sighs. "So much for a distraction. The princess is much easier to needle than you are."

That surprises me into a huff of laughter. I'm not sure anyone has ever said that about Saiyana—certainly not to her face—and the hit clearly lands, because Saiyana draws back under her customary cool and imperious façade.

At least it seems Lorwyn will be able to fend for herself against my sister from now on, which is one less thing to worry about.

My position is less clear.

"I'm impressed you managed to get assigned here," Saiyana says to Ostario, "considering your failure to apprehend Miyara, which you were ordered to do."

"Ah, but I was also ordered to let nothing interfere with my investigation," Ostario says. "And Miyara was an invaluable resource. Had I betrayed her confidence, she never would have helped me."

"That's the logic you used? Have you even *met* Miyara?" Saiyana scoffs. "She's the most helpful person in the world. You think she would have refused to serve people in that way?"

"I would have," I say quietly. "I wouldn't have trusted someone with delicate information who I knew couldn't be trusted with mine. I would have gone around him, and probably gotten into even more trouble. I don't do what I'm told anymore."

Her gaze searches mine, as piercing as it's always been.

"What happened to you?" Saiyana asks softly.

Yet somehow it manages, as always, to miss the heart of who I am.

"Do you truly not recognize me?" I ask, my voice smaller than I would prefer.

She shakes her head. "I always knew you had a spine. I'm frustrated you're wasting it like this, and I don't intend to let you."

My heart leaps to my throat. "You don't have a choice."

Saiyana laughs. "Oh, my dear sweet innocent sister. You gave up your ability to stop me."

Panic tightens my chest. This is what I've feared for weeks.

"I'm a tea master," I force out. "You cannot command me."

"Your mastery is a sham, and you know it," she replies, dropping into a chair, apparently unconcerned with all the people still standing around her.

Which means she's confident enough she can afford us the subconscious advantage.

"You think I didn't earn it?" I ask.

"I think the tea guild is not as aloof from temporal politics as it likes to pretend," Saiyana says. "I think if I push, they will give you away without a fight. Do you think I'm wrong?"

Shame burns through me. But anger, too.

I, too, take a seat.

Not because I'm confident, but because I can't afford to appear otherwise.

"Not at all," I say evenly, and her eyes narrow. "Lorwyn, Ostario, would you give my sister and me a few minutes, please? I think we should continue this alone."

Lorwyn clearly doesn't want to leave, but after a moment her face clears.

My stomach roils so violently I almost retch.

"What did you just do?" Saiyana demands of her.

Lorwyn's shark-smile is in full force. "Try to leave the premises with Miyara and find out. I was there the last time an assassin tried to kidnap her, and I don't trust you."

"Now if you apply that kind of precision to your magecraft exercises, we may get somewhere," Ostario says wryly. "Your Highness, my apprentice has erected a bubble around the room keyed to Miyara. If she attempts to pass through the barrier, whoever is inside will experience an immobilizing shock. Otherwise, nothing will happen." He looks at Lorwyn. "It's good work. I see you were paying attention to more than I realized when we fought Kustio."

Lorwyn shrugs self-consciously.

"You don't have a problem with your apprentice threatening me?" Saiyana asks.

Ostario bows to her, and even to me it looks mocking. "You must agree, my apprentice has reason to distrust the intentions of the crown. But *I* trust you, your Highness, and so I have no reason to fear for your safety." While Saiyana's deciding how to respond to that, he tells Lorwyn, "We'll give them ten minutes, and then you'll take that down."

Lorwyn nods, not arguing. Before she goes to the back, though, she looks at Saiyana one more time.

"You never apologized," Lorwyn says. "Not that I expected one, but I hope you realize Miyara will remember that forever."

And then it's just the two of us.

"Ostario still toes that line with you, I see," I say.

Saiyana looks at me sharply. "Oh?"

"Between keeping you on your toes and also not giving you enough grounds to feel compelled to do something about it."

"Nice try, Miyara, but we're not here to talk about spirits-cursed Ostario, we're here to talk about you," she says, avoiding that topic so fast I can't help smiling a little. "You left off agreeing the tea guild won't fight to keep you. I will."

The smile helps me appear more relaxed than I am, because *keep* is the operative word there.

The battle for my freedom is upon me.

"So I did," I say, settling in. "You must have read that my mastery is provisional, because my official testing was disrupted."

"*You* disrupted it by leaving in the middle," Saiyana says. "Don't think you can evade responsibility by using passive speech constructions with me, little sister."

I roll my eyes. "Yes, *I* chose to leave in the middle of testing, knowing it would cost me the mastery certification that could protect me from your schemes, in order to stand up for the citizens of Sayorsen, because no one in the government you ostensibly manage was doing their job effectively. Better, elder sister?"

"You're a brat," Saiyana says, though to my surprise doesn't argue the point. She must have been more disturbed by the news about Sayorsen's recent events than she's been letting on. "Continue."

"The tea guild has arranged a test for me to enter their ranks in truth," I say.

She frowns, then heaves a sigh as in an instant she connects the disparate pieces of information she must have already had. "They brought the spirits-cursed tea tournament into it."

"I've already been entered into the tournament officially," I say. "You might still be able to remove me, of course, but I invite you to imagine the ramifications with the tea guild if you cost them such a public loss of face, not to mention public perception of the royal family."

"But the tournament started moving before that, which means you hadn't yet agreed," Saiyana says, missing nothing. "You know what arrangement the tea guild worked out with the tournament organizers if you didn't agree. What was the deal?"

"The tea master didn't wish to share that information, to make sure it wouldn't influence my decision as to whether to participate," I say.

Her eyes narrow. "But you know something."

"Of course," I agree, "but I see no reason to share. Especially as it's not pertinent. If I can be a tea master in truth, how could that be a waste of my skills and upbringing?"

"Because you wouldn't be working for the crown," she snaps. "You wouldn't be helping your family."

Your sisters, she doesn't say. *Me.*

"Of course I would be," I say. "Because I'd be serving people in a way I don't hate. In a way I'm good at. In a way that allows me to be myself and still *matter*, which means I will be significantly more effective. I could never have that in the palace. And you don't truly need me to."

"How can you seriously make that argument after all your sniping about what's been going on in Sayorsen? If you'd been a princess, everything would've been different."

"Different enough it's impossible to say with any certainty how events would have played out," I say. "But Saiyana, I dedicated my life, before the spirits, to finding my own path. This is part of it. You can't gainsay that."

"Playing at tea in a tournament. One the tea guild itself has disdained for years. Come on, Miyara. How can you sit there and tell me *this* matters?"

"I made my choice," I say. "And I know you don't like it, and may never understand it. But I will fight for it. And since I don't believe for an instant you came all the way to Sayorsen just to yell at me, I think you can afford me the chance to prove to you that my chosen path *does*, in fact, matter. And not just to me.

"Let me participate in this tournament without any need for my friends to fear you'll steal me away. Once it's all over, we'll talk."

"And if you can't prove it, you'll come back to Miteran?"

I laugh. "If I can't win the tournament, my case against you will be much weakened."

"I don't care if you win the stupid tournament," Saiyana says with sudden heat. "I care that you think you have to make a case against me."

"I know," I say. "And I'm not going to promise you how that conversation will go. All I promise is that I'm going to fight."

"Which is what I've been trying to get you to care enough to do for years," Saiyana says. "Yes, very clever."

"I always cared," I say quietly. "I just lacked a purpose that suited me. I've found it here."

"That remains to be seen," she says, drumming her fingers on the table. "If the tea guild inducts you into its ranks, it will of course present a firmer obstacle toward removing you."

"I will not speak as to what the tea guild will or won't do," I say.

Her eyebrows shoot up. "What a surprising lack of faith in the people you hope to join, whom you expect to save your little life here."

"It's not little," I say. "Not to me."

"Then you'll have to prove it," Saiyana says. "Fine. Participate in your tournament. I look forward to seeing what you show me."

She's backing off not because she thinks she'll be convinced, but because she thinks *I* will be.

I don't know what the next weeks will bring. Perhaps we'll both think me insignificant by the end.

But I have my shot.

My stay, at least for a little while.

"You'll be staying in town, then?" I ask.

"After his investigation, Ostario was in a good position to get himself appointed to oversee the transition with the Te Muraka." Saiyana rolls her eyes. "Every time he's given an assignment meant to snub him he emerges in an even better position. It defies belief."

"Ah, so he can rub the stodgy elders' faces in his success *and* be on hand to train Lorwyn," I say. "Well played of him."

"Indeed," she says dryly. "He'll be focusing on working with the Te Muraka to design infrastructure that accommodates and protects everyone."

"And you're taking charge of the whole endeavor of integrating them," I realize.

Saiyana leans back. "Yes. Ostario will report to me, but I'll be focusing more on the legal infrastructure. The goal is to guide this integration to prevent a repeat of how the Gaellani have been marginalized. If it's possible, I'll do it."

I believe her. Saiyana is impossibly focused when she sets her sight on a goal.

Of course, one of her goals is also extracting me from my life here. But she doesn't yet understand what it looks like when I fight; in truth, I barely know.

"I'm surprised you waited so long to come," I say.

She doesn't misunderstand. "Mother had another operative in mind who's more familiar with the region, but there was a complication."

"And complications are your domain," I murmur.

Saiyana snorts. "Yes."

"So the actual reason you came to see me first, or so I gather since you hadn't run into Ostario yet," I say, "is not that you wanted to send me back immediately, but that you wanted to conscript me as a local resource."

Saiyana gives me her piercing look again and then sighs. "Spirits, you would be so *good* at this if you would just bother," she says. "Yes, I thought it would ease you back into the role you left behind and the specific duties you'd be picking up. And since I'm coming in cold, being able to use the reputation you established in this city and our relationship as a jumping off point for my trustworthiness would have made this a lot easier."

If I were truly suited to her job, I would have guessed her angle from the start. Instead, I focused on protecting Lorwyn. Despite our overlapping training, my instincts trend in a different direction. "I will still be here," I say.

"But I can't discuss my work openly with a civilian," Saiyana says. "And I assume you don't want me to announce your identity publicly."

My chest tightens. I thought my absence wouldn't affect her work, and in some ways that's true. But while I didn't want to be part of that work, not being able to be privy to it, either, feels, unexpectedly, like a loss.

It's not the work. It's the wall that now exists between me and my sister that wasn't there before. Because I put it there.

And no matter how she asks, I'll never take it down.

That's the choice I made at my dedication ceremony, and it's one I've committed myself to making, again and again, every day, for the rest of my life.

Perhaps I do deserve more of her scorn than I've considered.

Saiyana frowns suddenly into our silence. "Okay, I have to ask. What is that smell?"

I close my eyes. I've smelled it so much this morning I've become inured. "Spirit poop."

"Come again?"

"Excuse me a moment." I head to the tea counter, where Yorani has knocked the lid off a teapot, perched on its spout, and aimed her posterior where the lid should be.

"Do I want to know how long you've been at this?" I ask her pleased face.

Yorani turns to face me proudly but loses her balance and falls off the pot.

I catch her before she crashes into the shelf of ceramics below her—

—and Saiyana catches the teapot. Peering inside she says, "Wow. I thought you were joking."

"Would that I were," I say.

"This is fascinating. The spirit eats solid food as well as magic, then? So this—"

"You can take it if you'd like," I say, lifting Yorani to my shoulder. "It's authentic and one-of-a-kind. You could even preserve it for future generations of mages to study."

"Working in sales has not improved your sense of humor," Saiyana says.

"Regrettably true."

"But the spirit..." My sister finally manages to look up and falters, getting her first good look at Yorani. "Spirits," she whispers.

Yorani chirps in the affirmative.

"No, I mean," Saiyana starts, then shakes her head, not taking her eyes off of Yorani. "You know what I mean."

I smile. It would take Yorani to render my sister incoherent. "Yes, she's real, really a spirit, and was born out of my tea ceremony. Her name is Yorani."

Saiyana hesitates. "Will she bite me if I touch her?"

"Only if she doesn't like you. Or thinks it would be funny."

"So, maybe." Saiyana nevertheless carefully extends one finger.

Yorani boops her with her nose, and Saiyana smiles.

Reaching out to pet her scales, Saiyana says, "I can't believe this is your life."

"I know," I say. "It's not a life I could have conceived of before. I could never have expected the spirit poop."

"That's not what I mean," she says.

"I know."

Part of what she means is, *Is there a place for us in this life of yours?* And I don't know.

But in this moment, where we're not fighting, where she's exercising extraordinary restraint to at least pretend to let it all be, I want to find one.

"Are you having any trouble taking care of her?" Saiyana asks.

I can't decide if she means that to be a swipe at my current status, but it nevertheless hits. I have no idea how to care for Yorani, but being lectured by my sister on the subject isn't likely to improve matters.

So I deflect. "Are you volunteering to take that teapot off my hands after all?"

"It is all yours, to do whatever it is you do with... spirit poop," she says, rolling her eyes. "By the way, I do like your hair. It suits you. I wouldn't have expected that. Did you dye it yourself?"

I laugh, though her rapid transition into compliments makes me think she *did* intend the hit and learned by my deflection it's a sensitive subject. "Risteri—that is, my roommate—"

"The Taresim daughter? You're living with her?"

I pause. "Are you shocked that I have a roommate or that I'm living with someone connected with the Kustio scandal?"

Saiyana pauses. "You were saying?"

She's trying. Perhaps she is trying to play up our sisterly relationship for her own ends, but it doesn't mean it's not true. "Risteri helped me try to dye it, but it was a disaster. And then we learned the tea master was going to be evaluating me that day, so Lorwyn took pity on me and fixed it."

Saiyana is silent a moment. "We never did anything like that," she finally says.

A lump forms in my throat. "I never knew who I wanted to be before I was here," I say.

"Visible and memorable and distinct," she says. "Yes, that's a change for you."

I frown. "If you're thinking it'll make it easier for me to separate myself later—"

"I wasn't," Saiyana says. "I already said the green suits you."

"Oh," I say. "That's good, then."

Her eyes narrow. "Why is that good? No, don't tell me. It's witchcraft."

Spirits, I've forgotten how quickly she makes leaps of logic. "It was an emergency," I say, "but I'm not sorry. Risteri and Lorwyn have both saved me."

"Lovely," Saiyana mutters. "Anyone else I should know about?"

I'm not entirely certain how to take that. "The messengers' guild has been nothing but discreet in my experience, but if you have something particularly sensitive and want to make sure it's handled by someone with brains in her head, ask for Glynis," I say.

Saiyana's eyebrows lift. "Noted. Anyone else?"

"Thiano," I say.

She nods. "I saw his file. As slippery as he sounds?"

"Probably worse," I say. "I'm not sure what his interests truly are yet, but so far they seem to be in alignment with ours."

"Or at least yours," she says, "which might not be the same."

That stings.

Oh, spirits grace me, best to do it now.

"There's also Deniel," I say.

"And I should know Deniel because...?"

"We're..." What is the term for this? I can't think of it. "Courting. Whatever that's called."

"You're *what*?" she yells.

Lorwyn bursts through the door to the back, followed closely by Ostario.

"Everything's fine," I rush to say.

Yorani squawks and paces on my shoulders in agitation, belying my words.

Saiyana demands, "Who is this Deniel?"

Lorwyn's glare melts into mirth. "Oh, we've reached that part of the conversation. Carry on then."

"Well as long as I have your permission," I mutter.

"Miyara," Saiyana growls.

"He's an incredibly talented potter, and he's now also on the city council," I say. "I'm sure you'll meet him if you're in town very long."

"My little sister expresses interest in *courting* for the first time in her life, you'd better believe I'm going to meet him," she declares.

Oh dear. I may have made a tactical error. "Not without me if it can be possibly avoided."

"I promise nothing of the kind."

Behind her shoulder, Ostario mouths at me, *I'll help.*

Spirits be thanked.

"Are we done then?" I ask. *Please let us be done.*

"For now," Saiyana says, her tone dark.

I sigh, and she grins, then turns to Lorwyn.

"I'm glad to know my sister has people here who care about her enough to attempt to stand in my way," Saiyana says. "And she was right, earlier. I apologize for my actions and my words; you do deserve better from me."

Lorwyn nods. "It's an extremely irritating habit of hers, being right. Maybe consider she might be right about other things, too."

I notice Lorwyn hasn't accepted the apology, but I'm not sure I want to step between them in this moment.

"I hope you're right," Saiyana says seriously. "I hope she hasn't ruined her life as badly as I believe. I'll hold back for now, but know if I can save Miyara, I will. Whatever that means."

"Noted," Lorwyn says.

With final bows, my sister takes her leave.

As soon as the door shuts behind her, I collapse into a chair, burying my face in my arms as Yorani skitters down my back.

"That did not go how I expected," Lorwyn says. "How come your sister talks like a normal person, but you have to work at it?"

My voice comes out muffled. "Saiyana cultivates a no-nonsense façade in contrast to court culture because she finds her ability to unnerve people saves her time."

Lorwyn snorts. "Okay, that sounds more like what I'd expect from a sister of yours. But I did think she'd be harder to read."

"She is," Ostario says. "Don't be fooled. She only lets her guard down on purpose with Miyara. And she knows how to feign letting her guard down, too."

"That's..." Lorwyn pauses. "Reassuring?"

"Come on," Ostario says, hauling me upright. "Let's see what we can do about your spirit poop problem."

CHAPTER 4

TALMERI IS BESIDE HERSELF after having been visited by a princess ("Did you perform the tea ceremony for her, Miyara?" "Perhaps we can erect a plaque, to commemorate the occasion!"). Saiyana will want to announce her presence in Sayorsen her own way, so to keep Talmeri from dashing off to brag to her friends—at least, beyond what I assume she managed while Saiyana and I spoke—I leave her in charge of the tea room while I take off with Yorani for the tournament meeting.

It's being held in a conference room in City Hall, an unassuming building except in that it stands apart from the rest of the block. I can't tell by looking, because presumably mages would have been on the design team erasing the traces, but my guess is that buildings were razed to make that room after the influx of refugees into Sayorsen. Past the perfectly pruned garden, I have a clear line of sight to the police station one direction, and I'd bet Entero could tell me all the other avenues open in an emergency.

Yorani flaps her way through the garden, mostly sniffing and eating bugs. I'm here early enough that we can afford the time to meander, so I leave her to it, only making sure she doesn't dig around in the dirt before our meeting.

Which means I'm present to watch the other competitors arrive.

The first is a Velasari man—not as stocky as most and his brown skin looks paler than average, but his short height and tightly curled, dark hair are distinctive. He's sleekly dressed and strides right up to the door like he expects it to blow open from the force of his efficiency. I can't make out what he says at the entry, only that his tone is cutting before he vanishes inside.

Not, I think, a man with whom I can be friends. But I'm not here to make friends, and perhaps he exercises more patience when brewing tea.

He's closely followed by a matronly Istal businesswoman moving easily and confidently, like nothing in this world could cause her to doubt a step. She bows to the two assistants flanking her and heads inside—and then they walk my direction.

"Grace Hanuva hoped you could give us a tour of the gardens while she works," one of them says to me with a slight bow.

My eyebrows shoot up. Interesting—the grace gave no sign of noticing me.

But if she did, I don't believe she didn't also see Yorani. Which means she didn't mistake me for a groundskeeper, and this request is not made innocently.

"I regret my time is spoken for," I say. "But please give her my regards. Yorani, it's time for us to be going."

Yorani zooms over, passing by the assistants' faces closely enough they stumble backward, and one glares at me while the other mouths appropriate pleasantries.

But they are not surprised by the presence of a tea spirit. They definitely know who I am.

I pet Yorani as she settles on my shoulder and head for toward the door, where a shaggy-haired adolescent wearing too-formal Taresal men's garb hesitates.

"Are you looking for something in particular?" I ask, and he jumps, turning to face me.

And then stares, seeing Yorani.

His jaw begins to drop, but before an expression of wonder can fully form on his face he snaps his mouth closed, scowling instead.

"That's the tea spirit," he says flatly.

Not the reaction I usually get to Yorani.

Her tail begins swishing, so I prepare to rein her in if she decides to take issue with his tone.

"Yes, this is Yorani, and my name's Miyara," I say. "It's an honor to make your acquaintance. Do you mean to be at City Hall?"

"What, do I not look nice enough to belong with all you people?" he asks, gesturing down at his fancy clothes.

He does not, in fact; he looks like he has no idea how to dress himself. "Your clothes are very fine," I say. "I only wondered why you might not be entering the building, and thought perhaps the lack of clear signage was the issue. I only moved here a few weeks ago myself, and—"

"Whatever, let's just go," he says, pushing open the doors.

Yorani has gone still, watching him carefully, but she doesn't appear ready to pounce yet.

"I take it you're participating in the tea tournament as well, then?" I ask.

He shoots me a glare over his shoulder. "Don't expect me to believe you don't know anything about it."

I wonder if he's always like this, or if it's a reaction to dealing with people as evidently underhanded as Grace Hanuva. "Believe what you wish," I say, just before a City Hall functionary arrives to meet us in the lobby and escort us to the appropriate conference room.

I peer around as we go, trying to imagine Deniel in these halls. I'm struck by the disconnect between two images: Deniel as he is, and Deniel as he could have been had he attended a school for law. The former stands out among the people here, and the latter can never exist.

Deniel is right about how his ability to negotiate this space will affect his work. I'll have to think on it. And soon, before the councilors' impression that he can safely be ignored is so firm it will be even harder to change. Spirits.

My adolescent companion bows as he enters, a jerking and sloppy movement. Not mocking custom, then, but untrained in etiquette and trying to mask it. I appreciate his effort but doubt it's having the effect he wishes it to.

But we are competitors, and if he won't accept even greetings from me he won't accept help, either.

I already dislike this competition.

Nevertheless I pause in the doorway, a weighted moment for attention to turn my direction but not so long it becomes awkward, and I bow gracefully.

Let them see I will compete as a tea master.

"It's my honor to meet you," I say to the tournament official, who scrambles away from his conversation with Grace Hanuva. "Thank you for having me."

"Oh, the pleasure is all ours," he assures me, his eyes straying between Yorani and me, clearly unsure how to treat her. "We're beside ourselves with excitement to be conducting the finals with an actual tea master."

"Quite," the Velasari man says sharply.

"Would you introduce me to my colleagues?" I interject before the official can do more than frown nervously as Yorani skitters over to my right shoulder to glare at the Velasari. "I'm afraid I've been so consumed by my studies lately I've not had the opportunity to follow the tournament as closely as I would have liked."

"Oh, such a shame," the official says. "We've had such top talent this year, too, but only the best make it to the finals, as I'm sure you know!"

Grace Hanuva smiles politely at this apparent compliment, while the bad-tempered Velasari man looks down his nose and the young Taresal tries to keep his expression neutral.

Because of course, they have demonstrated that they are the best, and I have not.

"Yes, well," the official says, "Grace Hanuva has been running a popular tea shop for years, and she brings quite a lot of experience to the brewing station!"

Hanuva's expression remains polite, but tightens: she doesn't think this is a compliment, perhaps because experience is all the official can think to flatter her with.

But to me it says she may be my toughest opponent, because experience is exactly what I lack.

"Ari here is one of our youngest competitors to date, and the only one to make it to the finals," the official says. "When you see how inventively he applies magecraft to the art of tea, you'll understand why."

Flashiness is also extremely outside my skillset, Yorani's manifestation excepted.

"And last but not least is Lino! If you use any modern tea tech, Lino probably had a hand in its invention," the official says.

"She doesn't," Lino says confidently. "Tea masters are famously backward."

Backward? "Tea masters do focus on the simplicity of traditional techniques, it's true," I say, "but I hope we can learn from one another in the course of the coming events."

"Exactly, that's exactly our goal, to foster tea culture worldwide," the official exclaims. "Please, let's all sit. I'm sure you're dying to know about the first challenge."

Worldwide seems a bit of a stretch when only three nations can be included, but I dutifully take my seat. Yorani won't settle on my shoulders, so I pull her into my lap, her head poking up over the table so she can rest her chin there.

"As you all know, we like to make use of the unique features of our host cities," the official says. "So I'm sure it won't surprise you that for the first round of the finals, we'll be heading into the Cataclysm."

Hanuva is calm, like she knows she can deal with anything thrown at her, and Lino looks as though the Cataclysm would hardly dare waste his time. Only Ari clenches his fists, but he, too, doesn't seem concerned; if anything, he's angry.

Yorani watches them all, and so do I.

"As the first part of the challenge, you have until tomorrow morning to secure a guide to the Cataclysm," the official says. "Grace Miyara, I don't have the roster for your team yet, but since you have contacts in this town I want to make sure you're aware your guide cannot be a team member? In the interest of impartiality, you understand."

Of course I'm going to ask Risteri, but that means she won't be able to help with any of the other aspects of the tournament. Spirits. "Thank you for letting me know," I say.

He nods. "We'll meet at the central guide station at sunrise tomorrow, and you'll all have until midday to collect ingredients to create a tea flight. After that, you have until midday the following day to prepare. I'm sure I don't need to say this, but remember, this is the finals, so go bold."

"Ah, just to test my understanding," I say. "We are to create entirely new blends using Cataclysm ingredients?"

"Yes, that's correct," the official says. "Will that be a problem?"

"Poor dear, you must not have much practice with that, since your studies were so... rushed," Hanuva says sympathetically.

"Please," Lino scoffs. "As if someone aspiring to tea mastery would have any experience creating something new when they can cling to *tradition* instead."

I wait for Ari to chime in, but he apparently doesn't feel compelled to rub his inventiveness in my face.

"What a splendid idea," I say to the official. "I look forward to the challenge."

The remainder of the meeting passes in much the same manner. Once the details are attended to—namely signing stacks of liability waivers in case of dismemberment in the Cataclysm—we disperse.

I head for the messengers' guild headquarters straightaway. I want to make sure Risteri is willing to be my guide before any of the others can learn enough to request her.

"Oh, I know where to find her," Glynis says, hopping off from her seat atop a counter.

Her tone makes me think it's neither the guide station nor our apartment. I raise my eyebrows. "I suppose I can't ask."

"Not me," she says—but with a grin.

Since I left my official tea mastery exam to stand up to Kustio, she's stopped looking for offense to take in my comments. After the meeting I just left, it's a relief.

But I wonder if perhaps Risteri and I have more to talk about than the tea tournament.

I send another messenger to Talmeri's with an update about the first round of competition rather than going myself. I've already taken the afternoon off, and I'm going to make fruitful use of it to center myself.

Events are moving so fast I want to visit the shrine before anything else happens.

Yorani lifts off my shoulder, fluttering ahead of me. As I reach out, I realize she's leading me in the direction of the shrine. As if she knows where we're going already and can't wait to get there.

Smiling, I let my arm fall. To the shrine it is, then.

I am growing used to the shrine's near-emptiness. It is the middle of the day, when most people are working, but still a few pass through to reflect on the blessings of the spirits in their lives. I'm glad they, and I, can come.

I pay my respects to the spirit of air but don't feel called there. At the pool of water, I pause, dipping my feet inside. The spirit of water has been strong with me for the last few weeks, its aspects of calm and surging. But I feel at peace with those, today; reflecting on water is not what I need now.

Before I can stand, Yorani plops into the sacred water. I reach out instinctually, because that is *not* respectful behavior towards the spirits—

—except Yorani is a spirit.

She floats happily, using a wing to spin herself in a circle.

Probably the spirit of water doesn't mind, I decide.

And I'm not sure it's good how quickly my reaction to Yorani's choices has been to reach out to stop her. It is necessary to hold her back some of the time, but how much?

Once she's clearly out of my reach, Yorani promptly wings her way across the pool to the only other person at this altar, and I sigh.

But to my surprise, that person is Sa Rangim.

He opens his mouth to say something but closes it, bowing his head in acknowledgement instead.

"Speaking is permitted here," I say, "as long as we're quiet. Just understand, there's nothing to prevent anyone from overhearing. It's considered sacrilegious for them to repeat outside, but..."

"But I am an object of fascination for many of my new neighbors yet, as are you," Sa Rangim rumbles. "I understand."

"Yorani missed you," I note as she nestles in between his feet.

He smiles faintly. "The water around my feet is heated."

Yorani already spends all day around hot water. And it will probably always feel like home to her.

I watch her contentment. "I believe I need to spend my time at the altar to earth."

"May I accompany you? I have been lingering here, in part I think because I am not ready to approach that one alone."

So many pieces to that. I explained at our first visit that a priestess would always be available as a guide if needed. Either the priestess will not help him feel less alone before the spirits—and as this practice is new to him, this does not surprise me entirely; I was not sure he would ever return on his own—or he wishes my guidance in particular.

In either case, to be asked to serve as a guide or companion in this fashion is an honor, and I sense Sa Rangim knows it.

I bow. "Of course. Do you think..."

He smiles. "Yorani can be left alone here without cause for concern."

I nod, taking his word for it, and together we dry our feet on towels and pad to the bed of earth.

"This is where my focus needs to be today, for perhaps similar reasons as you," I say, immersing my feet in the rich dirt, feeling the rocks underneath. "How can I put roots down deeply enough that no one can sway them?"

He peers at me, carefully settling his own feet into the dirt. Slowly, as if each sensation, each moment is new and unique and precious.

"Are they trying?" he asks. "I find that distressing to hear."

"It's not related to you, if that helps," I say, running my fingers through the dirt, "but nevertheless. I knew attempts would be made. I am... questioning my ability to meet them. To know when to push, and how hard, in which direction."

I find a stone amid the dirt and lift it out, turning it over in my hands.

"Trees here," Sa Rangim says suddenly. "Their roots work differently than in the Cataclysm. As do most things, of course, but trees... I remembered trees outside the Cataclysm as stable, unmoving things. But they do bend, in strong wind. Their leaves blow, and sometimes are lost, but the trees themselves only snap in rare circumstances. Because their roots anchor them. What are your roots?"

My first instinct is to say I have none here, and that is the problem. But here with my feet in the dirt it feels like a lie, so I contemplate the stone in my hands.

My life as a princess is my background, but I have sawed myself free of it, for—

"My commitment to service," I murmur. "That is the core. Service to people, above all else."

"Ahh." Sa Rangim sighs. "That I do understand. Nurture your connections to those people, then, and in serving them you will have your roots."

Of course, he should know. He's spent a lifetime putting his people before everything. For all that I've lamented not having time to settle in Sayorsen, he's had less. "Is that enough?"

He glances up at me, amused. "Roots are not trees. I have been fostering connections among the Te Muraka for years, but that does not change, for instance, that one of our youngest acts against our interests and his own. He feels guilty about it, and so do I—we are his family, but he cannot find his course among us. He is symptomatic of a problem I do not yet have a solution for."

"His roots are with the Te Muraka, but that doesn't help him grow out into the world beyond," I say. "This particular world, at least."

"Yes," Sa Rangim agrees. "I wound us all inextricably together for our survival. I do not yet know how to incorporate us into the outside world."

"Or the world into you," I murmur. "I think it must work both ways. We will all have to change."

"But the Te Muraka will have to change first," he says. "Because we are fewer, and I can control our actions more directly. We have hoped for the possibility of this occasion for some time and are more prepared than the other residents of Sayorsen."

"But if you move too far, too fast, you may lose your own people, the roots that make you Te Muraka," I say. "Not to mention it sets a precedent that you will change even if the rest of the world does not."

"You see." Sa Rangim gestures. "It is a conundrum."

I nod. "In some ways, listening, and sensing what people need to hear, grants me a great deal of power," I say. "In others it serves only to underscore how deeply powerless I can be. I fear I do not yet know how to reconcile that gap."

"You will never feel confident you know," Sa Rangim says. "In fact, such confidence is an indicator you should reconsider. But I think you know that."

"I know to be sure my work is toward the end of serving others. But when that overlaps with serving myself, or at the *expense* of serving myself, it becomes murkier." I close my eyes. "I've learned to change with the water, but I've forgotten how to feel the solid ground under my feet."

"It isn't," he says.

I open my eyes. Look at him, look at the earth, and close them again.

He's right. It's not just that the earth can be moved, but that there's always movement happening that no one sees, incremental, invisible. Life. Always happening at every moment, and still we must stand on this foundation.

"I gather you are new to feeling you have power," Sa Rangim says. "That carries its own challenges. Being an old hand at it has different ones, but there is some overlap."

"When is it worthwhile to demonstrate what you're capable of, and when will it frighten people into the wrong kind of action," I say.

His golden eyes glow as he looks at me. "Indeed."

I need to dig in, to bolster my roots so every wind doesn't threaten to blow me over. Not standing stiff against the wind so I break, but not bending all the way for the winds of change, either; moving with the wind, but not away from myself.

Sa Rangim doesn't need to set roots. He needs to move them, entwine them among the community's, mine, so the Te Muraka can learn to thrive in new earth.

Earth that is still changeable; perhaps that comment was as much for himself as for me. It is not so anathema to what he knew in the Cataclysm. Just a different pace of movement whose rhythm he needs to learn to match.

"You'll be meeting one of Istalam's princesses before long," I say, mindful not to name her as my sister because while there aren't many people in the shrine, there are a few. "She arrived in town today to take over the integration effort on behalf of Istalam."

"The crown princess?" he asks.

I shake my head. "Saiyana, third in line for the throne. Administrative crisis management is her purview, and she's nearly as strong in magecraft as Ostario, whose proficiency is nigh unmatched."

In Rangim nods, waiting.

"Saiyana will see your power easily, because she sees much," I say, "but she will also see you as a problem to be solved. It is a consequence of the nature of the work she has dedicated herself to."

He frowns. "Are you advising me to resist her efforts?"

"No, the clearer you can be with your concerns, the more she can help you. But while you should demonstrate that you will work with her, be wary of any change she asks of you that is not accompanied by a next step *not* from you. It is a negotiation for her. Be easy to negotiate with, but make sure she must negotiate on your behalf, too."

Sa Rangim's eyes narrow thoughtfully. "Meet reasonable changes with reasonable expectations. She will deal in good faith?"

"Yes, but holding her to it will make her job easier, which will ultimately help you," I say. "And if she gives you any trouble, or the course flows in a troubling way you would redirect, please don't hesitate to call on me. I will intercede on your behalf."

"Against your—" He pauses, assessing how close any other people are to us, and drops his voice to ask quietly, "Against your own sister?"

"My sister is representing the institution of Istalam, which exists to serve its people. If I feel she is not representing it faithfully..." I shrug. "Yes, against my sister. My roots extend to you."

The statement feels obvious to me, but Sa Rangim bows low.

"Then perhaps there is hope for us yet," he says. "Though I will endeavor to not put you in a position against your sister."

"Don't feel the need to endeavor too hard," I say. "I would not be sad to have occasion to demonstrate my new understanding of my power to her."

Sa Rangim laughs. "I'll keep that in mind. Your advice has eased my mind, Miyara. Is there a way for me to return the favor?"

I open my mouth to ask him about tea spirits and what I thought I saw in the ceremony yesterday, but stop. I'm not certain I didn't imagine it. Sa Rangim will still be in Sayorsen if I change my mind once I know more.

Instead I ask, "Do you have any suggestions for how I can help Yorani? I didn't even know until yesterday she would play with something as non-destructive as yarn, but then she ate some unique treats and—you're laughing at me."

"Out of sympathy, I assure you," he says. "You've never raised a child before. In some ways Yorani will be like one, and in others she'll be both more and less explicable. You are learning to listen to her, and she to you. It will come. Your instinct to keep her close is good, I think, for now. But broaden her horizons as much as you can. As your familiar, she learns and grows with you. Long after you have passed, her life with you will form the basis for how she understands the world."

"No pressure then," I say, setting the stone back in the dirt and moving to stand.

Sa Rangim's gentle fingers on my wrist stop me. "It is, and it isn't," he says. "Who you are will shape the spirit she becomes as you demonstrate your self to her. I have seen who you are, and I have no fear of her future."

I bow my head. "I fear I do not merit your faith in me."

The heat of his fingers lifts. "That is also what it means to wield power, my friend. If I am not too bold to term you such?"

"You are not." I smile. "If we are friends, I don't suppose you'd be willing to help extract Yorani from her bath?"

His eyes glint. "I will leave you the pleasure of extracting her, but I'd be happy to offer my services drying her scales."

"I accept," I say quickly, and he rumbles with laughter.

CHAPTER 5

WHEN I ARRIVE AT DENIEL'S, he answers the door spattered in clay.

"Miyara! I wasn't expecting you. I mean, not that you normally message ahead of time—or need to—"

He lifts his hand to run it through his hair, and I grab his wrist before he can cake his hair with clay.

Even that, the touch of bare wrist, makes my own breath catch. Wearing security bracelets for so long, and then being stripped of them, has left a strange impression on my psyche. But my wrists are comfortably encircled now by the bracelets Deniel had crafted for me, giving me a sense of peace I hadn't realized I needed.

And making me peculiarly aware that he is still exposed.

Deniel pauses, smiling a little and changing his hand's course to clasp mine. "I do that a lot around you, don't I?"

He means running his hands through his hair, but I wouldn't mind if holding my hand became more common, too. I swallow and manage, "It's charming, but I'm now wondering which unexpected substances have found their way into your hair over the years. Is this a bad time?"

"Oh, no, I was actually hoping you'd come over this evening," he says. "I'm just running behind and was in the middle of something. Do you have a little while? Is it okay if I finish what I was working on?"

"Of course," I say, following him inside.

And Yorani takes off from my shoulder, flying straight for Deniel's clay.

Oh dear. I dart forward. "Deniel—"

He's already ahead of me, dragging Yorani away from his work station. "I... well, I almost got to her in time."

"Is your work—?"

"Fixable," he says, peering intently at what he was working on while holding Yorani aloft. "Or workable, anyway. If nothing else this will be an especially unique piece. But you."

He faces Yorani, lifting her up. Her tail swishes happily, and she is absolutely covered in clay.

"How did she manage that so quickly?" I ask in a mixture of wonder and exasperation.

Deniel laughs. "She's more prone to trouble than a kitten."

"Yes, because she seeks it out," I grump as Deniel passes her to me.

"So do kittens," he says dryly.

Oh.

"But in fairness," he continues, "Elowyn didn't go looking for trouble and still managed to end up a mess when she was little. It's something about being young."

"Elowyn," I repeat. "Your little sister?"

Deniel nods. "Speaking of, I have something to talk to you about later."

"So do I," I say.

He frowns. "Is everything okay?"

"For the moment," I say. "I'll tell you once you've wrapped up. I suppose I'm now going to use this time to give Yorani a bath, if I may?"

"Good luck," he says. "There are a couple special products under the sink that may help with the clay, which tends to cake. Though it may interact differently since Yorani doesn't have skin. Oh, but maybe grab the cooking oil?"

To polish her scales. "Good idea. I promise I'll replace it, but may I take one of your scrubbers, too?"

"Yes, scrubber, towel, whatever you need," Deniel says, already focusing back on his work. "My home is at your disposal."

The simplicity, the ease of his words arrests me. Words fail me, so I bow.

But Deniel doesn't notice. It's as if I can see him falling back into an artistic trance, focusing on his work, the rest of his surroundings falling out of his vision. I'm glad he can relax enough to make art with me here, that my presence doesn't keep him from himself.

So I leave him to it, requisitioning anything I can think of and sealing Yorani and me in the bathroom.

I would have said, before, I was comfortable using Deniel's bathroom.

But washing in another person's bathroom feels more intimate, and I'm not entirely certain why. Going through the same motions he must, perhaps. Delving into his cupboards, using his products. Like I'm wearing his clothing. Though why I should blush at that prospect is equally odd. I do, nevertheless, imagining how I would look in his shirts and trousers—and how he would look at me.

Yorani splashes around as I run hot water, and I purse my lips. I am not optimistic about how my own clothing will fare. I strip out of it, hiding it inside a cupboard before Yorani can think to get to it, and grab a piece of string I believe to be one of Talsu's toys to mostly draw my hair out of the way before crawling into the bath with Yorani.

At first, she is delighted by the entire experience, and I make a mental note to run baths for her at my own apartment. She enjoys splashing games, and I untie my hair to use the string for games, too.

But the clay doesn't come off at all; it adheres more firmly, if anything. When I scrub harder, Yorani's good mood frays.

After much trial and some error, it's clear water has not helped matters, regular soap has no effect, and the pressure of focused scrubbing bothers her; her scales are too delicate. With a silent apology, I steal Deniel's toothbrush to slowly work his ceramic-removing lotion over all the many affected areas.

Yorani doesn't fight me, much, but she squirms a great deal—out of boredom, I think, rather than discomfort.

But eventually she is clean—and dried, and wet again and unhappy because the water has turned cool, and dried, and only lightly rubbed with oil because she is out of patience and puffing smoke into my face.

"Is it safe for Yorani to come out?" I call. Surely it must be; my skin has shriveled, and I am shivering.

"Yes, it's all clear here. Is everything okay?"

"I'll be just a minute," I say, opening the door just enough for Yorani to zoom out and for me to smell that Deniel has started cooking.

My hair did not make it through the ordeal unscathed, and I dry it as best I can. Regarding myself in the mirror, it still looks bedraggled. I am too cold to worry about it, though, toweling myself off and dressing again rapidly before attempting to run Deniel's comb through it.

My efforts are not effective.

I sigh. I can't leave Deniel alone with Yorani any longer, but at least my clothes are on straight.

I head out and promptly snatch Yorani out of the air above a hissing Talsion, carrying the tea spirit to the other side of the room.

"We do not pick fights with our friends," I say. Yorani leaps up, and I place her right back down again, glaring right back as she puffs smoke at me. "No. It's not Talsu's fault you got yourself into trouble and had to face the consequences."

After two more rounds of this Yorani subsides, hunched over with her butt facing me but still twisting around to eye me narrowly.

I turn to the kitchen, where Deniel is biting his lip to hold back a smile while he deftly maneuvers a pot on the stove.

It's unconscionable that he should be so attractive when I look like this.

"Yes, I know I look ridiculous," I say.

His smile breaks crookedly free across his face. Spirits.

"The word I would have chosen is 'adorable'," he says. "Come here."

I trudge over. "What's all this?"

"This one's just to get some steam going for Yorani to bask in," he says. "She looks like she could do with some warmth without the water. And that pot is the soup I started earlier. I suspected we might both be harried again, though the reason for it I could not have predicted."

I stare, wondering, at this man who is unreasonably perfect.

Then he kisses me, compounding the problem. Such as it is.

"Turn around," he murmurs, and somehow I find it in myself to do so. I hear a drawer open, and then he is smoothing my hair, running his hands over it. I close my eyes, savoring the sensation.

Then he gathers my hair and twists it. I frown, trying to figure out what he's doing, and feel him insert sticks into my hair.

"There," he says. "That should hold you. Your hair is much more cooperative than Elowyn's."

"The texture of it changed when Lorwyn fixed the color." I tentatively reach a hand back to touch. I've seen women with this sort of hair twist in the Gaellani market, and I itch to rush back to his mirror to see how it looks on me. "I am both grateful and mortified by how much more capable you are than I am. Thank you."

"It's nothing," he says, but he sounds pleased.

"Do you do Elowyn's hair often?"

"Not anymore, since I don't live at my parents' home anymore and she's old enough to do it herself now, but I used to." He shrugs. "I'm good with my hands, and my parents weren't always available. It was easy enough to learn. Would you like me to show you?"

"Another time," I say, and while I'm serious I find myself hoping he'll still want to play with my hair again. In part for the physical sensation, but also the feeling of being actively taken care of warms me. I am slightly surprised it doesn't bother me—perhaps it's because it's unnecessary care, so I am comforted rather than embarrassed by his effort. "My hands are too cold to be dexterous for a while yet."

For a moment I think he'll wrap me in his arms to warm me, but to my disappointment after a moment he seems to win some internal struggle and steps back, hands twitching. "Then let's get Yorani situated and have some soup."

Yorani is displeased at being placed somewhere, but since it's warm she grudgingly stays, glaring all the while.

"I suspect as soon as she feels warm again she'll start looking for trouble," I say as we move to the table. "We'd better eat fast."

"Perhaps next time we should try firing the clay off her scales," Deniel muses. "She is in some sense a dragon, after all."

I wilt into my chair. "Spirits. I didn't think of that. That... would have gone much more easily."

"So optimistic," he murmurs. "I assume you weren't largely responsible for caring for your younger sister?"

Lorwyn said almost the same thing. "No. She's not that much younger than me than I am to Saiyana, but her... political circumstances are different, because of our parents' involvement with her. Where they could not be with the rest of us. More of our care was left to tutors, in general."

Though that isn't fully true—Iryasa and Reyata are rumored to have been close as children. Saiyana had more interaction with them than I did, but I've always thought it was in part because she lacked the same closeness that she strove to force her way into my world when our tutors would have happily kept us separate.

And then I walked away.

"Are you and your sister close?" I ask.

He tilts his head from side to side; sort of. "Yes and no. We've always understood each other in some ways, I think, but we're also almost ten years apart."

My eyebrows shoot up. "That's not a common age discrepancy among successive siblings." I've studied enough historical censuses to know that.

"No, my parents had so much trouble conceiving with me they stopped worrying about precautions against pregnancy as they got older. So Elowyn came as a surprise." He sighs. "They love her, of course, but she's perceptive. She knows her birth created complications for them."

"In what way?"

Deniel hesitates, glancing at me. "Time and money," he finally says, uncomfortable but not mincing words for my sake. "It's easier now that I'm making money, too, but for years they supported not just my upbringing, but my training. If our family had been any bigger they couldn't have."

Lorwyn has five sisters. Spirits.

Deniel is being far less careful than usual when speaking about his parents, so I dare to ask, "What do your parents do?"

"My father had trained as a structural engineer back before the Cataclysm, but as a Gaellani here the only work he could get was as a manual laborer. No one with investors will trust Gaellani with more serious work. His jobs are exhausting but also unreliable and don't bring in that much money."

"And your mother works in a bakery," I recall.

"Yes, she's an assistant. It's long days with weird hours compared to much of the community and carrying heavy loads. The income is reliable, at least, but it... drains her, artistically, because she has no input. It's all drudgery, every day. Someday I want to help her get a loan to start her own shop, but she thinks it's impossible. I told you she shapes candy?"

"Yes," I say. "I'd love to see someday."

"That's actually what I wanted to talk to you about," Deniel says. "I was hoping tomorrow you could come for dinner at their apartment to meet them."

I am warm and full of soup, which happily means my body can't work up the energy to react with the shock I feel.

"You want to introduce me to your family?" I ask faintly.

Ah, with the words comes the panic I was expecting.

"I want you to know them," he says. "Since we're seeing each other seriously."

That's the term. "Seeing each other," not "courting." I mentally file it away, even as it warms me to hear him name our relationship in those terms. Not that I didn't know, of course, but something about their being a term that applies to our relationship makes it feel strangely more defined, more real.

We are not just two people who want to care for each other, we are seeing each other. We have a relationship predicated on no one but ourselves.

Which is both a comfort and, in this specific context, a pressure.

"I want to know your family, too," I say. "But I... am moderately terrified by the suddenness. I don't know what they will expect of me. I don't know what to expect of them."

To my surprise, this seems to amuse him. "Miyara, you're a tea master. Dealing unflappably with any situation is literally your specialty."

Put like that, he has a point. "But this matters."

I thought he might be cautious about how I'd react to information about his family circumstances, given the discrepancy in our upbringings, and that had made him want to handle this slowly, carefully.

"And that's why I don't want to wait," Deniel says.

When he spoke so openly about his family I should have known right away something had changed.

"I know we're both busy, but I'm not sure when we won't be," he says. "I want to make time for what matters, no matter what."

And put like that, there's no way I can refuse. "You are devious and wise."

Deniel smiles. "So that's a yes?"

Somehow I will make the time.

To my further surprise, with that thought, something in me settles.

This is my place, and I won't let this tournament—this pressure from the tea guild or my sister—deter me from the life I've chosen.

I will fight, and I will live, and I will have to learn to do both at once.

"Yes," I say, "but it will have to be a somewhat late dinner, since tomorrow is the first day of the tea tournament."

"Oh," Deniel says. "I didn't realize it was starting so soon."

"Nor did I," I say dryly.

"Are you sure—"

"Yes," I say. "You're correct. I only apologize for my schedule constraints, and hope it won't unduly burden your parents."

"Don't worry about it," he says. "I'll speak to them. We'll touch base tomorrow afternoon about the get-together, then?"

I sigh. "Yes, but. Speaking of family. Saiyana arrived in town with an ultimatum."

Deniel sets down his spoon carefully. "Tell me."

I do. When I'm finished, Deniel says, "I think that explains a couple customers I had today. Not your sister, but visitors who seemed more interested in me and my business than my work."

"Are you sure it wasn't my sister?" I ask. "She can be... difficult to deter."

As I am becoming. An odd thought.

"Yes," he says. "After you confessed your identity to me, I looked up the royal portraits."

I blink. "What for?"

"So I'd have some idea what your sisters looked like if they came looking for you, since you've been so worried about it," Deniel says.

Oh.

"Do I look different from the royal portrait?" I wonder. "Aside from the hair, I mean."

"Yes, actually. You were poised in the portrait, but you looked..." He thinks. "Lost. Sad. Less vibrant. Even if you hadn't told me you needed to leave the court, I would have known."

I blink sudden tears back. "Then you would have been unique."

He shakes his head. "I admit, it's difficult for me to understand how. Having met you, trying to reconcile the distance in your family relationships is..."

I never hear how he intended to finish that thought, because Yorani chooses this moment to swoop down and steal the ball of yarn from Talsion. What was a game before is clearly a challenge tonight, and Deniel and I separate them before their claws can do real damage.

But nothing I do can make Yorani settle, leaving Talsion agitated. "I think I'd better take her... back, for the night," my mouth hesitating over using the word home.

Home isn't just Sayorsen, or with my community, or even this house. It's specifically where Deniel is.

While I'm reeling from that realization, Deniel says tentatively, "There were a couple of legal cases I wanted to ask you about, actually. Here, wait just a moment."

This is easier said than done; Yorani does not want to be held, so I end up clutching her tightly, feeling her claws gouge into the clothing I'd so carefully protected earlier. Alas.

Deniel tries to pass me a sheet of paper, but I shake my head. "I can't put her down right now. Put it in my kit? I'll write out what I know tonight and make sure a messenger has it to you first-thing tomorrow."

"Then I'll have time to actually clean up and get myself a new toothbrush," Deniel says, and although he's smiling I feel like I've let him down.

"I'm sorry," I start.

But he silences me with a kiss. "All is well. Good night, Miyara. Dream sweetly."

If I am to dream, I hope it is of him and not pressuring claws.

CHAPTER 6

WHEN YORANI AND I arrive at the agreed-upon entrance to the Cataclysm, it's immediately clear something is wrong by Risteri's stiffness and the tournament official rushing over, another guide in tow.

"Miyara! Good, good, I was beginning to worry you'd never make it," he says.

I frown, as Yorani shifts on my shoulder—I think she enjoys how her movement draws the official's attention to her and makes him nervous—because I'm not late; I am, in point of fact, early.

Yet I'm still the last one here. Risteri left to scout the lay of the Cataclysm today early, so I knew she would be waiting. But that the other contestants, as well as a small crowd, are already here, tells me I have missed something.

"Was the meeting time adjusted after our meeting?" I ask. "I understood we would not be starting until sunrise, which I've arrived well in advance of."

The official's polite expression freezes when Risteri answers me.

"It's a common technique deployed by people wishing to curry favor with a certain kind of authority," she explains tonelessly. "They arrive far earlier than needed to signal the degree of import they accord the person they're meeting, in hopes either that person will be flattered into special favors or they'll have an opportunity to obtain information outside the scope of that meeting."

Ah. I have, of course, witnessed this at court, though I've generally not been on the receiving end personally. I simply didn't expect such jockeying for position in a tournament ostensibly to judge our ability. Foolish of me.

Now I wonder which judges are part of the mingling crowd, and which I've offended by not arriving early to attend on them.

And how I can belatedly turn this if not into an advantage, then at least back to a leveler playing field.

"But we all signed agreements not just committing to an impartial contest, but asserting we would enter the Cataclysm with the same resources," I say. "Would informational tips not count?"

"Evidently not," Risteri says. "Fortunately you've been in the Cataclysm before, because the official here has been dropping hints for the last hour or so."

"That's outrageous," he says, flushing.

I cut off that line of conversation before it can gather kindling. "You seemed in a hurry to reach me. Is something amiss?"

"Ah, that." The official gathers himself and pastes on a smile. "We understand you're new to this competition. Since you haven't had the same experience to get to this point as the other contestants, we wanted to offer you a guide whom you may find more suitable for the purposes of this challenge."

Risteri says nothing, but her jaw clenches. We've landed on the true problem, then.

"I have no qualms about being held to the same standards as the other contestants," I say. "These are the finals, and I was expected to find my own guide. I have done so."

"You understand, there are..." The official lowers his voice. "Certain realities at play, in a public competition like this. How particular gestures and choices influence judgment."

Carefully, I take Yorani off my shoulder and pass her to Risteri, who accepts her out of habit.

For the next few minutes, I think it's best I have no potential distractions.

"If I may test my understanding," I say, "are you implying that Risteri of Sayorsen is not permitted to accompany me as my guide, or that her presence will adversely affect my judgment?"

"Risteri of *Taresim*—" the official begins.

"That is not her name," I interrupt coldly. "Risteri is not implicated in Kustio of Taresim's crimes. You will refer to her by the name she has chosen."

The official blinks, clearly startled by my tone—and my volume. We are beginning to attract onlookers.

"Be that as it may," he says impatiently, "you must see why our producers have concerns about promotion when legal proceedings concerning her association are still ongoing."

"If there were concerns my choice was not in accordance with tournament allowances, I don't see why I wasn't informed before now, when all this should be well settled," I say.

"We did attempt to contact you, but there was some confusion with the messengers' guild." Frustration leaks into the official's voice. "You'd never see such business in Miteran, let me tell you that."

"I have lived in Miteran," I say. "I am confident the messengers' guild here is not inferior."

In fact I know nothing of the kind, having never had occasion to frequent the messengers' guild in Miteran. But the superiority in his tone as he casually dismisses the competence of anyone outside our capital city galls me.

"And I assure you I have never had to scramble like we did this morning," he snaps. "They were unable to deliver our messages to you in advance! I've never heard of such shoddy business."

Nor have I, which tells me it was done on purpose.

I am nearly concerned, until he continues, "I suppose it's what I should've expected, all things considered in this place. A child like that should never have been entrusted with such responsibility."

Glynis. Why didn't she warn me she was blocking the tournament messages, so I'd know they planned to target Risteri? Did she think I wouldn't appear convincingly ignorant?

Maybe she's not done testing me after all.

"As I said, we've already done the work of acquiring an alternate guide for you, since we couldn't reach you," the official says. "I had simply hoped you'd be here earlier so we could work this out... quietly."

Oh, no.

Quiet he will not have from me.

"Miyara," Risteri says, at which point I finally realize perhaps there is more than one reason *she* has been quiet throughout this conversation. "Maybe you shouldn't jeopardize your chances. I know what's at stake for you."

Yorani nips at Risteri's fingers, interrupting anything more she might have said.

"You see?" the official says. "She understands. Let us look out for your best interests."

And then I think Glynis isn't testing me after all. She risked her reputation, and further judgment of the Gaellani, to help Risteri, who has done her best to support Gaellani when few Istals with any semblance of power do. Who has done her best to support *me*, when she had nothing to gain and everything to lose.

This isn't about me at all, but about Risteri, and what she needs. And Glynis has trusted me to handle it.

We have an audience, all of whom are pretending not to listen in.

"A tea specialist who sacrifices friendship for advancement surely cannot be the best, so I am not jeopardizing my chances on that count," I say to Risteri. "And losing you as my guide would *surely* jeopardize my chances, because as you know perfectly well you're the most knowledgeable guide in Sayorsen. I will not accept any other, and I see no reason to."

This last I direct at the official who hisses, "I am trying to help you. Do you want to win this tournament or don't you?"

I bow, and do not lower my voice. "Thank you for your concern, but if I cannot win as myself, then victory is meaningless to me. This tournament purports to select the best tea specialist, and I intend to demonstrate what that means."

"*Best* is always a subjective category," the official tries once more. "The tide of public opinion plays a role. This will not play out the way you think it will."

Public opinion again. That's the tea guild's concern, too; distressing on its own. But if I can't earn approval with the way I mean to go on, though, surely it will only hurt me later.

I've dedicated myself to finding my own path of service. Compromising my values will not be part of it.

"Nevertheless," I say. "Risteri of Sayorsen is my choice."

"Well." He signals to someone behind him. "We'll see."

No. I have been forced into this contest, but interference like this, I will not tolerate.

I incline my head. "I had wondered," I say, "at the tea guild's long separation from this illustrious contest. I do hope there's no basis for them to doubt the sincerity of its commitment to its stated truths."

The official freezes. "What are you saying?"

And then I smile.

Not Lorwyn's shark smile, but my own version that appears at once both sweeter and more dangerous.

The official freezes.

"Ah, but I see this is another part of the test, isn't it?" I ask. "No doubt the others have endured tests of character throughout the earlier trials. How do I fare, do you think?"

I wink at the audience, who collectively hold their breath.

The official watches me narrowly for a moment and then he, too, smiles—a bureaucratic, empty smile. "Well done!" he says grandly, and the audience bursts into applause. "We'll have to see what the judges think. But now that that's settled, let's make sure all the candidates are ready for this challenge, the first of the finals!"

The audience applauds again as the official wanders off with one last long glance at me.

"I'm not sure you should have done that," Risteri says to me quietly as attention shifts.

I hug her impulsively, Yorani apparently utterly content to be squeezed between us. "I'm sorry you had to stand here for so long knowing what they were all thinking. But while I have many doubts about this contest, this decision is not among them."

"Miyara, it could cost you your tea mastery if you don't win!"

I rest my hands on her shoulders and hold her gaze, wishing it could confer to her the same sense of security my bracelets give me. I focus on that feeling, will it into my voice. "I meant what I said. Every word. If joining the ranks of tea masters requires abandoning you, I will not do it. No prize would be worth it. Never doubt that."

She takes a deep, shuddering breath, wiping her forearm across her eyes. "Okay. Spirits, okay. I hope you realize now I'm going to take you so deep into the Cataclysm your judges won't even be able to fathom the ingredients you end up with."

I smile, collecting Yorani back to my shoulder. "Then I believe we are on the same page."

I keep one hand on Yorani's warm scales and place the other in Risteri's, focusing on the connection between us, imagining my tree's roots supported in them.

We are ready.

Other guides accompany officials and a portion of the audience into the Cataclysm to witness the proceedings. I purse my lips, considering. Hanuva is making a show of playing to the audience, which would probably be a wise move for me as well. The judges and audience don't know me, and if the official is right that will matter. This could be an opportunity to endear myself to them.

But this is not why I selected Risteri as my guide. It's too late for me to compete on emotional investment from the crowd; for the moment, what I have going for me is the opposite: mystery.

So before any onlooker notices to object, Risteri and I slip away. I catch measuring glances from other guides, but they see the direction we're taking, exchange looks, and shake their heads.

They know better than to follow an explorer of Risteri's caliber with untried passengers.

We soon leave the safe borderlands behind as Risteri leads me deep into the Cataclysm. Quickly, too, because she knows she can trust me to follow her directions without question.

Eventually, we begin to encounter mysteries neither Risteri nor I can name, and these I collect samples of.

When I can. There is only so much time, and I will not waste it on magical defenses so strong it would take a witch to overcome.

I wish Lorwyn were with us to help me be more discriminating in my selections, but for now I can only do my best. My strength in tea brewing is not in the harvesting of ingredients, so I will rely on Risteri to make sure they are sufficiently unique and Lorwyn to help me experiment with them safely. My own acumen will be needed later.

"We're in luck," Risteri tells me at one point, though she looks troubled. "Normally the Cataclysm would be too unstable by this point to bring you without assistance from Lorwyn. It's like it's more... focused, somehow. I wonder if it's because of Yorani?"

Yorani's assistance has been mixed—she flutters ineffectually around teasing vines, but a single puff of smoke from her renders dancing stones inert. I keep a close eye on her, but to my surprise she seems at ease here, interacting with the chaos.

Perhaps it shouldn't be shocking. Yorani was born within the Cataclysm, after all, but she's spent far more time in the world outside the Cataclysm at this point. It makes me wonder about the nature of spirits, and what is truly natural.

So when both her and Risteri's heads snap up at the same time, I know something out of the ordinary even for the Cataclysm has occurred.

Risteri closes her eyes, focusing on listening. When she opens them, she frowns.

"I don't know who that is, but they're Velasari, and there's more than one."

I remember the Velasari spies she rescued on my first visit to the Cataclysm. "Are they in danger?"

"It doesn't sound like it, but I also don't hear any voices I recognize—namely a guide—which I don't like at all."

I don't, either. The last thing I need is for Velasari to bring an international crisis to Sayorsen on top of the Te Muraka's resettlement and this preposterous tournament. "Then perhaps we should go see."

She hesitates. "But, Miyara, the tournament—"

I pat my bag. "I'm doing well. We can continue to forage on the way. It's not as though we don't have a perfectly legitimate reason to be exploring."

Relief melts into her expression. "I'll make sure you have all the best stuff before we leave. This way."

Yorani settles on my shoulder without prompting, gaze intent in the direction Risteri is leading us, the quiet readiness of a predator.

The Velasari aren't nearly as deep in the Cataclysm as we were, but still far farther in than they ought to be. Risteri locates them without any trouble, and we hide a little ways off. I take a centering breath to steady myself, focusing on the weight of the bracelets on my wrists, a gift of roots to hold onto my self.

Risteri's right, I realize. As if there's a kind of ripple effect, the Cataclysm around us seems more solid. But it could just be a matter of perception, preventing me from seeing further into the chaos. I'll ask her thoughts later, when we're not spying.

On spies.

The Velasari tea contestant, Lino, is one of the figures here. And he's accompanied not by one, but two others, both Velasari: an old, tough-looking woman and a well-muscled, serious young man.

Neither, critically, is a Sayorseni Cataclysm guide.

"This is needlessly risky," the young man says, hacking away a swarm of branches that attempt to surround him. "You hardly have enough information about the supposedly safer sections of the Cataclysm. We have no idea what the effects will be here."

"Exactly," Lino snaps. "I have scarcely any information of merit about the Cataclysm."

"You have the combined intelligence of years of Velasari agents." The man looks around for the next attack.

Risteri isn't, I realize. Where she stopped us, nothing is moving to harm us.

This is the difference a true guide makes.

Lino sneers. "Yes. That's exactly what I mean, Aleixo. Keep up."

Aleixo draws himself up. "You may be a genius, but that doesn't make you superior."

"And yet you think I can make your foreign tech work, just like that? You're as stupid as you look."

"If you can't, there's no reason for us to risk our lives here." Aleixo gracefully side-steps a cloud that erupts into teeth and feeds it the discarded branches before it can reach the charge he's arguing with. Entero would approve.

"Lino's a genius," the old woman says idly, "but not a magician."

Lino's face tightens. "Yes. Velasar has made well sure of that."

"You know what you were promised," she says. "Do your part, and you'll be knighted, and the magecraft collegium will be open to you."

Interesting. Unlike Istalam, where—at least in theory—anyone can study magecraft, Velasar restricts education to only the aristocracy and wards sworn to the service of the state. Their control of magical learning has only grown tighter since the Cataclysm and Velasar's escaping relatively unscathed, giving the government the justification it's always craved for hoarding knowledge.

Taresan has increasingly trended in a worryingly similar direction, but there at least people can practice magecraft informally on their own without sanctions, even if they're not able to attend most educational institutions or earn credentials that would allow them to make money from their work.

More than one scholar in Istalam has argued our openness—such as it is, I'm coming to understand—in training anyone with the requisite dedication and talent in magecraft is the core reason why, until the Cataclysm, Istalam's empire was able to grow so vast.

Which in turn means, of course, since Istalam was disproportionately affected by the Cataclysm in comparison to Taresan and Velasar, fear and opportunism now drive people to hold our openness responsible for our loss.

I do not know Lino. Feeling trapped, locked away from opportunity, that I can empathize with. What he appears to have led himself to on account of that feeling... that is more difficult for me to accept in any gracious terms.

"Imagine," the older woman continues, "not having to pay people like me to implement your designs ever again."

"Fail and I'll take the fall, yes, this is not new information, Ignasa," Lino says.

She smiles faintly. "I didn't think it was. But as Aleixo says, we've taken a risk here. It had better be worth our while."

"Your experiments thus far have been ineffectual," Lino says. "I need to understand why, and my repeating what you've already done won't give us new information. So while there's a perfectly reasonable excuse for someone of my prominence to be in this spirits-cursed place, I'll learn whatever I can. Now, hand me that."

Aleixo just glares at him.

"Or stand there and force me to fail," Lino says, irritated. "That will definitely get results that will impress your superiors."

"Aleixo, stop wasting time," Ignasa says. "That's an order. What would your precious commander Braisa say about neglecting your duty?"

"Nothing," Aleixo says, though the mention of the famously harsh commander seems to relax him. "She would simply look at me with such disappointment that no further admonishment would compare." Aleixo unloads a huge metallic contraption from his back. "I've committed to our cause, and I will see it through."

The older woman watches him narrowly, I suspect wondering if she will need to handle her junior officer like she is handling the asset they've recruited.

Lino frowns down at the contraption, adjusting pieces I can't see. "All right. Let's try this."

A loud whirring sounds.

Sparks shoot out of the contraption, and the Velasari all jump back.

"Shut it down!" Lino yells, hiding behind a tree.

"This is your experiment," Ignasa growls at him, snagging him back as the tree attempts to cocoon him.

"And I'm your cover story," he says.

It's Aleixo who darts in, risking getting close to the dangerously fritzing machine to somehow stop it. "You're a coward, is what you are," he says to Lino. "Congratulations. That's an even worse reaction than we got."

"Then we've learned something," Lino says, approaching it again as if he hadn't fled moments earlier. "All right. We're going to try this another way. Turn it around."

"I think you forget," Ignasa says, "who is in charge here."

"I am, unless you think you can get by without me," Lino says. "No? That's what I thought. You're the muscle, Ignasa. I'm the brain."

She gives him a long look before nodding sharply at Aleixo to hoist the contraption.

"I thought you'd be glad," Ignasa says. "I scouted you myself. This is a chance to serve the crown most Velasari could never dream of, and you'll get everything you've ever wanted out of it. Is helping bring down this backwards nation that foments witchcraft not worth it to you?"

Lino snorts, messing with the contraption again. "Istalam can burn to the ground, for all I care. This is a distraction from my work."

"It's always about you," Aleixo snipes.

"When I have my magecraft certification, you'll see why it always should have been," Lino says, and fires up the contraption again.

I watch light gathering inside and realize it's pointed in our direction. "Risteri!" I hiss.

Risteri grabs me and Yorani and yanks us to the side, and we go down tumbling.

Only this time the contraption doesn't just spark.

A beam like lightning cracks out, past us.

It fritzes like it's reached a wall—the barrier?—and fritzes again to another nearby spot, and again, like it's trying to gain purchase.

But then the whirring powers down, and it's clear that whatever the machine tried to do, it failed.

My heart is still beating rapidly when a shadow leans over us, and Risteri rolls us all out of the way before coming to her feet with her knife in a graceful move just as Ignasa calls out, "Aleixo, hold!"

"They could have overheard us," Aleixo says. "They're liabilities."

Yorani's claws tighten on my shoulder, but she doesn't make a move. She's frightened, I realize. Like when Talsu's fur fluffed up, which Deniel explained was a signal that his hackles had been raised and he was considering the opportune moment to strike.

I can't say I blame her, in this scenario, but I'm not sure it's the wisest course of action.

"If you want them, you'll have to go through me," Risteri says, falling into a ready stance.

"With pleasure," Aleixo says, hefting his short sword.

"Well, well, the tea pretender herself," Lino says, "with her creature of wickedness and the house traitor. How delightful to see you so deep in the Cataclysm."

I'm startled enough by the bile in his voice when he speaks of Yorani in particular that Risteri gets her mouth open an instant before I can.

"Oh, Lino, this isn't deep," Risteri says. "You'd need a guide and magic for that, and you don't have either, do you?"

As his expression tightens, I ask, "What have you done with Risteri's colleague?"

Lino snorts. "The so-called 'guide'? Nothing but make him happy. Talented addicts are easy enough to bribe." Risteri's expression goes stony. "But let's return to your previous point. I do, in fact, have access to a mage." He gestures at Ignasa. "So how deep into the Cataclysm could you take us?"

"Absolutely not," Ignasa snaps. "She could lead us wherever she wanted and then abandon us there or worse. We can't trust her."

"I disagree," Lino says. "She was willing to sell out her own father, after all. Perhaps she'd be willing to negotiate for her own life now, since she must realize otherwise there's no compelling reason for you not to kill her."

Risteri's hand tightens on her knife. I know enough from Entero to be sure it's not a knife intended for combat, and Ignasa and Aleixo are both clearly trained. Risteri's odds against them aren't good, and I'm no help there. What Yorani could do, we should never have to find out.

Which means this cannot come to a fight, and that *is* my work. I focus on the weight of the bracelets on my wrists, let the awareness of their comforting presence make me confident and calm.

"How interesting," I say. "The best genius Velasar can scrounge to send on such an ignoble mission, and this is what your deduction amounts to? Your ability to read people is dreadful, and your handler has too much sense to kill us, which is why she stopped Aleixo. Perhaps, Lino, you're not qualified to be in charge of yourself after all."

His eyes narrow. "Is that what you think?"

I smile pityingly. "I think the princess Saiyana is in town, and I think the mysterious disappearance of a tea master on her watch will attract exactly the sort of investigation you don't want."

"She's right," Ignasa says. "And there's nothing she can do to stop us in any case. Reporting would only make her look like she was trying to sabotage the tournament, and no one will believe her friend here, all things considered. Our position is secure."

She's right, too.

Spirits take her, but she's right.

No official reporting channel will believe I haven't just invented a Velasari conspiracy out of desperation to retain my mastery.

I'll still tell Saiyana, of course, but with no evidence and just Risteri and me as sources there will only be so much she can do.

"Then perhaps," I say, "you should return to the safer edges of the Cataclysm now."

"Why should we?" Lino counters. "You can't hurt us, or you would have done so. I think we'll continue about our business."

"Because you won't injure us, either, but Risteri can track you through the Cataclysm wherever you go and turn it against you," I say, and shoot a deliberate look to Ignasa as if to say, *Take your charge in hand.*

Ignasa looks thoughtful, which is concerning, but her reaction in this moment isn't the most important one.

Lino's expression twists. "Your dependence on others will cost you this competition."

"That I understand the benefit of listening to guidance and trusting sound judgment is why I will win," I say. "Now go."

Without waiting for his companions to decide, Aleixo slowly backs away with his weapon, keeping his eyes on Risteri, who doesn't move. He hefts the contraption onto his back, and in moments they're gone.

I close my eyes, letting out a breath.

Yorani nuzzles my neck, and I gather her into my arms. "It's all right, little one. It's all right."

"It's not all right," Risteri growls. "What are we going to do? What were they up to?"

"Nothing good," I say. "But I don't think there's any need to follow them. Let's do what we came to do."

"That's it? Miyara, who knows what they could be doing to the Cataclysm! That light—"

"No, Ignasa won't let him push any further today." I'm confident in that much. "An agent doesn't get that old unless they're careful. Not to mention I just gave her what she needed to rein him in. She'll take the opportunity. The Cataclysm is safe from their machinations for now."

Risteri shakes her head. "They've already done something," she says. "Miyara, look around you. This deep in, the Cataclysm shouldn't look this stable around us."

"You said earlier it looked unusually stable," I say.

Risteri regards me seriously. "And what if this is why? And what does it mean for the rest of the Cataclysm?"

"Let's find out," I say. "You said you'd take me deeper. Let's take a look." I peer at Yorani, burrowed in my chest. "If you're up for it, little one?"

Yorani pokes her head out and rubs her nose against my arm deliberately.

I take this to mean yes.

Risteri takes a breath. "Have I mentioned you're never boring?"

I smile, but given all I've learned over the last few minutes it's half-hearted.

Velasar isn't just plotting against Istalam; they're putting those plots into action. And they're going to go through the Cataclysm to do it.

I tighten my hold on Yorani as we delve deeper. I will stand as firmly in the face of their machinations as Risteri just did.

They will have to go through me.

CHAPTER 7

THE REMAINING CATACLYSM INGREDIENT-GATHERING portion of this tournament challenge concludes without further incident, though there are veiled comments afterwards from the officials to the audience about how their guides lost track of both me and Lino. I know I will pay for my choice in the first match.

The officials put on a show for the spectators, who largely couldn't follow us inside. My showmanship is perhaps not what they'd prefer. But at least I'm confident in my poise, from my upbringing as a princess, and in my ease at speaking without preparation to an audience, from working in customer service.

Risteri, likewise, handles herself well. Not because of her aristocratic education, which she largely avoided, but from entertaining tourists with accounts of the cataclysm for years.

By the time we're out of the Cataclysm, the officials have also crafted a narrative of Risteri as a victim of her father, like a princess trapped in a tower, and her quest for independence and to separate herself from his legacy.

As soon as the show is over, though, the officials don't acknowledge us; I expect they resent me for putting them in this position. I don't know what effect that will have on the judging.

As the crowd disperses, I catch sight of Glynis and make my way to her. Yorani has been subdued, quiet and watchful on my shoulder, like she doesn't trust all these strange people. I can't say I blame her. I want to get her to a familiar and secluded location as soon as possible.

"Make this quick," Glynis says gruffly. "I have lots of news to spread."

"Thank you." I bow. "If in the future it's ever possible to warn me, I would greatly appreciate it, but thank you all the same."

"Hard to pretend total incompetence if an investigation reveals I got a different message to you," Glynis points out.

I'm not sure whether I should be pleased or bothered she thinks I cannot pretend total incompetence.

"Was that it?" she asks.

"No, to my regret," I say. "I need you to get a message to Princess Saiyana."

Glynis' eyes widen. "You don't mess around, do you? Do I want to know what this is about?"

I purse my lips. "Probably, but I'm not sure it's safe for you to know."

She frowns. "You don't trust—"

"Other people to not hurt you if they think you might have the information, no," I interrupt.

Her face goes blank. "Oh. Is this like Kustio again?"

Better and worse. The Velasari don't have their feet on the throats of everyone in Sayorsen, but an international incident has the potential for very damaging ramifications. "Yes. Can you ask her to meet me here please?"

"No," Glynis says. "Spirits, you still really don't understand how messengers' guilds work, do you? The princess doesn't accept messages from just anyone."

Ah. I should have expected that. "Mage Ostario, then?"

"Also no, not now that he's part of an official princess-headed project." She stares at me hard. "Do you really think a princess of Istalam would just show up and meet you because you asked?"

"We've been in communication about the treaty with the Te Muraka," I explain quickly. "And I met her yesterday. I believe she would. How do I get a message to her, then?"

"Don't you have special mage schooling?" Glynis scowls. "There's a code her guards use to filter messages."

I close my eyes, thinking back. Most of my messages at the palace were carried by guards; I'd had no need to spell them myself. And since I'm no longer a princess, it would be a great affront to everyone, from my sisters to the spirits themselves, if I were to attempt to use a royal code. I'm not certain it would work, regardless. Mages who work for the crown are issued codes for specific missions, and I ought to have asked Saiyana for one. Since I didn't...

I think back, and I remember visits with my grandmother.

I remember my grandmother, who knew before I did that I know how to listen.

Who, unbeknownst to my past self, retired only from serving as queen and instead serves as spymaster.

I remember time with her, and messages she received, and how they felt.

Although magecraft is not my strength, Saiyana has always said that's due to my lack of interest, not ability, and in this matter I concur. Unlike many aspects of magecraft, in this case I do know the applicable theory to work out a reasonable approximation of the structure of a message spell.

"What are you doing?" Glynis asks as I hunt around for sticks.

In the corner of my eye, I see Yorani's ears perk up with interest. Although her position doesn't change, that's a small relief.

"This is too important to wait for the usual channels," I say, glad the audience has left such a mess: there is ample detritus for me to work with. "Have you paper, perchance?"

"You are so weird," Glynis mutters, but her expression tells me I've aroused her curiosity. She passes me her guild-issued magecrafted quill full of ink.

My message is to the point, though I write it with a princess' artistry so Saiyana will not doubt the source. The structure for the magecraft is even less ornamental, a set of multiple overlaying but simple diagrams, presumably because a mage in the field might not always have time or resources when messaging the crown.

Glynis peers over my shoulder. "What's this?"

"Secret," I say. "I will rely on your discretion. If I'm doing this right, it's a seal used by spies to communicate with the crown."

She stares at me flatly. "You are not telling me you've been a spy all this time."

"No, but I've met several," I say, "and once I've spoken with her, I believe the princess will agree with my reasoning for coopting the seal."

I clap my hands, and it shimmers into place.

"Clapping," Glynis mutters. "Should've guessed."

I glance up at her, caught by surprise. I hadn't realized how seriously she'd taken my suggestions of her potential skill at magecraft, but I should have had more care. "Clapping was always most comfortable for me, but it's not the only way. Snapping is common as well, and some mages prefer really dramatic gestures. Ostario can mark the casting of a spell with no more than narrowing his eyes, but that is a more advanced skill."

"What about people who are completely paralyzed?" Glynis asks.

"That's difficult," I admit. "To my knowledge, physical movement is a limiting factor for magecraft, like the physical structures themselves. Ostario would know more about that, if you—"

"No," she says.

She'll only reveal so much of herself at once, but there's no rush for this. I study the spell in my hands critically, and I believe it's at least close enough to pass muster.

"That should do." I hand it to her.

"Someday," Glynis says, "I have a lot of questions I want to ask you."

I smile faintly. She can't ask about my background now and how I know to cast a spy's seal without betraying her messengers' guild oath of discretion. "Someday, Glynis, I imagine you won't need me to answer them."

She scowls. "I'll be back with the princess, unless you're setting me up."

Before I can assure her I'm not, she takes off.

Glynis doesn't need my answer, because she already knows I'm not setting her up, and despite my worries—and despite how suspiciously she's seen me behave—that warms my heart.

I turn away, looking for where Risteri's gotten to, and instead notice Ari, the young Taresal tea contestant, frowning at the Cataclysm, his image reflected in the rippling mirrored surface of the barrier.

I glance around, but the area is nearly deserted now.

Good.

I approach him quietly so as not to disturb whatever he's thinking about so seriously. But when I get close, the object of his attention becomes evident.

The barrier looks like a bubble, a wall that extends all the way to the ground, and far into the sky. Farther up than I can see, teams of mages have determined it bends inward, a dome containing whatever caused the Cataclysm inside.

But here, at Ari's feet, the presence of the barrier is not what's remarkable.

It's the deadness.

It's a patch of earth extending right up to Ari's feet that is gray and cracked, like the land itself has turned to charcoal.

It's a patch that extends from inside the Cataclysm, outside of it. Yorani edges closer to the warmth of my neck, curling inward.

I shiver and whisper, "Spirits defend us."

"They won't."

I tear my gaze away to look at Ari. "What?"

"The spirits won't do anything," he says.

I search his profile. "The methods of the spirits are not always straightforward, but—"

He looks up at me, and the hardness in his young face stops me cold.

"This is what farms in Taresan look like," Ari says. "Within the last generation, spots of land that look like this are gradually covering farmland. It's magical drain, pure and simple. This is the legacy I've grown up with, thanks to that." He jerks his chin at the Cataclysm.

My eyes widen. Taresal farms have become famous for their rates of production in the last generation; if he's right, this is a frightening correlation. "The farmers haven't noticed and taken steps? Surely—"

"Of course the farmers have noticed," Ari says. "The small ones, the poor ones can't do anything about it except make their land die slowly."

"Make?" Risteri asks, coming up behind me.

"We—they're poor because they've been beggared affording the mage-tech that allows the land to produce enough crops to compete as independents with the big farming conglomerations, but it's killing the land," he says fervently.

"You didn't mean," I say slowly, "that the spirits won't defend us because you think they don't exist."

Ari snorts. "No. They won't help because we're the ones attacking them. And I know they won't, because they haven't."

A chilling thought. That the spirits would abandon us is beyond nightmarish, and I shy away from contemplating it too deeply just now.

"Why doesn't the state put a stop to it then?" Risteri asks.

"You can't be that naïve," Ari says.

Yes. The institutions of state will shy away, exactly like I just have.

"They must realize," Risteri argues, "that they're just dooming themselves in the long run? I mean, yes, I get that it would be inconvenient for their profits now and people hate that, but—"

"That's how the world is," Ari says. "Most people can't do anything, and the ones who could, won't."

His words hit me like a rock to the chest.

And that's before he says, "And it's going to get worse, because of you."

It takes me a moment to catch up. "You think the dragons leaving the Cataclysm will accelerate this... phenomenon you've observed?"

"The evidence," Ari says, gaze flicking toward Yorani, "speaks for itself. The dragons are new, and so is your land death. That's not a coincidence."

I reach a hand up and pet Yorani, shielding her from his accusation. If what Ari's saying is true, and the land can't afford to lose any magic here, we do have a problem. I've promised the Te Muraka can live here at equilibrium, but they do eat magic.

Have they since crossing the barrier, though?

Ari takes a step closer to me. "You may be in this tournament for fun, lady. I'm not. This is my shot to get the sponsorship I need for people to take me seriously, so I can do something about this before it's too late. Because no one else will. So as far as I'm concerned, you're not just another contestant. You're the enemy."

He shoves his hands in his pockets and stalks away, shoulders hunched, as I stand there frozen, reeling.

This day has been too much.

Risteri whistles low, turning to watch him disappear into the city center. "I can't believe I'm saying this about a tea tournament, but I think you need to watch out for him, Miyara."

Because a boy who cares so much, who's trying too hard to help, sees me as an enemy.

Because he is not, precisely, incorrect to.

I have been mentally disparaging this tournament since I learned of it, viewing my participation as a... punishment, an offense.

If I am going to participate, I owe it to Ari, to the other contestants who've put their all into this chance, not just to take it seriously, but to find a way to not be the enemy.

Easier thought than accomplished.

But of course, there is an exception. "What are the chances," I ask Risteri as I pull Yorani into my arms and hold her close, "this isn't related to what the Velasari were attempting inside the Cataclysm?"

Risteri sighs. "Honestly, high," she says. "Look, Velasari spies make me angrier than anyone even when they don't actually threaten me with bodily harm. But the Cataclysm is so volatile and so poorly understood, not to mention we have no idea what that tech they were using even was, it's way too big of a jump to assume that at this juncture. If you tried to legally accuse them you'd be laughed out of court."

A cloud passes over her face, and it's hard not to imagine she's thinking of how cases against her father would have been dismissed, too.

"Rightfully laughed out of court," she amends.

A fair assessment. Convenient answers are not necessarily true ones. Ari has jumped to conclusions too, but if he's right, I will have to do far better than accepting what's convenient if I am to serve the way I mean to.

"Is he right?" I ask. "Have you seen anything like this before?"

Risteri shakes her head. "No. Never. And, I mean, I don't mean to brag, but I don't think it's a stretch to say I'm more familiar with the nuances of the Cataclysm than anyone else alive." She pauses. "Excepting the Te Muraka. I can ask Sa Nikuran what she thinks."

"That might be wise," I murmur, staring at the patch once more in silence.

So it is that familiar footsteps sound loudly in my ears, and my heart clenches in remembered pressure, already anticipating disappointing her, and relief, because in my bones there is a part of me that will always believe my older sister can fix anything.

"You have a lot of nerve," Saiyana says.

Ostario is with her, thank the spirits, with Glynis leading the way looking not even slightly whelmed.

"Thank you for coming, and my apologies for the suddenness," I say.

Yorani squirms, and I help her back onto my shoulder, glad she's showing some initiative and also that she's comfortable with my friends. My family.

Perhaps her discomfort is a reflection of my own feelings. A troubling notion.

"When exactly did you learn to do that seal?" my sister demands.

"Several minutes ago," I admit.

Saiyana swears. "You little—I am going to throw you back at mage school," she growls.

Ah. I hadn't considered that consequence. "I couldn't think how else to reach you quickly."

"That's on purpose," Saiyana says dryly. "As a general rule, royalty are not supposed to be at the beck and call of any random person."

"But I am not a random person," I point out, "and royalty should, in fact, be open to being of service to all people."

"Are you kidding me right now?" Saiyana explodes.

"Maybe a little," I admit.

Saiyana stares.

Ostario laughs softly.

"Uh, I hate to interrupt," Risteri says.

"Oh! Yes, of course. Your Highness, this is Lady Risteri of Sayorsen, my roommate and also the foremost expert on navigating the Cataclysm. Risteri, Princess Saiyana of Istalam." I glance over at Glynis. "Were you introduced?"

"Yes," Glynis and Saiyana say at the same time. They exchange a look, and neither looks embarrassed about it.

I smile. They're both so blunt they were either going to hate each other or get along famously, and I'm glad to see indications it may be the latter.

But Glynis sighs. "Are you going to have any more messages for me? Because if not, unfortunately I'm already running behind, so—"

I bow. "My gratitude, Glynis. I won't keep you from your business any longer."

Saiyana adds, "I may have work I think you'd be suited to in the coming days, if you're willing. Shall I have someone call on you at the messengers' guild?"

"That would be best." Glynis bows. "It's my honor to serve, your Highness."

Saiyana returns her bow, and Glynis is gone in a flash.

"Spirits, that girl is fast," Risteri mutters.

"Also unflappable, and she misses nothing," I say, and point at the gray patch at my feet.

Saiyana nods. "What are we looking at?"

"I'll get to that," I say. "But I think it's best I start a little earlier."

I recount our encounter in the Cataclysm and Saiyana has to walk away for a minute, on account of the targets for her anger are not present.

When she returns, she takes a breath, looks me in the eye, and says, "You're fine."

"Quite," I say.

Risteri puts in, "Miyara has nerves of steel."

"I'm aware," Saiyana says. "I also may strangle her myself if she continues putting herself in situations where her life is threatened."

"I was never in any true danger," I say.

Saiyana looks at me again, and my arguments die on my tongue. She's not just angry; she's afraid for me.

"I'm fine," I say again. "And you need to hear the rest."

When we've finished, Saiyana glares at me for almost a full minute before crouching over the dead patch with Ostario.

"Should we isolate it?" Saiyana asks.

"I think better to not," he answers. "We don't know if we *can* isolate it, except from humans, and it will be more useful to watch how it develops."

"Monitoring beacons, then," Saiyana says. "Do it."

"I notice you said 'humans'," I say. "Do you not think the Te Muraka would respect your wishes not to interfere?"

"No, I think I don't yet fully understand how the Te Muraka affect their environment unconsciously," Ostario says. "Even if they haven't been eating magic outside the Cataclysm in the past few weeks, they still may be the source."

"Don't even start, Miyara," Saiyana says, holding up a hand. "I don't want it to be them, either, but the fact remains their presence is the only major factor that's changed in the magical makeup of Sayorsen in recent days. And here we have a magical consequence. It's logical to investigate the possibility that they have something to do with it, even if their intentions aren't malicious."

Yorani shifts on my shoulder. "I object to immediately assuming association with the problem—which, you must admit, is circumstantial—merits immediately investigating the Te Muraka as the potential cause," I say.

"And that's why you're not an investigator, isn't it?" Saiyana shoots back. "Did you call me in to take care of this or didn't you?"

Once upon a time, her admonitions alone would have made me silent with shame. Even I'm surprised at how quickly I have changed that I don't even consider staying silent, let alone believing she's correct.

"I trusted you," I say, "to treat the Te Muraka fairly."

"I am, Miyara. I'm not assuming they're guilty, I'm just gathering information."

"Then I hope," I say, "you'll also be looking into the Velasari, who are experimenting with strange technology in the Cataclysm?"

Her expression tightens. "That's more complicated and you know it."

"I do," I say. "I never took you for someone who only took easy solutions. I see the Te Muraka will already have to work to keep your efforts from institutionalizing their marginalization in our society, just because you have power over them and it's easy."

"Don't snap at me because you decided not to be a princess and now don't get a say in the work you renounced," Saiyana says. "You know, I didn't trust you not to compound your stupidity, but you've surpassed my imagination on that front."

"Enough, both of you," Ostario says, standing between us. "We all have work to do. I think we're all aware of the challenges, and we will all do our best. Let's be about it, shall we?"

Yorani has gone quiet and careful again. I turn on my heel without another word, and Risteri runs to catch up, a silent shadow as I brood.

All my roots are tangled.

Saiyana isn't wholly wrong. My first instinct was to alert the crown to the risk the Velasari pose. I can tell myself it's because it's the crown's responsibility to handle foreign relations, and I can tell myself it's because I trust my sister to handle thorny problems.

But it's also habit. The kind of habit, it seems, that will take more than a few weeks for me to break my reliance on.

The crown considers its responsibility to be serving its people as a whole, not as individuals. This is the fundamental break between us.

If I want something done in a particular way, I must do it myself. I must have both the ability and power to do it myself, because it is not my sister's job, not anyone else's but mine.

I cannot simply do my best, as Ostario said. I must, as I resolved in Ari's wake, do better than that. I must move beyond my best and become yet another new Miyara.

"The timing of this," I say to Risteri.

"Are you verbal again now?" she asks.

"Yes," I say. "Thank you for giving me a few minutes."

"No worries. You and your sister are kind of intense together though."

Perhaps another day, being described as 'intense' for the first time in my life might make me smile. But not now.

"The Velasari used the entire tournament as a distraction to work their machinations on the Cataclysm," I say. "What are the chances, do you think, that they might be using the Te Muraka in a similar fashion?"

Risteri goes rigid. "Taking advantage of the new refugees connected to the Cataclysm to pin the effects of the Velasari's experiments on the Te Muraka?"

I watch her think through the implications of the framing, given the edge of wonder and fear in Sayorsen since the Te Muraka's arrival. Watch her nod.

"Oh, that is nasty, and definitely in character for at least Lino and Ignasa," Risteri finally says. "You think their weird tech worked after all?"

"I think it did something I don't understand," I say. "I think Lino is exceedingly clever without the ethical core to match. And I think I'm going to find out for certain, one way or another. Are you with me?"

The timing is bad for her, too, to have anything to do with a dangerous and unofficial investigation. If I were a good friend, I wouldn't have asked her.

But I hope she thinks me a better friend, because I know she would never forgive me for counting her out without giving her the choice—to decide her own fate, to make her own path, and let no one else restrict or define her.

"I'm in," Risteri says.

CHAPTER 8

I GIVE LORWYN AN abbreviated version of my encounters both in and just outside the Cataclysm, and she helps me find a large kettle to settle Yorani inside for a nap. With my tea spirit settled in I should be free to focus on creating blends for the tournament tea flight, but so far it hasn't mattered.

"You're overthinking this," Lorwyn says. "Sit down, Miyara."

"I don't want to sit down. Something is off, and if I could just—"

"Did I phrase that as a request? Your pacing is annoying me. Do you want your witch annoyed?"

I throw up my hands and throw myself into a chair. "If you actually were my witch in any way it wouldn't matter." Then I sit up. "Lemon! If we add a dash to the tea—"

"It will turn from blue to purple because of the butterfly pea flower, which might impress the audience but won't at all draw out the flavor of the new grated death vine you brought back. A death vine you still need to name I might add, since 'death vine' has been taken for decades. Stop. What's gotten into you?"

I close my eyes, taking a breath. My roots may be tangled, but tugging at them thoughtlessly will only tighten the knot.

"I need to win this tournament," I say.

"I'm aware," Lorwyn says. "Your tea mastery is at stake. Which is why you need to focus."

I open my eyes to fix her with a look. "How well does that line work on you when Ostario says it?"

"Poorly, which is why we're having a conversation instead," she says.

"Does *that* work for Ostario?"

"Definitely not," Lorwyn says, "but you actually like talking."

"So do you." Though not, it must be said, about her feelings.

Lorwyn smiles sweetly, and my gut twists. "Would you like me to demonstrate how focused I am on you getting to the point?"

That means I don't want to know what kind of witchcraft she just prepared for me. I sigh. "It's not just one thing. I know enough about how this game is played to know I won't win without spectacle, and that's outside my skillset."

She frowns. "What do you mean?"

"They're not selecting the best tea specialist," I say, "at least not by any objective measure. They want the people who please the crowd, and the crowd is most delighted by narrative upsets, surprise, daring choices. I may have brought back the most unique ingredients, but if the audience and judges don't recognize their uniqueness compared to the more... pedestrian, if we can call them that, Cataclysm ingredients, it gives me no advantage."

"But no worse off than the other contestants," she points out.

"Except that I offended the show runners today," I remind her, "so they'll be looking for reasons to keep me from winning this challenge. Ari will do something with dazzling effects, because he's a mage—"

"But he's the only mage," Lorwyn says. "The other two whatever their names are—"

"Lino will impress the audience with his mage tech and has already positioned himself to show me up as excessively traditionalist. And if that fails, Hanuva has laid the groundwork to demonstrate my inexperience. I need to not just put together a competent, coordinated tea flight, I need to refute them so firmly the judges won't be able to go along with whatever plan the show runners come up with to put me in my place."

Lorwyn eyes me narrowly. "Your place," she finally says. "Where do you think it is?"

"Here," I say without thinking.

Lorwyn blinks, then rolls her eyes dramatically. "I suppose I should've seen that one coming," she drawls.

Ah. She's speaking in a less spiritual sense. I flush. "You mean in the tournament."

"Yes, I mean in the tournament. If you want to control the narrative, you have to cast yourself first. Are you the underdog? Are you the outcast? Are you the one to beat?"

"That's why you know so much about fashion," I realize. "Your style reflects your narrative. I knew you put thought into it, but not that you thought like this."

Lorwyn scowls. "You say that like you don't expect me to be capable of it."

I frown at her. "You're one of the smartest people I know. That has nothing to do with how you think about the world. It's just that you always project an air of deliberately not caring what anyone thinks—but that's part of it, isn't it?"

"You don't get to be an unregistered witch in your twenties with a steady job without thinking very carefully about what parts of you the world gets to see," Lorwyn says. "But most people do this to varying degrees. I know you do, because you crafted how you were going to present yourself as a tea specialist your first full day here. So why haven't you approached this tournament the same way?"

She's right. I need a strategy, and it's silly not to have been deliberately operating with one. But all the roles she mentioned pit me in relation to my fellow competitors, and that is... off. I am one of the people, and I should be accessible—but also unassailable.

"At the top," I finally say. "But on my own level."

Lorwyn nods slowly. "Okay. We can work with that. But you know what? You don't get to the top by pandering, Miyara."

True. "This is a game for bold choices," I say. "And the boldest choice is not to play by their rules, but still win by them."

All the tea specialists are fighting for something, but so am I. It is about my tea mastery, of course, but the tea mastery matters not just for my own sense of self-assurance, but for what I can do with it: namely, serving people.

That's why I got into this at all. It's the whole point.

I need to win this for all the people who've come to see me as a representative of the Lostari, and the Te Muraka. I need to be unassailable so the people I want to defend can't be hurt by my loss.

Lorwyn is right. I've let my focus be pulled in too many directions, lost my center.

If I am to win in the only way that matters, I must win indisputably as myself.

"Let's start over," I say. "I have thirteen ingredients you don't recognize that are safe for human consumption."

"Might be able to get two of the others," Lorwyn says.

"Can you guarantee it can be done in the next few hours?"

Lorwyn purses her lips. "Probably not. At least not without witchcraft."

"Then we'll leave them aside. So. I need four teas or tisanes for a flight, and they need to both complement each other and demonstrate what both of us together are capable of. What's the best way to approach this?"

Lorwyn blinks. "Wait. You're asking me?"

"Of course I'm asking you. You're the one who's blended hundreds of Cataclysm teas. You're also the one who was just telling me I needed to focus, and you were right. So what's our first step?"

"Not asking me for steps." She crosses her arms. "I don't construct tea flights, Miyara. I don't know anything about performance or serving guests or whatever. I just experiment until I get one that works. I don't work with *processes*."

I open my mouth to ask what she wanted from me in that case when she demanded more focus, but I close it with a clack as I realize why she's suddenly on the defensive. "That's what's wrong with your magecraft exercises, isn't it? It's the actual process."

Lorwyn throws her hands in the air. "It's that there's a process at all. Spirits, if *you* understand, why can't he? He's a witch too!"

"Admittedly I don't know how good of a witch he is," I say. "Perhaps he took to magecraft more naturally."

"He's good enough," Lorwyn says. "I don't know what changes he's made to his body, but he can pass as male easily. From our conversations I can tell you he didn't start there. That's not something you can do with magecraft, is it?"

I shake my head. I've never known what body transitions Ostario made, and it has never once come up in conversation between us. So it's interesting to me that he's spoken of it to Lorwyn, who is not exactly overflowing with fond feelings for him.

"So what does he tell you to do?" I ask.

Lorwyn sighs. "Honestly, not much. I think he's trying to avoid telling me how to do anything because he wants me to find a process on my own rather than feel justified telling him that his doesn't work. But I don't use processes or systems or whatever. Witchcraft just isn't like that."

I admittedly don't know witchcraft, and I can't contradict her experience. But it seems her perception of witchcraft minimizes her own part. Her control has grown over the years. She's been able to practice skills. Some of that may be innate, but she's crafted her witchcraft, too. An art, perhaps, if not a science.

I think of Deniel, how the familiar trained motions of his hands produce ceramics that are each utterly unique.

I think of myself, and tea ceremony: how within the correct forms, I draw out nuances to build bridges between different people.

But it's not enough for me to be able to build bridges for others: I have to be able to help them learn to make their own.

Perhaps Lorwyn's conception of the nature of magic is her barrier.

"What about tea, though?" I ask.

She glares at me. "You think I approach tea brewing methodically? Were you not listening, and have you not met me?"

"You always make sure Cataclysm ingredients are safe for human consumption or can be rendered so first," I say. "Actually, I suppose first you make sure they're not going to attack you somehow."

"Yeah, and sometimes I'm wrong and you and Entero have to come back here—"

She breaks off, sucking in a breath.

Entero, who is still gone, whom we've still not heard a word from.

The silence is suddenly taut with the knowledge I have not yet made good on my promise to help him.

"With the seal I learned today," I start, "I may be able to send a message—"

"Don't bother," Lorwyn says. "If he wants to talk, he knows where to find me."

Oh, spirits, she's blaming him—or herself—for his absence. "It's not that simple," I say. "He may not be *able*—"

"Then what would be the point?" Lorwyn demands. "Either he can run his own life, and he'll find me if he wants. Or he can't choose to find me, and that's not my problem. I can't let it be, Miyara. I *can't*."

I swallow my words.

This is another bridge I don't know how to build; it's also one I'm not sure I have any business meddling with. But it's hard to believe that when I see her—and the strength of her reaction to even the mention of his *name*, by all the spirits—knowing how careful Entero was trying to be of exactly this situation, that it would be unfair to ask her to accept never being able to come first for him. When I'm the one who caused them to be thrown together and also torn apart.

"So," Lorwyn continues as if our conversation had not been derailed, "if I have a process at all, it's a broken one. I start experimenting by what feels right, not by going down an organized list of steps."

I take a breath. One bridge at a time.

And perhaps with the potential to discuss her relationship with Entero looming and how badly she wishes to avoid *that*, we may get further with magecraft.

"But you know the properties of tea," I say. "You know how to dry or roll tea leaves. You know how hot to pour the water, how long to let the tea steep. You know that lemon juice will turn butterfly pea flower from blue to purple, not any other color. You know fairy dew extract will complement a tisane that's light and sweet, and jacksnake ichor assuredly will not."

Lorwyn stands abruptly, pacing herself. "You want to start with a vague notion of the flavor as a goal and work towards it?"

"Yes, exactly," I say. "Let's go over the ingredients again, and I'll tell you my impression of their salient notes. That way I can make sure we have a good set—one light, one robust, or sharp, or smooth, that sort of thing—before we waste time developing teas that will fall into the same category. If we think of their characteristics like rules to—"

"No." Lorwyn shakes her head. "That ruins it for me."

"Then don't think of magecraft structures as rules, either," I say. "They're the properties you need to account for to hone your creativity. And I know you can do this, because I've watched you since literally our first meeting where you fed me beetle scale tea."

"Worst tea of your life," she reminds me.

"Only until it worked," I say. "Sometimes awfulness is the only way through." I remember some of my abominable tea ceremony attempts when preparing for my mastery exam with a wince.

"I'm still not sure I like this," Lorwyn says. "The obvious idea isn't always the right one. I mean, sometimes it works, but it's... boring. I don't brew boring blends, Miyara, and I'm not going to let you, either."

She won't accept the easy path, the one everyone expects, and neither will I.

"That's it," I say. "That's our in. I'll incorporate the ingredients separately into the service, so the judges can appreciate what we've done. The other candidates have never worked with Cataclysm ingredients and will probably focus on making something tasty out of them at all. We take the ingredients and do the unexpected: find the hidden nuances, uncover what's hidden under the surface, what no one else looks for. We take the set expectation and surpass it. Your brewing experience with my ability to taste nuances."

Lorwyn stops moving sometime during my speech. "Okay," she says. "We've made this work before. Let's see how your idea fares in action."

We've blended tea together before, but not like this. This time, it's not just tea we have to create, but tea for a fickle audience and antagonistic judges, tea that must somehow still be true to who I am.

How will we make this work?

No, that's the wrong question:

What will we do?

What can we bring ourselves, in practice, to do, in pursuit of our goals?

"Lorwyn," I say slowly. "I have a bad idea."

She grins shark-like over her shoulder. "I mistrust it already. Tell me."

❧

Lorwyn and I work with focused intensity throughout the afternoon, finalizing the flight only minutes before a knock at the back startles us both from where we've sagged, slumped over with exhaustion from our efforts.

"You go," Lorwyn mutters.

I sigh, dragging myself to my feet. "Yes, your Witchiness."

Lorwyn snorts but evidently isn't willing to risk my noncooperation with any further remarks, so I trudge over to the back door.

When I open it, I blink into Sa Nikuran's face and the dim light behind her.

Still, it's been so many hours since I've seen sunlight I have to shield my eyes. "Spirits, is it this late already?" We'd planned to meet only shortly before I need to leave for Deniel's to meet his family, as late in the afternoon as possible to give me and Lorwyn time for blending.

"Sunset, as we agreed," Sa Nikuran says tonelessly.

I move my hand and squint at her. "Is something the matter?"

"The boy up front told me I could only come in through the back," Sa Nikuran says, the undercurrent of violence in her tone barely constrained. "I would like an explanation."

I close my eyes and bang my head lightly on the doorway. "Lorwyn, when you're willing to move again, would you do me a kindness and strangle Iskielo please?"

"I will happily put it on the top of my to-do list," she replies.

"I'm sorry," I tell Sa Nikuran. "Lorwyn and I locked the door to the front of the tea shop so he wouldn't keep disturbing us every few minutes. Had there been an emergency, he would have needed to come around the back, too. However, this never should have happened: I thought we'd be done much earlier to unlock the door. If you were here as a regular customer rather than to speak with me specifically, and in fact on any other day, you of course would have been welcome in the front of the shop. My sincerest apologies."

I catch the gleam of a fang as Sa Nikuran flashes a smile. "I'm relieved. Sa Rangim has encouraged us not to jump to conclusions. I would have disliked being at odds with you."

I let out a breath. I have no doubt I would have disliked both the adversity and the consequences. "Thank you for your understanding. I'll speak with Iskielo before we go and make sure the whole front hears that we will be offering you tea on the house at your next convenience as an apology for this rudeness."

Sa Nikuran inclines her head. "I accept."

"Then please, come in. Yorani had a trying morning and has been taking comfort in a teapot most of the afternoon. She's had enough of a nap now that I'm afraid she may be something of a handful this evening."

"That is the correct state for dragons," Sa Nikuran says. "Anything I should know about?"

I think she means about caring for Yorani, but the events in the Cataclysm are perhaps more pertinent. "Actually, there are some developments I would like shared with Sa Rangim at the earliest opportunity, if you have a moment to listen to me recount them."

Sa Nikuran's eyes sharpen. "Do tell."

"Miyara," Lorwyn interrupts. "Not that I disagree that you should tell her, but is Saiyana going to make trouble for you over this?"

"Possibly," I say. "If so, we will fight about it then. But I don't think so. I suspect no matter what she is bound to say officially, she'll be glad of a way for you to learn this information without her having to twist around violating any oaths."

"Do you have time to talk and get cleaned up?" Lorwyn asks.

I glance down at my formalwear.

I am a mess.

"I suppose my hair looks just as bad," I say.

"Worse," Lorwyn says helpfully. "Come over here and sit still. I'll witch you while you explain."

I move quickly before she can change her mind. "You are my favorite witch in all the land."

"Flattery won't get you as far with me as permission to strangle boys who interlope into my lab," Lorwyn says.

Ignoring the roiling of my gut as Lorwyn works her witchcraft, I bring Sa Nikuran up to speed on what we learned in the Cataclysm: my suspicions that the Velasari agents may be framing them, their strange device and its reaction to the Cataclysm, the magically drained patch outside, and Saiyana's investigation. Sa Nikuran grows stiffer in the telling, drawing herself up like she expects to stand against an attack alone.

I find myself drawing up straighter, too, but for me it's as though Lorwyn's drawing the stains and muss out of me leaves me ordered.

"There," Lorwyn says. "Back to your customary immaculate self. Honestly I probably should have left you as you were; you're going to intimidate Deniel's parents this way."

I will feel less intimidated this way, and I am selfish enough to need that for this meeting.

I fetch Yorani's teapot for Sa Nikuran. "Feel free to just borrow this. It's probably easier than extracting her."

Sa Nikuran snorts. "You are spoiling her." Then her gaze softens. "But although she will have to learn to face situations like this morning's, she is young yet."

"I don't want her to have to learn that," I say quietly. "It is my failure that she should ever have been put in such a position."

"Are you responsible for the world?" Sa Nikuran asks.

"I'm responsible for my role in changing it," I say.

She nods. "And Yorani was born out of that. So. Perhaps consider there will be no more keeping Yorani from danger than there is with you."

At that moment, Yorani's head pokes up out of the teapot, knocking the lid off so she can stare at me bright-eyed.

Sa Nikuran may have a point.

"Hello again, little one," I say, stroking her nose gently.

She chirps and slips back into the pot.

I retrieve the lid from the floor and settle it back into place. "Do you need anything else?" I ask Sa Nikuran.

"No, I'll take her back to your place," she says.

"Oh," I say. "Dear. I'm not sure I have time to detour on my way to Deniel's, and Risteri may not be home to let you in—"

"She is," Sa Nikuran says. "She agreed to keep me company as I—what do you call it? *Dragon-sit.*"

Did she? Odd; she didn't mention anything. I suppose we did have other concerns on our minds this morning, but—

While I blink, Lorwyn clears her throat, and I return her pointed stare in bewilderment.

What—?

Oh.

Oh.

"I'm glad!" I exclaim. "I hope you both have a lovely evening. Ah, all, that is. Dragon-sitting."

Lorwyn snickers. Sa Nikuran's eyes gleam with amusement.

"I think I'll be on my way, then," I say, "as I am clearly prepared to face any nuanced conversation with grace."

"Have you set up an altar in the tea room yet?" Lorwyn asks as I make my way toward the door to the front, my gut roiling as she unlocks it. "Maybe we should offer prayers for you—"

I shut the door on her laughter.

CHAPTER 9

DENIEL OPENS HIS DOOR before I can knock. "Are you ready to go?" he asks. At my nod, he steps out immediately, locking the door behind him. "Then let's go."

"Do your parents live far?" I ask.

"It's a bit of a walk," he concedes, "and we should probably hurry, if you don't mind. I don't want to keep them waiting any longer than necessary."

The longer it takes us to arrive, the longer they'll have to stay up to host us, and they both start work early in the morning. I wish either Deniel or I had the chairs in our apartments to have hosted them instead, but they will probably be more comfortable in their own home.

"Fine by me," I say, picking up the pace. "Less time for me to fret."

He casts an amused look over his shoulder, looking unfairly attractive as the wind tousles his hair. "You'll be fine."

"Easy for you to say."

"Do you think so?" Deniel asks. "I may someday meet your family."

He says that tentatively, like he thinks I may not wish to introduce him. I would only hesitate for his comfort, but I respect Deniel too much for that to prevent me. "I hope I can introduce you one day," I say to relieve any doubt. "They may be more intimidating in the abstract, but not, I think, in context."

"How do you mean?"

"They're public figures," I explain. "You can make educated guesses about how they'll behave, and vice versa, because they're trained to behave a certain way. Whereas I have no idea what your parents expect of me, or what I should expect from them."

Deniel rolls his eyes. "Miyara, are there really forms of etiquette that will encompass meeting the refugee your disowned daughter is seeing?"

I purse my lips. There are forms of etiquette for all situations, but, "You may have a point."

He huffs a laugh, but then stops abruptly. "Oh, that reminds me. Spirits, I should have thought of this earlier."

"What?"

Deniel looks uncomfortable as he explains, "I don't know about Istals, but for Gaellani, it's customary to bring a small gift for the host when you visit. I'm sorry, I normally don't because my parents get so uncomfortable accepting gifts from me, but—"

"Oh," I say, relieved and nervous at once. "I wondered about that, actually. I didn't have time to buy anything, but I brought two coupons for a free tea ceremony with me at Talmeri's—I thought perhaps, if they weren't comfortable accepting them for themselves, they might be willing to pass them on to others in your community who might enjoy or benefit from a session. Do you think that would be appropriate?"

Deniel blinks, and a smile blooms on his face, warming me from head to toe in spite of the wind.

He steps in close and there, in the middle of the street, he kisses me, warming me even further.

"You are too perfect for words," Deniel says. "It is an endless marvel to me that you have come into my life and seem to wish to stay here."

I take his hand, smiling myself. "That's my line." I kiss his hand gently and look into his eyes, where the intensity of his gaze stirs me.

He kisses me again, longer this time, as the world passes us by.

Finally we disengage, breathing raggedly, and he says, "We really should hurry."

I keep a hold of his hand the whole way.

Deniel's parents live in another Gaellani quarter of Sayorsen, which I expected but haven't visited. From my time searching for apartments with Risteri, I know it's one of the poorest areas in the city. It's not unkempt, exactly, but to my amateur eye, it looks as though no one has invested money to maintain the infrastructure here in decades. Any ethnically Istal community would have rioted years ago over conditions like these, and rightfully so.

I must have involuntarily tightened my hand in Deniel's, because he asks quietly, "Are you okay?"

I nod and say only, "Istalam—and my family—has not done right by the Gaellani, and this must change."

I wonder if I have given up the ability to make that change happen by leaving the royal family.

No. I would never have begun to learn my power had I stayed a princess. And the power, and burden, to make any meaningful change should not exclusively belong to my family. I'll find a way as I am, or I'll change to become someone who can make that change.

Deniel's hand squeezes mine in return and doesn't answer.

I'm glad of his grip as the alleys narrow and we pass more and more ash-haired Gaellani who stare at us and whisper. I am not invisible anymore, with my emerald green hair and brightly colored silk formalwear, a stark contrast to the cloth our onlookers can afford.

I focus on standing by Deniel's side, the warmth of his hand in mine, and try not to feel as though my presence is garish or embarrassing. Deniel wants me here, and I must let that be enough.

But I move to stand slightly behind him as he approaches his parents' door through a dimly lit hallway in their apartment's building, the lone light flickering.

"You don't have to hide," he whispers.

"I'm not," I say. "It's a point of etiquette for the guest to follow two paces behind—"

Deniel smiles. "No one here is going to expect that, let alone recognize it."

I think he means this to be comforting, the knowledge that I don't need to worry about the minutiae of etiquette.

However, it has the opposite effect, and I freeze.

One of my great strengths as a tea master, how I know what to say and when and how, is by manipulating etiquette. It's the basis for how I exercise what talents I have. Without that—and without people who appreciate those forms—what am I supposed to do?

Lack of etiquette isn't liberating for me; it is terrifying.

"Miyara?" Deniel asks, smile fading.

The door opens.

"Deniel, welcome!" a man who must be his father says warmly, reaching immediately for a hug. When they separate, he says, "And you must be Miyara. Be welcome in our home."

I bow, the movement so habitual I've already bent before it occurs to me this is exactly the sort of etiquette his parents evidently don't expect from me. "Thank you for your hospitality. My apologies for our tardiness."

As I feared, Deniel's father looks faintly gobstruck by my formality.

"Think nothing of it," he says, ruffling a hand through his hair. "We're glad to meet any friend of Deniel's."

I glance from his father's hair to Deniel, and Deniel laughs aloud.

His father looks surprised a second time, and this time that makes me hide a frown. Is he so unaccustomed to the sound of Deniel's laughter? It's a sound that moves *me* every time, but can the same be true for his parents?

"I do the same thing," Deniel explains to his father, running a hand through his hair to demonstrate. I sigh, and he grins at me. "Miyara is forever trying to keep me from doing so when my hands are covered in substances I've forgotten about."

"Aha." His father smiles. "I suppose I should be relieved you learned *something* from me."

"Yes, Miyara, please direct dissatisfaction you have with any of my habits towards my father," Deniel says.

"Hey, now!"

Deniel is more outgoing with his father, and I wonder if that's habitual for him or if he's making an extra effort to ease the conversational burden for my benefit—or perhaps for his parents'.

We leave our shoes in the entryway, and while of course my shoes, purchased only weeks ago and to accompany formalwear, naturally ought to look nice, the juxtaposition of seeing them next to Deniel's family's, which are falling apart, gives me pause. Deniel's are at least sturdier, if not quite as fancy as mine. When I look up his father is frowning down at us, though his expression clears as soon as he catches me looking.

Then Deniel's father pulls back the door to let us in, and the smell of cooking hits me like a blow.

"Your mother's outdone herself," he warns, then looks at me. "Are you all right?"

I nod, wide-eyed, my senses still overwhelmed and I haven't even tasted anything yet.

Deniel comes to my rescue. "Miyara is sensitive to smells, and she's probably more aware than usual right now because she's been fine-tuning new tea blends all afternoon."

"Is this too much?" his father asks quietly, anxiously.

I get a hold of myself. "Not at all," I say. "It smells exquisite. My apologies for worrying you."

"No need to apologize," his father says, running a hand through his hair again.

I bite my lip. At this rate I will be apologizing every other minute and his father's hair will be in complete disarray. I can't keep letting Deniel rescue me.

I take a breath. This cannot be impossible. People meet the families of those they're courting every day.

And often it goes disastrously wrong.

"Pardon me, but how may I call you?" I ask.

"Oh, just Cadell will do," his father says, reaching up to run his hand through his hair again.

Deniel catches his arm, and Cadell glances down at his son in amused exasperation. "You trying to take on your mother's work, now?"

"Her hands are occupied," Deniel replies. "I needed something to do with mine."

This elicits a chuckle from his father.

Deniel explains to me this time, "It's a long-running joke in the family, because my mother and I are always doing something with our hands."

"Ah." I nod. "Like when you tie Talsion's string into elaborate flowers without even looking while you read."

"Yes, that sounds right," Cadell says. "You spend much time watching him read, then?"

Is this teasing or an accusation? "I could not even aspire to create on purpose what he does by simply existing," I say. "I sometimes can't help but watch."

I wish I could tell what he thinks about that, but after looking once between us he merely shakes his head and brings us further into the kitchen.

I catch Deniel's sleeve. "Do they not know we've been studying together?" I whisper.

"They do, but they probably don't understand how much," he answers, patting my hand. "I've always been... reclusive, not to mention focused on my work. They're not used to thinking of me spending much time with anyone. Don't worry about it."

I am absolutely worrying.

The apartment is small. There is no getting around that, even knowing from my own search with Risteri that having multiple rooms at all makes ours bigger than many in the Gaellani quarter. My discomfort with my current place is ludicrous in comparison.

I'm horribly impressed by how Deniel's mother moves in the small kitchen—no movement wasted, let alone dishes, timing everything perfectly so she never runs out of space. Perhaps someday I'll be so graceful behind the counter in Talmeri's, but I doubt it's something I'll ever achieve in a customary kitchen.

Deniel's parents have a table that can seat four, so we will sit close together, though they only have three stools. They've pulled a threadbare chair from the corner of the room to add a fourth setting to the table, which they insist be my seat. The fifth, Cadell explains, they borrowed from a neighbor for the evening. There's no reason to clutter their space with more than three dining seats on a regular basis.

"Deniel, would you fetch your sister? We're about ready here," his mother says, pulling off her apron.

I tense at the prospect of being left alone even for a minute, which is so silly I hold my tongue.

Deniel scoots his chair back to go without protest as his mother folds her apron. "Please, call me Ronwyn," she says quietly but with assurance, and I recognize right away whose temperament Deniel takes after. "I'm sorry I couldn't greet you right away."

I bow slightly, reflexively. "Thank you for having me, especially on such short notice. My apologies for the trouble."

"Deniel has always been a source of joy for us," Ronwyn says, "never trouble."

In light of Deniel's comment that his sister knows her existence made trouble for her parents, this strikes me as less gracious than I think Ronwyn means.

"I didn't realize how closely he resembles you," I say, which is true. They have the same willowy grace, long fingers, narrow chin, and dreamer's eyes.

She smiles slightly, and this is Deniel's smile too.

Before I'm faced with producing another conversational gambit Deniel returns, his sister peeking behind him. No wonder he thought I was hiding.

"Miyara, this is my sister, Elowyn," Deniel says, stepping aside suddenly so I can see her fully. "Elowyn, this is Miyara."

He doesn't introduce me as *his* anything, I realize, but only for a moment, because in the next I recognize Elowyn and suck in a quick breath before I can control my reaction.

She's the girl who was following me in the market.

Elowyn's eyes go wide as saucers.

I incline my head. "It's my honor to meet you, Elowyn."

She tries to mimic the gesture, and as her parents exchange glances Deniel asks me, "What was that about?"

Spirits, of course he caught my reaction. "It's nothing," I say, shaking my head. Deniel narrows his eyes, so I add, "She just looks like someone I saw the other day at the night market, is all."

"Well, it couldn't have been our Elowyn," Cadell says. "She's much too shy to be out and about in a crowd like that. And she's too sensible to be out so late."

"In my experience," Deniel says, looking at his sister, "Miyara doesn't make frivolous connections."

And without having said a single word, Elowyn flees the room.

"Elowyn!" her father cries. "Spirits, what's all this now? I'll go—"

"Let's give her a minute," Deniel says, frowning as he returns to the table. "Miyara, what exactly happened?"

"Nothing," I say. "Truly."

"You didn't notice nothing. And I don't believe she just looks like someone else you noticed."

I don't want to get her in trouble. "I thought she was following me. I only noticed her because she was doing such a good job of not being noticeable," I explain. "It's... something I have some small skill at." At his parents' look of patent skepticism, I add, "The green of my hair is in part a deliberate choice to make it harder for me to fall back on that habit."

They exchange troubled glances and sigh.

"I'm sorry for the trouble," Cadell says.

"Truly, it wasn't," I say. "I don't know what she was doing there, but she didn't cause trouble for anyone, myself included."

"You're kind to say so," Cadell says, "but it never occurred to me she'd sneak out at night." He looks at his wife. "Do you think she's done it before?"

She tilts her head. "Perhaps, though I can't imagine she's had much reason to before."

"Why would she now?" Deniel asks.

"This was before this dinner was planned?" Ronwyn asks me. When I nod, she says, "Then I expect she was trying to get a glimpse of you."

"Of Miyara?" Deniel asks. "Why?"

His parents exchange glances again, and this time I notice they're deliberately no longer looking at me.

"She's gotten it into her head that she could have a career in tea," Ronwyn says to Deniel. "That girl Lorwyn works at the shop, and she's Gaellani. And her own brother knows the local tea master personally. It's made her believe a girl like her can rise so high in this world. It's so rare for her to be excited about anything we haven't wanted to burst her dreams, but we're worried she'll get her hopes set too high."

With a sinking feeling, I ask carefully, "Have you told her it's impossible?"

"We've just hinted around the issue a bit," Cadell says.

"Elowyn's always been perceptive," Deniel says, his voice brittle. "That would be more than enough."

Ronwyn glances at me quickly and then away, as if ashamed, but her voice is calm enough. "I can't change what reality is. You're an artisan, Deniel, but a tea career—that's a high-class trade. It's not like your craft."

"No," Deniel says coolly, "it's like my dreams of practicing law."

And that does it, tips my sadness at this hard reality, at his parents thinking they're looking out for their daughter, into anger that they would discourage her from trying to reach her dreams. I know it is a luxury for people, like me, to be able to do so, that they probably *are* being practical, but that, too, makes me angry. It should never be right to discourage children from aiming for the sky.

"May I speak with her?" I ask.

His parents jump in tandem.

"Oh, no, please forgive Elowyn's behavior," Ronwyn says, and Cadell speaks over her, "I'll go have a word with her now, don't you trouble yourself," and I stand up.

And bow, formally. "Please do not increase her shame for my sake," I say quietly, still bowed. "I would find that more distressing than anything."

Ronwyn and Cadell subside in stunned silence.

"I think," Deniel says carefully, "they're worried about what you'll think of their home. I can tell you they've gone above and beyond to clean out here, but they can't possibly have had time to do so everywhere."

Had he hoped the late notice would prevent his parents from overworking for my sake? Even I could have told him otherwise. But I'm grateful that he's plainly stated the problem so I can address it, that he's recognized I might not understand the nuances of his parents' behavior in this.

"Deniel," his father protests with a glance at his wife, mortified.

I bow again. "I promise you there is nothing about your home that would cause me to think less of you. The only shame I see is that the systemic failures of Istalam have caused you to be ashamed of your home. It is warm and cared for, and I am truly honored you've invited me inside."

His parents blink at me, at Deniel, at each other. It's as if I see the moment they begin to grasp how two people so apparently different as we are connected.

With Ronwyn's slow nod of consent, I extract myself from the table.

"She'll be in the closet," Deniel says quietly as I pass.

It's not hard to figure out where this is. There aren't many doors, and I knock on each. There's only one that shoves closed again when, not receiving a response, I try to open it.

"It's Miyara," I say. "May I join you?"

There's a long silence.

Finally, the weight holding the door shut vanishes, which I take as a yes.

I open the door just wide enough to slip inside, catching a glimpse of rags and a broom as I crouch down, shutting the door again behind me. Very little light seeps in through the cracks around the door, but there's enough for me to make out Elowyn's shape next to me until my eyes adjust enough that I can see her face.

"I'm sorry for giving you away," I say. "Your brother is familiar enough with my reactions it's difficult to hide them without preparation, but I'll endeavor to improve my skill."

Elowyn shakes her head. "It's not your fault," she says quietly. "I shouldn't have been there."

"Why not?" I ask.

I feel more than see that movement of her shrug. "My parents say I'm too young to navigate the night market."

Why do their parents have so much faith in Deniel and so little in Elowyn? "With respect, I must disagree. An assassin of my acquaintance would have been deeply impressed by how well you navigated the market unseen."

"You know an *assassin*?" she breathes.

Oh dear. I sigh. "Also, if someone as inept as *I* am can navigate the market, you certainly can."

She's silent for a beat. "You're not going to tell me more about the assassin, are you."

"It's not because you're young," I say. "It's not my story to tell. But perhaps I should be more distressed you won't protest my ineptitude."

"What?" Elowyn scrambles. "Oh, I'm sorry! But. Weren't you joking? I mean. You're a *tea master*."

"I am a tea master who in trying not to be intimidating has just managed to accidentally let slip my association with assassin," I say dryly, and my eyes have adjusted enough now that I see Elowyn's quick smile. "Also your brother keeps suggesting I should bake with your mother sometime, meanwhile yesterday I spattered more than one pancake across his kitchen. As you can keep your counsel and not embarrass yourself in the kitchen with your mother, that is at least two counts where you have far surpassed me."

After a moment, she mutters, "I'm not that good at cooking."

"Compared to whom?"

"Why are you doing this?" Elowyn asks abruptly.

I don't pretend to misunderstand. "I want to know why you didn't approach me in the market."

"You *were* waiting for me," she says. "I knew it."

"I figured you would."

Elowyn turns to look at me. "Why would you think that? You had no idea who I was."

"Because you were too aware of everything around you," I say. "You can't slip through a crowd invisibly like that otherwise."

"*You* saw me."

I settle back more comfortably. "I had the benefit of a tea spirit looking interestedly in your direction to clue me in. And I've spent most of my life moving the same way."

"*You*? Why?"

"Because I haven't always been a tea master. Only weeks ago I couldn't have imagined this for myself. But I am not much of a tea master if someone who wishes to speak with me feels she can't approach."

"It's not that," Elowyn says automatically, then pauses, I suspect having noticed a moment too late how I compelled a response from her.

I smile. She really is as perceptive as Deniel said. "See, I can't even slip that by you."

Elowyn turns away, hunching in on herself. "I just thought, maybe if I watched you long enough, I could see how you do it."

"Do what?"

"Everything! We're stuck on the edge of this cataclysmic disaster zone, and you make it seem like magic. With *tea*."

"Ah, that I can't take any credit for," I say. "All the tea we serve at Talmeri's is blended by Lorwyn, not me. Do you know her?"

Elowyn hesitates. "No, but I've seen her. She looks... hard."

I nod. "I thought so at first too. It's more like she's covered a soft center with spikes."

"See, that's what I want to know," Elowyn says. "The magic I'm talking about... it's not just the Cataclysm ingredients. You make people feel like they matter just by being there!" She waves a hand to encompass us sitting in the dark closet and adds, in a smaller voice, "I wanted that."

Not just to feel that, I realize, but to be able to convey that feeling to others.

It's not enough for me to help people for the space of a tea ceremony if I can't make them feel like they can help themselves.

"You're two parts of the way there already," I say.

Elowyn looks up at me.

"I gather," I say, "your parents don't think pursuing tea is a wise course for you. While I cannot discount their knowledge of the world and its realities, I submit that they do not understand tea or how far you, personally, can go in that world."

"You're just saying that—"

"With respect, Elowyn, I would never," I say seriously, and she goes quiet.

Then almost inaudibly, she asks, "Why?"

Why her, why do I know, why am I saying this. The answer is the same.

"Aside from the physical skills of brewing tea, there are three qualities tea masters need," I say. "The first, and perhaps the most fundamental, is the ability to listen. To listen with your ears and eyes and heart. Without that, there's no point in continuing, but you need no help there. You couldn't have been so aware of every nuance to keep yourself invisible in the market if you didn't already possess that ability.

"The third is the willingness to take action. Perhaps that ability is newer for you, I can't say, but you cared deeply enough to make the choice to sneak out of your home, despite what your parents thought you should do, to pursue me. So I am confident of your potential there, too."

Elowyn processes that silently for a moment. "You skipped the second."

"That's because the second is belief in yourself and your abilities," I say, "which takes time and practice. You don't have that yet. But if I can learn that, I think you can, too."

And maybe, if I can teach Elowyn, I can teach someone else, too.

"You?" she asks.

"Believe it or not, it truly wasn't so long ago that I was blending into crowds wondering what to do with myself."

Elowyn nods, slowly. "I can see that you believe that. It's difficult for me to imagine you as anything besides poised."

"I'm delighted my acting is so effective," I say, "but your brother can tell you the first time we met I was literally incoherent with tears."

She startles. "Really? He talks about you like you... ah, perhaps I shouldn't say. But very highly."

I very much want to ask but restrain the impulse. "Deniel speaks highly of you, too, you know. Though perhaps not in the same way."

Elowyn laughs quietly, which I take as a victory.

"Oh, I suppose technically that was the second time we'd met," I realize. "The first I had managed to botch waiting in line to buy a book, so it's something of a miracle he ever decided to take me seriously."

"You really think I wouldn't be wasting my time?" she asks seriously. "Considering tea mastery?"

"Not even a little," I say. "In fact, even if you someday decide on another path, the skills you learn along the way will help you in the long run. I may, admittedly, have some bias, so I don't think I'm the best choice to convince your parents it's a worthwhile use of your time."

"No," Elowyn says, "I think that has to be my task. But I'm not ready yet."

I nod, agreeing with her assessment on both counts. "Would you like to visit the tea shop? Things are in a bit of disarray at the moment because of the tournament—"

"Would it be a bother?"

"—but things are always in some kind of disarray, so there's no reason to delay."

"I'd like that," she admits, "a lot. If it really wouldn't be any trouble."

"Leave that to me." I stand carefully and reach a hand down to her. "Shall we return to dinner, then?"

Elowyn accepts my hand without ducking her head, and she opens the door for us both.

By unspoken agreement, Elowyn and I make no mention of our new pact to her parents. Although I'm sure they'll have words for her later, the rest of the meal passes with more ease than it began.

Still, when Deniel and I are on the street again, I let out a breath of relief.

"That bad?" he asks.

I shake my head. "No. Your parents are remarkable." Cadell is warm and welcoming, and Ronwyn takes care with everything she does. It's easy to see how two such people produced Deniel—and Elowyn, too. And when I returned with Elowyn, their guard relaxed, the glances I caught from them in my direction more thoughtful and less worried.

Though still assessing. Perhaps Elowyn would tell me how I measured up in their view, where Deniel might try to assuage my fears.

"And Elowyn?" Deniel asks. "I assume you came to some kind of understanding."

"I invited her to the tea shop," I admit. "She's not ready to tell your parents yet, so that is between us for now."

He blinks, then smiles. "I should have guessed. She doesn't normally talk, you know."

"At all?" She's clearly quiet, and I assumed she could keep her counsel, but she was perfectly articulate in the closet. Though she did not, it must be said, waste any words.

Deniel nods. "Very nearly. That she actually participated in dinner at all will go a long way toward convincing my parents once she's ready. I assume you didn't just offer that out of pity."

"Of course not. If I have any ulterior motives, they're selfish."

Deniel takes my hand as he starts leading us back. "In what way?"

I'm so arrested by the simplicity of his gesture, the casualness of his acceptance in demonstrating that he wants to be with me, in public, after I've just implied that meeting his family was trying and that I have selfish motives, that I am momentarily at a loss for words.

Deniel glances back with worry lining his brown. "Are you okay? Or—is this not okay?"

"It's very okay," I say too quickly.

Deniel pauses, a smile crooking across his face. "Oh, I see."

Flushing, I roll my eyes skyward in amused disbelief at myself while Deniel laughs and steps in closer and kisses me.

"You were saying?" he asks, eyes dancing.

I reach my free hand up to press my palm against his cheek, and he shivers slightly at the touch. "I'm selfish," I whisper, and this time I kiss him.

When we separate, Deniel manages, "I find I can bear that prospect with equanimity."

I grin, and he mutters something I don't quite catch and kisses me again.

After a little longer, I grudgingly say, "Regrettably I have to be awake to win a tournament tomorrow."

"Pity," Deniel murmurs, and this time I shiver. But we start walking again, hand in hand, and he asks, "So?"

"It's part that I want to know your sister better," I admit. "I was never close to my younger sister, and Elowyn—it's silly, as I've only just met her, but she feels almost like a sister already, or that she could be. Perhaps it's because in some ways she reminds me of myself."

Deniel nods. "That makes sense. I'm—truly glad you got along so well. But what's the rest?"

I sigh. I will have no secrets from this man. "I think I can help her. Perhaps I'll just make everything harder for her, but—I want to be *able* to help her."

"Ah," Deniel says. He doesn't agree or disagree for a moment. "You were right, before. I didn't really understand why you were so worried about tonight, and I apologize."

I shake my head. "It's fine."

"No, I should have realized," Deniel says. "I mean, I'm used to thinking nobles don't understand what our lives are like here, but I knew you have too much care to be rude. But it's also a class thing, modes of interaction. Given what I've been struggling with on the council, I should have realized it would work both ways. At least with someone who is actively trying not to be offensive."

"Did I fail so badly?" I ask.

"No, not at all," he says. "I just wish I could have made it easier for you."

Spirits be thanked. "For me, but not your parents?"

Deniel's smile turns rueful. "You're Istal, and you have status. They know what that means. Nothing could have convinced them you weren't going to accidentally act badly around them other than you yourself." He shakes his head. "I can hardly imagine what they'd have been like if they'd known I was bringing a princess with me to their house."

Will our two families ever meet? Even if it were possible, would it be possible to manage without everyone being unbearably uncomfortable?

I wince. "My awkwardness might have been more explicable, but I think it's fair to say everything else would have been even worse. But if you're sure I didn't make a total hash of things, perhaps I can get more practice at interacting like a competent person with them another time?"

"You mean it?" Deniel asks, looking over at me. "I don't want to force you into uncomfortable situations."

"Perhaps it's more like helping me into the water so I learn to swim," I say. "But you're not worried about Elowyn?"

He smiles and shakes his head. "If you want to help, you'll worry about her enough there's no point in my expending extra energy over it."

I huff out a laugh. I suppose he isn't wrong.

"Besides," Deniel adds, "I've hoped, for a long time, that someone would truly see her. I can't be sad or even surprised that it's you."

CHAPTER 10

THE MORNING OF THE first match of the tournament dawns, and this time, I am the earliest.

In part, this is because I had trouble sleeping: there is too much for my brain to process, and it would not quit chewing on problems enough for me to relax.

But this is also part of my plotting.

Talmeri and Meristo are preparing to open the shop early. Taseino and I will relieve them later, but in the meantime I've conscripted Iskielo and all his enthusiasm to weave through the crowd and hand out lovely cardstock on which I've written the business details of Talmeri's Teas and Tisanes in calligraphy, the image replicated onto each card with magecraft technology.

The audience doesn't have an emotional attachment to my winning like they do for the other contestants, and I mean to change that. I can't share my true backstory with them, but I can invite them into a community space where they will feel welcome and my skills will shine.

I'm also early because my setup for this event will be more involved than the requirements specified. As the other contestants and their teams arrive, I see that this was a wise choice, because they are all tailoring their booths, too.

We set up on the stage where the council sits during community meetings. Each contestant has an individual tea blending station, not dissimilar to the nook in the ceremony room at Talmeri's, with the ability to heat water, along with a kettle, a selection of teapots and cups, and a few of the most basic tea accessories. There is a raised surface between the brewing station and the audience like a bar, with three chairs behind where I presume the judges will sit to taste.

Everything else, the contestants have brought themselves.

And when I see what the 'everything else' includes for them, I see why sponsorship is such a critical part of this contest.

It's the ingredients, not just the tea, but the honey and lemon. The equipment, like temperature thermometers and timers. And the marketing—banners and special shelves behind the counter and cups with logos.

Hanuva is, in some ways, the most obvious, and also the most dangerous. She sets her team to work efficiently, and within minutes her booth is transformed into a clean tea room. The ease with which she can create this physical space is a testament to a great deal more practice than I've had.

Ari carries in two bags by himself: one with jars of ingredients, and the other, larger one full of sticks, rocks, leaves, and the like. In short order his booth looks exactly how I'd expect from a reclusive genius magecrafter's lab, with a fancy illusion in the background. Rather than bringing his own equipment, he even uses magecraft to change the appearance of his cups.

I tense when Lino arrives, but he makes a point of ignoring me. Aleixo, though, is with him, and my heart thumps when he makes eye contact with me.

I hold his gaze for a beat.

Then, by unspoken agreement, we continue about our tasks. He will not be attacking me here, nor I him. At least not directly.

As Aleixo unpacks a host of modern tea equipment—presumably, but perhaps I should not assume that—I've never seen before, I wonder where Ignasa is.

I focus on making the final adjustments to the shelves I'm setting up behind my booth. They are borrowed from the shop warehouse, because during the inventory reorganization I got ample practice reassembling them and changing their shelf heights on my own. I wheeled them in on a delivery cart this morning, but they are not decorative.

Fortunately, Risteri arrives with, to my surprise, Sa Nikuran in tow. Or perhaps it's the other way around: Sa Nikuran is carrying crates on her own, while Risteri trails behind making an obvious effort not to wring her hands in discomfort.

Meanwhile Yorani bounces between their shoulders, full of excitement and "helping." Sa Nikuran agreed to watch her for the duration of the match, but I expected that to occur elsewhere.

"Lorwyn asked me to make a delivery, but I didn't realize it was for this," Risteri says. "But I can't, because—"

"Because since you're my guide you can't be part of my team," I say. "Spirits, I don't think I remembered to tell Lorwyn."

"I knew it was almost time, and Sa Nikuran was available at the last minute," Risteri explains.

I won't ask how she knew, though Sa Nikuran casts her a distinctly amused glance.

I bow toward Sa Nikuran. "My sincerest apologies, and thank you for your assistance. I'll have to add you to the roster for my team, but I won't ask you for any more. And I will take steps to make sure such emergencies don't fall on your head."

"It's no trouble," Sa Nikuran says. "Where do you want all this?"

"Let's do the cloth first." The booth is bare, but Lorwyn kept the strips of green cloth leftover from when we first went shopping for my formalwear. Last night she sewed them into something resembling draperies that we can use to dress up the lines of the booth in a coordinated fashion: the edges of the shelves, as well as the top of the booth and the bar.

Risteri reaches to help, and I bat her hand away.

"Sorry," she mutters. "I just want to help."

Her and Yorani both. Quicker than I can see, Sa Nikuran deftly snags Yorani out of the air before she can bite the fluttering cloth.

"Then by all means," I murmur in Risteri's ear as I pass, "keep an eye out for Ignasa. If she's not here, I want to know. And if she is, I want to know what she's paying attention to."

Risteri's gaze sharpens, and she nods.

Sa Nikuran holds Yorani in one hand and the drapes in place with the other so I can attach them as Lorwyn showed me, and when that's finished we break into the other crate.

"What's all this?" The official's alarmed voice sounds behind me.

I turn with a bow. "Part of my display. It is perfectly safe, I assure you."

The second part of the delivery from Lorwyn is not the tea blends ready in their canisters. Those I brought with me this morning. These are large glass jars that each feature the raw form of the ingredient: what it looked like before our experiments, suspended in witchcraft.

And it is obviously witchcraft, because if magecraft could do this safely, there would be Cataclysm museum displays around Istalam.

This is another part of my plot.

The official's expression is forbidding. "Under what authority do you assure that, tea master? Are you an expert in magic now too?"

"Their safety has been verified by Mage Ostario, who holds the highest mage certification and oversees the work of my partner Lorwyn personally," I say. "He has already verified the work, but I'm sure the princess won't mind if you need to pull him away from his work for her so you can be sure."

He glares. I suppose that was a trifle blunt.

"My apologies," I say smoothly. "I fear the realities of what this tournament truly requires are more challenging than I initially understood. I have a great deal of respect for the other candidates for managing so well for so long, and for you for tracking all the minute details. Shall I send for a written affidavit of the magical working's safety?"

The official considers me narrowly. "After the match will be sufficient, as long as you're sure."

"I am." It's why I didn't have this delivery before this morning—Lorwyn insisted Ostario look over her work if it was going to be in the public eye, and I think her caution is warranted. Not because I don't trust if she tells me it's safe, but because it matters that Istal officials don't fear it, too.

"Then we'll have more to discuss later. Your roster included."

I bow. "Yes, I have adjustments to make."

"Oh, indeed," he says, moving off before I can unpack the nuances of his statement.

"You've made an enemy there," Sa Nikuran notes quietly.

"On the contrary," I say. "He made an enemy of me when he disrespected Risteri."

Risteri sighs. "I appreciate that you're angry on my behalf, but you need to be on his good side if you're going to win."

"I disagree," I say. "Specifically, I refuse to accept that as a condition of victory. If I can't win despite his best efforts at undermining me, I do not deserve the title of tea master."

Risteri frowns. "I'm worried you're hanging too much on what it means to be a tea master, Miyara. Tea masters are respected, and rightfully so, but they're not infallible."

"Perhaps not," I say, "but they must be able to turn the most unfavorable conditions to their advantage."

"Their advantage?" Sa Nikuran asks sharply.

I wave a hand. "Only in the sense that they have sufficient leverage to serve adequately."

"What is your phrase?" Sa Nikuran asks. "'Cutting hair finely'?"

"You are definitely splitting hairs," Risteri confirms. "Semantics aside, my point stands. You're holding yourself to an unreasonable standard."

"My point also stands," I say. "This is necessary, and I will not accept less for myself. Certainly not without first trying."

"I don't know how Lorwyn tolerates you," Risteri says. "You're even worse than me. How did you talk her into being part of this, in the open?"

"I didn't," I say seriously. "I wouldn't have pushed her into this."

Risteri snorts. "Yes, you would."

Hmm. "Only if lives were in imminent danger and I was sure hers wasn't. The stakes are high here, but they are not, to my knowledge, life or death."

Risteri and Sa Nikuran exchange a look. Risteri glances quickly away when she realizes what she's done without thinking, but Sa Nikuran flicks her gaze to mine and holds it.

I raise my eyebrows in response. I don't know why Risteri hasn't told me that they're keeping company, but although her secrecy bothers me, the prospect of the existence of a relationship between them certainly doesn't.

Sa Nikuran smirks and nods.

Well, then. At least we're on the same page.

Or so I think until she adds, "You were right to inform us of your suspicions."

I frown. Here in public, I hesitate to ask whether she means in dealing with Saiyana, the Velasari's strange tech—

Risteri says, "The looks we got coming through the streets were a lot more suspicious today than they have been before."

—Or the brewing anti-Te Muraka sentiment. "New rumors, or is it coming from all the recent visitors to Sayorsen?"

"Definitely new rumors," Risteri says. "I recognized a lot of the people whispering."

Spirits, the tide changes quickly. "Any sign of our Velasari friend?"

"She's not here," Risteri says grimly.

I don't have time to worry about what that means, because the match begins. Risteri joins the other guides present, and Sa Nikuran drags Yorani into the audience.

Ari's flight is the first to be judged, and from the perspective of showmanship I immediately see why. Each of his teas is flashy, and with the Cataclysm ingredients his magecraft can augment their effects explosively. I can't help gasping in awe, and the audience goes wild.

The judges are less impressed.

"You've certainly captured the wildness of the Cataclysm," one explains, "but you've focused on spectacle to the exclusion of flavor. This is the finals now, and if you're going to win, the primary thing we really need to see from you is growth beyond that aspect. We know you can wow us. Let's see that in your tea."

Ari is quiet at that, subdued. For all his passion and skill he is still a young boy who's being publicly criticized for the benefit of an audience. He put himself in this situation on purpose, but he didn't think he had a choice. Even if his reaction is crafted, and I don't think it is, that is a lot.

It is possible I'm projecting, but there is no fear of that when Lino's turn comes up. I can sympathize that Lino feels stymied from the path he would have chosen for himself, but given options, he has deliberately made the choice to value no one but himself.

I pay more attention to the team of guides this time who—grudgingly, which I suspect is because they've recovered their colleague and are not pleased with Lino—verify that each tea does use a genuine ingredient from the Cataclysm.

I exchange a look with Risteri. All of his ingredients are from the rim of the Cataclysm, which means that's one less way to prove where Lino and the Velasari spies went. And his ingredients are so easily verifiable the guides can't reasonably pretend not to know them even if they wanted to sabotage him.

"We lost you track of you for a while in the Cataclysm," the official remarks when the guides note the surprising source of his ingredients. "Decided it was too adventuresome for you?"

"I am not in the business of crafting tea that is not fit for human consumption," Lino says, and I keep my expression pleasant. It's just one more sally I'll have to refute with my flight.

That's fine.

Then Lino demonstrates the use of his contraptions, and I can't deny they're impressive. Unlike Ari, who emphasized magic—in fact manufactured magic separate from the Cataclysm—Lino has designed machines that render the magical effects of the Cataclysm ingredients inert.

"On one hand," a judge says, "what you've done with the flavor here is incredible. If I didn't know it wasn't made with entirely familiar ingredients, I might not be able to tell. But that also means you haven't highlighted the Cataclysm in your flight."

"I've highlighted how people, humans, can triumph over it," Lino says, and this time I do stiffen.

That's a slight against the Te Muraka, and a deliberate one.

"We don't have to accept wild magic as inevitable or outside human control," Lino says. "We have the technology. We just have to be forward-thinking enough to use it."

This response keys the audience up, too, but not in a way I think the officials want any more than I do.

And yet as far as the tournament goes, Hanuva is the one who concerns me most. Her Cataclysm guide helped her find ingredients that could be rendered magically inert easily so she could focus on flavor.

"Plucking, snipping," a judge echoes. "You're choosing your words carefully, but the fact is you killed the sources of each of these ingredients, didn't you?"

Hanuva bows. "I could dispute whether anything that can only subsist in the Cataclysm should be considered as living at all," she says.

"But the facts, as you say, are that ultimately, I'm not willing to risk my customers. This was the most efficient way for me to ensure that they are safe, and that is always my first priority before anything else."

I am the safe option, her deportment screams.

The safe option whose bigotry against the Te Muraka is carefully couched in terms that will be easier for people on all sides of the issue to accept, to consider thoughtful.

"As always," a different judges notes, "you've tailored your tea for our tastes. We have one designed to appeal to each of us specifically, and the last to appeal to all of us. That's fine work, but what I want to see from you in the finals is what you're capable of when you're not trying to please people. I want to see what your taste is."

Like Lino, and unlike Ari, Hanuva does not let this criticism stand. "I always curate my taste with the goal of my customers in mind," she says.

It is, perhaps, all she can say. Because what I now understand of Hanuva is that she will say and do anything she thinks will help her.

Unfortunately for me, in a contest like this, that quality, combined with her skill, might be enough. Hanuva's blends use ingredients that we carry at Talmeri's, and her flavor choices are similar to what Lorwyn worked out. Hanuva knows her business, all sides of it.

And then there is me.

The Cataclysm guides exchange looks when they come to my ingredients.

"Well?" the official asks.

One of the guides smiles ruefully. "I can assure you that they're Cataclysm."

The official pounces on that. "But not what they are?"

Another guide speaks up. "Risteri knows the Cataclysm better than any of us. It's not surprising she'd find creatures we've never seen." He grins at Risteri, who now stands off to the side of the booth. "Though I'm going to ask you to show me where you found all these later."

"A professional guide couldn't find them, but Risteri was right to bring an untested tea specialist there?" the official asks.

"Hardly untested," the first guide argues. "She's brought Miyara far deeper inside. It's not their first time working together."

She doesn't mention this was about finding the Te Muraka, and no one clarifies; perhaps she thinks everyone will assume. She may be trying to protect me from perceived association with them, given how not-badly the previous contestants' bigotry has been received.

She doesn't know what I have planned for my tea flight.

"You asked us to verify the ingredients originated from the Cataclysm," the first guide says. "We're doing so. This is our area of expertise, sir."

Risteri's colleagues will stand by her. Beneath the counter, I clench my fists in triumph and let no one see how smug I am at how they've thwarted the official.

Still, I am a tea master, and it's time to turn this.

"This is why, as soon as we learned of the challenge, I requested Risteri serve as my guide," I explain. "As the judges may be aware, I serve tea at a local shop called Talmeri's Teas and Tisanes that specializes in tea made using Cataclysm ingredients. We use all the ingredients my colleagues have displayed today in our tea blends—and I should mention the shop will be opening early today upon the conclusion of this match, so anyone curious about what these ingredients really taste like can partake in the fun."

That gets the excited reaction from the audience I hoped for, though the official bears down on me.

"This isn't the venue to promote your shop," he tells me. "Let's stick to the matter at hand."

"What's relevant is that, as I said, my role at the shop is to serve tea," I say, "not to blend it. Starting today, Talmeri's will offer a special on the tea flight I've crafted for this match while supplies last. But every other tea and tisane that Talmeri's carries was blended solely by my partner Lorwyn.

"Lorwyn isn't on stage with me today, but she has long been the secret behind the success of Talmeri's. She's worked with hundreds of Cataclysm ingredients, including all the ones you've seen today. My contribution to her process has historically been confined to refining in tasting."

I bow toward Hanuva first, then incline my head at Lino: it is a deliberate slight, and I see the official note it.

"When we first learned of this challenge, my fellow tea specialist Lino suggested my tea practices were, to their detriment, mired in tradition. Grace Hanuva noted there was some question as to my experience. A valid question, since, as a latecomer to this tournament, I've not had the opportunity to serve any of you tea. So for this challenge, for the tournament finals, I wanted to challenge myself. I challenged myself to take the lead in blending. I challenged myself to use ingredients wholly unfamiliar to me. And I challenged myself to craft you a tea flight that will show you not just that tradition need not be detrimental, but that will give you a taste of what I can do."

A tea flight is traditionally made up of four teas: one for each of the spirits, and one that combines them into a whole. Today I will make use of every literal and metaphorical interpretation: made from earth, formed in water, released into air.

As the tea brews, I continue, "Deeper into the Cataclysm, many ingredients, as my colleagues have intimated, are exceedingly dangerous. Sometimes even more so than they appear. But they are still magical and wondrous, and that is not antithetical to humans. I wanted to capture how that wonder fits into our world, and sustainably, without any irrevocable damage to the Cataclysm or to us."

Although this isn't a tea ceremony, I have still timed my brewing perfectly so that I pour in succession from each of the specialty tea ceremony pots suited to their respective blends. I'm not performing the tea ceremony, but each tea uses a traditional tea ceremony blend as its base.

"We begin with Deep Roots, a variant on the traditional black earth blend," I say as they taste the rich and warm flavor. "If two of the judges would be willing to hold hands, there is another property of this tea you may appreciate."

The audience murmurs, but the judges, being good sports about odd tournament displays, take each other's hands.

"The judges," the official comments for the audience, "have apparently just experienced something profound, if their expressions are anything to go by."

"The unique property of this tea is that when holding hands with another person, the person who has drunk the tea will feel a deep sense of connection and contentment," I explain. "This is a consequence of the oil of what we're calling snareroot. In the Cataclysm, snareroot emits this oil to attempt to use a creature's own emotions to lure and entrap them, making them feel relaxed and comfortable so they don't fight back."

The judges let go of each other's hands with forced laughs.

I continue, "That isn't the effect of the oil in the form we've distilled, however. What it should do is force those feelings onto whoever is touched. If the official would kindly offer a hand, you can verify that this does not occur."

After some good-natured ribbing from the audience, the official does offer a hand.

"That effect of course would be the height of invasiveness and against consent," I continue, "which is what the use of witchcraft prevents."

At that, I have everyone's complete attention.

"Not only are these teas all variations on the most traditional teas used in ceremony," I say, "they all make mage-tested use of witchcraft."

Risteri gapes at me from her station, but in the audience I see Sa Nikuran smile.

The official is far less pleased, and there's a commotion until he can restore order to the proceedings.

I pick up with the second blend as if nothing unusual has occurred, and after some hesitantly exchanged glances, the judges drink again.

"The traditional green water blend is associated with adaptability and change," I say.

"Still smooth and mellow," a judge notes, "though not in exactly the same way as the water blend. And there's another note underlying that with a bit of zing, almost like citrus."

"The ingredient in this tea is mirrorlake vapor," I say. "You can see it bottled behind me. The lake surface in the Cataclysm shimmers constantly, always shifting to project images onto its surface according to its prey as if those images were a true reflection. The liquid releases chemicals that make prey think they're among their own kind and let down their guard. The witchcraft application in this case is also preventative, in that it will not affect your mental acuity. However, this time, I invite you to touch your own skin. Although there's been no physical change, the sensation of the texture of your skin will feel different with every sip you take. My favorites were petals, fur, moss—and scales."

The official glowers at me. That I've dropped in scales when the Te Muraka have indirectly come up in conversation is no accident, and he knows it.

But I want the audience to get used to the idea of dragons as not off-putting—and also that witchcraft can be used in their best interests.

We move onto the lightwing white air blend, a light and sweet tea made not from the bones, but the essence of feathers from a snowy greatwing. Drinking it makes a person literally lighter, and more buoyant; with any step, they almost float.

This time, the witchcraft is less subtle, though still not as showy as Ari's magic. A sip produces the fleeting image of wings at the drinker's back—and if the drinker makes any movement, the wings flap until the magic of the sip fades.

This, the audience loves.

"Last but not least, we come to a variation of the blue dragon's blend," I say, "which, as the tea that birthed my spirit companion, has become near and dear to my heart. It is my honor to serve you."

The tea is full-bodied but with deeper spice notes that increase its robustness. Immediately after sipping, the judges emanate a hazy glowing aura, shimmering for all the audience to see, the edges flickering like fire: this flaring effect is the witchcraft's doing.

"In this case, the witchcraft is not the most interesting part of the tea. You can see in the display case behind me what looks like a large rock," I say. "Of course, it's not just a rock: it's animate, for one. For another, chunks can be scooped off without damaging it—the magic of the Cataclysm pops it back fully formed, so it takes no damage. But most of its compatriots in the Cataclysm are enormous boulders, surrounded by some pebbles we suspect might be their children. As a group, they emit a powerful haze that causes prey to become dazed—but importantly, not the rocks' prey. The disabled prey attract other predators, from which the rocks absorb nutrients through their surfaces without disabling those predators. It's a symbiotic relationship, and we were able to isolate the component that produces only the visual effect."

"When you say 'we'," a judge asks, "how much of this is the witch—Lorwyn, was it? How much is her doing?"

"Quite a lot," I say. "Although I took the lead in creative direction and worked hands-on with all the ingredients, I will always defer to her expertise when it comes to the safe-handling of Cataclysm ingredients."

"So despite what you said about your challenge to yourself at the beginning, then, it sounds like you can't do it by yourself after all," the judge points out. "You've made use of Risteri's expertise in the Cataclysm, working with ingredients we are forced to take at your word." The audience boos, and although I see the official note it the judge continues, "You've made use of witchcraft, rather than your own skills. So exactly what sort of tea master are we to understand you are?"

It's the perfect opening. "The kind who brings people together and doesn't put myself above anyone else, and the kind who is always striving to learn to serve people better. I could not have created this tea flight without Lorwyn and Risteri's assistance, but nor could they have created this without me."

And the audience cheers.

I have made us all people in their eyes—and people who they're invested in. No matter the verdict, I'm already victorious.

CHAPTER II

IN THE END, THE RESULTS of the first match of the tournament are not surprising.

Because it was my first match, the officials wanted to introduce me, the new variable, in a risk-free situation. Risk-free to them, that is: they can stave off complaints about favoritism by making sure no one is unduly disadvantaged by my inclusion without knowing how it's going to play out, myself included.

Of course, for suspense, no one was told this in advance. But as I suspected, although we are ranked, in this bout no contestants are eliminated.

Ari is at the bottom of the pack, which surprises me—I thought his spectacle would go further. But while the audience enjoyed it, I suspect he suffers from overexposure: they have seen this same approach from him before, and it no longer has the same awe value. Or as the judges put it, although he may have captured the experience of the Cataclysm, he failed at actually blending tasty teas, which should always come first.

Lino is next, a fact that has him looking haughtier than ever. His blends were not in the spirit of the assignment, and despite his impressive gadgets that can render Cataclysm ingredients inert, the judges make it clear he ranks above Ari in this contest only because the flavor of his tea blends was superior—but he took no risks in their flavor, either, and that point seems to hit home where the rest don't.

I do not take first place in this match, which I expected. Even if I were the clear winner, it is not a good move for the standing of the tea tournament's organization to have an outsider appear and outstrip all the contestants they've invested resources in making the public believe are the finest tea specialists. For their narrative to work, I need to have to work for first place wins—and I shall.

And I was not the clear winner in the abstract. Although the judges dock my rank for utilizing witchcraft and disregarding my audience's potential discomfort, the fact is that Hanuva's tea flight was perfectly executed without any tricks. Not flashy, just effective.

But ultimately, I did accomplish what I needed from this match, because the judges' opinion of my performance meets with dissent from the audience.

I didn't win the match, but I've laid the groundwork to win the tournament.

When the match concludes, the contestants—and Yorani, whom I collect back from Sa Nikuran with surprisingly little fuss—and our official liaison reconvene to discuss the parameters for what comes next.

Somewhat to my surprise, even coming straight from our judgments, everyone's attitudes are much the same as at our first meeting, but heightened: Lino behaves even more like he is the only one in this room worth anyone's time; Ari looks even less like he knows what to do with himself and is ashamed about having to try and failing; Hanuva is completely put-together but somewhat more smug and less desperate about it. They all have more experience with this than me, but I suppose I'm no different.

I will always comport myself as a tea master, and everything that means.

But in short order, I discover there was another advantage for the judges in not eliminating any of the four of us before the second match.

"The second match of the tournament," the official says, "is a team match. You will be judged together. Whichever team wins will advance to face each other in the finals; both contestants on the losing team will be eliminated at once."

Lino demands, "We're to be held responsible for the other contestants' inferior performance?"

"You may choose to look at it that way," the official says. "Put another way, they will be responsible for your inferior attitude. Consider for a moment that if the bottom two contestants had been eliminated in this match, Lino, you would be one of the ones gone."

My eyebrows lift minutely. There's no hidden venom in the official's voice like there is when he speaks to me, but it's interesting he feels comfortable reprimanding Lino so openly.

"And ultimately," Hanuva says mildly, "we are all here in the interest of promoting excellence in tea worldwide. For that, it is to our advantage to be able to work together, is it not?"

My attention focuses on her sharply, and I notice Ari tenses too.

She knows something we don't.

Lino narrows his eyes at her and then subsides with poor grace, apparently catching on to whatever nuance I've missed.

"Grace Hanuva has the right of it," the official agrees. "That is what this tournament is all about."

Lino rolls his eyes, but when he doesn't offer any further commentary the official continues, "The first team will comprise of Hanuva and Lino; the second Ari and Miyara."

Ari sits bolt upright. "That's not a fair divide. Based on the results of the last match, it should be me with Hanuva: first and fourth place together, against second and third."

I barely feel any distress that Ari considers me such an enemy that being paired with me actually merits his speaking up, which he clearly hates, because I've already moved on to imagining what it would be like to have to try to work with Lino.

My hands inadvertently tighten on Yorani in my lap, who squirms.

Then again, being paired with Lino might afford me more opportunities to learn about Velasar's scheme with the Cataclysm.

"The prize for winning first place in the match was not just a monetary bonus the contestant may use in the second match," the official says. "Part of Hanuva's prize is an advantage in that match, partnering her with the third place winner instead of the fourth."

That was *not* a stated prize, and everyone in this room knows it.

"Really, Ari," Hanuva chides. "You should know the way these things work by now."

Ari flushes angrily—at the implicit insult in his inability to learn, but also, I think, about the world.

Because he's right: despite the tournament's pretenses, it isn't about fairness; it's about ability to work the system. Hanuva excels at that, and Ari and I don't.

At least, I haven't done so clearly, but I'm not out of the game yet.

"I will, of course, defer to the tournament's wishes," I say.

"Of course you will," the official says, tone smug although he watches me closely.

Because of course I have not deferred to their wishes when it benefitted me, and he can't decide if my words are ironic or if I've learned my lesson now that I've been positioned on the losing team.

So I only bow as the official continues his explanation.

"Hanuva and Miyara will be the captains for their teams, as the highest ranked winners of the previous match," the official continues. Not surprising: despite the fact that we will be judged as a team, the officials will wish to make it appear that the loss is on my head, and Hanuva has demonstrated she can beat me. "Despite the advantage to Hanuva, we also like how these teams are organized because of the ongoing debate Lino in particular has highlighted in this year's tournament, between traditional and experimental brewing techniques. Each team has a contestant that specializes in one or the other."

It doesn't escape me that this also leaves all the monetary resources firmly on my opponents' team, and I can't think this is accidental when the official explains the nature of the second match.

Pitting me against Hanuva's experience, the match will consist of a pop-up tea shop, and we have only days to prepare.

Ari rushes out of the meeting, and Yorani launches off my shoulder to flap right up to his face, causing him to stumble back as he swats at her.

"Stop that," I say, and though I meant that to be directed at Yorani, who while I suspect is trying to be helpful by buying time for me to catch up is not creating a great impression of the sincerity of my wish to work together, it's Ari who rounds on me.

"This is how low you'll stoop? To send your abomination after me?"

My abomination.

My movements go very slow and deliberate as I draw myself up.

Surely, he did not.

Ignorant of etiquette he may be, but Ari is not stupid, and whatever he sees in my stature in that moment gives him pause.

"This *thing*—" Ari starts.

"You will apologize," I say. "Yorani is a living, breathing creature, and your disrespect is unconscionable."

This is not the tactics I intended to employ to get him to work with me. But on this, I will not compromise, and more than that I believe it important he *knows* that.

He scowls. "It's not like she knows what I said."

"Not that such a reason would make your behavior more acceptable," I say, "but she is sapient as well as sentient. Yorani, will you come back, please?"

Yorani flaps back to me, and although the flutter of her wings is irritated, she won't look at Ari. Giving him her back may be a gesture of disdain, but I think it's more than that.

She's hurt. Which I dislike intensely, but that she isn't just angry makes me believe she may agree with my assessment of Ari.

That unlike Lino, Ari's mind is worth changing.

"I won't apologize to something that represents everything I'm fighting against," Ari says.

If I don't let her exhale sparks in his face first.

No. If I truly believe his mind is worth changing, then it is up to me to accept responsibility for changing it.

I don't know if I can fix all of what is broken. But I know I can't do it from a seat removed from my people, like Saiyana imposes policies. I start with people. I build bridges with tea for customers, neighbors, friends and their families. I can serve them, and help them, one at a time, bit by bit.

Here, today, I will commit to changing this one life.

And to do it, I'll treat him the one way that will make him take me seriously:

"Yorani is some*one*, not some*thing*," I say coldly. "Tell me, do you think it's right for people to jeer at those living in impoverished circumstances, who didn't choose to be there, as representatives of a poverty they detest? Of everyone involved in this mockery of fairness, you I expected better from."

Uncompromisingly, with blunt honesty, and forcing him to confront that he is not smarter than me, and thus I am not lesser. These are all he values, and so these must be the pillars I use to support any bridge between us.

How I connect them will be trickier.

Ari bristles. *Good.* "You think you can scold me because I'm younger than you?"

"No, I think there's a chance your behavior isn't a lost cause because you're not transparently self-interested," I say. "Though perhaps I'm wrong about that after all. You do understand we will have to work together to win this match?"

"I'm not working with you," Ari says, predictably.

"Then what a pitiful commitment to your lofty goals it is, if this is as far as it extends," I say. "Will you give up so easily?"

"This is your fault!" he yells, then flushes again as he realizes how childish that sounds. "You believed you were above the rules, and now they're punishing you for it."

He's partially correct. Positioning me on the losing team is payback for making the official angry.

"I'm not the only one they put on this team," I tell him. "They're not positioning you for the final battle because the audience is bored of your appeal, or else there would have been more protest against the judgment. You've depended on magic spectacle too long, which has led them to choose Lino over not just me, but *you.*"

Ari folds in on himself a bit.

But he's thinking.

Except what he finally comes back with is, "Better Lino than you."

Maybe I won't be able to make this work after all. But I fight the urge to slump and reply, "Surely you realize Lino's victory would be far worse for you than mine."

"Lino may not care about sustainability," Ari says fiercely, "but he's not actively making the problem worse."

I clutch Yorani closer as a thought seizes me. "Did *you* help start the whispers against the Te Muraka?"

Ari scowls. "I would have, if I thought anyone would believe me."

That's worse, not better. But almost as soon as the thought escaped my lips another followed on its heels.

Kustio didn't operate his black market of Te Muraka-created objects alone, and he must have worked with others who share his anti-Gaellani sentiments—the same that Velasar espouses.

Those contacts aren't in custody, which means there's no reason they can't now be facilitating the Velasari agents.

A troubling thought, but my immediate problem is the intransigent child before me. Because if I don't take the time to try to reach him, no one else will. He wouldn't be here if they had.

"If empathy is beyond you, consider this," I say.

"Beyond *me*?" Ari protests. "*You're* the one who doesn't care about anything but her own glory."

That arrests me for a moment, but it is not as far of a stretch as I would like to see how he came by such an impression of me.

"I'm the one who believes we should all be able to live fairly, and addressing the magical drain you've observed is part of that," I say. "I will not settle for less. But whatever you may think of my true beliefs, consider that I have skills you lack."

"Tea ceremony won't help with the next match," Ari snorts.

"I didn't need it to outrank you in this one," I point out. "What I needed was exactly what you lacked, which was to get the crowd on my side."

That makes him frown. "The audience doesn't like Lino, and he's now on the winning team."

"They may like Lino less, but he gets strong reactions from the crowd, which gets the tournament engagement," I explain. The official's behavior in our meeting made clear he's comfortable being open with Lino because he always knows where Lino stands—and Lino is useful to him. "Pitting him against Hanuva, and making sure she wins decisively, will be a resounding validation of their philosophy of selecting the so-called all-around best tea specialists. Or, to put another way, a refutation of Lino's philosophy, a selfishness they officially oppose."

Ari narrows his eyes, studying me. *Listening*, or at least trying.

"So what do you propose?"

I let out a careful breath.

"I propose you apologize to Yorani," I say. "And then we can make a plan for how to beat them, together."

I can see he hates it with every fiber of his being, but finally practicality wins out over his prejudice. "Fine," he grinds out. "I'm sorry. Happy?"

"No," I say, "but now we can get to work."

We head for Talmeri's, because Ari has even fewer resources at his disposal than I do and no knowledge of how to deploy them. I want Lorwyn to be involved in this part of the strategy, too, and will need to be on hand for the work I set up for us this afternoon.

Ari and I walk there in silence. I do make a detour into a Gaellani courtyard for sustenance, though Ari waits at the edge of the alley rather than accompany me.

Still, I bring him back a portion of dumplings, too. I know he doesn't have available funds, and I hope that a belly full of dumplings may at least temporarily fill the acidic hole inside him.

But although he doesn't refuse the dumplings, Ari scowls mightily when I present them.

"What now?" I ask with a touch of exasperation.

He shakes his head. "You talk all high and mighty, which I guess makes sense, since you're just another rich person."

That stings, in part because he's not precisely wrong. And yet.

"It wasn't that long ago I had no money, not a single coin, to my name," I say. "Once I did I still had to count every coin for some time, and I only survived by relying on the kindness of others. Please don't imagine you don't know my circumstances."

"Maybe not," Ari agrees as he chews. I definitely need to find a way to get him to accept some basic lessons in etiquette. "But I know you didn't think twice about spending that, which means you weren't in that poor of a position long enough to think of it as normal. And you *had* people you could rely on."

I nod slowly. "You are partially correct. But those people were strangers to me, and I will never forget. So if the cost is negligible to me but notable to you, then no, I will not think twice about paying."

After that, the rest of our walk is silent.

Ari and Lorwyn immediately get off on the wrong foot when Ari notices the piles of sticks Lorwyn has in her workspace.

"You're a mage?" he demands.

Lorwyn knocks the structure over, sweeping the sticks away before Ari can criticize whatever she was working on. "I'm working on it," she growls.

Ari eyes her skeptically and then says to me, "I assume you expect me to be civil to her, too."

"Yes." I heave a sigh. "Do you hate witches, too? How do you keep track of everyone you hate?"

"Witches caused the Cataclysm," he snaps. "You can't pretend this is unreasonable."

"Ah, so you accept the rhetoric from those comfortable people who've driven your farmers to use technology that drains the land and have a clear vested interest in not being held responsible?" I ask. "What a curious choice."

That startles him. "Everyone knows witches created the Cataclysm."

He may be smart and determined, but he is still young, young enough he probably hasn't met a great many people who can appreciate that without being unduly impressed. But I hope he is still young enough at heart to be in the habit of curiosity.

"You've already said that, which I take to mean you have no further evidence to offer," I say calmly. "That has never been conclusively proven, and I fail to see how they could have. Witches channel magic just like mages do."

"They do *not* channel magic like mages," Ari says. "Magecraft works through mental discipline."

He has a high opinion of his own intelligence, and I imagine for a long time it's all he's had. But it also means targeting it is the only way I'll get through to him.

"And a witch's ability comes from within as well, but those are only determinants of capacity for magic," I say. "Mages and witches both still channel magic from the world around them. A witch can be no more responsible for the drain of the land than a mage, so if you're not blaming yourself, it is hypocritical to hold witches accountable for this."

"So now you're an expert in magic too I see," Ari says.

But he still hasn't refuted me, and I hope, perhaps in vain, it's because he has the self-awareness to realize he can't.

I consider telling him that Sa Rangim himself provided a similar explanation, and it would be silly to deflect attention away from witches and mages if he were in truth responsible, but decide this won't persuade Ari.

"I do not possess your skill at magecraft," I say, "but I suspect I've had access to more theory."

His eyes go wide. "Wait. You went to mage school? And—dropped out?"

Spirits, that was a mis-step on my part. Generally those who attend mage school intend to go far there.

"The circumstances are complicated, but I needed to pursue a different path," I say. "That's as much as you need to know."

"Fine," he says after a moment. "So what do I need to know?"

Lorwyn answers before I can. "How to dress," she says. "Miyara, please tell me you're going to get him new clothes. It hurts to look at him."

"I am definitely going to get him new clothes," I assure her.

"What's wrong with my clothes?" Ari demands.

I sigh. There are few ways to answer that without insulting his childish pride. "Fashion is a skill, and it's one you do not yet possess. There's not sufficient time to teach you in the days we have available to us, so I'll ask you to trust my judgment."

"I am not wearing clothes like yours," Ari says.

"Nor do I expect you to."

"My sponsors didn't say anything was wrong with them, either," he tries.

"Given your age, they probably find your attempts charming," I say. "However, I don't think that's the impression you wish to convey."

Ari flushes and shrinks in on himself again. "Whatever," he mutters. "What does this have to do with your plan, anyway?"

Plan is a strong word for what I have now, but it's a start.

"The officials believe they've set us up on the losing team," I say, "which actually works to our benefit, since people love to root for those who aren't the obvious choice to win. Since the officials were never going to award me first place today, this move is actually the best way they could have helped me."

"Wait a minute," Ari says. "Are you saying you didn't even try to win today's match? Because if you're not serious about this—"

"It's not that I didn't try to win, it's that I adjusted my goal based on reality and what I truly need," I say. "What I needed was for the audience to care about my victory. I did not need to actually come in first place, so forcing matters in that direction would be a poor application of effort when I already knew I wasn't going to be eliminated."

"You knew," Ari says. "Sure."

"She knew," Lorwyn confirms.

"How do *you* know?" he demands.

Lorwyn shrugs. "She's always right about stuff like this. It's her thing."

"You expect me to believe she just knows everything?" Ari scoffs.

"No," I say. "I pay attention, and I'm good at reading people. That's all. Magecraft is your greatest skill; this is mine."

"How does that help if you can't use it to win?" Ari demands.

A fair question, which I intend to answer, but Lorwyn beats me to it.

"Because she's very good at getting around people to do what she wants when they refuse to actually behave like reasonable people," Lorwyn says, "including when their actions run counter to their stated goals."

"Then can you explain why people are like this?" Ari asks me. "Why do they have to operate on a set of rules no one says out loud?"

"Because when you also know the rules, it tells them they can trust you," I explain. "It's like a secret password. And if you know exactly what everyone expects from you, you can use that to your advantage."

"It's a tea master thing," Lorwyn adds. "Don't think about it too hard; it'll only upset you."

I can see Ari about to object again and continue, "Lino and Hanuva are going to aim for a haute cuisine shop, so we will distinguish ourselves another way."

Ari turns to Lorwyn. "How do you stand her?"

Lorwyn shrugs. "It's incredibly satisfying when she aims her power at entitled wealthy people."

"Glad to be of service," I say dryly. Of course they're now getting along at my expense. "I admit my first idea was to play to our strengths, committing fully into a formal mode—"

"No," Ari says immediately.

"But," I continue as if he had actually waited, "not only would it be hard to set up a shop that way, it's what everyone will expect from us. I think that will work to our disadvantage. So we go the other way."

"Make a contrast to Hanuva's gentrification aesthetic," Lorwyn muses.

"Exactly," I say. "We make a point of using local products, nothing exorbitantly expensive. Especially since we don't have Hanuva or Lino's resources, we demonstrate we don't need them."

"Don't you live here?" Ari asks. "I thought the officials were trying to keep you from being able to use your contacts in the community unfairly."

"My resources amount to the shop supplies and the boys who work here that are trained to serve tea," I say. "I intend to make full use of them for this challenge, but beyond that my contacts are few. I have not actually lived here that long."

He crosses his arms. "And they relocated the whole tournament finals for you?"

"That was not my idea, and it had already been done by the time I was informed of my participation."

Lorwyn interrupts before Ari can get momentum going arguing with me on yet another front. "I think it may help more than you're thinking, Miyara," she says slowly. "With our budget and deadline, Gaellani seamstresses are probably your best bet anyway. And after what you did with Kustio, they'll do it for you." She considers. "If you want to be really bold, you can probably even set up shop in a Gaellani courtyard."

Lorwyn tosses that last out like a wild suggestion, but I know her well enough to hear that she believes it would be a powerful move in the Gaellani's favor but isn't sure how it will be received—by me, or by the audience.

"That would wonderful," I say, "but you don't think that's unfairly taking advantage of them? The people I'd be displacing in the courtyard, and the ones who'd be helping us with their services?"

"Unlike Deniel, I don't have to try to represent the views of all Gaellani," Lorwyn says. "You should ask them."

I look at Ari.

"No," he says.

"Yes," I counter. "We're a team, whether you like it or not, and that means you need to be part of this."

"Then let's be clear: I don't like it," he says firmly.

"I don't care," I say calmly, "because your feelings are not the most important thing at stake for you, are they?"

In this moment, though, they are for me.

Ari scowls, but I am coming to be able to read them, and this one says that I've won this bout. And that means he's beginning to listen to me, which means I can afford to hope I will be able to help him.

One fight at a time. Person by person, bit by bit, maybe I truly will be able to serve people, and in so doing save myself.

For now, I focus my hope on whether he can manage to keep his rudeness in check when we meet our potential Gaellani saviors.

CHAPTER 12

WE HEAD FOR THE Gaellani courtyard closest to the barrier of the Cataclysm. It has the advantage of being the least densely packed, given its proximity to the Cataclysm, which means more of the tournament audience will be able to partake of our shop. I'm confident Hanuva and Lino will cultivate an experience of exclusive access, which makes taking the opposite approach of reducing barriers not only morally correct but also good tactics.

But as we approach the courtyard I catch a glimpse of someone heading toward the barrier I did not expect to see.

Lino.

I yank Ari and Lorwyn to a halt, ignoring Ari's outrage, and grab Yorani's foot when she tries to take off in Lino's direction.

"Miyara, we can't go after him," Lorwyn says, immediately fixing on the sight that arrested me instants before he passes out of view. "It's not public knowledge you're here this time, which means he could make it look like an accident."

"Or set it up to frame you if you defend me," I say. "Yes, I know. Spirits. I don't suppose you see Glynis anywhere?"

Lorwyn rolls her eyes. "She doesn't just wait around for your convenience."

"I'm aware of that," I say, "but she's the only messenger I know with access to Ostario."

"Wait, Ostario the *mage*?" Ari asks.

"Don't sound so impressed," Lorwyn snaps, and then to me, "Give me a minute."

She shoulders her way into the crowd, leaving me with a seething Yorani and Ari.

"What's going on?" he demands.

I weigh the merits of telling him. Show trust, when he's shown me none? Perhaps he could help us find evidence against Lino and the Valsari that Saiyana can act on.

But while he may be capable of changing his mind, he hasn't yet. In the service of that change I am willing to expose more of myself than is warranted, but I do not owe him anything or everything.

"You are not the only one with more at stake in this tournament than a title," I say.

Ari narrows his eyes. "I'm not interested in being a part of a plot I don't know about."

"I'm not convinced you'd be interested if you did know about it, and I will do my best to keep you out of it entirely."

"How reassuring."

"I don't make promises I can't keep," I say. "I will do my best. But until I understand all the pieces in motion, I cannot guarantee I will not be outmaneuvered."

Lorwyn reappears. "I sent a couple kids to find her and get Ostario here. There's nothing more we can do. Or that we should do, anyway."

"Kids?" Ari asks.

Lorwyn raises her eyebrows. "Do you think you're the only child in existence who can be trusted to perform basic tasks?"

He glares. "You're involving children in your plot, and you're trusting their discretion but not mine."

Lorwyn considers him. "There are some lessons we learn young, here," she finally says. "Solidarity. Who can be trusted and who will say all the right words but look out for their own interests. I'd have thought a poor farm boy like you would understand that."

Ari points at me. "But you trust her, after she brought the dragon people here, and not me."

"Yes," Lorwyn agrees. "Maybe you should reflect on why that might be."

"Enough," I say. "We have a job to do. Lorwyn, who do we need to talk to?"

"Everyone."

I look at her. "I'm sorry?"

She shrugs. "There are a couple grandmothers who could give you permission and make everyone else go along with it, but they won't if they think you're trying to take advantage of them."

"Demonstrate commitment first, that we don't think we're better than them." I nod. "That makes sense."

I rub my wrists, feeling the reassuring bracelets there. I was trained to give noncommittal answers to people, not to make human connections. We'll see how far I've come.

"We don't have time for this," Ari protests.

"We'd better make it, then." I roll my shoulders back and take a breath. I'm not just a tournament contestant; I'm a tea master, and if I'm serious about helping people, I must always be ready to prove it. "Let's go."

※

As we introduce ourselves to shop owners, I don't have to feign my excitement. The cuisine, the craftsmanship—everything from cloth to chairs to flower arrangements—is new and wonderful. Yorani charms everyone. Lorwyn's acerbic presence at my side keeps me grounded, and I think it is less her than the fact that I am demonstrably unafraid of her that also seems to put the people we talk to at ease.

Ari is mostly silent as we explain what we're interested in, but the longer we're there the more I notice all the furtive looks when people think I'm not paying attention.

Finally I bow and say, "Your pardon, but am I causing an inconvenience? I have no desire to force myself on you, and it seems as though there is something no one wishes to say."

Under her breath, Lorwyn mutters, "How is it that between the two of us you got the reputation for being the tactful one?"

I don't smile. The exchanged glances in front of us are too serious for me to take lightly.

"She might be able to help," one man finally says.

A woman shakes her head rapidly. "It's not her problem."

I dare a glance at Lorwyn, but she shakes her head, frowning. She doesn't know either.

I bow. "With respect, one could argue Kustio wasn't my problem to begin with, either. But I am happy to be of service."

They exchange glances again, and my heartbeat accelerates. It's not just that I am sure something is going on that I should know about—it's that this is a test, for me. Can I really be a person the community will turn to? Will they trust me, and do I deserve to be trusted?

Finally the man makes a decision. "Come with me."

It's too soon to feel relief, but we don't have far to go. He leads us behind one of the edge stalls to a narrow alley, barely wide enough to walk through. Yorani stiffens and scrambles around on my shoulder before he holds up a hand to stop our approach.

Prismatic red eyes glow out of the darkness.

"What is that?" Ari asks quietly, calmer in the face of this than he's been with all the people.

"It's a creature from the Cataclysm." I look at the man. "Isn't it?"

He nods wearily.

"But what is it doing here?" Ari persists. "Are you sheltering it?"

Behind us, the woman who protested snorts. "We are keeping out if its way. We rounded up a few for those with experience of the Cataclysm to escort back, but the problem is they keep coming. Some seem docile enough, but this morning a houseplant attacked a pregnant woman." She looks at Lorwyn. "You should go see her."

"I'm not a medic," Lorwyn says. "Healing is not my expertise."

"Then maybe you should take this opportunity to acquire it."

"Well, as long as you're okay with me possibly blowing up the developing baby—"

"Lorwyn," I say firmly.

She scowls. "Just because I'm a witch doesn't mean I'm a healer."

"You are an expert with Cataclysm life forms and keeping them contained," I say. "You may not be able to do anything for the pregnant woman's health, but you could probably do something for her home."

Lorwyn purses her lips, probably irritated she didn't think of that, and nods sharply.

I turn back to the Gaellani man. "When did this start?"

"The first attack was yesterday, as far as we know," the man says. "But the incidents are accelerating rapidly."

"So creatures have been here longer than that?"

He looks unsure for the first time, as though I'm trying to get him in trouble for not knowing, or not reporting.

If anything, I should be apologizing, for the fact that they've been in this position and felt they had no one to turn to.

But none of us—not me, not Lorwyn, and not Ari—ask him why they felt that way. We all know better.

"Maybe a week," he says at last.

Spirits.

"We think many of our homes are now infested," he says. "And if they're here, they'll probably be further along into Sayorsen before long. But if they come from here..."

"You'll be blamed," Ari says.

I can't read his expression, but he digs into his pockets and begins placing sticks on the ground.

Yorani's head whips around.

"Hold that thought," Lorwyn says.

Ari glares up at her from where he's crouched. "You want to just leave it here?"

She points upward, at the sky, and all our eyes follow.

"Spirits," the man breathes.

The barrier shimmers in the light, like a rainbow reflecting off a bubble.

Its surface warps.

And then it's like acid has eaten away at the surface: a hole stretches.

"Lorwyn, shield," I say.

"I can't control a big enough one steady with witchcraft," she says. "Ari, Ostario showed me the pattern, but I'm not good enough at magecraft for this. Lay it out how I say."

"If you think I'm taking orders from a witch—"

The red eyes behind him flash, and before Ari has finished turning to face it Lorwyn has already knocked it out with a sizzling bolt of witchlight.

Ari swallows.

"You're better than me at magecraft, kid," Lorwyn says, "but I've been in a lot more fights than you."

At her words, nebulous waves of magic spill out of the hole in the barrier, resolving into creatures and strange plants as they pass through, aimed straight at the courtyard where we stand.

"And this is now a fight," she says grimly, calling witchlight to her fists.

I kneel down beside Ari, who's shaking, and start moving his pile of sticks and rocks around.

"What are you doing?" he asks.

"Lorwyn needs to focus, but I know the theory of this shield, too," I say. "This is the pattern. We'll need to echo it all around the courtyard." I look up at the Gaellani who led us here. "We need to get this in position fast. Will you help?"

"Tell us what you need," the woman says.

I scan around us. "Take those poles—"

"Her business will collapse—"

Ari cuts in, "She won't have a business if you don't."

"I personally guarantee you will be reimbursed for damages by the government," I interrupt.

"That's a promise you *can* keep?" Ari demands.

Yes. If I have to bully the city council, if I have to shame my own sister, no matter the cost, *yes*. These people should not have been unprotected, and Istalam will answer for it and commit to do better.

As will I.

"We'll get the structure in place," I say. "Be ready."

Lightning arcs in the sky as Lorwyn takes out one attacking creature, then blasts a vine into winding around the surging blob nearest it.

I run, issuing directions as I go: take apart this post and place it there. Carry the small children to that place, where they'll be most protected from debris until the shield is up. Move. Keep moving.

It feels like we've taken forever. In reality, it's minutes at most.

The shield goes up. Ari's disheveled hair floats around him, and for once, he seems totally at ease and natural in his skin, channeling inordinate amounts of power.

"This is not the shield I was going to make," Lorwyn says as a greatwing lands on it and sizzles.

"Me either," I say. "Ari tweaked the core. Just as well."

She frowns, but when Yorani hisses Lorwyn is ready with witchlight.

The Cataclysm creatures already inside are erupting now too. Yorani squawks, and Lorwyn defends, and I hurry around hustling people out of the way of danger.

Until at last, it's quiet.

The hole in the barrier fills in again, like the barrier is liquid rushing to fill a lake.

We wait, and wait, and finally, I give Ari the nod. He drops the shield without a word of protest and doubles over, panting.

Instants later, Saiyana and Ostario burst into the courtyard.

I bow quickly and rush out of it faster than I should, crossing to meet them. "Did you get my message?" I ask.

Saiyana stops abruptly. Takes a breath.

It occurs to me that her first question might have been some variant on 'are you all right'. But I am, and we don't have time for that.

"Yes, and there's nothing there, and I can't investigate further on your word alone," Saiyana says. "The timing looks a little convenient. Do I need to put a tracking spell on you?"

I raise my eyebrows. Yorani flares her wings and flaps them rapidly in what I suspect is intended as a gesture of intimidation. "Only if you intend to clear it with a judge, and I will contest the move in my capacity as a tea master."

"Miyara!"

I bow again. "Your Highness."

She sucks in a breath and stomps a couple steps away, surveying the damage.

The Gaellani are all silent. Some look her in the face, but none speak. None expect her to hear them.

That's what I'm here for.

"The city of Sayorsen should reimburse the people here for damages," I say.

Saiyana glares at me. "Do you have any evidence the city could have known the barrier could be imperfect?"

I tense. "No."

"Then they won't pay." Before I can argue, she holds up a hand. "*I* will, Miyara. I'm the highest ranking official on site, and it's my responsibility to handle it. I'll send assessors out as soon as we're done. Does anyone need medical care?"

Miraculously, there are no serious injuries beyond a few scrapes and sprains. I pet Yorani to settle her, as she toddles back and forth on my shoulder, scales lifted slightly like hackles. Ostario beckons for Lorwyn to attend him, and she scowls.

"I'm not interested in healing," she says.

"I don't recall asking, and I don't recall you being in a position to refuse my lessons," Ostario says. "And from what I witnessed, you've expended a lot of witchcraft in the last few minutes. That may make it easier for you to rely on magecraft now. Come."

"Ari," I say, "would you like to go, too?"

Ostario raises his eyebrows as Ari freezes like a startled cat. "The shield was your doing? Impressive work."

Ari looks away. "Miyara started it."

"He's being too modest," I say, noting that's uncharacteristic, remembering how he reacted to the mention of Ostario earlier. "I showed him a basic pattern and he refined it all on his own, and he also held it on his own. To my knowledge he has no formal training."

I catch Ari's mild flinch. Does he think Ostario will think less of him for coming from a less privileged background? If anything, the opposite is probably true.

Ostario looks him in the eye as he says so quietly I don't think his voice carries to anyone farther than me, Lorwyn, and Saiyana, "My apologies, but I can't help but notice you wince every time we use a male pronoun for you. Would you prefer a different one?"

I freeze my lungs against my instinct to suck in a sharp breath.

Ari's discomfort in his own skin. His frustration with clothes. No reason that should mean anything in the abstract, and yet Ostario has instantly identified the cause.

And I didn't.

"I'm not a girl," Ari protests.

"But are you a boy?" Ostario asks.

Ari crosses his arms angrily. "Don't play games with me. I'm young, not stupid."

"I don't think you're stupid in the slightest," Ostario says. "But I'm wondering if you're aware there are other options than boys and girls?"

Ari looks flabbergasted—confused and hurt and angry all at once, like he can't tell if we're having a joke on him or if the world has been having a joke on him all this time.

I wanted to help Ari, and I thought introducing him to a trained mage who'd listen to him would help. This isn't what I intended, but it's what he needed. Which is good as far it goes, except that I didn't manage it on purpose.

I'm still fumbling around. I still don't know enough to help people the way they need.

Holding Yorani firmly so she doesn't startle Ari, I step in. "You don't have to be a boy or a girl. You can be somewhere in between, or something else entirely. Your gender doesn't have anything to do with what body you were born with. That's part of why we now understand not all witches are women."

"What—" Ari swallows, flushes. "What are the other options?"

Ostario says, "You're the only one who gets to decide. Your gender, and how your body matches it both. Some people choose different pronouns, too."

Ari looks lost and overwhelmed, so I step in again; Yorani is, for once, holding conveniently still, like she recognizes the importance of this conversation. "If you want, we can try out a neutral one like 'they'," I say. "Maybe just among our group, so you can get used to it and see what you think?"

Wide-eyed, hesitant but decisive, Ari nods, and I mentally make the switch from 'he' to 'they'.

Ostario clasps their shoulder briefly, an instant of contact, and straightens. "Let's get to work then, shall we?"

I turn back to Saiyana as Ostario, Lorwyn, and Ari head toward the Gaellani who need medical attention. I wondered if she would object to interrupting our report for Ostario to intervene with Ari, but her expression is closed off.

For Saiyana, 'neutral' means powerful emotion. She must realize, as I have, what it would mean to Ostario to be able to help another child the way no one helped him.

Finally, she looks at me. "You messed up," Saiyana says quietly.

The volume makes it no less a rebuke.

Nor does the lack of emotion in her tone make it dig any less sharply. So too do Yorani's claws, perhaps in indignation, but I pet her gently.

"I did," I agree, and Yorani stills into a crouch, the ear closest to me twitching. Listening.

It was only an hour ago that I thought I could come and persuade the people here to give me space. Oh, I'd realized something was amiss early on, but I hadn't pushed—and once they showed me the infiltrating creature, what was I going to do? Leave it there while I went to organize aid? Ask my friends to take care of the problem? A kind of help, to be sure, but not the kind they need.

"If you were a princess," Saiyana says, "you could have fixed this without risking their lives."

I do glare at her for that. "Did I miss the lesson on repairing holes in the supposedly inviolable barrier?"

"You apparently missed being able to summon guards and mages at will," Saiyana says. "Or whoever else is needed. You don't always have to be able to solve the problem yourself. You're the focal point."

I catch my breath, and something in me shifts, clicks into place.

I feel like I have to solve the problems myself to matter—but being a focal point is what I use to solve problems as much as my weaponized etiquette.

Another function of bridge-building, allowing them to lead to me. I'm not as far along as I made it sound, talking with Elowyn.

"This isn't the first indication the barrier has weakened," I say, and explain to Saiyana what people have noticed over the last few days.

She swears, but before fixating on what that means says, "If you think that's going to distract me from how you could have handled this is a princess, you're wrong."

"If I were a princess, I wouldn't have this information for you," I say.

"Do you think I'm like Iryasa, or Reyata? The answer is no, Miyara. There's more than one way to be a princess. There's no reason you couldn't talk to people as a princess."

"Yes, there is," I disagree. "They trust me as a tea master. They would not trust a representative of Istalam, which has failed them so badly."

Saiyana's expression tightens, and she runs a hand through her hair, as if untangling the problem could be as easy as untangling her gathered hair. "Nor should they, I suppose. Spirits, this is a mess."

"I'm glad you're here," I say. "I'm not going back, but I'm glad it's you."

Saiyana narrows her eyes. "What do you want?"

I sigh. "Nothing. Or rather, I didn't say that comment thinking it would earn me favors."

She raises her eyebrows and waits.

"You know this wasn't the Te Muraka's doing," I say. "You know."

"We don't actually have proof their presence here isn't connected to the deterioration of the barrier, and frankly just saying that phrase makes me feel ill."

I've hardly had a moment to process the implications myself. It's not just a magical drain on land, as if that weren't bad enough. If the barrier is failing, what does that mean for all of us?

"You can't make the Te Muraka go back," I say.

"I probably could if it really came down to it," Saiyana says, "but I have no intention of doing so. In fact I'm hoping they'll be amenable to helping evacuate the city in case the situation with the barrier deteriorates further."

"I imagine they will be," I say, "but perhaps consider stopping the people you know are interfering with the Cataclysm before it gets to that point?"

"You're either a princess or you're not, Miyara," Saiyana tells me. "You can't have it both ways."

"No," I agree. "I'm not a princess. I don't share your limitations."

"Don't let me catch you interfering with the investigation," she warns. "I'll arrest you if I have to."

I smile faintly. "I'm glad you're here, Saiyana."

Then I leave the magic to her and turn my attention to the community.

I know my sister. I know how she'll proceed, what she'll miss.

I know how to interfere without being caught.

CHAPTER 13

WHEN I'M SATISFIED THINGS are under control in the Gaellani courtyard, I get directions to Deniel's family's apartment, which isn't far away. Cradling a deeply sleeping Yorani, who is suddenly so exhausted she can't maintain her regular perch on my shoulders, I make it to their apartment only needing to course-correct twice.

His parents aren't there, but I don't expect them to be. It's Elowyn who answers the door, out of breath, her hair disheveled and smelling of soot.

"How long were you at the courtyard?" I ask.

She winces. "You saw me?"

"No," I say, "but you're covered in evidence."

Elowyn purses her lips, looking down at herself. "Oh."

I wait.

"Before the breach," she admits.

I hold still against a shiver. *The breach.* I suspect soon we'll be pronouncing it with capital letters. I only hope the article remains definite.

"I heard you were visiting and... I wanted to see, but I was going to say hello this time," Elowyn says. "But then you looked like you were working and I didn't want to be in the way, and then everything started happening, and I knew my parents would be mad if they knew I was there, so—"

"So you hid, and you left," I say, closing my eyes.

Spirits, she really does remind me of myself.

Elowyn ducks her head. "Are you mad?"

"No, though I do wish I were half as good at communication as the Gaellani community evidently is." She'd heard I was at a courtyard and made it there within an hour. It occurs to me that if she isn't already, my grandmother really ought to be tapping Gaellani as spies.

But that is a princess thought, and I'm not here to be a princess.

"Then, um. Why are you here?" Elowyn asks.

One conversation with Elowyn isn't going to be enough for her to feel like she can trust me, or that she has a future, or that anyone cares. Nor will it be for the community at large.

Trust is earned, and if I'm serious about earning it, I have to do the work. One person at a time, proving it to them through my actions.

And to myself.

"I wanted to see if you might be available to visit the tea shop this afternoon," I say.

Her jaw drops. "*Now?*"

"I know it's late notice, but—"

"No, I mean—after the courtyard, and the promises you made at the tournament, isn't today going to be busy for you?"

Worrying about me again. "If I wait for a day when the shop isn't busy, you'll never get to come," I say. "This will perhaps be an extreme case, so you may rest assured that if today doesn't scare you off, nothing will."

Elowyn takes that in. "What if it does scare me off?"

I smile. "Then we know, and we go from there."

Her expression doesn't change, and in that I know her decision has already been made; she simply doesn't trust it. "Do I need anything? Should I change clothes?"

The thought clearly distresses her, and I wonder if she has any she considers fine enough, or if she's simply overdue on laundry.

"You're fine," I say. "I thought we'd start you in the back today."

"So my clothes aren't fine, then," Elowyn challenges.

"It depends what your goal is," I say. "My choice of formalwear is deliberate for marketing and branding, but no one else wears it, nor do they need to. The tea boys all have special aprons, because Talmeri's selling a particular vision of her shop to her wealthy friends. Underneath, the tea boys' clothes vary, but they dress in line with that aesthetic. Lorwyn can wear whatever she wants not just because she stays in the back, but because her eccentric style matches what people expect of the artist behind our unique tea brews.

"As far as I'm concerned, if you want to serve customers in the front, you can choose how to present yourself. But although I hope to change this over time, I can't promise yet that our current customer base won't judge you on it. So since we haven't had a chance to talk about what you want, let alone how to deal with that possibility so you're not caught unprepared, I thought starting in the back made the most sense. Especially since it's where Lorwyn, our greatest tea expert, practices her craft." I gauge her reaction as she considers that and add, "Would you rather start at the front, serving customers? We—"

"No," Elowyn says quickly. "Definitely not."

I pause and decide to be direct. "Did I just scare you off the notion?"

She shakes her head. "No. I'm glad you're not lying to me about what to expect. But since I never know what to say to people anyway, I would *much* rather start with the tea."

One step at a time, for her and for me.

"Then let's go," I say. "Though I will have to rely on you to find the way there."

She blinks. "Why?"

"I'm gathering knowing which direction places are situated is considered normal," I say, "but this is a quality or skill I definitely do not possess."

"Oh." Elowyn sounds totally surprised. "I can show you the way, then."

Of that, I have no doubt.

"*There* you are," Lorwyn says without turning around when we come in the back door of the tea shop. "There's already a line at the front of people waiting."

"Good," I say. "That was the goal. Are they talking about the breach yet, or just the tournament?"

"Do I look like I've been listening?"

"You know they're there," I point out.

"Yes, because certain tea boys are interrupting me with updates every few minutes," she growls.

"You also could listen."

"To customer chatter? Do you think Talmeri pays me enough for that?"

I suppose not.

A thought strikes me, and I glance at Elowyn. "Actually—would you be willing to filter through and let me know?"

She realizes at once what I mean. "You don't think I'll stand out too much like this?"

Lorwyn startles, turning for the first time. "Wait, who did you—"

"I think," I say, "the people who would care you don't look like them will choose not to see you at all."

Elowyn purses her lips, then nods, sharply. "I'll find out."

Silent as a shadow, she's vanished out the back, and it's the first time I've never heard that door close.

"Is that Deniel's sister?" Lorwyn asks.

"Have you never met?"

"Not in ages, and she definitely didn't talk," Lorwyn says. "What's she doing here?"

"She's interested in learning about tea," I say.

"No," Lorwyn says. "Today of all days, I don't need any more interruptions."

"She's so quiet you literally didn't even know she was here," I point out.

Lorwyn scowls. "That's not the point."

"It is for me," I say. "She's so fixated on not causing anyone trouble she goes out of her way to make herself invisible."

Lorwyn stares at me hard. "That's what this is about?"

It's about so many things I'm not sure which she means, but I figure it's safe to say, "Yes."

She opens her mouth to say something else, but I hold up a hand, having caught the new sliver of light out of the corner of my eye. "You can come in."

Lorwyn's eyes widen, and she swears under her breath. She hadn't noticed Elowyn's return. "Well that spell's getting adjusted," she mutters.

"So far they're just talking about the tournament," Elowyn reports as she flits back to my side.

"That's something," I say. "We'll ride this deluge in waves. I'd better get up front. Elowyn—"

"Elowyn," Lorwyn snaps.

Elowyn's eyes go wide, and she freezes at my side.

"Oh, for spirit's sake," Lorwyn says. "Use words."

Elowyn swallows. "Y—yes?" she whispers, eyes darting up at me uncertainly.

"Get over here," Lorwyn commands. "Don't get in my way, but stay close enough to see what I'm doing. If you're going to be here, pay attention."

Somehow her eyes go wider and she nods, a jerk of a movement.

"Elowyn. Words."

I cut in, "She'll use words when you deserve them."

Lorwyn's eyes flash fire at me.

I ignore her and tell Elowyn dryly, "You can ask her questions as she works. If she snaps it's not personal. She's just like a spiky Cataclysm creature protecting its underbelly."

"Which is also made of spikes," Lorwyn says. "Or scales. Like your familiar I don't have to agree to dragon-sit."

"Lorwyn's not as cute as Yorani, either."

"Miyara!"

"I'm going," I say, and to Elowyn, "Thank you. Now you know you can come find me if you need anything without bothering anyone." If she doesn't want to be noticed, she won't be.

Elowyn blinks and nods, hesitantly. "Okay," she says at an almost normal volume.

I smile and leave them to it.

⚮

The next time I have a moment to step into the back, Lorwyn is calmly explaining how she's rolling leaves to Elowyn, who perches on the nearest surface and stares in wide-eyed fascination, utterly still.

The time after that, Elowyn is standing next to Lorwyn as I first did only weeks ago, working alongside her, both of them silent and focused.

It occurs to me I may have inadvertently acquired an assistant for Lorwyn. Which Lorwyn desperately needs, especially given how much time her mage lessons with Ostario now take on top of everything she was doing before.

Talmeri has only recently agreed to raises for me and Lorwyn, and she still doesn't pay the tea boys regular salaries; it's part of her arrangement with their parents. To get her to go for this, I'll need to make sure the shop is consistently busier and more successful than ever before, fast.

I add convincing Talmeri to add another salary into the mix to my mental list, steeling myself with a serene smile as I return to the front. The plans I laid to transform this business to fight Kustio will be put to a much better purpose now.

The third time I stop by the back, Elowyn is gone.

"I sent her home," Lorwyn says. "It took a while before either of us realized how late it's gotten, but since her parents don't know she's coming here yet she needs to be where they expect."

And just like that, Lorwyn joins the plot. I am beyond lucky in her friendship.

"How did she do?" I ask.

"If my sisters listened half as well as Elowyn, I'd have all the time in the world," Lorwyn says. "And she doesn't mind working, which is also starkly different from my sisters. She doesn't know much yet, but I thought you were bringing me a charity case, not a natural."

"I did," I say. "It would be poor charity if the arrangement weren't beneficial to you both. Did she enjoy herself?"

"I don't know why you ask me questions like that."

"Lorwyn."

"She agreed to come back tomorrow," she says. "Ask her yourself."

Which means the request came from Lorwyn, which will mean a great deal to Elowyn. She may come back over fear of Lorwyn's reaction if she refused, but tomorrow the tide of customers will have ebbed enough I can talk to her myself.

The door to the front opens. "Miyara," Taseino says firmly.

There are too many people for him to hold the front alone. Plotting can wait; now, I have work. "On my way."

Weary in my bones after this day, I trudge to Deniel's. So much has happened, and even in my exhaustion I feel as though I'll erupt if I can't talk to him.

Then again, I'm so tired I'm not sure how coherent of a conversation we can have, and yet—I still want to see him. To sit with him, and be with him, together.

But Deniel's is dark. The day has been long enough it takes me a few minutes of waiting to notice, but for once, he's not home.

Unreasonable tears prick the corners of my eyes. Silly and presumptuous for me to assume he'll always be available for me. And it's not like I can't see him another day when both of us have been less busy.

Still, I stand there for several more minutes before I can bring myself to leave.

But if I can't be here, I'm going to make the most of this time so that when he does have time, I can be fully present.

Glynis arrives at my door early the next morning. "Ready to stir up trouble?" she asks.

I'm going to make myself someone the Sayorseni community can count on, and that means helping people individually, because I can.

It also means inserting myself into my sister's business to make sure the right people are held accountable.

Because I can, and I will.

"I'm just going to talk strategy with Grace Hanuva, which is to both of our benefits," I reply sententiously, which is ruined as Yorani forces me to chase her around the room to catch her.

Glynis actually cackles. "I'll make sure to tell the princess that if she asks."

"Has she been inquiring into my movements?" I ask as we head out, a hand firmly on one of Yorani's feet as she flaps around my head. I don't know where Hanuva and Lino have set up operations, but I thought

Glynis would be willing to escort me there in the interest of knowing everything that's happening.

"Oh yes," Glynis says. "Her Highness got a lot subtler about it once she realized I understood what she was doing, but she is definitely keeping an eye on you."

"I'm surprised you didn't give her the line about confidentiality," I say.

She shrugs. "Wealthy types sometimes take it less seriously. Like if they pay me enough it'll matter. Wasn't sure if she was one of those, and anyway, I usually keep my mouth shut around clients. I learn more that way."

"You've never kept your mouth shut around me," I point out.

Glynis scowls. "You're a special case."

I contain a smile. "So am I to understand the princess didn't protest your being unavailable for her work this morning when you mentioned I'd requested your assistance?"

She glances at me narrowly. "You understand her game awfully well for someone who didn't even know how the messengers' guild worked a few weeks ago. Who *were* you, Miyara?"

"No one that mattered," I say. "It's who I am *now* that the princess should worry about."

In a city where space is at a premium, Hanuva and Lino have exclusive access to a "community center" in what Glynis explains to me is the most expensive business district in Sayorsen. It is not, in fact, a community center, but it is in legalese, which gives the "right" kind of people privileged access. It's not the greatest injustice in this city, but I add this to my mental list of things that have to change.

I'm not sure how to change it—a tea master has no business issuing edicts at a city council, and Deniel will have more immediate work on his plate. But if it's never the most important issue, who will ever take responsibility for fixing it?

Yorani finally stills on my shoulder, gaze intent like a bird of prey's. I wonder if she senses danger or just understands that I'm up to something.

Glynis gets me all the way inside to where Hanuva's team is hard at work before anyone alerts her to my presence, cutting her off in the middle of criticizing a minute piece of work I can't see from here.

There are no Velasari in sight. Good for my purposes here today, but I wonder where they're at instead.

"Grace Miyara," Hanuva says, striding over. "What an unexpected surprise. Come to scope us out?"

An almost courteous greeting to a competitor, except that she's left off my title, and I don't believe it's an accident.

"Not at all," I say. "I can take your assistants' excellent work as a matter of course without inspecting it." Her face tightens as the nearest girls perk up, but my riposte calling into question *her* work is subtler than her sally, enough that she can leave off addressing it. I press on. "I was looking for Lino, actually, and had thought he'd be at work. Do you know where I might find him?"

"And what could the esteemed tea master want with him, I wonder?" Hanuva asks.

Definitely not an accident.

But I'm not talking to her accidentally, either.

"I saw him heading for the Cataclysm just before the barrier breached," I say. "And now he's not here, working, and nor is his team. Do you know where he is, Grace?"

We have the attention of the whole room, now.

"Is this your strategy, then?" Hanuva asks calmly. "You know you can't beat us at tea, so you plan to spread rumors?"

I sigh with obvious impatience. "Starting to spread rumors with *you* would be silly, wouldn't it? And coming from the opposing team, no such allegation would ever be taken seriously. I can't personally gain from being here."

"Ah," Hanuva says, "but an accusation from *me* would be listened to, because Lino and I are on the same team. I see. And what do you think I would gain?"

Integrity, I want to say, but instead ask, "What do you lose? You don't need him to win, clearly. But if he does have something to do with the breach, you stand to lose your life."

"Don't be ridiculous. No one in the afflicted area died, and the princess herself has taken responsibility for ensuring our safety."

I search her face. "You haven't yet told me I'm wrong," I say softly. "I wonder why you didn't lead with that."

Hanuva tenses. "Because it doesn't bear saying, obviously. I don't owe your spurious claims a response. But out of respect for a fellow competitor, I will set your fears on this count to rest: Lino was with me all afternoon yesterday. You must have seen someone else."

Her girls are well-trained, but they don't have her control yet. Their sudden furtiveness gives away the lie even if I hadn't known it.

I hold her gaze. "Duly noted, Grace," I say.

Hanuva knows enough to know she has to cover for him. And since someone as adept at this game as she is could slip me hints if she were under duress, I know she's willing to be his cover.

She's not only not going to help me, she's complicit.

"Now if that's quite all," Hanuva says, "some of us are doing real work, and I think you'll find, eventually, that matters."

A snipe on my inexperience from multiple directions. I'm impressed despite myself, but there's more than one way to play.

"Is that why you're willing to go along with this?" I ask her. "Do you believe you're owed victory at any cost for lasting?"

She freezes, and so does everyone in the room.

"You are such a child," Hanuva says at last. "What a wonder that Talmeri lost control of her business to an upstart like you."

In that dig, it hits me all at once: *She hates me because I'm young.* Not because I have talent or power, but because I have more future ahead of me than she does.

"No, you're nothing like Talmeri," I agree. "You would have let a bully roll right over you and parroted whatever bigotry he demanded to save your own skin. I'm glad to know where you stand, Grace."

"Indeed," Hanuva says, opening the door behind me. "You know as much as a child about the world, and you belong with them—out of my tournament."

The door shuts behind us firmly, and I think furiously.

"You are never boring." Glynis sighs with satisfaction. "What now?"

"Hanuva never says anything by accident," I say. "I'm not sure that last dig was about Ari—the tournament liaison made a leading comment yesterday about needing to change my team roster. I didn't think anything of it at the time, because I thought we were talking about Sa Nikuran, but..."

"Oh," Glynis says, switching gears from nebulous conspiracies to the politics of competition. "You think there's a rule against the tea boys participating?"

"I think I'd better find out fast," I say. "Because if they can't be part of this match, Ari and I aren't going to be able to manage."

"Well after that display, I am especially invested in that horrible woman not winning," Glynis says. "Not to mention that she's collaborating with someone you clearly think is trying to kill us. I'll get my hands on that information for you if you'll tell me why."

I wonder, continuously, about my path, and how I'm choosing to pursue it. My grandmother may have wished me to follow in her footsteps as spymaster, and here I am, with Elowyn and Glynis both easily fetching information for me.

And happily. Because truly, here I am, with two people who have more cause than most to be suspicious of intentions, yet are willing to trust me enough to help, even knowing I haven't shared all my information with them.

I may not be there with Ari yet, but it wasn't that long ago Glynis glared every time she saw me. This trust is a gift, and I must make sure to be worthy of it.

"Let me bring you up to speed on the Velasari situation," I say. "It'll give you context for messages the princess has you carry, too."

"I'm not passing those messages on to you, Miyara," Glynis warns.

"Nor would I ask you to," I say. "But I trust your judgment, and you can't make informed judgments without information. Are you ready?"

The steadiness of her gaze tells me she understands what she's consenting to be aware of even as she says, "See, this is what I like about you. You treat me like I was born ready. Let's move."

CHAPTER 14

WHEN I ARRIVE WITH Yorani at the back of the tea shop, there are more people gathered than I'd expected.

Lorwyn, scowling, is predictable.

Ari, also scowling, likewise.

Elowyn is a happy surprise, albeit that she is wide-eyed and still, like she's afraid to make a move.

But I was truly not expecting Sa Rangim, let alone the young Te Muraka next to him, who looks embarrassed and grouchy at being here. But when Yorani launches herself off my shoulder at Sa Rangim, the stranger's eyes widen in wonder.

"Sa Rangim, what a pleasant surprise." I bow. "How may I serve you?"

And then sigh, as Yorani continues fluttering around his head excitedly.

"I suppose I know my first task, if not the way to accomplish it," I say dryly.

Sa Rangim smiles, lifting an arm that Yorani promptly lands on like a hawk, chittering at him excitedly. "Hello, little one," he murmurs. "Yorani, Miyara, I'd like you to meet Tamak. I mentioned him the other day."

That's right, the Te Muraka child who's adrift among them. Though "child" is perhaps the wrong word; he looks to be in his early teens. It occurs to me the "Sa" in Sa Rangim and Sa Nikuran's names must be a marker of status, but I don't know what it or its lack indicates.

Sa Rangim moves his arm down so Yorani can get a close sniff of the adolescent beside him.

Like all Te Muraka, Tamak is alabaster-skinned with eyes like jewels—in this case, aquamarines, making them look like chips of ice. His black hair has the barest hint of red in it. Red streaks symbolize power among the Te Muraka, so the fact that Sa Rangim's entire head is crimson is noteworthy. I don't know if the faint tint in Tamak's hair is an indication of likely future power or simply the normal precursor to any streaks whatsoever.

There is so much I still don't know.

"It's my honor to make your acquaintance, Tamak." I bow, and he returns the gesture rigidly but without hesitation—still not saying a word.

Embarrassed to be singled out, by his leader no less, and trying not to misstep, to not be rude even though he doesn't want to be here. Oh, dear.

"May I ask what brings you both here today?" I ask.

Ari cuts in. "We have work to do, and they're not a part of it. If you wanted to talk, maybe you shouldn't have been late."

I take a breath.

Of course Ari's like this in front of the Te Muraka. I should not expect any different, but we had made such progress yesterday.

"I'm impressed," Lorwyn says dryly. "Ari managed to hold their attitude in without saying something rude until this second. Five minutes is quite a record."

"They lasted longer yesterday at the courtyard," I point out.

"Oh, I know," Lorwyn says. "I'm tracking their nastiness. Good behavior is really more your domain."

Ari looks caught between anger and confusion, and I realize this will be the first time they've heard their new pronouns used aloud and without comment.

"Sa Rangim, Tamak, were you introduced to everyone?" I ask.

"Briefly," Lorwyn supplies. "Please take the conversational burden from here."

Tamak glances up at her at that, like he can't decide whether to be offended.

"This is an unusual crowd for us here," I explain, "but aside from Sa Rangim I believe I may be the only one present who doesn't find the prospect of all polite conversation daunting."

"I'm not daunted," Ari says.

"No," Lorwyn says, "just rude."

"Hey!"

"Ari, if you wish to be treated as a child, I will adjust my expectations," I say. "But you are smart enough to realize what you're doing, and as we're colleagues I don't see any reason to exempt you from being responsible for your behavior."

They cross their arms. "That's rich, coming from someone who's shirking her responsibilities to make small talk. And you're not talking to anyone else that way."

"If they were behaving like you, I would be," I say. "Lorwyn has witnessed enough of my handling of customers to testify to that."

"Can confirm," Lorwyn says. "The pompous rich lady you offended by serving free tea to the old lady who gave you the dragon pot is still my favorite. Especially when you managed to back her into such a corner the fallout couldn't land on you. Good times, good times."

Sa Rangim says, "This is the same teapot you brought into the Cataclysm? I have never heard this story."

"Maybe," Ari says, "she can tell you some other time. When I'm not here waiting on her to get to work."

"Ari is my designated partner for the next match of the tea tournament," I explain to Sa Rangim, and then to Ari: "And we do not need to get started immediately, because I've been looking into some tournament rules this morning and we need to wait for clarification, which Glynis will be arriving with momentarily. I believe we may have to change out plan rather drastically, so it would be inefficient to continue on our current understanding. May I offer you some tea while we wait?"

"My apologies," Sa Rangim says while Ari mutters. "I hadn't realized this would be quite such a fraught time."

I smile wryly. "What time would not be, I wonder?"

He laughs. "Indeed."

"That is partially why I invited Elowyn to join us now, though," I say, gesturing to where she sits utterly still. Ari jumps, apparently having forgotten she was there, while Sa Rangim and Tamak both fixate on her like she's fascinating as she ducks into a quick bow. "If she is interested in a tea career, I thought perhaps to give her a glimpse of what it could be like at our most chaotic so she cannot be accused of having falsely romantic notions."

"You are assisting Miyara?" Sa Rangim asks, his tone indicating that he's impressed.

Elowyn shakes her head rapidly.

Then she seems to realize Sa Rangim is waiting for a response from her, and her fingers clench on her clothes. She glances at me, wide-eyed—

But before I can intervene she swallows, squares her shoulders, and says quietly. "No, Grace. It is only my second day here, by Miyara and Lorwyn's grace. I could not aspire to be a true tea master's assistant so quickly."

Lorwyn nudges her gently with her shoulder. "Learning fast though."

Elowyn blushes deeply and looks down.

"I see," Sa Rangim says. "Would this be an inconvenient time to take on another apprentice, then?"

I suspected that was where this might be going. With all Sa Rangim's worries about the ties between communities, roots between where we've come from and where we are to go—well. I should have anticipated this.

"Are you interested in tea, Tamak?" I ask.

"The practice of tea is a noble art with a long tradition," he recites.

Oh, he definitely does not want to be here.

"My goodness," I say. "I hope we're not as boring as all that."

Tamak looks up, startled, as Sa Rangim's eyes glint in amusement.

"This tea shop is unique in Sayorsen in that all of our teas are brewed using ingredients from the Cataclysm," I say. "Lorwyn here is our master brewer. Many ingredients that come to us are a surprise, and so it is often somewhat more adventuresome than you might expect."

"Dealing with the Cataclysm isn't a challenge for me," Tamak says, a hint of haughtiness creeping into his tone.

"I'm sure it isn't," I say. "Does that include containing magic in ways that don't destroy it, or affect everything around it, though? Because I admit that level of control would be a great boon to us here."

His face tightens, which is the answer I expected.

"We rely overly on Lorwyn and her witchcraft," I say, "but all of us here learn ways to deal with the Cataclysm even without magic. And although I think this is where the fun comes in for a few of the boys who work here, the greater challenge is not in handling the tea as much as it is the interactions with people. As a newcomer to Sayorsen, and since you're not actually interested in tea, that might be a more interesting position to you."

I wait to see his reaction, but his jaw is clenched hard—I suspect he thinks he can't object with Sa Rangim standing right next to him, so I continue.

"We currently have three other tea boys on staff," I say. "As we recently lost our fourth, there is an opening for you there." Out of the corner of my eye I see Lorwyn tense, and so does Sa Rangim, but it passes almost instantly. "I suspect you're about the same age or possibly a year or two younger. They're all quite different, but all of them started from no knowledge of tea or working with customers and have been learning."

"Even if you've never talked to an Istal before today you'll be starting in better shape than some of the boys I've seen come through here," Lorwyn says. "Trust me."

"I don't believe any of our tea boys have ever gone onto a career in tea," I add. "This isn't that sort of apprenticeship. But you will learn useful skills that will transfer to other paths, as well as establishing connections with people who might come to help you in the future when you make a different choice."

"Thank you, Miyara," Sa Rangim says. "If you are willing, I believe we will take you up on this offer."

"With respect, not today." I bow as Sa Rangim stills, his gaze sharpening on me. "I trust your intentions, Sa Rangim, but I will not have Tamak forced into this through pressure. When the tournament has concluded, he may come to me on his own to discuss the matter. If he hates it, perhaps we can figure out another solution that might suit him better."

Sa Rangim and Tamak both search my gaze as Glynis bangs open the back door.

"You were right," she announces. "The tea boys can't compete in the tournament."

Spirits.

"*What?*" Ari bursts out. "Your whole plan for our shop depended on their ability to serve a crowd, when you *knew*—"

"I didn't suspect until this morning," I say.

"And I suppose you have a new plan?" they demand.

I ignore them and turn to Glynis. "Why can't the tea boys be part of my team?"

"Age restrictions," she says. "Doesn't apply to contestants, because prodigies play well to audiences, but it does apply to the team members, because of child exploitation litigation. The tournament makes exceptions under certain circumstances, but basically anyone under the age of eighteen is out."

I look at Lorwyn. "How old's Meristo?"

"You think I know?"

I roll my eyes and turn back to Glynis. "Is there anything else I should know?"

"Yes." She grins. "I'm an exception."

I blink. "Why?"

"I have a special permit in order to work for the messengers' guild," she explains, "and it applies here. So as long as I was at it I went ahead and added myself to your team."

"Are you sure?" I ask. "I don't want to get in the way of your work."

Glynis hops up on one of Lorwyn's counters, earning a glare from the resident witch. "I told you I was committed to taking down that woman even before you brought me up to speed. If I have an opportunity to strike back at these jerks, I'm taking it."

Lorwyn says, "Glynis, it's a tea tournament."

"It's more than that and you know it," she shoots back. "So if Meristo isn't old enough, you're going to need at least two more tea servers, right? And you can't ask Risteri, since she was your guide in the first match."

"Can you handle a tea serving tray?" Ari asks.

I tense, wondering if Glynis will take offense at such a bald question of her abilities. But for once, Ari's tone isn't sharp, and although it doesn't change what they said, I don't think they meant to be offensive.

"Not easily," Glynis says with a shrug. "But I bet I can take orders faster than any of you."

I hadn't thought of that. As a messenger, she's not only fast, she's unobtrusive—and as I've learned, she's used to listening closely for gossip.

"Even if Meristo isn't old enough, he and Taseino can help train you in what to do," I say slowly. I wouldn't charge Iskielo to, but our other two tea boys know their work.

"I won't need two trainers," Glynis says and looks at Ari. "Are you going to be serving? Your poise needs work if you won't be doing magic."

"What's that supposed to mean?" they ask.

"That you've spent a lot of time focusing on magecraft and not as much on dealing with people," she says point-blank.

To my surprise, Ari doesn't dispute her.

Well, I'm glad they both seem to instinctively know how not to offend each other, though I admit to some irritation I've had to work toward that outcome with both of them.

"We talked about having Ari focus on brewing, but that might not hurt," I agree. "Especially given what the judges said after the first match, they'll be looking for them to demonstrate non-magical skills. Perhaps we should show them more."

"Someone still has to brew the tea," Ari points out.

"Lorwyn is with us, too."

"Why doesn't she serve then?"

Glynis snickers, and Lorwyn shoves her off the counter.

"It sounds," Sa Rangim says, "as though you are still short on tea servers for this match, however. Perhaps I might be of service."

That silences us all quickly, and we stare in shock.

"No," Ari says, but at Glynis' scornful look they subside.

At least there's *someone* whose opinion they value, even if it's coming from a sudden and unexpected source.

"While your help would be invaluable, I wouldn't want to trouble you," I say with a bow.

"It's no trouble at all," Sa Rangim says. "On the contrary, I think being seen to work with the existing community in service is perhaps the most important thing I can do for my people right now."

Tamak protests, "There are other Te Muraka who could do this."

"A leader leads by example," Sa Rangim says. "Let no one say I am above the tasks I expect of my people."

When Tamak looks away, Sa Rangim focuses on me and winks, with the kind of deliberation that tells me he's still learning the gesture.

Aha. So this is for Tamak's benefit, so he won't think Sa Rangim is encouraging him to be a tea boy as some sort of punishment—or that this work is beneath Tamak's dignity.

"And," Sa Rangim adds gravely to Tamak, "I hope you will derive considerable amusement by my trials in learning."

Tamak snorts, but the first hint of smile I've seen from him emerges.

The back door creaks open once more.

Lorwyn sucks in a breath, and I turn.

I recognize the silence of his tread before I can believe my eyes.

"If you're in need of a temporary tea boy," Entero says, "perhaps I could be of assistance."

I stare, wide-eyed and stunned wordless.

He's fine. He's here.

I take two steps to fling myself into a hug and then think better of it, dropping into a deep bow instead.

Entero's tone is amused as he says, "My head won't explode if you hug me, but I appreciate the thought."

I rise upright again, scarcely daring to believe he's here, definitely not daring to look at Lorwyn's reaction. "I'm so sorry," I say.

"I know," Entero says. "But I forgive you. You made the best choice you could. That you could make it is no fault of yours."

"Yes, it is," I say seriously.

He nods. "Thus the forgiveness. But I'm back."

At that, Entero stares over my shoulder, and I finally look at Lorwyn, who hasn't moved.

Until she does:

By turning her back on him and beginning to brew tea.

"Elowyn, pay attention," Lorwyn orders.

Oh dear.

"Quietly, please, Elowyn," I say, looking back at Entero, whose face has gone stony. "Will you be here for long?"

"Yes," he says, still watching Lorwyn. "They expedited a long-term assignment. I'll be a special agent attached to the local police force in Sayorsen going forward."

"Until?"

"Until I quit," Entero says simply. "I had to testify publicly, which means my previous role is no longer open to me. I was supposed to go through more training on how to work with the police, but there's an urgent investigation they need someone to lead, so, here I am. For good."

Lorwyn slams the knife she's chopping with down. "And the next time your real boss has another urgent assignment for you?" she demands.

"The assignment is permanent," he says. "It's the particular investigation that's urgent."

Lorwyn turns her head. "You are not that naïve."

"If you won't believe anything I say, I don't know what you want from me," Entero says.

"Nothing," she replies coolly, turning back to the chopping board.

Although I started in the middle of their relationship, my instincts tell me I should resist the nearly overwhelming urge to intervene in it now. And yet.

"Before I get to work on whatever your plan is," Entero says, "I'd like to talk to you about my investigation, Miyara. If you could step outside for a minute?"

Lorwyn chops.

Over her head, Elowyn nods at me gravely.

I catch Glynis' eye, and she says impatiently, "We're fine, Miyara. Just get back here."

"On your own," Lorwyn snipes. "I'm not saving you this time."

"Things have changed," I say, "and I no longer need saving."

Though perhaps the children will save us. I bow to them and follow Entero out the back.

༄

"Are you leading us back to the alley where you tried to kidnap me?" I ask.

"Absolutely," Entero says. "I brought a mage device back that establishes a private bubble of sound, so no person or competing magecraft device can eavesdrop. It's set up there."

I smile. "Look at you, being sentimental. I assume it's not proof against witchcraft."

"No," he says. "The mages don't really know how to make a device like that, probably because they're not willing to ask Ostario for help. I'd see if Lorwyn knows, but it doesn't look like she's going to be willing to talk to me anytime soon."

"Lorwyn is much less willing to accept feelings than you are," I say. "She'll come around."

"Or she'll stay angry forever," Entero says. "She tried with Risteri."

"And now they're friends again."

"After you meddled." He slants me a look. "Stay out of this."

"I intend to," I say, "but if it turns out I have to fabricate a way you can both only escape a terrible situation by working together, I will."

Entero snorts. "She'd rather die."

Possibly. "Let's hope it doesn't come to that."

"Your grandmother said something similar, you know," he says abruptly. "About me and accepting feelings. It's a little uncanny that no one has ever said that about me before and now I've heard it twice in the span of weeks."

"Really? But your awareness is your greatest asset," I say. "Of your body, of space, of interactions around you and what they mean. Of course you'd know how your reactions fit and affected your mission so you could account for them. I always thought it was the secret behind your terrifying efficiency."

He blinks at me, nonplussed, then shakes his head. "She says hi, by the way."

My chest tightens. "I don't suppose she said anything else?"

"No," Entero says, "just to say hello."

I don't believe him. Not that this is unbelievable, exactly, but I know Entero, and even though he's been a spy for years I can tell when he's lying.

I raise my eyebrows. "Well all right then."

He snorts, acknowledging my disbelief, and then we step over some invisible line into a bubble with no sound.

No birds, no cart wheels turning, no background chatter.

"What's going on?" I ask. "Why did my grandmother expedite your return?"

"She had another agent in mind she was planning to send to uncover Kustio's contacts here, but that one was delayed," Entero says. "And then the barrier breached, and this couldn't wait. Since I already know Sayorsen, I was the obvious choice."

I wonder who her first choice was, but it's not immediately important. "You're investigating what happened with the barrier?"

"Yes," he says. "What do you think?"

I purse my lips. I'm hardly a professional investigator, and yet, I *do* have thoughts on this. "I don't want to tell you how to do your job."

Entero smiles faintly.

Spirits, I missed him.

"Miyara, you're the best source of intelligence I could ask for," he says. "I'd be shocked and disappointed if you didn't have ideas about this. In fact I'm counting on it."

I blink. "What?"

"You listen to everyone, and people trust you," Entero says. "I may know Sayorsen, but no one here knows me. And I'm coming in cold here."

I wince, thinking of how well I've been listening to people for the last couple of days. "I think you may be exaggerating my abilities."

"I'm definitely not," he says. "Recall that I watched you for weeks."

I sigh. "I suppose it is only in retrospect that those weeks seem clearer, but my faith in my ability to find my path, let alone tread it, has waned these past few days," I admit.

"Have you seen Deniel?" he asks.

I finger my bracelets. "Not in a day or so. Why? Do you think my sense of purpose is dependent on him?"

"No," Entero says. "Just that you always seem re-centered after seeing him. If he's busy, visit the shrine."

That's a very good idea, and one I should have thought of myself.

"I missed you," I say.

"No charge," he says. "And you haven't lost your knack."

"How do you know?" I ask.

"I just happened to walk in on your having gathered a witch, the best messenger in Sayorsen, a Taresal magecraft prodigy, a teenage dragon, a king, and a shadow," Entero drawls. "People of different genders, races, and abilities, and while they might not all have been friends, they were talking and not fighting. That's what you do, Miyara. You bring people together."

The bridge. I close my eyes, focusing on the feeling of the bracelets on my wrists. I've been spoiled: it's hard to remember sometimes that important work takes time. Not everyone or everything can be changed with one dramatic conversation.

I promised Master Karekin I would devote my life toward doing the work. I will make good on that, but I must improve my ability to maintain my sense of clarity while in its midst.

"What do you mean by shadow?" I ask.

"I mean she's like me," Entero says.

She isn't, and yet in a way she is. It was only yesterday I sent her to spy out information for me.

"I'm beginning to think what she is is a mirror," I say. "Both I and Deniel have had the same reaction to her, seeing reflections of ourselves in her."

"Never let your grandmother know," Entero says seriously. "She would dearly love to use a girl like that."

Use. He should know.

"She's Deniel's little sister," I say.

"I know," Entero says. "Do you really think, as your bodyguard, I didn't look into his family?"

Oh. "I met his parents."

"Oh to have been a mage device on that wall," he drawls. "But let's get back to the part of this conversation where you with your uncanny instincts tell me what you know about what's going on with the barrier."

I explain my theory that the Velasari are trying to frame the Te Muraka, taking advantage of the strains caused by adding another refugee population to the area to try to scapegoat them.

"Why now seems obvious, but they can't have had time to prepare this only after the Te Muraka's arrival," Entero notes. "So why?"

I close my eyes again, offering a silent prayer to the spirits.

Entero, who has more cause to distrust than most, trusts me and believes me when I have no proof. I must make sure to be worthy of it.

"What do you know," I ask, "about Taresal farming technology?"

His gaze sharpens. "Very little. Go on."

When we return to the shop, Lorwyn, Glynis, and Ari are engaged in a hot debate over some piece of magecraft, while Sa Rangim with Yorani on his shoulder calmly asks leading questions that further the discussion. Elowyn and Tamak both linger outside the circle, listening avidly but quietly and occasionally exchanging shy glances.

As we watch silently from outside, peering through the crack in the door, Entero bumps my shoulder lightly, and I take a breath and nod.

Perhaps I'm not doing as bad as all that.

Perhaps doing the work, and dedicating myself to continuing to do the work no matter what, *is* the path.

CHAPTER 15

ENTERO AND I ENTER the lab, which I expect to stall the enthusiastic debate about magic Lorwyn, Ari, Glynis, and Sa Rangim are having, while Yorani wanders and flutters contentedly among them, pausing now and again to head-butt for petting or poke something she shouldn't.

It does not.

"By your own explanation, witches and mages can only channel magic," Ari argues to Sa Rangim. "So they can't be taking it away. *You* can."

"I can," Sa Rangim agrees equably, "but I have not. Nor have any of my people."

"You don't know that."

"Yes, he does," Tamak says. "We were trapped. We had to ration magic. We know how to tell where someone has been, trust me."

"Tamak," Sa Rangim says, and Tamak looks away.

That is an interesting piece of information. I raise my eyebrows at Sa Rangim but say nothing more.

"There must be other ways to harness magic," Glynis points out. "Mages imbue objects with magic all the time; if magic isn't infinite that must involve some kind of transfer."

"It's not permanent with magecraft, though," Lorwyn says. "The physical structures sustain it."

"And with witches?"

Lorwyn shrugs. "My willpower."

"Can't be just that," Glynis says. "Willpower is part of magecraft too. And I don't believe that you're actively thinking about Miyara's hair every day."

Ari startles. "Her hair? You mean she let a witch change her body?"

"I promise," I say dryly as I approach, "it's an improvement."

"Does witchcraft last after you die?" Glynis asks.

"How should I know?" Lorwyn asks. "Do you think I know many witches?"

"It does last," a voice comes from behind us.

Ostario opens the door, and the silhouette behind him is my sister's.

"Does no one here know how closing doors works?" Lorwyn demands.

"Too many people know how to exploit your spell," Saiyana tells her.

Everyone scrambles into bows. Saiyana looks amused until she realizes I've done so, too, and her expression closes off.

It's not as satisfying when she doesn't believe a person should be bowing to her at all.

"Thanks for the insight, your Highness," Lorwyn says tartly. "Apparently it's time for me to explore new secrecy spells. For the security of your queendom, of course."

Saiyana narrows her eyes, but Ostario speaks before she can respond and Yorani distracts her by fluttering around her head in greeting. "To answer your question, workings created with witchcraft do survive past the witch's lifetime."

"Because they're unnatural," Ari says.

Ostario raises his eyebrows. "That is a theory. It has not been tested. For reasons you may understand, witches have not been willing to volunteer to undergo study at the hands of mages who consider them less than human."

Ari flushes.

"We were talking about the barrier breaches," Glynis explains. "If something magical is causing them, something magical ought to be able to stop them, right?"

"Are you a mage as well?" Ostario asks.

Glynis shrugs with an edge. "No. Do I need to be?"

"I only thought you might be suited to the work," Ostario says, "if you had any interest. I admit I was listening for a few moments before we entered, and your logical approach to the problem is the kind of thinking that facilitates magecraft."

"Which is why I'm bad it at it, yes, we know," Lorwyn says.

Glynis studies him suspiciously and glances at me. Perhaps she didn't believe me when I told her I thought she'd be a talented mage.

"He's not lying," Ari says abruptly.

Glynis looks at them and nods sharply, apparently deciding their opinion she can trust. "I just thought if we could agree on the cause, we could stop it," she finally says.

"Except we don't have to agree," Ari says. "What a group of people decides doesn't change the cause."

"It can help solve it, though," Ostario says.

"Especially," Saiyana says mildly, setting Yorani down gently on the ground, "if you think you're going to experiment on the most dangerous magical working in the world, in my nation, you had better be planning on obtaining my consent. Because if *I* don't agree, I can stop you with extreme prejudice."

Ari pales.

I sigh. "Back to threatening already?"

Saiyana shrugs, watching Yorani toddle back over to us. "Don't discount it as a tactic. There's a real art to threatening."

"Thank you for the information. I will certainly take that under advisement."

Lorwyn rolls her eyes. "I'm beginning to worry you won't even realize when Miyara's threatening you, Princess."

"Then it would be a poorly crafted threat," Saiyana says.

"Why are you both here, exactly?" Lorwyn asks. "Did someone decide my workplace was a party and forget to ask for *my* consent? Because I can also make everyone regret that." She looks at me. "Do you think everyone got that one?"

"Perhaps crackle a bit of witchlight," I suggest. "Adds a sense of ominous ambience, the promise of violence."

Sa Rangim's lips twitch.

"We are here," Ostario says, "because I will be here to train you, my apprentice, whenever I so choose. And as Miyara is often here as well at this time, I thought perhaps she and the princess might wish a chance to discuss recent events privately."

"Again?" Lorwyn asks dryly.

He thought I would prefer his presence to mediate as we talk.

Or perhaps he thought Saiyana would prefer it.

"I think, perhaps, that may have to wait," Sa Rangim says.

Saiyana steps forward. "I would not have expected you to interfere in my affairs, Sa Rangim."

"Your Highness," I say.

"You have mistaken me, your Highness," Sa Rangim says, though whether he means he's not interfering in this moment or that he would not is unspecified.

"Oh?"

I'm not sure what to make of the strange expression on his face, but Yorani has fixated on the door to the front as Sa Rangim says, "I believe there is a visitor."

The door to the back shuts, and Entero pulls Elowyn inside.

Spirits. I hadn't even noticed they were gone. And if Entero is drawing her back—

He looks at me heavily, and says, "You need to have a conversation with this one."

Evidently so.

"It wasn't dangerous," Elowyn protests. "At least not for me."

I can't talk to Elowyn about respecting danger in front of my sister without her catching on that Elowyn could be an asset.

A thought chills me: in my current position, there is nothing I can do to keep Saiyana from taking Elowyn if she chooses to.

"Elowyn is a good judge of character," I say without commenting on her ability to sneak, "but I gather this is not the usual sort?"

"It's the old lady," Entero says. "The one who gave you the teapot."

My eyes widen.

"The teapot you created a spirit with?" Saiyana asks.

And starts for the door to the front.

I dash in front of her. "Don't you dare," I say, and then add, "your Highness."

Her eyes narrow. "I'll give you once chance to rephrase that, Miyara."

"I am going to serve her tea, your Highness," I say. "That is the promise I made to her."

"Then I will ask my questions while she drinks it," Saiyana says, trying to shoulder around me.

I mirror her step, blocking her again.

"You will not," I say. "Your Highness." Every time I append her title with weight is a stab.

Yorani has gone very still, like when she senses a threat. Lorwyn scoops her up and holds her close.

Saiyana sys, "I am a princess of Istalam—"

"I am aware, your Highness, and you may imagine how deeply unimpressive that is to me," I say.

Lorwyn whistles.

Ostario steps up next to us. "I think what the princess means is—"

"That this is a state affair, and I will do what I wish," Saiyana interrupts. "That woman produced an arcane magical artifact on Istal soil, and I will have an explanation from her."

"No, your Highness," I say, "you will not. Because my promise is to serve her, and part of what that means is creating a satisfying experience for her. I nearly failed the last time she was here, and I will not have you interrupt us today."

"Will not have," Saiyana echoes dangerously.

"This is not an issue where I can or would compromise," I say, heart rate accelerating, because this, all of a sudden, is it:

I can either hold my place, or I can't.

"Believe me, I have questions of my own," I say softly. "But you will either respect me in this, your Highness, or you won't."

"I can force you to move aside, Miyara," Saiyana says.

"Perhaps," I say, "but you will have to use force, because I will not move otherwise. And if you do, I will know who you are, and what your word means. Your Highness."

She stares at me. "You are both sanctimonious and out of line," she finally says tightly. "I am working on behalf of Istalam. You are obstructing me."

"What is Istalam if not its people?" I ask. "What is Istalam if it will break promises of hospitality made in good faith?"

"Istalam is the guardian that could have told you not to make a promise like that," she snaps.

"Then Istalam would be wrong," I say, "and I do not wish for that to be true, your Highness."

"This is the contempt you hold the crown in?" she asks softly.

"The great spirits themselves could appear in the doorway this instant, your Highness, and I would still serve this woman tea," I say.

I have sworn my path to service, and I will not be swayed from it. Not even by Saiyana.

We stare at each other, and I can feel the others watching.

They aren't just people I gathered; these are all people who are counting on me in one way or another. I can't let them down.

I can't.

"If I may," Sa Rangim says, "time could be of the essence. We do not know how long she will stay."

"Princess," Ostario says.

Saiyana's expression twists in disgust. She turns on her heel and leaves without another word.

"That went well," Lorwyn mutters, setting Yorani down and petting her gently.

"Maybe you should actually plan a time to talk," Glynis says. "There are messengers' guilds for a reason, you know. It doesn't have to be a stressful shock every time someone appears."

I let out a breath.

I can hold my place with help. That's a start; perhaps it's even the entirety. I will think on it later.

"Miyara," Ostario begins, his tone disappointed.

But Sa Rangim looks at me and says, "Go."

I can't think. I spent a lifetime thinking, and now I have to move.

༄

I light and unlock the front just as the old woman is beginning to turn away.

"My apologies," I say, "I hope you weren't waiting long. Please come in."

Her eyes crinkle. "What would have happened if you hadn't been here?"

"If any of the shop employees are here when I'm not, they know to seat you and send for me," I say. "There are times when no one is here, however."

"I do know," she says, and I believe her.

She looks just as she did before, like not a day has passed, clothes still in tatters, still hauling an enormous sack that could contain the world.

I offer my arm to her shaking one and when she takes it, help her inside.

"Would you prefer the ceremony room today?" I ask.

She chuckles. "With knees like mine, let's not get fancy," she says. "Just tea, if you please."

I bow. "It would be my pleasure."

I move around the room swiftly, touching it up as I go. I flare several mage-candles to light, cue light classical music to keep the silence from being oppressive, and bring her a glass of water while the kettle heats.

"May I ask what brings you here today, Grace?" I ask.

"I was in the neighborhood and thought I'd drop by," she says.

I don't remember her playing the game so obviously last time. Now, however, it's unmistakable.

She's here for me.

This, after knowing everyone in the back is in some fashion here for me, too, begins to feel overwhelming. I swallow the feeling with a bow.

"I will endeavor to see that this portion of your journey does not disappoint you," I say, going to ready the tray.

"Tea is enough," she says.

Not for me.

"With respect," I say, "I believe tea is a beginning."

My questions will wait, which is almost for the best: I scarcely know where to begin, except with tea.

I make my selection, return, and with a bow, begin the ceremony in truth this time. We're not kneeling on the floor of a ceremony room, but if I can't adapt for the comfort of my guest I am no true tea master.

I don't know what her true goals are, but I do know this: she is here for respite, for respect and comfort and a chance to ease the great burden she bears, whatever it consists of. This is a job for the spirit of earth, the traditional black blend, for grounding and warmth, and robustness for the vigor to keep going. I may not feel grounded, but whatever roots I have, I will dig in on one side and reach out with the other so she, so anyone, can feel moored and stable and safe with me, too.

I open my eyes as I pour.

And so I see the steam rise out of the tea as it flows out of the dragon teapot.

I meet the old woman's eyes through the wispy animal shape as it forms, just for an instant, and then shimmers away.

I am speechless as she lifts the cup and takes a sip as if nothing is amiss.

She knows what this is.

"Grace," I say.

"Not bad," she says. "Not bad at all."

"A tea spirit, Yorani, is in the back with friends," I say. "I would be happy to introduce you, if you'd like."

"I would like that, but not today," she says. "Not yet."

No questions about what a tea spirit is. No surprise. She could have heard news elsewhere, but I don't think this is a woman who interacts with people in any sort of normal fashion.

"The teapot," I say. It's a guess, but not exactly much of a reach.

She raises her eyebrows without a word, and I subside.

I've served her tea, but my work does not stop there: it is still my role to serve her, not the other way around. I wouldn't let Saiyana interrogate her, and nor should I, even if I did not precisely phrase that as a question.

"What is tea without ceremony?" she asks me.

A riddle. It's not the same game I'm used to at all.

Except arguably, it's my own. Perhaps I deserve this. On one level, she's implying the teapot on its own does not create spirits, but requires the ceremony.

That is not the answer, though.

"It is enough," I say, "but *enough* does not move us forward. It sustains."

"Is forward the only direction that matters?" she asks. "Is sustenance so inconsequential?"

Another click in my mind, and I'm momentarily stunned.

Sustenance fills us up; it keeps us going. If we can't sustain, we can't move. But sustainability is variant on circumstance, too.

Roots grow in different soil, soil changes, and we adapt. We hold, and we strive, not one or the other.

"No," I finally manage. "Sustenance is everything. But we must always change and grow in order to do so."

The old woman sips her tea, her eyes closed. "Remember that 'we'," she says, "but remember your 'we' won't be the tea spirit's."

The friends in the back. I blink; it hadn't occurred to me to conflate them, in fact. "I think there's at least one in the back Yorani would count as a friend, though her favorite friend is a cat who does not visit us here."

"A cat?"

"This will definitely only end well for us all," I say.

She chuckles. "So be it, then. And no, I'm not going to give you any more than I already have. I've given more than enough."

This time, I don't think she means the teapot. This is something to do who she is or must be.

"With respect, Grace," I say, "I believe you've given everything I need."

She closes her eyes again, just for a moment, but a different kind. She sets down her cup. "Then help an old lady to the door, and I'll see you again."

I think she means it to sound like a threat.

It feels like a benediction.

⁂

"Well?" Lorwyn asks when I return. "Any new arcane magical artifacts?"

"No," I say. "She may have more, but I don't think I'll be the recipient of another."

"What? Did you offend her?"

"No," I say. "There's something else going on with her."

"As if we needed another mystery," Lorwyn says. "Does she need help, too?"

I purse my lips. "I think we are the help."

"What?"

"Did you sense anything during the tea ceremony?" I ask, looking around. Saiyana is still gone, but Ostario is here. "Any of you?"

"A burst of magic that almost immediately vanished," Ostario says with narrowed eyes. "I admit I thought nothing of it because there are waves of magic all the time, but now that you mention it, this was less of a wave and more a sudden presence."

"It was a birth," Sa Rangim says quietly. "That was creation."

"Not like when Yorani was born," Lorwyn says, frowning, "but yeah, I did feel something like that, too. Why?"

"I don't think it's anything to worry about," I say, "but Ostario, may I talk to you outside for a minute?"

"Miyara," Lorwyn growls.

"Later," I say.

"When, exactly?" Ari asks. "Because we're doing an awful lot of waiting while you talk to people."

"There's no reason you and Lorwyn can't be strategizing blends without me," I say. "Glynis, would you let Meristo and Taseino know I need them both at the shop as soon as they can get here, please?"

"Sure," she says. "We'll start training when I get back then?"

"One more thing," I say. "Please let your family know we'll have several rush orders incoming later today?"

Glynis grins. "We'll charge accordingly."

"I expect nothing less," I say. "Let's go."

Outside, Ostario casts a quick bubble around us. "What's going on, and why didn't you tell me?"

"Because I haven't seen you without Saiyana since I was aware something might be going on, and I might have been wrong."

Ostario frowns. "Saiyana isn't your enemy."

"I certainly hope not, but nor are we precisely on the same side right at the moment," I say.

He sighs. "I don't like you two being at odds. I know in my head that your relationship has to change, and it isn't going to slip into place seamlessly. But in my heart it feels viscerally wrong, and I know you're both unhappy, too."

"I'm sorry to put you in the middle of us," I say. "I do appreciate your trying to help though, truly. I'm not sure we should be alone together right now."

"I know," he says, "but I don't have to like it. Now, what should you have told me?"

"Two things," I say. "The one you mean, though, is that when I perform the tea ceremony it appears I'm creating spirits. Not like Yorani—there's a vague mystical figure in the steam when I first pour, and then it floats away. I thought I imagined it before, but this time I know the old woman saw it too."

"Only twice?" he asks.

"I tabled my tea ceremony slots temporarily so I could focus on the tournament," I explain. "I've practiced since with the teapot and haven't noticed anything odd; it's only when I perform for guests. The old woman indicated the teapot is at least a factor, if not solely responsible. Could you examine it?"

Ostario looks up at the sky. "I can't believe I'm about to say this, but as much as I'd love to, that teapot is magic I don't understand. I would like nothing better than to take it apart, but that's what it would be, Miyara. I can't promise the teapot wouldn't be broken in the process."

"Definitely not, then," I say. "Sorry to tempt you. I'll find another way."

"Are you sure there is one? You don't know anything about this woman or what she wants from you. I have some concerns."

"As do I," I say, "but not about her. I don't know everything she wants from me, but I know what matters. The rest is mine to figure out."

"And you're sure you can."

I nod, and I realize I am, absolutely. The tea ceremony grounded me as surely as it did her, and I believe I am equal to my task here.

I'll seize this feeling of vigor while it lasts, because the second part I am far less sure of.

"I also wanted to ask if you and Saiyana might be available and interested in joining me and Deniel for dinner in a couple days," I say.

Ostario blinks. "Are you sure?"

"Extremely not," I say, "but I'm asking anyway."

He huffs out a laugh. "I suppose I can trust you still have your wits about you, then. I'll talk to her, but you should know after today she's going to be spoiling for a fight."

"I have met her before," I say. "And I know what her style of combat looks like."

"You never really fought before, though," Ostario says. "You resisted, and redirected, but you never used to confront her head-on."

"I've changed," I say, which is true, but only in the sense that I'm more myself than ever before. I've put down roots, and they in turn have changed me. "She needs to understand how much, and what it means, or we'll be caught like this forever."

Ostario searches my face. "I hope you're right. But I hope you also know that she's not the only one who needs to accept what your new relationship means."

He's right. What are we like as tea master and princess? And if I'm not a tea master, what is our relationship then? How can we relate to each other without the formal protocol of established hierarchy?

"I'm working on it," I say.

He takes his leave.

And I turn to Elowyn, leaning silent and invisible against the wall.

"Now that," I say, making sure the door is closed firmly behind us so Lorwyn's sound-blocking spell will function, "was dangerous. And also rude."

Elowyn's eyes are wide, but she lifts her chin. "You're sisters," she says quietly. "You and the princess."

"Which you'd already realized before you decided to eavesdrop on the most powerful mage in Istalam," I say.

She nods hesitantly. "You look different, but you make similar facial expressions," Elowyn says. "And then when you blocked her—you were so in tune, like you're used to moving together."

I sigh. If only that were true. "You know I'm not any different than before though, right?" I ask, not sure what this will mean for the budding trust between us. "I'm still the same Miyara."

Elowyn cocks her head to one side, and I hold very still, awaiting her verdict, waiting to see what this will change.

"After seeing you with your sister," she says, "I understand why you were never afraid of Lorwyn."

That makes me laugh.

"Does my brother know?" Elowyn asks.

"Yes," I say. "I told him the first night we met."

"...I have questions."

"I think I will redirect you to Deniel for those," I say, "but Lorwyn, Risteri, Entero, the Te Muraka, and Thiano know, too. Oh, and the tea masters."

"Thiano?"

"Don't go anywhere near him," I say. "I'm fond of him, but Elowyn, some of the people I deal with—they'll recognize what you're capable of, and they may not give you a chance to choose whether you want to be part of their plots."

"You didn't want your sister knowing what I did, earlier," Elowyn says, because of course she noticed. "Neither did Entero, did he?"

We're having this conversation now, then. "I believe you can be a tea master if you want to be," I say. "I also believe you can be a spy."

She startles, and her eyes widen in understanding. "Entero?"

"Former spy and assassin," I confirm, and somehow her eyes get huger. "Elowyn, tea master and spy are not necessarily mutually exclusive, but they do both have one thing in common, which is people will always want you to work on their behalf rather than your own. They will always test your boundaries, and they will always try to influence your choices. The difference is, the people who will want to use you as a spy have the power to start making that happen *now*. Until you understand what that means, and if it's something you want, you must take care that you don't let everyone know what you can do, how easily and quietly you can blend and sneak and listen. I want to make sure you have the opportunity to choose what *you* want. Does that make sense?"

"Are you a spy?" she asks.

I blink. "Not in a traditional way," I say slowly. "I suppose, in a fashion, I am. I will have to think on that. But I also don't report to anyone I don't choose to, and as Entero could tell you, that is a great luxury."

Elowyn nods slowly. "What now, then?"

Finally, I feel like I can smile. I lead her back to the door.

"Now," I say, "we see if I can change the world with tea."

CHAPTER 16

BY THE END OF the day, I'm exhausted yet restless. But I would like to think I'm capable of learning, so this time I message ahead to Deniel to see if he's available and to ask if he has any city council questions I can help with.

Truly, I just want to say hello, but that seems like a waste of messengers' guild resources. I wonder if they'd refuse such a message on those grounds but can't ask Glynis without arousing her suspicion regarding why I don't already know the answer.

The quickly dashed off return message is disappointing. He will be working late tonight, too, but is willing to share some questions with me. I ought to find the latter encouraging, that when I actively make the space he is comfortable bringing problems to me. But I am mostly sad he still won't assume he can count on me.

Yorani has been "helping" us with preparations for the tea tournament match all day, and all the activity has left her attention more satiated than usual. While I don't have to rein in her antics, I decide to walk.

With my map of Sayorsen in hand, I meander with Yorani through the local Gaellani night market. I'm not wealthy, but my new terms with Talmeri put me in a comfortable enough place that I should be able to see to Yorani's needs, if I can figure out what they are.

Ari would no doubt judge me for spending money "frivolously" when we have limited funds for the tournament. But I refuse to let this arbitrary contest I've been forced into take precedence over my life.

In short order I have embarrassedly paid a fortunately amused vendor for a rope Yorani accidentally set on fire, and I decide to commission a protective flame retardant lotion from Lorwyn at the earliest opportunity. Yorani's desire to play with her fire seems to be growing, and while my priority should be making sure she learns not to damage, some emergency protection is a sensible precaution, especially at our apartment.

Yorani is also delighted to discover feathers, at first scrambling at them with her claws as if she wants to gather them into a nest. But when she sees that they float, and not in predictable patterns, she's fascinated, every one a toy to bat at (and, before I rap her gently on the snout, to attempt to set on fire). I spare a worry for our local bird population, but her prancing is innocently delighted.

I end up with a large but inexpensive sack of feathers so small and poky they're evidently not ideal for blankets or clothes. I remember Yorani's ease in the Cataclysm and wonder if Risteri, or perhaps Sa Nikuran, can recommend an erratically bouncing Cataclysm magic that isn't horribly dangerous for her to play with.

Yorani's claws have by now poked through the first pair of socks I gave her, so we look for a new pair of those, too. I like the green socks with the pattern of fluttering blue leaves, but Yorani has recognized the shape of a cat in a pair of socks and is adamant. Each sock shows half the shape of a cat, so when she puts her toes together they display a whole that makes her chirp in delight. I decide to get both—I need new emergency socks for the tea kit, after all.

Through it all, I listen.

There are worries here, but not about me, and not about Yorani. Not even about the Te Muraka, exactly, though there are whispers about competition for resources and who Istalam will favor. There is suspicion about Saiyana's attempts to help and Ostario's magic intruding into their lives, surveilling them.

And, of course, there is no end of discussion about the breach, and what it means. The restless feeling swells in my chest, and I grip the bracelets on my wrists, breathing deeply.

I buy Yorani and me both a few dumplings to sample—hers are the same flavors but miniature—and decide to follow Entero's advice.

To serve people, I must center myself. It's not enough to listen if I don't also know how to act on what I hear.

I head to the shrine. In a way it's a natural course for me, a comfortable practice I can fall into easily. And yet, while the spirits live in everything, their contemplation should not be a fallback, a routine rendered ordinary. Reflecting on them *should* be part of my everyday life, though, and while I've brought a shrine into my home, the spirits and my relationship to them don't belong only sequestered there.

There are a few people at the shrine, and we bow to each other. I pay my respects briefly to the spirit of air, where I pull Yorani away before she can accelerate the melting of the candles, and water, where Yorani promptly dives into the pool. But once again I find myself drawn to the spirit of earth.

I reach for Yorani, but she splashes away.

From the other side of the pool, a woman says, "I will watch her." Her shoulders are hunched, but there is a soft smile on her lips as she watches Yorani frolic.

I make a snap judgment and bow deeply. "My thanks."

She returns it with a small nod, and I go to the earth, to putting my feet in the dirt and teasing out my roots here.

What does it mean to be connected to the spirits?

For the first time, I wonder what it feels like to the Te Muraka to eat magic, as opposed to eating food. Their connection to magic is through making themselves into channels to the spirits of their ancestors that allowed them to survive the Cataclysm.

My connection has never been magical.

Except that now when I perform the tea ceremony, I bring spirits into the world.

My hands go absently to my wrists, and feeling the metal there I focus on the bracelets—on the gift of an anchor and a shield and Deniel.

Entero observed I am always more centered after being with Deniel. Is that why I've visited the shrine less in Sayorsen? Because I've replaced them in my heart with Deniel, made my internal balance dependent on an external source rather than drawing it from within?

I turn the thought over in my head a few times. It feels inaccurate, but I can't think of any good reason why.

Ruefully I realize I want to ask Deniel what he thinks of the idea.

And then I realize it's not because I need him to parse this out for me, but just because I want to hear what he thinks. That's the difference.

I just want to spend time with him.

I want to tangle my roots up in him until he's at the base and I'm at the base of him, until we can support and lift each other up and know that we will always, always be there.

I bow my head, laughing at myself.

I miss him. That's all this restlessness is. We're out of sync, and I need to do something about it.

If I want roots, I have to make them.

If I want them to reach out on a particular path, I must walk it.

That's all; that's everything.

Shaking my head, I return to the pool, but not to pray or contemplate, and not to collect Yorani, either.

"Grace, you've been here long enough your toes are turning blue," I say to the woman gently as I open my tea kit. "May I serve you tea?"

Startled, she at last accepts.

When I pour, the spirit that emerges into the air between us is clear. Yorani flaps up to it, and they circle each other, spiraling upward, until the spirit disappears.

The woman stares at me, wonder in her gaze, and then regards her cup silently.

She drinks the tea, and her whole form shudders, releasing wave after wave of tension.

I stay with her, and when she's done she bows and says, "Thank you, tea master."

I bow, and Yorani lands on my shoulder as I stand, leaving her to her thoughts. "It is my honor to serve you, grace."

~

The next day is a flurry of activity. My efforts are mostly logistical preparation for the actual physical structure of the pop-up tea shop: what space we can use and how to integrate into it with the least amount of disruption, tables and decorations and aprons.

In the morning, I hand Glynis and Ari off to Meristo for training, as his attitude can easily keep theirs in check. Sa Rangim and Tamak I leave in the hands of Taseino's calm competence. Taseino manages his nerves well, and I have no doubt if he falters Sa Rangim is experienced enough as a leader to draw him back out.

In the afternoon, they get their first try at serving actual customers, and it's clear we have a lot of work to do—for their individual training, but also how to work together seamlessly. Iskielo arrives to take over the burden for an actual shift so the lesson can wrap up for the day, and Ari retreats grouchily to argue with Lorwyn about tea and magic—but under Elowyn's watchful gaze, they do so civilly. Ari's first experience of what sort of work customer service actually entails has been educational for them.

Entero drops by in the afternoon to check in, but I miss it entirely. Elowyn informs me that Lorwyn wouldn't say a single word to him, and after promising to stop by again the next day, he left.

They're still not speaking. Then again, rather more by accident, neither are Deniel and I, and that has to stop.

Exhausted in body and mind this time, I go to Deniel's.

The cottage is dark once again, and I want to cry with frustration. I ball my fists and knock on the door out of sheer stubbornness—

And it moves.

The door isn't firmly closed.

"So Talsion can push it open, if there's bad weather," Deniel once explained to me sheepishly. "Since it's also my business there are security spells in case of a real break-in, so I don't worry about that. Talsu knows how to close the door behind him again, because he's cleverer than a fluffy ball of claws has any right to be."

I bite my lip, pondering for a long moment.

Perhaps the real reason I'm spending less time at the shrine now than I did when I lived at the palace is that I don't need to spend as much time thinking anymore. I've spent my life contemplating.

Now, I need to act.

Deniel has said I'm always welcome, and I will take him at his word. If it's a problem, we'll talk, and we'll move forward.

But we will move, and we will do so together.

I enter Deniel's home and see glowing eyes in the darkness.

Yorani flies off my shoulder, and I clap the lights on in time to see Talsu wiggling before he pounces at Yorani.

She chirps, and they tussle, and I am home.

Talsu even left the door open for us, and I can't help but wonder if it was on purpose.

I set my things down and head into the kitchen. There are pre-cooked chicken livers I can feed Talsion and Yorani, and although there isn't much else, with a smile I realize Deniel still has everything on hand needed to make for chicken and egg bowls.

The first meal he made for me, and the first he showed me how to make. Tonight, I'll prepare it for him.

The three of us eat, I clean up, and I put Deniel's bowl in the cooler.

He's still not home. Here, with me.

I look around the strangely quiet room. Yorani and Talsion have curled up together in the big chair.

I'm not going to keep going and coming back. This has gone on long enough.

I curl up against the side of the couch and close my eyes.

※

Hours later, I wake to find that I'm not alone. Talsu sleeps in the crook of my elbow on the arm of the couch, and Yorani is in my lap.

And Deniel is next to me, his arms wrapped around me.

I blink back sudden tears. *He's here.*

"I'm sorry," Deniel says softly in my ear. "I didn't want to wake you."

I turn to look at him, and he's so close. My heart thumps.

I lift my free hand and palm his cheek. "I didn't mean to make you uncomfortable. You should be in your own bed, so you can rest—"

Deniel catches my hand. "I would rather be here with you than alone in a soft bed, Miyara."

My chest is so full I can't breathe, and it hits me all at once.

I love him.

That's what this is all about.

The suddenness of that revelation rockets me to wakefulness, and I'm almost too stunned to respond when he kisses me softly.

Almost, but not quite.

"Thank you for dinner," Deniel whispers.

"Thank you for the use of your kitchen," I say. "I hope you don't mind. Talsu let us in."

The cat in question stands up, stretches, and lies down on his other wide, setting a paw on my arm to hold me in place.

"I don't mind at all," Deniel says, "though it was a little surprising to find you here."

"Sorry," I say.

"Don't be," he says. "I'm glad."

"We just kept missing each other," I say. "And I didn't want—to keep missing you. I know you're busy right now, and I am too, but I'm worried if we let the world get in the way of us being together, then it always will. I don't want that."

Deniel's eyes go unfocused, and I look away, suddenly unsure.

"I—that sounds extremely presumptuous and lofty now that I'm saying it out loud—"

Deniel kisses me again, cutting me off. "I agree," he says. "I was actually just thinking maybe I should get you a key. If you want one, I mean. Obviously we still need to work on making time and coordinating with each other, but I wonder if that would help."

I blink, and then let my head loll forward onto his shoulder.

"This is why we have to talk," I say, my words muffled against him. "That hadn't even occurred to me."

Deniel chuckles softly, petting my hair. "Is that a yes to the key, then?"

It seems like such a big step, and yet it feels utterly natural, just an extension of what we already have; another connection, tangling us together.

Moving down the path of our choice, together.

"Yes," I say. "What's been going on?"

Deniel sighs and leans back against the couch, though he moves to hold my hand. "A lot," he says, "but I'm realizing the particulars are less important than the fact that I've let myself be bogged down by them."

"Focusing on the details and not the whole," I murmur.

Deniel flashes a weary grin. "I'm mimicking your learning pattern with the tea ceremony, aren't I? Too bad I'm not clever enough to take the advice I gave you before."

"Sometimes you need to focus on the details in order to see the shape the whole can become," I say.

"The shape," he says, "is that the council is intentionally inundating me with more details than I can cope with to keep me frozen. I'm not sure how to not play their game." He pauses. "I felt you tense there."

I huff out a laugh. "You can read me too easily."

"I like to think of it as the correct amount," Deniel says. "Did you have an idea?"

"I invited Saiyana and Ostario to meet you for dinner," I say.

It's dark, but there's enough moonlight for me to see Deniel's eyebrows shoot up.

"It's just an idea," I say, "but if anyone can bust up a political network it's Saiyana. And then it not only wouldn't look like you were only there because of me, you'd have the implicit support of the crown behind you."

"I'm still caught on the idea of meeting your sister," Deniel says.

"Because she's a princess?" I ask. "If it helps, she's very blunt. If you don't know the etiquette, she won't care. She'll only make an issue of it if she wants to annoy me."

"Which to hear you tell of it, she may," Deniel points out. "Unless you think she'll be trying to court your good opinion."

"I'm honestly not sure," I admit. "I've never been interested in anyone before, so I don't know how she'll react. And even if I had, with how things are between us—"

"Never?" Deniel interrupts.

"Never," I confirm simply. "You're unique."

He sighs and leans over, resting his forehead against mine. "You know I can't say no to you."

I frown. "I did not, and I don't think that's a healthy basis for our relationship."

A laugh erupts out of him. "I mean about what matters deeply to you," he clarifies. "And I disagree—so there you go—because I think it is good to be willing to accommodate a partner's needs if it is to be a partnership in truth."

"Oh," I say, and should probably follow that with something pithy, but I'm fixated on the fact that he's called our relationship a partnership.

"But in this case that's also what I'm worried about," Deniel says. "I don't want to interfere with your relationship with your sister. Things are difficult between you now, but I know she matters to you."

"She does," I say, "but if we are to have a relationship in the future, she must be willing to accept me as I am now. That means she must be able to accept you, and me with you. Because you are important to me, and I will not hide that from her." I purse my lips. "And also because if I don't introduce you soon, she may take my ability to control the encounter out of my hands."

Deniel's hand tightens on mine. "All right, then. I trust you."

I close my eyes, letting my reaction to that sweep through me.

Then I jerk them open, because I realize that, the stress of my worries allayed by his presence, I'm falling asleep again.

Deniel shifts off the couch, kneeling in front of me. "I know this is sudden, but the bed really is more comfortable. Shall we move upstairs?"

His bed, in his room. I've never been.

Somehow, unlike the key, this doesn't feel like a natural step, but a terrifying leap.

I realize we were just sleeping together on the couch, so it shouldn't be *so* different. But it is.

"We should talk more first," I say. "We still haven't worked out how—" I break off on a yawn.

"We will," Deniel says, "but I think we both need to sleep. I promise not to leave tomorrow morning without talking to you first. Agreed?"

"Okay," I say, to all of it.

Deniel releases my hand to pick up Talsu, who merps softly as he cuddles into Deniel's chest. I hug Yorani to me and follow Deniel to the stairs.

Before I go up, though, I turn back, and bow deeply to the shrine. *I will do better by him*, I think. *I swear it.*

I will leave offerings tomorrow as a symbol of my commitment.

I sway. *Tomorrow, when I am awake.*

Upstairs, Deniel opens the door to his room, and I follow him in. "It's nothing special," he says as he sets Talsu down on the bed. I put Yorani down, too, and then predictably they both refuse to stay put. "I don't really spend much time here, honestly."

There's the bed, a small desk, and a chest. An entire wall is shelves full of books. Tidy and organized, with his priorities front and center, surrounding him, always. It is quintessentially Deniel.

Behind me, Deniel has opened a chest of drawers. "Do you want to sleep in something else?" he asks. "If you don't have a change of clothes, you'll probably want your current ones to be presentable when you head back to your apartment tomorrow."

I stare at him. "You sound like you know what you're doing."

He pauses and looks back. "You're the first person I've ever had up here, if that's what you're asking."

"It... is and it isn't," I say. "I admit I hadn't thought forward as far as the state of my clothes tomorrow morning."

"Ah," Deniel says. "Princess."

Something about the teasing note in his voice makes me flush. "I suppose."

"If you're going to make a habit of staying over unexpectedly, you may want to leave a spare set of clothes," Deniel says.

My heart stutters. *I could stay here* habitually. "You don't mind?"

"Definitely not," he says. "Or else I wouldn't have offered you a key. Here."

Totally flummoxed by the course the evening has taken and not quite awake enough to process it any longer, I stare blankly at the cloth in his hands.

"It's just an outer robe," Deniel says, running a hand through his hair. "But it should be long enough to cover you."

I will be completely wrapped in his scent.

"Is this the... done thing?" I squeak.

Deniel pauses again. "As I understand it," he says. "But you don't have to if you don't want."

I swallow. "I'll go... try it on."

I dart out to the bathroom and change clothes quickly, recognizing that I'm going to drift off soon whether I want to or not. And also that I might lose my nerve if I think.

Act, I remind myself and my hammering heart.

Deniel is not... wrong, exactly, about the robe, but though it covers me technically I feel naked. It is soft, and it is his, and I am going to be in his bed.

I take a deep breath.

I grab our new socks while I'm downstairs, tug mine on, and bring Yorani's back up with me.

Deniel turns when I open the door again. He's now wearing pants and a short robe on top, not practically different than anything else he's worn in my presence and yet we both freeze, staring at each other.

He swallows. "I did not think this through."

A laugh bubbles out of me. "Oh thank the spirits, I thought it was just me."

Deniel snorts. "Definitely not. Turn around?"

Heart hammering, I do without question. Then his hands are in my hair, and I close my eyes, savoring the feeling as he quickly gathers my hair into a braid.

"There," he whispers.

I shiver, and turn, and kiss him.

He withdraws with a soft sigh, and I decide it's probably for the best we're both so tired or I would never stop kissing him.

Stepping back, I gather Yorani up in my arms and put her new cat socks on. She chirps and wriggles into them, thrusting her feet out to show off to Talsion, who does not apparently know what to do with this information.

After a moment Talsu approaches and head-butts Yorani, who chirps again, and I set her down to cuddle with her friend.

When I turn back, Deniel has pinched the bridge of his nose as he watches us.

"Are you all right?" I ask softly.

"You are impossibly adorable and I'm not sure I can cope," Deniel says.

I smile, and Deniel takes a deep breath.

"The next done thing is to decide who gets which side of the bed," he says. "Do you have a preference?"

I blink. "I don't think so."

"Then you take the window side," Deniel says, pulling the covers back.

I slip inside, and he follows, and then we're together, in his bed and—

His body eases up behind me, and he wraps an arm around me. "Is this okay?" he whispers.

More than.

"Yes," I whisper back.

A feeling of bone deep contentment sweeps through me. I relax, and settle in, with him, and am asleep in instants.

CHAPTER 17

"MIYARA?"

I am so cozy, but I can sense a greater source of warmth and curl into it.

A huffed laugh. "Miyara. If you want to have time to talk, you should probably get up."

Deniel.

Spirits.

Bolting awake, I jerk upright, startling Talsu off the foot of the bed.

Swearing, Deniel scrambles backward, narrowly avoiding being unintentionally head-butted.

Crouched across the bed from each other, we stare. As my face begins to heat, Deniel bubbles into laughter, and I can't help but join him.

"As a tea master, I am an epitome of grace and awareness," I mutter.

"Tea will probably help," Deniel teases. "Yorani is downstairs helping me with breakfast if you'd like to join us."

"By helping, you mean—"

"Helping in the cat sense," he confirms. "Interfering with maximum adorableness. I'll, ah, leave you to get dressed." He averts his eyes shyly.

Glancing down I see that the robe he leant me has slid loose while I slept. I am... not completely scandalous, but certainly not in a state that qualifies as modest.

Deniel glances back up, and the pink in his cheeks eclipses any burgeoning embarrassment I'd expect to feel.

As always in his presence, I feel warm.

But this is a warmth accompanied by boldness, and the edge of promise.

I smile slightly and raise my eyebrows.

Deniel's eyes widen.

Slowly, he shifts on the bed, crawling toward me.

My heart hammers with anticipation.

His face breaths from my face, he looks into my eyes.

And he kisses me. It starts soft, but in instants turns harder, hungrier. I wrap my arms around him, holding him closer, feeling the pulse of warmth zinging through my body.

Then I am on my back, Deniel's weight on top of me, and all at once I realize this has turned into something I'm not sure I want.

I tense, moving a hand to push Deniel's shoulder, and he pulls back immediately, both of us breathing heavily.

"Sorry," we both say at the same time.

"Don't *you* be sorry," I say while he's blinking. "I wanted you to kiss me. I still want you to kiss me."

A smile flickers over his face, and he bends over and kisses me again, this time gently. "I'm happy to," he says, "but you don't get to be sorry either. I never want to make you uncomfortable. Please don't hesitate to tell me what you want."

"I wasn't uncomfortable," I try to explain, "it's just—"

"That did escalate quickly," Deniel agrees, running a hand through his hair and looking sheepish.

I nod, relieved he understands, that he isn't taking this as a rejection, because I am definitely interested in where that was going, just—not right now.

As he moves to one side I sit up, adjusting the robe because this time I really am scandalous. Then I catch him watching and flick him lightly in the cheek with my fingers. Before he can decide whether to be embarrassed or amused, I follow it with a kiss in the same spot.

He catches my lips in another real kiss, and his fingers drift down to my hands.

"At this rate we're never going to make it downstairs," I note. "Not that I'm complaining, you understand."

Deniel smiles, but he's looking down, and I notice he's caught my wrists in his hands—and the bracelets.

"You sleep in them?" he asks.

The question startles me. "It never occurred to me to take them off," I admit. "In the palace, the security cuffs had to stay on at all times."

"I don't want you to feel like you have to—" Deniel starts, but I cut him off.

"I want to," I say firmly. "It makes me happy to wear them. Is there a reason I should take them off?"

Deniel purses his lips and finally says, "Only my own insecurities about myself, I suppose."

I squeeze his hands. "Then perhaps the fact that I wear them always can be a reminder to you, too, that I have no doubts about you."

Deniel's hands tighten on mine, and then he slides off the bed. "I'm going to leave before I really never leave. Breakfast will be ready when you are."

Was that too much, too fast as well? I realize I don't want even this much distance between us, and perhaps that means we need it. "Very optimistic, considering how long you've left Yorani unattended," I say.

Deniel rolls his eyes but pauses at the door. After a moment, he finally turns and says quietly, "I want to wake you up with kisses every day."

Oh, my heart. I meet his eyes and answer, "I want that too."

His fingers twitch, like he wants to reach for me, and mine tighten on the blankets in answering anticipation.

Deniel swears and laughs and ducks out of the room quickly before we can distract each other again.

Distract is the wrong word. It is more that we are focused on each other, drawn like magnets.

I take a moment, covered in his blankets and his scent in his space with the memory of his warm hands and lips and smile, and revel, holding onto this feeling that's only more perfect when he's actually in the room.

I want to keep this. I want the key to his home, and his heart.

And if I am to stay, I have work to do. With a sigh, I extract myself to start the day.

❦

My clothes are sitting on top of the dresser, only a little rumpled. I have no memory of folding them and assume Deniel must have at some point. I leave my hair braided for now and head downstairs.

Yorani and Talsion zoom past, and I cross to where Deniel is setting the table with trays of different dishes for breakfast: rice, pickles, egg soup, and tea.

Each is in a gorgeous ceramic and placed deliberately on the tray as if set for tea ceremony. Did he buy an etiquette book?

"Did you make all this just with leftover ingredients?" I ask. There was hardly enough last night for the chicken and egg bowls—if he can make egg soup with so little I should ask him to teach me.

"I meant to get up early and pick up proper ingredients," Deniel admits, "but waking up next to you was too comfortable, and I lingered."

"I'm delighted to hear it," I say, "not least because you shouldn't go to any special trouble after I surprised you."

"After you made me dinner and took steps to make sure we could be together, special effort is certainly merited," he disagrees.

"And then you offered me a key to your home, leant me a robe, and let me sleep in your bed."

"Are we going to argue about obligation again?" Deniel asks.

Oops. "Probably. I don't think it's a habit I'm going to break any time soon."

"Duly noted," he drawls. "Please, eat. I gather you have a lot to tell me, and we don't have long."

I pause with the soup spoon almost to my lips. "Did something happen?"

"A certain bodyguard of our acquaintance got me up this morning by tapping on the window like a bird," Deniel says, "so if you neglected to mention Entero is back in town and needs to speak with you urgently, I imagine there's a lot happening."

Oh, spirits. Deniel's been worried about him too; I should have led with that.

I try not to think about the fact that Entero saw us sleeping together.

"I think having him back with us felt so right that in my sleepy state I forgot how important it was," I say. "This is his third day back, and he's—"

"On assignment," Deniel finishes. "He gave me the basics."

I frown. "He's not my bodyguard anymore, though. Was he trying to warn you away from me?" While I'm glad Entero cares about my wellbeing, I cannot be glad if he's decided it's his place to interfere in my choices.

"No," Deniel says, calmly sipping his tea. "I think he approves, actually. This was more... I think he wanted to check in, as a friend, and make sure we were okay. Admittedly I'm not an expert on friendship, but nor is he. So that's my take. Anyway, he's coming back with a change of clothes for you so you don't have to go back to your apartment."

Entero must have a lead he wishes my company on, then, and doesn't want to lose any more time.

So I fill Deniel in on the developments of the last few days, and he shares his with me. I'm able to give him references for a few answers to council queries, and he volunteers to cook for Saiyana and Ostario's visit.

"You're certain it will be acceptable to leave council work early?" I ask. The other councilors surely do, but I imagine Deniel feels he must work harder—to overcome his ignorance, to overcome their failures.

"I won't be able to help anyone if I can't take care of myself," he says firmly. "And I can't let them keep wasting my time. It will be fine. Even if it's not, the answer isn't to lose my life to council politics."

I want to tell him a day won't make a difference, but it would be a lie. Too often since coming to Sayorsen I've seen first-hand just what a difference a day can make.

Still, he's right. If he doesn't start reclaiming his time, eventually he won't have any left.

We strategize the meal, working together toward a common goal for once, rather than helping each other with our separate ones. I can't help but hope it's not the last time.

We do the dishes together, talking right up to the last moment, but too soon, Deniel needs to start work in truth.

I am so glad I decided to stay last night, and at Deniel's home shrine I offer a prayer to the spirits, for wisdom and resolve and faith.

<hr />

At some point while I'm cleaning up, new clothing appears on the counter. I consider, and decide to take my time dressing before stepping out to the sitting area, where Entero is waiting, dragging a string for Talsion and Yorani.

"You're not usually that slow," he says without preamble as Deniel looks on from his work area.

"You've forgotten courtesy," I say. "I'm glad to have you back, but that doesn't mean you get to invade my privacy."

"I was your bodyguard, Miyara," Entero says. "You realize I have seen you naked."

"You clearly did not ever finish bodyguard training, or you would know it's impolite to make an issue of such access."

"I went all the way back to your apartment to bring you clothes," he grumbles.

"For your own purposes, and you did so unasked," I say. "Since I assume you didn't knock on the door and ask to be admitted, that means you broke in instead, without permission."

"You would have given it," he says.

"But I *hadn't*," I remind him.

"What do you want from me, exactly?" Entero asks. "Should I have made you aware of my presence so it would be awkward? Is that less of an invasion of privacy?"

"Yes," I say. "Because it involves my explicit, active consent. I trust you, Entero, but you're not my bodyguard anymore. Treat me like a person, not a charge."

His face shifts in understanding, but all he says is, "Ah. Can we go now?"

Nearly. Deniel's hands are occupied with clay, his gaze focused. For a moment I worry a kiss might distract him and interfere with his process, but then I remember he was able to recover after Yorani flew through one of his works in progress.

I come up behind him and kiss him on the cheek.

He glances up, smiles, and nods his head in an acknowledgement.

I hadn't thought my chest was tight, but it feels like it eases. Spirits, I really do love him, don't I?

I'll have to decide what to do about that, but—later.

For now, I collect Yorani, and we're off.

I knock on the door to Thiano's shop. If he has another home somewhere, I don't know it, and, more to the point, neither does Entero.

Still, there's no answer. It's early enough that it's normal for his shop to not be open, but not so early that he wouldn't normally be here setting up.

"It's Miyara," I call.

Still nothing.

I purse my lips. "Are there any spells on the lock?" I ask Entero.

He frowns, taking it in, looking around, consulting something I can't see. "No."

I don't have to ask to know that's unusual. I try the door; it's locked. "Can you pick it?"

"You want me to break into a foreign spy's territory?" Entero asks. But, scowling, he's already started to work.

In less than a minute, the door is open.

"Is that a normal speed to be able to open locks?" I ask him.

"No," Thiano answers dryly, "it is not. Your muscle is a unique specimen, which is why your grandmother went to such trouble to keep him."

Entero tenses, and I lay a hand on his arm.

Thiano still hasn't revealed himself, hiding somewhere in the stacks.

"Aren't you going to come greet us properly?" I ask. "We went to such lengths to make sure you hadn't fallen and injured yourself and couldn't come to the door."

Thiano snorts, emerging from the darkness. "Can't even let an old man have his amusements without poking at them, I see."

"I wouldn't want you to get bored of me," I say, bowing in friendship.

"Never that, child," Thiano says. "I admit I'm impressed by how quickly your boy here thought to bring you in. I'd have expected him to have more pride, but I guess such things can be trained out of you."

"I should know," I remark with false casualness. I don't know why he's intent on boring into Entero, but I won't stand by and allow such rudeness to pass without comment.

And truly, if anyone here has had reason to have no pride, it's me. I've been working toward the world I want only in recent weeks; Entero's been doing what he can for much longer, and so, I think, has Thiano.

Thiano looks at me sharply, and I raise my eyebrows.

"And he's not my boy, as you know," I say.

"No?" Thiano scoffs. "Not still working for you as a tea boy? Not still sworn by blood oath? Not still doing your bidding?"

Spirits, I'd forgotten about the blood oath. Before we knew each other, I'd demanded it to ensure Lorwyn's safety, but it isn't necessary now.

To my surprise, Entero says, "The blood oath stays."

I realize in an instant: for Lorwyn. So she always knows he can't hurt her, even when she doubts his intentions.

Spirits. I may have to do something about them after all.

"Entero's mission is his own," I say. "I'm here today as *his* asset."

On the way over, Entero explained, "The character of the city has completely changed in the time I was gone. That kind of chaos can be good for shaking information out, but in this case it's also masking what's really going on. If anyone knows what's really going on in this city, it's Thiano, but he won't talk to me. I think he will for you, though."

"Why won't he talk to you?" I asked, surprised. I don't pretend to understand Thiano, but he's always, in his way, tried to help me.

"I don't know," Entero says, "but he knows something I need or he wouldn't be playing around. One way or another, I'll know more if you talk to him."

In the present, Thiano asks, amused, "Is that what you think? That you're here for him? Ah, Tea Princess, you know better."

"Do I?" I ask. "Must I continue, endlessly, to keep up an accounting of obligation among my friends? Can we not simply help each other as ability and necessity allow?"

"Subtlety, Miyara," Thiano chides me.

If I am any less direct I'll have no idea what his responses mean at all. "Are you sure a dose of bluntness wouldn't be a nice change of pace?"

"Why do you think I'll tell you what I didn't tell him?" Thiano asks promptly.

Finally. "I have better questions. What do you know about Taresal farming equipment?"

That gets an honest pause from him. "I hate to disappoint you, but farming equipment is outside my expertise."

"I admit I wouldn't have been surprised if you did have that trivia," I say.

"Flatterer," Thiano says. "Why the interest in agriculture?"

"I'm specifically interested in the technology used," I say, "and more specifically, the barren patches of earth it leaves behind, as if the sustaining life magic of the world has been sucked out."

As I speak, Thiano's eyes flash fire for an instant before his expression is under his usual sardonic control.

"I've seen such a patch here," I say quietly, "and Ari explained what he's seen in Taresan. There is also, as I'm sure you're aware, the coincidental timing of the first barrier breach I've ever heard of. So my real question, Thiano, is where Entero might acquire similar tech for our mages to study."

Thiano is silent for a long, fraught moment.

"Better," he finally says gruffly, "but still not the right question." He raises a hand to forestall my inevitable response and says, "But I will give you the answer to the question you should have asked, which is this: did you think Kustio sold objects spelled by the Te Muraka alone?"

I had. Now I wonder what else Thiano means—I doubt it's magecraft, or mages would've caught Kustio's network earlier. If it were witchcraft, he'd have had a witch to work against Lorwyn. So then what—

Thiano stares at me, hard, and I go cold as I realize: he has not been able to share information.

Thiano is a spy.

Specifically, he is a spy for the Isle of Nakrab.

Entero says, "The investigation into Kustio's network is still ongoing."

"Then I recommend you see that it goes faster," Thiano snaps.

"Thiano, help me buy something," I say.

His dark eyes flash in my direction. "What happened to not accounting for obligation?"

"I can also do nice things for no other reason than I wish to," I say, "and I will revel in that freedom."

"Nice for whom, precisely?"

"Deniel's younger sister," I say. "I'd like something special for her to wear."

"Ah, buying the family's affection?" Thiano smirks.

"As I'm sure you're aware, I have no need to," I say coolly. "But sometimes pride can do with a little help."

Thiano looks at me again for a long moment, and then he sighs.

"I can't decide if you make me feel unbearably old or young," he complains. "Come on. I have just the thing, obviously."

※

As soon as we leave, gift in hand, Entero wastes no time. "Tell Risteri to have the guides take extra precautions watching the border of the Cataclysm," Entero says. "They care, and they'll do a better job than anyone else can."

"Can't you arrange that through the police?" I ask. "Isn't that what you're here to do?"

Entero shakes his head, a jerk of movement like a slash. "No time. I'm too new, and there's too much bureaucracy. Risteri can make it happen. But the fastest way to get the information I need is going to Taresan."

The Isle of Nakrab is as much a cipher as Thiano. I know very little about Nakrabi magic, but I know while the continent was scrambling in the aftermath of the Cataclysm, the Isle of Nakrab was unaffected and took advantage of the chaos of the markets. The pressure they can assert on commerce has long been a concern for the Istal government, and the same must be true in Taresan and Velasar.

But for Nakrabi magic to be involved, and with Kustio no less... I like this not at all. We need more information, badly, but I'm not sure the most crucial of it is to be found anywhere but here.

"And tell Lorwyn... I'll be gone a while," Entero says.

"No," I say.

"Miyara—"

"No, Entero. You left me to tell her the last time you left for an extended period with no estimate on when you could return—"

"Have you forgotten that leaving was your idea?" he interrupts.

Not for a moment. "Face her yourself this time."

Entero scowls. "That's the problem. She doesn't want to talk to me."

"Consider why," I say.

"I know why," he says. "I left her."

I roll my eyes. "Reconsider."

"We're not all superhuman at knowing what people are thinking, Miyara," Entero snaps.

From anyone else that would be fair, but Entero is normally more perceptive—particularly where Lorwyn is involved.

On the other hand, while I'm trying not to interfere, surely helping friends understand each other is harmless enough? I can practically hear Thiano's snort in my head and wince. I don't believe myself either, but nor can I convince myself it's truly better to leave Entero to flail for answers on his own.

"You weren't willing to face her when it was hard," I say simply.

"I didn't exactly have time for a long conversation," Entero says.

I just look at him, until finally he sighs and looks away.

"I still don't know what I can offer her," he says quietly. "I'm trying, but what she said the other day... isn't exactly wrong."

Clearly not, as he was just about to leap at the chance to leave Sayorsen.

"Then tell her that," I say. "Whatever my grandmother wanted, you started police training to come back here for your own reasons, didn't you? You've done this much already. If she's that important, before you go into deep cover or leave the city, you can take the time to see her."

Entero is silent.

"You managed to find time to play with a dragon and a cat this morning," I remind him.

"Lorwyn will take considerably more time," he says wryly.

"And it will be worth it," I say quietly. "I promise."

CHAPTER 18

THE DAY PASSES IN a frenzy of activity. It's almost time for the second match of the tournament, and everyone has so much to do, from logistical preparations to training on individual skills and learning to work together as a group.

To my surprise, this challenge has made me less irritated with the tournament as a whole. I am learning, and so are my people. I will take advantage of this tournament and use it as a lever to promote my own goals: helping everyone feel welcome, empowered, and worthwhile.

Too soon, though, Risteri arrives to pick up Yorani for dragon-sitting, and I am scrambling away from the tea shop to pick up the offerings I promised to the spirits and thence to Deniel's.

It's already time to host Saiyana and Ostario for dinner.

Already, this dinner is not what I hoped, but perhaps what I expected.

In scheduling, Saiyana's messages pushed for as early of a time as possible, trying to catch us unprepared. In a way it is a blessing, because I am substantially less nervous and more determined to answer the challenge she has posed.

Dinner has become a duel, and not one I can afford to lose.

"I assume it's occurred to you," Deniel says as he transfers his attention to a different dish, "that you don't have to play by the terms of engagement she's set?"

I nod, concentrating on chopping vegetables. He's chosen to take responsibility for dinner, perhaps to have something he can control, or to focus on what he feels confident in where he does not in formal etiquette.

In a way I am also glad Saiyana forced the issue early, so that neither I nor Deniel had time to fret about the best way to approach this. We will do only what we can.

Still, I marvel at how many different dishes Deniel can cook, let alone all at once.

My contribution is dessert: the first dessert I ever made. I'm not sure how Saiyana will react, and I'm afraid to think about it. I suspect this is why Deniel asked me to help with chopping, rather than any true need for my assistance.

"Yes," I say. "If I can hold my own against her head-on, she'll respect my choices. It's speaking to her in a way she can understand."

"Except that she's not used to losing or accepting, to hear you tell of it," Deniel says. "And head-on is not the mode in which you prefer to operate."

"I'm not sure this precisely counts as head-on in any case," I say wryly. "I am setting her up, and I'm preparing to serve her. This isn't how she would have chosen to engage, either."

As soon as I say that, though, I frown. In her work for the crown, she does have many uncomfortable political dinners with people she needs to manipulate. It may not be her preferred dueling ground, but it is not one she's inexperienced with.

It is only me with my new sense of self she hasn't found a way to hook her claws into.

"You're having a thought," Deniel says.

He knows me well. "Being a tea master is part of who I am now," I say, "but in a way, it is a mode of engagement I can hide behind."

He nods. "Using etiquette as your weapon of choice."

"Yes. If my sister and I are ever going to have a personal relationship again, though, I can't rely on that tonight."

I will have to be vulnerable, knowing she is coming here to attack, without letting her undermine me.

Deniel sets down his spoon—what is that utensil?—and looks at me. Waiting.

"I want my sister," I whisper, "but not at any cost."

An awful, liberating realization. Only weeks ago Saiyana was the person closest to me; the person I asked to stand for me at my dedication ceremony for personal reasons rather than political.

Deniel takes my hand and with his thumb strokes my wrist under the bracelet. I close my eyes, letting the warmth of him and his presence with me sweep through me.

"I'll do what I can," he says, which is sweet but also bitter, because he is already doing this for me at great discomfort for himself.

I squeeze his hand. "I know what's most important. That matters the most."

Deniel ducks his head. "I appreciate the sentiment, but please don't throw your sister over for me. I don't think that will make you happy. Can you bring me the stacked boxes please?"

It's not like him to try to distract me from a serious conversation, which is how I know it's his own nerves about what he's just said.

"Do you make ceramic versions of these?" I ask, carrying them over. They're lacquered trays with individual compartments for different dishes that stack and, I gather, expensive, normally used only for special occasions. He has exactly four: one for each member of his family.

Tonight, we will use them for my family. I wonder if Saiyana will know to appreciate the gesture.

Deniel shakes his head. "No, ceramic would be a very difficult medium to make..." He trails off, head cocked to the side. "You know, I wonder if I could—at least a version of them. I'll have to experiment."

"Happy to help," I say. "And you're not coming between me and my sister. If she chooses to make herself an obstruction in my life, I will act to defend my choices, and you are part of that. But my goal for tonight is to prevent it from coming to that."

I don't want to have to choose between them. But if I do, I know which way I will go: it is the same choice I made when I dedicated myself to this path, and I will not deviate or go back on my commitment. It's simply a matter of whether I am strong enough in myself to make that stick: whether I've planted my roots deeply enough, or whether I am still a twig to be swayed by a strong breeze.

Tonight, we will see.

"If anyone can make this work, it's you," Deniel says. "I'll try not to make it any harder."

I sigh, exasperated. "Deniel."

He winces. "Sorry."

"You should be," I say. "You are helpful by your very presence, and I am better for having you in my life. If you can't believe that of yourself, please trust the esteem in which you hold my judgment."

Deniel flashes a smile at that. "See? You are sneaky. Like a cat."

"Thank you," I say gravely, and he laughs.

Then there is a knock at the door, and we're out of time.

We exchange glances. Deniel squeezes my hand one more time, and I squeeze back, and together we head to the door.

Deniel takes a breath and opens it. "Welcome," he says. "Please be at ease in my home, graces."

Deniel bows, the perfectly correct angle to greet a princess. He's been studying.

It is immediately clear Saiyana is not taking this anywhere near as seriously. Ostario is wearing his formal robes of office—to intimidate, or to show respect?—but Saiyana is dressed exactly as she always is, as if this meeting is of no import to her.

As Saiyana fails to fill the silence, staring blankly, I touch a hand to Deniel's shoulder so he rises again. "I'm so glad we were able to arrange this at such short notice," I say.

"Yes, it must be such a trial to make time for me," Saiyana says.

Ostario sighs.

"Since when do you not want your visit to be a cause for deliberation?" I ask.

"Since when do you wear aprons?"

Is that what arrested her at the door? I step back, gesturing for her to enter, and Deniel lets me take the lead. "Since I started working with magical ingredients, couldn't afford more clothing, and didn't know how to wash silk," I say. "I've found I'm no more immune to stray oil spatters and showers of flour in the kitchen."

Saiyana gives me a funny look. "You?"

"I believe what her Highness means," Ostario says, "is she has difficulty imagining someone of your grace spattered in food."

"Or working in a kitchen," Saiyana says. "You cook?"

"You may rest easy knowing Deniel prepared tonight's dinner," I say, "but yes, I cook. It is less expensive than eating out for every meal, and I have limited funds. I've since found I enjoy it, even if I'm not particularly skilled."

"Miyara is a fast learner, your Highness," Deniel puts in. "Especially given her refined tasting skills."

My sister fixates on him, her gaze predatory. "Oh, so you're the one responsible for her performance in the kitchen."

She's bothered that I'm doing work like a commoner and not a princess.

"I also own a cookbook," I say, "and perhaps we should begin again. Saiyana, this is Deniel, who has graciously offered to host you tonight with very little notice and gone to great effort on your behalf."

"Has he," Saiyana says.

"No," Deniel says, and all of us look at him in surprise. "With respect, your Highness, you would not be here if not for Miyara. Whatever effort I have gone to is for her sake."

I feel a thrill at that—not just that he is being clear about his support of me, though of course that as well.

But that is also the kind of rebuke Saiyana can respect.

"Deniel," I say before my sister can respond, "I am less pleased to introduce my boor of a sister Saiyana, who I regret appears to have chosen to discard her extensive knowledge of manners. I hope you will not judge me too badly for her poor behavior."

"Oh, is that how we're doing this?" Saiyana asks.

"No," Ostario says firmly, "it is not. I'm disappointed in both of you."

"Who are you to be disappointed in me?" Saiyana demands of him.

"A person," I answer. "One who has known us for almost all our lives and wants the best for us. If you're going to stand here and reject Ostario as not worthy of being here as an equal with us, then you can leave right now, Saiyana."

"Don't make me your scapegoat," Ostario warns.

But Saiyana smiles, and I sigh in exasperation.

When Deniel looks at me quizzically, I explain, "She wanted to know what would get me to address her by name instead of title."

"Who knew your composure was so fragile these days?" Saiyana asks, still satisfied.

Because once upon a time, I never would have let her needle me like that.

I raise my eyebrows. "Is that what you think?" Without clarifying I say, "Please sit down, and I will bring tea."

"Dinner is almost ready as well," Deniel says, and together we retreat into the kitchen.

"Well that went well," he says softly.

I glance down at his hands and am encouraged to see they're not shaky in the slightest. Steady as a potter.

"It did, actually," I say. "We have both managed to hold our ground."

Deniel glances askance at me. "Is this what your family dinners are always like?"

"We didn't have family dinners," I say, "but it is what state dinners are like. I've simply never been an active participant in this way, and Saiyana will likely be pleased about that, too."

"Is that what you want?"

I consider. "Too soon to tell. But you were perfect. Thank you."

He stares at me for a moment and then smiles, shaking his head. "You're welcome, Miyara."

I frown at him. "You're relaxed now?"

"I know what I need to do now," Deniel says enigmatically.

If he's confident, I'm not going to poke him for more detail until later. Instead I carry the tea tray loaded with four cups over to the small table.

Deniel borrowed two chairs from a neighbor for the evening, and they're mismatched. But he has an artist's eye, and as I set the distinct pottery on the table, how it all fits together begins to emerge.

"Did Deniel make these pieces?" Ostario asks, taking a cup. "They're remarkable."

"Yes," I say. "After dinner we can take a longer look at the shop up front if you're interested."

"I'd like that," he says, and takes a sip. "Ah."

"No tea ceremony?" Saiyana asks. "I thought that was your thing, now."

I smile, and it is a polite smile she will know. "It is, but you're not open to receiving it. I can be patient."

"I'm not patient, as we all know," Saiyana says. "So enlighten me. What do you think you're doing here, exactly? Playing house with the first man who shows an interest in domesticating you?"

I blink, honestly taken aback by how offensive that statement is.

Ostario stares at her, but Saiyana lifts her chin and glares at me, standing by it.

Well then. Here we go.

"First of all," I say, "how dare you. Second of all, as you know perfectly well, there were any number of suitors who would have been only too happy to have a meek princess to add to their stable, and I was never interested."

"And now I am to believe that you are genuinely courting a man you met immediately upon abandoning your responsibilities, and adopting his lifestyle is unrelated to your intransigence? Please. You're not truly serious—you two clearly haven't even had sex yet."

I have never wanted to enact violence on another person more badly than at this moment. I am actually shaking with rage at the effort to restrain myself at the sight of Saiyana's self-satisfied visage.

At this moment, into the silence, Deniel's voice comes from behind me.

"I admit," he says calmly, "I couldn't understand how someone as sincere as Miyara felt there wasn't a single person in her family she could confide in, but now I see."

That gets Saiyana's attention.

In the now silent room, she sits up straight, her imperious glare boring into him.

Deniel sets each place at the table as if nothing is amiss, saying nothing further.

"How dare you," Saiyana finally says.

Deniel glances up at her, eyebrows raised, and shakes his head without saying anything, like she doesn't even merit comment.

Spirits, he is perfect.

Saiyana leans forward. "Miyara had a duty—"

"And you thought that meant she deserved to be unvalued for who she is?" Deniel interrupts, not even looking at her. "I can't imagine how you can be surprised she left an environment like that. The only surprise to me is how you cannot recognize her value as she is now, and the burden of that duty, your Highness, is yours."

"Oh," Ostario puts in, "she knows. Her Highness wouldn't be so mad if she weren't jealous of Miyara."

Saiyana scowls at him. "Don't be ridiculous."

"Compared to your company tonight, I don't see how I could be," Ostario drawls.

I'm still so angry I hadn't been planning on saying a single word more to my sister, but this revelation cuts through that.

Saiyana might play about this, but Ostario wouldn't.

"What in the world could you possibly have to be jealous about?" I demand as Deniel snorts softly, taking his seat. "You're good at everything."

Saiyana opens her mouth and winces.

Ostario looks innocently up at the ceiling, which makes me wonder what spell he just poked her with.

"But I'm not good," Saiyana finally says, her deepening scowl lending credence to her words. "I do good things out of spite, not because I care about people. Where you have this ineffable serenity that radiates outward. And don't try to tell me it's a tea master thing, because you have always been like this and you know it."

"And you," Deniel says to her, "have always tried to make her into something else. I am not the one at this table who has ever tried to change Miyara, Princess."

"Deniel," Ostario says, "this food looks wonderful. Is this traditional Gaellani cuisine?"

Saiyana glances down at her food for the first time and blinks at the presentation. Lifting her gaze, she scans the table, taking in the rest, and then rolls her eyes toward the ceiling.

"Of course you found the one man in the city with the soul of an artist and the incisiveness of a lawyer," she says. "Of course you did. Spirits."

Maybe she will be able to accept Deniel, at least, if not me. Perhaps the evening won't be a total waste after all.

"There is a lot I can learn from you," I say, "but I think romantic relationships are not among that number."

"What's that supposed to mean?"

I raise my eyebrows. "Do you really want me to answer that now? In this company? How forward."

Ostario's eyes widen, and for the first time in years I see Saiyana's cheeks flush. "You brat!"

"Try the sweet rolled omelet, for your disposition," I say. "Perhaps one of us should take your pickled vegetables, as you seem to be well full of vinegar—"

"I will throw these vegetables at you."

Ostario raps on her lacquered box quickly with his eating utensils to distract her into manners.

"Deniel," I say, "could you tell us what each dish is?"

"Can't taste it yourself?" Saiyana asks.

"People can offer information without my needing to poke around for it. There is more history to these dishes than I can taste on my own, and what people tell me about them is informative." I smile brightly and add, "But also I like to hear Deniel's voice."

"You almost had me going there," Saiyana says.

I may have said that to annoy her, but it doesn't make it less true. She subsides, though, and listens to his explanation. We responded differently, but our educations were very similar: she knows food, culture, and traditions shape people, and she knows narratives about those traditions matter in how we think. She doesn't know the Gaellani, but she knows Istalam has not done well by them. She would be foolish to reject this lesson, freely offered.

Saiyana is very angry, and perhaps shortsighted. But never foolish.

At the end, she looks at me and says, "If this is the real reason you brought me here, we could have done this differently."

"It's not," I say.

"Can the reason not ever just be the two of you talking?" Ostario asks.

"No," Saiyana says.

"I wanted to listen to her," I say, "and what I heard is that she is not prepared to listen to me."

"Oh, come off it," Saiyana says. "I have been sitting here quietly just fine, but you never tell me anything."

I have had it.

"I was listening," I bite out, "to see if I could in good conscience recommend you as a teacher to Deniel. Because policies in the government you represent have made it impossible for him, whom you yourself noted would be a gifted lawyer, to actually attend law school. Because now he is alone on the council of this city trying to keep our family's mistakes from repeating over and over and doesn't have the training he should. Because you can be a gifted teacher when you choose to be. And I thought, perhaps Saiyana will recognize that there are things in this world she has failed to see but can choose at any moment to start. Perhaps it will be this. And here we are, and Deniel has prepared this entire meal and explained it in depth and you still looked to me for what this has to do with you instead of first thanking him."

The entire table is silent for a minute.

"You know, Miyara," Ostario says finally, "I think you may actually be worse than she is. Spirits."

"I didn't ask you to set me up with a tutor," Deniel says quietly.

I look at him. "Would it have occurred to you to ask?"

"You still should have asked me first."

I remember my conversation just that morning with Entero and flush, nodding. "I know. I had planned to see how you two got on tonight and then ask you but... I lost my temper."

Saiyana snorts. "Spirits, even your temper is pure."

"No," Deniel disagrees, eyes still on me. "Her temper causes her to manipulate people into being what she's decided is right for them, even if they're not ready for it yet."

That gets me where Saiyana's sallies didn't. Oh, she got me angry, but she didn't cause me to doubt myself.

But I remember snapping at Lorwyn and Risteri and guilting them into joining me together on my quest to save the Te Muraka. Even more recently, I've been considering intervening between Entero and Lorwyn—and that's not even to mention how I'm behaving with Ari, Glynis, Elowyn, Tamak—

"You're right," I say quietly, bowing quickly. "I'm sorry. I'll work on being more aware of that."

"I accept," Deniel says, "and I'll work on keeping up so you don't have any reason to feel tempted on my behalf."

"You don't need to do anything more to keep up with me," I say.

"Nevertheless," he says.

Saiyana swears. "Spirits, you two are a good match for each other, aren't you?"

She glares at me, but instead of saying whatever is on her mind after a minute she finally just shakes her head.

"I know what books you've been reading," Saiyana says to Deniel. "They're a good basis, and I'll send you others that'll be more targeted at what you're going to need to know in the long run. But tomorrow you should come on rounds with me."

Deniel stares. "I have to work—"

"I know," Saiyana says. "Whenever you can manage it. But right away a crash course in practical politics is going to help you more than any theory."

"I'll try to figure something out, then," Deniel says. "Thank you for the offer."

Saiyana nods. "Thank you for the meal, and your patience. But I think I'd better get back to it, now. Ostario, feel free to take your time."

"Your wish is my command," Ostario says in a low voice.

Saiyana doesn't actually jump out of her seat, but I can see she badly wants to. She definitely does not want to hear whatever words Ostario has been storing up this evening. I nearly run to catch up with her at the door.

"Are you happy now?" she asks me abruptly.

I open my mouth; close it. "For the first time," I say, "I think I truly could be. But I have a lot of work to do."

Saiyana looks at me. "You always will."

"I know," I say.

Her expression twists, and she's gone before I can say anything more. Back in the kitchen, Ostario is getting ready to leave, too.

"I'm not sure whether I should apologize for her, or thank you for the entertaining evening," Ostario says.

"You could try dessert," Deniel offers. "Miyara baked."

Ostario's eyes widen. "It would be my pleasure."

I swallow. "I admit I'm not sorry Saiyana left before I had to present them to her."

"I'll wrap some up for you to take," Deniel says, looking to me for permission.

I'm being a coward. "If you can bear any more entertainment, could you give some to Saiyana, please?"

"Of course," Ostario says. "It would be my pleasure." He regards me for a moment and then adds, "Thank you for tipping me off. I never would have guessed and still wouldn't believe it, but for her reaction."

"I gathered," I say. "If I may, if you want your relationship to change, you will have to move first. She never will."

Ostario's gaze searches mine like he can't quite believe I've said this, that I am giving him my blessing to pursue my sister, a princess, romantically.

"I think you're right," he finally says. "But it would be wrong to move while we're on this project together, for professionalism's sake. So I will have time to plan."

"You are interested, then?" I ask. "I was never sure of you."

Ostario laughs outright. "I learned long ago how to keep my true feelings hidden, but Saiyana has always driven me to distraction. I didn't want to push where unwanted, but now..." His expression turns fierce. "I've never been beaten by impossible odds yet."

"I will pray for you," I say, and Ostario snorts as Deniel comes up with dessert neatly packaged.

But I don't think he'll need the spirits' help with her—and for the first time I think maybe I won't, either.

If my sister can see why I chose Deniel, maybe, just maybe, there is a chance she will be able to see me.

CHAPTER 19

AFTER OSTARIO LEAVES, Deniel and I start cleaning up silently by some unspoken agreement. I'm not sure what to say. So much of my life seems to be moving too fast, which perhaps I ought to revel in as a contrast to the stagnant dread of my life before, but—there is too much. I worry if I don't take my silences where I can find them, I will lose them altogether.

When the dishes are done, with regret I say, "I should go back to my apartment and relieve Risteri from dragon-sitting." I also have to do laundry, and perhaps choose clothes to leave at Deniel's place. The thought causes a flutter of anticipation.

Deniel nods, distracted in his own thoughts. "I didn't have time to get a duplicate key today."

Oh. "That's fine," I say. "Whenever..." I trail off. "Whenever you have time" is not a phrase that applies to either of us right now.

Deniel flashes a grin. "I'll make it a priority."

I search his gaze. "You seem... calmer than I feared you would be, after that gauntlet."

"Your sister has no idea how to approach you," Deniel says. "I think, if I were in her sights as a political enemy, she would be terrifying. But as a lost sister, no. Her venom misses the mark, because she's lashing out without understanding how to aim."

"You realized something, after she arrived," I say.

Deniel smiles. "And I'm not telling. At least, not now."

My heart thumps. His last attempt to keep secrets from me did not work as intended. "But you'll tell me later?"

He looks right at me then, and something about his gaze pierces right through me. "Yes," he says softly. "I will."

"Okay," I say, wishing I had a more graceful response.

Deniel crosses and kisses me. "I'll message tomorrow with how things go with your sister," he says.

"I'm not worried," I say, "but I admit I'm curious."

"So am I," Deniel says dryly. "Goodnight, Miyara."

His voice, low and intimate, makes me shiver. "Goodnight," I return. "And thank you."

"You are always welcome," he says. "Though we'll see about your sister."

That finally gets the smile out of me I belatedly realize he's been angling for, and after another kiss I make it out the door.

I trudge up the steps to my apartment feeling like a stranger in my own home. It occurs to me I haven't been here in over a day, and I don't especially miss it. I don't think of this as my home, not truly; if I am settling anywhere, it is at Deniel's. The thought is both a thrill and a concern, because I'm not sure, exactly, what I'm about.

Risteri, on the other hand, I am certain I have done poorly by.

When I open the door, though, she's not the only one there.

Yorani zooms toward my face, and I catch her by the leg before she escapes out the door, pulling her back in behind me.

"Miyara, you have to help," Risteri says. "Stop her or we're not going to have a kitchen left."

A moment later it becomes clear she's not referring to the dragon in our midst. Not the literal one, anyway.

"I haven't exploded a kitchen in years," Lorwyn says tartly.

"Only because your current lab is now warded. And consider that it's telling you've exploded a kitchen at *all*."

"I only exploded some things inside it. It's not like the whole building blew up."

"I'll never forget," Risteri says.

I set my bag down and take a look at what Lorwyn is doing in our kitchen. Most of the ingredients she's using are innocuous—which is to say, not of the Cataclysm—but the combinations are... dire. I suppress a shudder at their prospect.

"Am I to understand you had a stressful afternoon and are taking it out on these poor tea ingredients?" I ask. "Because that pepper is a terrible thing to do to such an innocent leaf."

Lorwyn squeezes more juice out of the pepper, and the leaf shrivels beneath it. "No such thing as innocence, at least that doesn't go unpunished."

I exchange a look with Risteri.

"I admit I thought Sa Nikuran might have volunteered to help with Yorani," I say, "but I was not expecting Lorwyn."

Risteri reddens. "Sa Nikuran was here earlier," she says, "but I sent her home when Lorwyn arrived looking like she needed to kill something."

And Lorwyn came here, to us.

My gut clenches. I've been neglecting my friends, and I don't deserve their trust. That has to change.

No: *I* have to change it.

"All right, that's enough," I say. "Yorani, would you be so good as to herd Lorwyn out of the kitchen?"

"How dare you," Lorwyn says. "I have dragon-sat this scaly baby for you, and you think you can sic her on me—ack!"

To my surprise and endless amusement, Yorani does in fact fly at Lorwyn's face—and starts whapping her with her tail.

Lorwyn dodges to no avail, then tries to catch Yorani who, now that she thinks this is a game, is decidedly slippery. When Lorwyn sends sparks of witchcraft in her direction Yorani slurps them up like they're candy and chirps happily.

"All right, all right, I'm going," Lorwyn grumbles with poor grace. "See if I come over again with this kind of welcome."

"Yes, I am a terrible friend who is going to force you to drink an actually palatable cup of tea," I say, darting into the kitchen and disposing of her dreadful experiments without looking any closer than I have to, because some concoctions are too abominable to bear consideration. "Somehow you will have to cope."

"I should have left you out in the rain," Lorwyn says.

"Are you going to tell us what's going on?" Risteri asks.

"No."

"Risteri." I shake my head.

"What?" she demands.

"I don't know why you think a head-on question is going to get her to talk," I say, "especially when obviously something has happened with Entero."

"You," Lorwyn growls, "are spiteful in your omniscience."

"Okay, even I knew Entero was probably involved," Risteri says. "Not a whole lot that would cause you to turn up at my door if you weren't literally running for your life."

Lorwyn glares. "Why am I here again?"

"Because you don't want to be alone with your thoughts, even if you don't want to talk about them," I say.

Lorwyn sighs, rubbing her temples. "That was rhetorical, Miyara. Spirits, you two might actually be worse than my sisters about this."

"Why, because we actually know enough to know how to needle you?" Risteri asks.

"Perhaps because we know enough that she feels like she might actually be able to talk instead of hiding, which she'd much rather do," I supply helpfully.

"I hate you both," Lorwyn growls.

"Pet Yorani," I say serenely. "It's very soothing."

"I'm going to *tackle* Yorani if she doesn't stop buzzing around my head."

"Here." The kettle has reached the right temperature, and with that prepared, I arrange my portable tea tray with the dragon teapot. I could probably afford a nicer set now, but this one feels uniquely mine—it's the setup I was able to make for myself when I could make very little, and I will always value it for that. Odd that I don't have the same reaction to my own apartment, but then I have always felt uncomfortable with gifts I can't repay.

I kneel opposite where Lorwyn is sitting.

She starts, "Miyara—"

"Just sit," I say, "and let me do this."

"Yorani will interrupt," Lorwyn says, then pauses to actually look at Yorani.

As soon as I knelt with the tea tray, Yorani settled down to perch on a nearby chair.

"Or not," Lorwyn says. "Is she always like this?"

"With tea ceremony? Yes," I say. "She never interrupts."

"You should perform tea ceremony constantly."

If only. "Tea is soothing. Now hush before the water temperature is wrong."

"If you—" Lorwyn breaks off when I look at her. "Fine."

That's all I need. Lorwyn may not fully understand what tea ceremony entails beyond the brewing and replication of physical movements, but she knows enough to be able to consent to my ministrations. I begin.

Lorwyn is in some ways easy to understand right now. I know what it is to be confused, and overwhelmed, busy and industrious and yet somehow still drowning. I know what it is to feel alone, to not know who to turn to or how to say what desperately needs to be said, to face what has been unthinkable.

But I do not know what it is to be a witch in our world. I do not know what it is to be a refugee. I have been poor, and I have been friendless, but never with opportunities barred to me like they are for her, never threatened for how I was born the way she is. I can empathize with her fear, and I can understand it intellectually, but I cannot feel what it is to live with it every day.

But although our fears and responsibilities are different, we both feel them strongly, and that is what I weave into the ceremony. There is duty and bravery, there are dreams and risks. But here, now, there is a person who will see them, and hear them, and not belittle their weight. I may nudge her toward happiness, but I will back off also, and no matter what I will stand by her choices and her ability to make them.

Lorwyn sought me and Risteri out; she needs to know she has friends she can rely on. She needs steadiness, and consistent support, and my movements take on deliberate weight and solid cadence, but they're also open, round and welcoming. With this ceremony I say, no matter the whirlwind of our lives, I will be here when you need me.

As I pour the tea, once again a steamy figure forms out of the spout, and as Lorwyn's eyes widen it dissipates into the air.

She drinks, and closes her eyes, and is silent.

I feel Risteri watching, waiting, and motion her to stillness.

Finally, Lorwyn opens her eyes. "Is tea ceremony always like that?"

I shake my head. "Not exactly. If I'm doing my work well, it should be different every time. This was the ceremony for who you are in this moment. Next time you will need a different one. Probably without an audience, but Risteri needed to be part of this one, too."

Lorwyn eyes me suspiciously. "Is this a spirit thing? Because that doesn't actually mean anything to me."

I don't think so; I think it's a human thing. But I say, "Something like that."

"You've gotten a lot better since the last time I saw you," Risteri says. "I'm not sure I could tell you how, because your movements were always clear, but even not being the recipient this *felt* different."

"Also," Lorwyn says, "you're creating spirits."

My heart thumps. "You're certain?"

She shrugs. "Witch's intuition. Something about the ceremony focuses the magic into a consistent form."

"So far all the spirits have been different," I say.

"And they only appear when you perform tea ceremony for other people using this pot?"

"Yes."

"That's..." She sighs. "All right, it's fascinating, and I'd love to be able to devote time to figuring it out, but I literally don't have it right now."

"How can we help?" I ask.

"What makes you think you can?" Lorwyn shoots back, automatically.

"Because you're here," I point out. "Also, between us we have managed to figure out some impossible things, so we may be able to come up with something together even if you haven't yet on your own. Would you like to come over here to work in peace without your sisters' distraction?" I glance at Risteri, and she nods, approving this offer, though it is after a slight hesitation.

Hmm. She must be worried about Lorwyn, then, but not actually enthusiastic about this prospect—which makes me wonder how things with Sa Nikuran are progressing.

"Entero decided to stay," Lorwyn says abruptly.

Oh thank the spirits.

"Was he going to leave?" Risteri demands. "Already?"

Lorwyn nods. "Yeah. Less than a week back and he was already planning how to go. But he changed his mind."

"Okay," Risteri says. "Why?"

"He decided there are other avenues of investigation in Sayorsen he hasn't exhausted that might bear out what he needs, and he should do more preparation before a deep undercover job anyway," Lorwyn says.

"So he's staying for you, is what I'm hearing," Risteri says, and I cover a smile.

Lorwyn nods. "I think so."

"That seems like good news, but you're not smiling," Risteri says. "I'm guessing because he was going to leave at all?"

"He's very used to running off wherever his work required without consideration of anyone else," I say softly. "I imagine that habit of inclination will take time to consciously break."

"Yeah," Lorwyn says, "but then what? I mean, *should* he break it?"

"Yes," Risteri and I say together.

Lorwyn shakes her head rapidly. "Obviously never repeat this, but he's so spirits-cursed good at what he does. And he has to give it up because of me? I don't want that. And he'll... what if he resents me for it?"

In that I hear, *I am sure he will come to resent me, because everyone does.*

"He's going to find new ways of using his skills, and he'll learn new skills," I say. "He's shockingly talented. But although he may miss some of that work, I think some he will not be sad to abandon."

"That doesn't change the fact that he's changing for me," Lorwyn says.

"And you're worth changing for," I say, "and so is he. But please also don't take too much of the blame here. Even if he wanted to go back, now that he's revealed himself publicly, he can't. That's *my* fault if it's anyone's."

"Great, so then he's changing because he has to, not because he wants to."

"That's not always bad," Risteri points out.

"And I think this case qualifies," I agree. "Lorwyn, have you considered whether Entero was happy before he met you? He was *comfort-*

able, certainly, in that he knew what was expected of him and could meet those requirements with aplomb."

"Aplomb?" Lorwyn echoes. "No one uses that word, Miyara."

"But he wasn't happy," I continue as if she hadn't spoken, because I know she's trying to hide from this again—though I take her point and note it for future reference. "Meeting you has given him a glimpse of what happiness might look like, and he's terrified he'll reach for it and fumble and always know it was his fault. But I believe he is earnestly going to try."

"Oh, well, no pressure," Lorwyn mutters. "I should definitely be responsible for another person's happiness."

"You're not," Risteri says. "You're what makes happiness seem possible for him. Actually being happy is up to him, not you. But your happiness is also up to you."

Lorwyn sighs. "And of the two of us, I'm going to be much worse about it. You know I am."

"Yeah, can't argue that one," Risteri says.

"I concur," I say.

Lorwyn snorts. "Thanks, friends."

"You're welcome," I say seriously.

Lorwyn rolls her eyes. "Have I told you lately you're a ridiculous person?"

"Possibly I am overdue for a reminder," I say. "But I am encouraged that you just termed us both friends of your own free will. To me, it seems perhaps your life may be changing toward happiness despite everything."

"By everything you mean me."

"I mean the world, and what it has taught you," I say. Looking at Risteri I ask, "Or was she born with a scowl?"

"Nah, her scowling definitely improved while we were children," Risteri says.

"Yes, and who do you think gave me the most cause?" Lorwyn asks.

Risteri grins. "I'm not sorry. Not even about that one time—"

"Don't."

"I am sorry about the other, though," Risteri amends.

Lorwyn rolls her eyes again.

"Can we make Lorwyn a copy of our keys?" I ask Risteri, which causes both of them to focus on me.

"Well well," Lorwyn says. "Look who else is having developments with a boy."

Oh. They know me well enough that they recognize the sorts of things I probably shouldn't know about, given my upbringing.

"Deniel is making a copy of his house key for me," I admit, flushing but pleased and also somehow nervous about sharing this with them.

"Are you moving in with him?" Risteri asks, and I can't quite place the emotional note in her voice—some mix of stress and hope.

"No," I say. "We've just been having such a hard time seeing each other lately. The only reason I managed to catch him is because Talsu had left the door open, and I let myself in to wait until he got home."

Lorwyn whistles. "Look at you, being forward."

Risteri grins. "I love it. So things are progressing with you two?"

I open my mouth to answer affirmatively but pause. "How do you mean?"

"She means sex," Lorwyn says bluntly.

"She's not wrong," Risteri says with more blandness.

Aha. I ponder what to tell them.

"Miyara?" Lorwyn asks, a note of concern in her voice.

"We have not had sex," I say. "I'm just not sure how to explain?"

"Do you want to have sex and he's not interested?" Risteri prompts as Lorwyn snorts, at what I'm not sure. "Or do you not want to have sex?"

"I am interested in having sex in the future but not right now," I say. "We... came close, the other night. But although I feel surer of Deniel than I have almost anything in my life, I am not sure I feel ready for that step at this time. Does that make sense? Is it odd?"

"Eh, what's normal?" Lorwyn asks.

"You know what I mean," I say. "And Saiyana implied—she said she could tell we weren't having sex by looking at us. Is that truly a thing?"

"I mean, is she also preternaturally good at reading people?" Lorwyn asks. "You two are related."

"She's good," I say, "but I wouldn't say she's better than me. But possibly I simply have a blind spot in this regard due to... being rather less worldly."

"Maybe it's the opposite," Risteri says slowly. "I think there are some subtle shifts in body language when two people are very close and comfortable with each other. Often it implies intimacy. But you and Deniel are already like that—you both just blush all the time, which is extremely adorable but also may have given your sister the impression that you're not comfortable with each other, and she couldn't discern the distinction."

"Or your sister was just bluffing to get a reaction out of you, because she's made it her mission to be awful," Lorwyn says.

"Oh, she was definitely trying to get a reaction from me, and she got it," I say, not disputing her assessment of Saiyana, all things considered. "Not that it did her any good. She just rarely does only one thing at a time, and I wasn't sure if she was fishing for information or something else."

"What do you mean, 'not that it did her any good'?" Risteri asks.

I smile, and feeling it spread across my face I know it's a derivation of Lorwyn's shark smile. "Deniel put her in her place."

Risteri whoops in triumph, and Lorwyn raises her eyebrows, impressed.

"Quiet little Deniel, shutting down a princess," Lorwyn muses. "Speaking of people changing, I suppose."

Is it a change? I think this is something that was always part of Deniel, and I have helped him draw it to the surface.

"But speaking of Deniel," Risteri says, "is he in agreement with you on the sex subject? You said you almost did."

"I think so," I say. "We haven't talked about it explicitly since, I admit, but everything has seemed normal between us."

"You know, normally I would tell someone to definitely have that conversation," Lorwyn drawls, "but you two are fine. If something needs to be discussed, you'll discuss it."

"Take your own advice," Risteri says to her dryly.

"I am absolutely not talking to Entero about sex," Lorwyn says. "We have so many other things to work out, that doesn't even need to be on the table right now."

"But you want to," Risteri presses.

"Of course I want to, but I don't trust him, or me, right now. I'm not going there, Risteri."

I divert the conversation before Lorwyn's defensiveness causes her to be less open. "So wanting to have sex right away *is* normal?"

Lorwyn waves this away. "People are different. You strike me as a person who needs an emotional connection in order to feel attraction."

I blink. "That's *not* normal?"

"I mean, it's not super unusual, but a lot of people feel physical attraction first and go from there," Lorwyn says. "Other people don't want an emotional connection before sex at all. Like I said, people are different. Risteri, weren't you going to give Miyara romance novels?"

"Are *those* normal relationships?" I ask, slightly aghast, and Lorwyn erupts into cackling.

"Sa Nikuran and I had sex," Risteri says abruptly.

That stops Lorwyn and me both.

"Seriously?" Lorwyn demands. "You had sex with a dragon?"

"So what if I did?" Risteri shoots back, sitting up straight.

"So that's awesome," Lorwyn says.

"Oh," Risteri says.

I turn my focus to Risteri, feeling guilty all over again that I haven't been around for her to talk to as she's going through so many changes in her life. Perhaps it's not so momentous for her, but, studying her, I think it may be.

"Are you happy?" I ask her. "You seem—like you don't know."

"I mean, it was fantastic," Risteri says.

"Not what Miyara asked, but good to know," Lorwyn says, amused.

"I have no idea what I am," Risteri says. "Things are going really well, but there's still a lot I don't know about her, and what I even want. I didn't go into this thinking of anything serious, but there's obviously politics, and she's coming from a whole different culture, and now I'm thinking maybe I might want something serious?"

"Breathe," I say softly.

She does. "I just—I like Sa Nikuran a lot, and I like sex, but it's... a lot all at once, you know? My father, stuff with the House, now there are the Te Muraka and your tournament and an actual royal princess in town deciding all our futures—I mean not that you're not an actual princess, Miyara, but—"

"I know," I say. "And truly, I'm not a princess anymore."

Lorwyn snorts. "You say words like 'truly' and 'aplomb' in normal conversation."

"There is somewhat more to being a princess than that."

"Okay nobody panic, but I'm with Lorwyn on this one," Risteri says. "There's a... I don't know, a weight to your presence and your focus that is really not common. It may be a tea master thing, but you learned it as a princess."

As I blink, Lorwyn nods her agreement.

In this moment, being a princess—both in my past, and the part of it that is still in my present—does not feel like a cage, but a source of... strength, perhaps.

Or roots.

"You do also have a habit of changing all our futures," Risteri says.

Well that's a bit much. "A *habit*? It's not like I go around negotiating treaties for foreign cultures in the Cataclysm every day!"

"You arrived," Lorwyn says dryly. "Everything after that has just been a cascading effect."

I frown, which I don't think is what she intended, but I recall what Deniel noted at our dinner. "Have I been pushing you into things so consistently?"

"Only in good ways," Risteri says. "I mean, mostly."

"When I have an objection, believe me, you'll hear about it," Lorwyn says.

What if they can't tell, though? What if I am so subtle in my manipulation—

But they have both already turned away, unconcerned.

"For the record, if Sa Nikuran treats you badly, I will—hmm," Lorwyn is saying. "I suppose maybe I won't set her on fire, what with being a dragon. This seems like a good time to figure out how to make a sandstorm, because I bet that would be super aggravating in her scales."

"Thank you, I think, and your mind is a strange place," Risteri says.

I give them too little credit. They know what I'm capable of, who I am.

And they trust me. It is humbling.

They are also my roots, as much or more as being a princess, and it is as wrong for me to neglect them as my responsibilities as a tea master.

"Which brings us back to Lorwyn having space to learn," I say. "Lorwyn, is there anything you could do with your hypothetical copy of the key to alert you when would be an unfortunate time to open the door?"

"You're right, I am definitely figuring that out first," Lorwyn says. "I might need to spell both of your keys, too, so you can mark the door as open or closed for sex."

Risteri sighs. "This will teach me to tell you anything."

"Or maybe you should have told me everything already, and then I wouldn't have to resort to innuendo."

"Lorwyn, it's not innuendo when you're stating everything explicitly," I say.

Risteri, more eloquently, throws a pillow at Lorwyn's head.

Lorwyn lobs a ball of witchcraft back at her, and that in turn rouses Yorani's interest, and for a while everything devolves, or perhaps evolves, into a mystical pillow fight, as I learn they're called. And then there is more tea, and some baking, and many more words sharing where all of us are in our lives until, finally, sleep overtakes us.

CHAPTER 20

I WAKE UP IN a chair in our sitting room, Risteri on the floor and Lorwyn on the couch. All three of us, still together. I'm amused neither Risteri nor I managed to make it to our perfectly functional beds, but this feels correct, even if my back protests.

I'm also amused that I'm the first to wake—Risteri is still accustomed to her schedule of secret late-night expeditions and accordingly late mornings, and Lorwyn probably never gets so much quiet from her sisters. I won't disturb her.

I begin quietly padding to the kitchen to start the kettle, but Yorani has other ideas.

I leap to catch her midair as she zooms toward Lorwyn's face.

"No more attacking Lorwyn," I whisper, already experiencing regrets. "That was a one-time license only."

Yorani chirps at me, and I fear I may have created a monster.

Perhaps, for our togetherness last night, it was worth it.

Lorwyn may never be able to dragon-sit again, though.

˜

At Talmeri's, Lorwyn's intuition for developing blends is shockingly apt, even for her, while I run mischievous tea spirit interference. Since Lorwyn likes to maintain an air of mystery, I decide not to mention that sufficient sleep clearly has salutary effects for her. It's possible she knows, anyway, and has developed her attitude of disregard for her wellbeing out of necessity.

(Yorani nose-dives from a high shelf above Lorwyn's head, but I am ready with a net and swipe her out of the air.)

It's also possible that after struggling through—but ultimately finding small successes at—Lorwyn's mage homework that morning at Risteri's and my apartment that returning to a more comfortable task is such a relief she can make great leaps.

(The net buys me several minutes of Yorani amusing herself by untangling herself from the net.)

Or perhaps stretching her mental faculties is good for her, though I will *definitely* not mention that.

(Then she destroys it with her claws and sets the remaining threads on fire.)

Besides, I am too delighted, between tea spirit interceptions, by watching Elowyn and Tamak interact. Our two quietest compatriots are drawing each other out of their shells, to everyone's surprise: Tamak listens to Elowyn seriously and attentively, intuitively appreciating the value of her judgment; Elowyn, meanwhile, is producing a shocking amount of sass, which Lorwyn confirms no one in the Gaellani community ever hears from her. It apparently delights Tamak, too, and whenever Elowyn smiles at him he freezes, just for an instant.

(Yorani isn't bothering Elowyn or Tamak in the slightest. She does, however, hide behind them to launch herself at a shelf of Lorwyn's tea paraphernalia with a glint in her eye toward clearing it all onto the floor. I step in between just in time to bundle her off toward a pile of sticks instead.)

Fortunately Lorwyn hasn't appeared to notice Tamak's reaction to Elowyn's smiles, or all my time would go into containing her teasing. But it reminds me so much of my reaction to Deniel I can't help but smile, too.

(I will need a new bag of sticks soon. Yorani's preferred mode of interaction today is target practice for her fire breathing. Fortunately, Lorwyn's laboratory of all places is well-spelled against fire damage.)

I also feel more confident they will both join us as true apprentices after the tea tournament after all.

"How long—" I start to ask Lorwyn as I scan the back for non-stick entertainment; Yorani is, literally, burning through my supply.

"Any minute now," Lorwyn says shortly.

She's perhaps more aware of the time than I am. Ari, Sa Rangim, and Glynis are practicing in the front of the tea shop on their own—or rather, under Meristo's supervision. Entero will join them shortly, in theory.

(Yorani takes advantage of my distraction to scurry along the floor towards Lorwyn's ankles. I quickly yank a dirty apron from the to-wash bin and toss it, covering her with it long enough that I can scoop her up in a squirming bundle.)

Any minute now I should be meeting Entero and Saiyana to share information on the situation with the barrier. Something momentous has changed, I know, because Glynis wouldn't tell me anything. When she caught me studying her, all she'd said was, "You'll find out eventually, but there are different rules for working with the police. Especially if you're Gaellani."

(One-handed, I start a kettle heating: this degree of mischief calls for Yorani to spend some time in a soothing teapot bath.)

In the present I ask Lorwyn, "Do you think I should tell Saiyana about the tea spirits? That I'm apparently manufacturing random magic with the tea ceremony?"

"You think it has something to do with the barrier destabilizing?" Lorwyn asks, eyes narrowing thoughtfully. "Doesn't seem likely."

"We don't know enough to make it impossible they're related, though," I say.

From behind me, Tamak cuts in, "What makes you think they're random?"

I turn to him in surprise—that he spoke up, mainly, and to me, but also that he wants to weigh in on this. "The form of every spirit is different."

"So is your ceremony, though, isn't it?"

"That's true," I concede. "Still, the timing does correlate. I created the first not too long before the breach."

Lorwyn says, "Don't get ahead of yourself. According to Ari the barren patches in Taresan predate that by years."

Tamak speaks up again. "Spirits aren't the same as chaos, and they're the opposite of emptiness. I'm Te Muraka. I know the Cataclysm, and the spirit you made here before isn't of it."

I blink, nodding slowly. He's not just Te Muraka, he's a *young* Te Muraka, which means he has known the Cataclysm all his life. If he says the tea spirits are different, he would probably know those magical distinctions better than even Sa Rangim.

"That's how you think of the Cataclysm?" I ask. "Chaos energy?"

Tamak shrugs, no longer even looking at me.

Apparently he's already said everything he intended to on the subject.

"Maybe," Lorwyn says, "that's why none of us noticed until you brought it up, Miyara. Even when I watched it happen, it didn't feel disruptive, like the Cataclysm normally does—cascading layered disruptions in the magical order of the world. It felt..."

"Stabilizing," Elowyn supplies. "Focused."

All of our eyes turn to her.

"Yes," Lorwyn says, "but how do you know that, exactly?"

It's Elowyn's turn to shrug. "I may not sense magic, but that's the sense Miyara's presence gives those around her. Cascading stability. It's a reasonable leap."

It's not a reasonable leap; it's a potential tea master's intuition.

But I am flummoxed at being called a source of cascading stability. As I flounder for my own roots, perhaps my branches are working better than I thought—perhaps they are indeed reaching out and grounding others to me, and that is just as important of a direction for me to grow.

Then I say, "You should learn to knock," while I deposit Yorani in a tea bath. She splashes around a bit but doesn't jump out, at least not immediately, and I take a deep breath.

"What for?" Entero asks, appearing out of the shadows in the warehouse. "Everyone in this room could tell I was here."

I review the people currently in the room: Lorwyn, who is probably attuned to Entero's presence anyway but also controls the spells around Talmeri's; Elowyn, who is also preternaturally aware of the movement of shadows wherever she goes; Tamak, whose Te Muraka abilities I don't understand; Yorani, who has never been surprised by someone's appearance in her life; and me.

He has a point.

"How are things going?" I ask instead. "Have you been able to find out more here?" *Without leaving for Taresan.*

"Some," Entero says grimly. "You need to hear—"

I cut him off. "Let's wait on Saiyana for that."

Entero lifts his eyebrows in mute query.

"She actually scheduled a time to meet without trying to make things difficult for me," I explain. "I'd like to encourage that behavior."

"Also," Lorwyn puts in, "Miyara's desperately curious how Saiyana and Deniel got on today and wants to maximize the chance of her sister telling her anything."

I cut a glance her way, and she grins, shark-like, unrepentant.

"I see," Entero says, sounding vaguely amused. "But then I'm not sure how you meant me to answer that question."

"I'm asking about your experience, not the substance of your investigation," I clarify.

"Ah." He ponders that for a moment. "New. Complicated. Operating in the open—in a way that can be observed and documented on purpose—is different. There's a great deal more talking with people than I'm accustomed to."

Lorwyn makes a sound that might be a snort.

"With your... former contacts, or with local investigators?" I ask.

"Both," Entero says. "Also neither. The resources overlap in some cases and are entirely distinct in others. I'm not efficient at this yet."

"Welcome to operating at a normal human speed for once in your life," Lorwyn says.

He gives her a look.

"Yes, I know time is of the essence," she says. "If you think that means I'm not going to take the opportunity to tease you when I can, you've misjudged me."

Entero rolls his eyes, but his lips twitch.

"And," I say, "you're arguably operating as yourself, rather than as a cover."

"Oh, it's still a cover," he says. "But yes, it's the first cover I've ever intended to keep actively operational long-term."

As opposed to an identity he would pull out as needed for certain jobs and let slide into obscurity for periods of time. "Which makes it effectively the truth," I point out. "Since you will be living it every day in the open."

Entero winces. "Which makes it bound to change me in truth, too, I know. I wish I had time to be more careful with how I established it."

"Fortunately you're new in town and starting a new job," I say. "People are bound to accept changes in your behavior as a natural consequence of settling in. Don't you think?"

"Within limits," Entero says, glancing again at Lorwyn, who raises her eyebrows back in challenge. "We'll find out."

Oh dear. That was unintentional and careless.

"Incoming," Lorwyn murmurs, and the back door opens to reveal Saiyana.

When did Lorwyn make *that* adjustment to her shields? Clever to have managed to detect my sister the mage; cleverer still to not have revealed to her that she can.

"Starting without me?" Saiyana asks without preamble.

"No, in fact," I say. "We haven't spoken about any particulars of the investigation."

Her eyebrows narrow. "No, you've just mentioned in front of three other civilians that there is substantive material in an active investigation the three of us should be discussing."

I regard her calmly. "If you mean Lorwyn, surely you realize it's a little late for that. She's apprenticed to Ostario in any case. As for Elowyn and Tamak—well, it's a little late for that, as well. They've been present for enough related conversations that it's hardly a secret to them that there is an investigation, that Entero is working with the police, or that you and I have a relationship. We haven't discussed anything more substantive in front of them."

"See that you don't," Saiyana says, which I take as acknowledgement of my points without going quite as far as being willing to apologize for her initial accusation.

That's almost like civility between us. I decide to leave it alone.

"Well?" Saiyana prods. "Are they going to give us the room so we don't disclose state secrets to people without clearance, or did you have somewhere else in mind for us to go?"

There is not a single chance in the world I am asking Lorwyn to leave her own lab.

"We could use the tea ceremony room, except anyone in the front who sees you is going to have a lot of questions."

Saiyana rolls her eyes. "I can make a look-elsewhere spell easily and so can you. Where's your stash of spell scratchwork structures?"

Most mages have a cache of accumulated sticks, rocks, and so on to mock up experimental spells on the fly. It had never even occurred to me to accumulate one after leaving the palace—the only reason I'd kept one there was to be prepared whenever Saiyana asked that question.

"Lorwyn, do you have any materials we can use?" I ask. "I think Yorani's burned the majority of sticks I would normally have offered."

"You need to keep your tea spirit out of your stash," Saiyana tells me.

I do give her a look then. "Don't tell me how to care for my tea spirit, particularly as you have no experience with it. And for the record, I keep the sticks specifically for her amusement, not for spells. I invited her to burn them on purpose."

That silences her long enough for Lorwyn to pass over a basket of various items Saiyana can use. "Here. It's not organized."

"That's fine," Saiyana says. I cover a smile: for all Saiyana's love of efficiency, what she really enjoys is *creating* that order out of chaos, so a mixed bag of ingredients will be soothing to her. But to my surprise she also adds, "Thank you."

Lorwyn watches her suspiciously for a moment before saying, "No problem."

While Saiyana sets up the spell, I turn to Tamak and Elowyn. "Could you two keep an eye on Yorani while I'm gone, please? Today she's—"

"We've noticed," Tamak says.

"We'll take care of her," Elowyn says, and as she winks I realize she means protecting *Lorwyn*. I stifle a snicker.

In short order Saiyana has cast the spell, and the three of us head up to the tea ceremony room. She clearly wanted to make me spell my own but restrained the impulse: she is trying to keep the peace between us too, in her own way.

I wish that made me less nervous.

Not even Ari, for all his prodigious skill as a mage, notes our passage. Sa Rangim's ears flick in our direction, which is not a thing I knew they could do, but he doesn't otherwise react.

So, Saiyana's dashed-off spell likely isn't enough to fool his Te Muraka magic, advanced as it is. I wonder if even a well-crafted spell could. And is that a feature of the Te Muraka's magic itself, or Sa Rangim's proficiency?

Too many variables; questions for another time.

In the tea ceremony room, Entero leans against the opposite wall, and Saiyana gestures toward the small table at the center.

"Well?" she asks. "Are you going to perform the tea ceremony for me this time?"

I smile and shake my head. "No. That's not what you need right now. But I will serve tea if you like."

"No, don't bother," Saiyana says, slightly irritated. Had she thought she was demonstrating being in a receptive frame of mind so I would perform the ceremony? Perhaps that's what she intended to communicate, but it is not the truth.

"I gather there have been some developments," I say, sitting across from her.

"Gathered how?" Saiyana asks.

I regard her calmly. "I listen."

She scowls.

"We've confirmed the barrier is destabilizing, but it's local," Entero begins.

"Inaccurate," Saiyana snaps. "And also not your place to tell."

That escalated quickly. I narrow my eyes, wondering what's set her off beyond the issue itself.

Entero deliberately cocks his head to one side. "Then by all means, feel free to talk about the matter at hand. I'll fill in as needed."

"You'll do as I say," Saiyana growls.

"I will not," Entero says. "I don't work for you. You're planning on keeping information from Miyara. I'm doing you the courtesy of making you aware I will tell her what you don't. She's an asset in this."

"What, you can't do your work without help?" Saiyana asks.

Calmly, Entero tells her, "Your grandmother sent me because she knew I'd work with Miyara. Now, can we work?"

Saiyana's expression is stormy, but she turns to me. "We've confirmed with other Istal towns along the border, as well as a few Taresal. The barren patches you observed are common in Taresan, but not here."

"But Sayorsen is where the barrier destabilization begins. Our working theory is the weakness is starting here and then being redistributed across the barrier as a whole."

I let out a breath. Bad news, and yet. "That's fortunate."

"That the weakness distributes, rather than simply punching a hole through?" Saiyana nods. "I agree—it'll make this easier to track down, and it also buys us time. Whoever designed the barrier was clever."

That startles me. "*Whoever?*"

She snorts. "A magical system that convenient doesn't just happen on accident."

I will never run out of questions about the world. It is a measure of how hopeful I've become about my ability to bring everything together that this is a wonder and not a worry.

"Tracking down the source will be especially easy," Entero says, "since Lino and the agents assigned to him have once again been spotted in the Cataclysm."

"Lots of assumptions and circumstantial evidence in your work," Saiyana tells him.

"The possibility of the barrier falling is too important not to act and you know it," Entero says. "I have enough evidence to bring him in for questioning and revoke his visa at the very least."

"Wait," Saiyana says.

"Only if you act," Entero says. "I've had copies of my findings sent to your people."

That's Glynis' involvement—though perhaps not all of it. Entero never said *who* saw Lino in the Cataclysm, and that can only be a deliberate omission.

"If you want this, I'll give you until tomorrow to make your play," Entero says. "After that, I'm taking it out of your hands."

I expect Saiyana to object to his threat, but she nods, one professional to another. "I'll handle it."

"Tomorrow is the tea tournament match," I say.

Saiyana smiles. "Oh, I know. I hope you weren't planning to lose?"

"You're not going to tell me what you have planned?"

"Definitely not."

Entero says, "I'll join the practice in the front then, if your Highness would be good enough to remove the look-away spell?"

"You're an agent of the crown," Saiyana says. "You can remove it yourself."

Entero flashes his almost-smile before ducking out.

Immediately, Saiyana sighs. "I don't know where Grandmother found him. I'd steal him if I could."

She always has valued extreme competence. "You were exaggerating about the problems with his evidence, then?"

"Eh, a bit." Saiyana stretches. "Didn't want him thinking his current level would be acceptable long-term, but he knows that and he'll get there fast. It's enough for me to work with."

My heart pounds. She sounds so casual, talking about an international covert operation bent on unleashing the greatest magical chaos our world has ever known.

And that will be that, all of a sudden.

Except I don't quite buy it—and she's not going to tell me what role she has planned for me in all of this.

"I had a fantastic day with Deniel," Saiyana adds.

She has to know how curious I am. "How'd it go?"

"I'm not telling," she says. Before I've done more than roll my eyes, she adds, "Unless you want to share what you told Ostario after I left last night."

I lift my eyebrows. "Beyond what I implied over dinner? Not much. Why, has he acted any differently today?"

"No," Saiyana says, studying me.

I smile suddenly. "You know, I think we will both have to live with our curiosity on this one."

"Miyara," she growls.

"I trust Ostario," I say simply.

Saiyana swears at length, and I fight the urge to laugh outright.

She's the one who's always had the most faith in my instincts, after all.

But she's not going to tell me any more about her plans without Entero here, and so, heart pounding, I ask about something else that shouldn't be harder and yet is.

"Did Ostario give you the dessert?"

Saiyana looks at me. Just, looks, for a long moment.

"He did," Saiyana says. "I ate a handful."

A *handful*?

"That's... *like* a compliment," I say lightly.

Because she hasn't said anything else, and I don't trust it.

"I want you to think about something," Saiyana says, "and I mean this seriously."

This is it: somehow I've brought her around to whyever she's been making an effort today not to make me angry. She wants me to hear her.

"I'm listening," I say, my whole body tensing.

"Can you really be a tea master and be this involved, this biased toward and settled in one community?" Saiyana asks. "You can't help poking your nose into problems that are none of your business. Those are princess instincts, Miyara. I think you've always had them, and I never really appreciated how strong they were. I want you to consider if maybe the objectivity of a tea master isn't truly your calling. Don't say anything now, just—think about it, okay?"

My sister leaves me sitting there, stunned.

Because with one sentence, my careful hope that I might finally be making everything work crumbles into dust.

She's right.

CHAPTER 21

IT IS SOMETHING OF a relief when the day of the second official match of the tea tournament finals dawns. In the whole consideration of the universe I may not know what my place is, but here is one day I can focus on that is perhaps not easy, but simple in the most abstract sense.

Today, all that matters is that I win.

Hanuva and Lino are up first, and I exchange a triumphant glance with Ari when I'm proved correct: they have opted for a sophisticated tea shop in a gentrified—by force of Risteri's father, most likely—part of Sayorsen.

Hanuva and Lino have blended their styles into modern, clean lines: simple, bare, and pristine, highlighting Lino's technology as well as the tea itself, its colors and flavors. Hanuva's touch at creating atmosphere as well as her skills as a hostess are well in evidence while Lino handles the brewing with enviable speed. Hanuva's girls are dressed all in white as they tend the guests quietly and efficiently, moving around like part of the scenery in a way that makes me tense.

It is a kind of movement I am well familiar with from my past at the palace in Miteran, and I dislike it being held up as aspirational.

Lino's watchers, the agents of Velasar, are nowhere to be seen. I have to hope Saiyana's defenses will pick them up if they seize this opportunity to try anything in the Cataclysm, because I will have my work cut out for me here.

Another flicker of irritation, with this tournament, for occupying me when our whole world is threatened, and then another with myself, for being irritated with a place I chose over concerning myself with royal affairs.

I know Hanuva will have arranged to have the first slot in the tea tournament out of confidence in her entry for this match and a hope of intimidating me and Ari.

"You really think the judges will choose us over that?" Ari asks me.

"It's exactly the performance we expected of them," I say. "If I predicted it, as new as I am to this tournament, it's likely the judges did, too."

"That doesn't mean it's not exactly what they were hoping for," they point out.

"True," I say. "But while it's well executed, it's not exciting. We have the benefit of a novel approach on our side. It will count."

"It will have to," Ari says. "Are you ready?"

I bow to them. It's the last quiet moment we're going to have alone together for the next few hours. "Always."

I smile at Ari and nod slightly. After a moment, they clap their hands sharply and nod back.

"Then let's go," Ari says.

As Ari's magic unfurls, we step forward.

To spectators, our pop-up tea shop will have just appeared as if clouds parted to reveal it: a glimpse into the magic of a Gaellani market. And when we're done it will fade back into obscurity, as if it was never here.

Like the people who've become an integral part of Sayorsen, the poor and the different: visible only when Istal spectators are interested, and invisible like they're not worth attention the rest.

It is as deliberate of a refutation to Hanuva and Lino's aspirational gentrification as I can manage.

But equally important, it's not only 'I', but 'we'.

It is the shop itself, designed like a Gaellani market stall but with our tea brewing station at the center of a circle, serving people from all around, literally and figuratively. The borrowed tables and chairs are mismatched but all share the same cloth covers Glynis' family made for us on commission to showcase Gaellani artisanship.

It is Entero, Istal and now a civil authority, working with Glynis, a disabled Gaellani messenger, and Sa Rangim, the leader of the Te Muraka refugees, all as equals. Three people of different ages, stages of life, abilities, and authorities, all demonstrating they can do work, and together, and safely.

They are dressed as individuals, with matching sunny yellow aprons: a welcoming color, and easy to spot. They take orders and serve the tea, making conversation and building relationships so that the customers, too, feel they have been seen.

It is Ari, a poor child from another world, deliberately allowing themself to be seen and known to people who have rejected them before. Sa Rangim tracks the flow of the room and identifies the correct time for Ari to visit; with a signal to Glynis, she can move quickly enough to bring Ari from their tea brewing to meet customers and share their knowledge; meanwhile Entero, more experienced with tea service, takes on a greater bulk of customers. Ari not only uses their magecraft, they overtly displays their knowledge of tea—and they work with a team and connect with strangers. All things the judges have yet to see from them.

It is Lorwyn, a witch, brewing tirelessly in full view of an audience that weeks ago would have called for her arrest, cool and collected and flawlessly using her witchcraft to clean every used cup and pot that comes back to the center without breaking a single one. She effortlessly picks up Ari's brewing tea whenever Glynis pulls them away, too.

But it is also me, because I am a tea master.

My role is to be aware of all the people in the shop, all the time; to filter through them, alongside the tea servers, and back to the tea brewing. Lorwyn and Ari developed blends in advance of this match that I helped refine with tasting, and apart from that menu from which the customers order, we have a selection of other ingredients.

Every pot of tea we serve today will be unique, targeted specifically for each customer or group. I am taking them in with nothing more than a glance, making snap decisions, and slipping into the flow of our service so everyone who needs to knows what I have chosen.

This is what I'm capable of.

It is not just my knowledge of tea on display; it is what separates a tea master from an adept brewer like Hanuva or Lino. It is a preternatural sensitivity and the ability to deploy it on command in the service of tea and all tea means.

Our shop is people coming together: it is community and the experience of being seen.

It is harrowing; this is not an effort any of us could sustain at this level of exertion over a long period. But we can last long enough.

We survive, because we have to.

As we near the end of our allotted time, I become aware of Hanuva and Lino at the periphery, observing like Ari and I had them earlier. Lino's expression is disdainful; he doesn't understand what we've done.

But in my focused state, I can see that Hanuva does. I have been more ambitious than she dreamed for herself, and she knows it. When our eyes meet, she turns and leaves, unwilling to face what that acknowledgement means.

All six of us collapse at the end of our allotted time. I am beyond relieved Sa Rangim convinced me we would be too tired to break down our shop set. The Te Muraka take over the invisibility as Ari's spell runs its course, and with volunteers from the Gaellani courtyard help Meristo break everything down quickly.

(We learned Meristo is in fact old enough to participate in the tournament, unlike Taseino and Iskielo. But not without parental permission, which was not forthcoming unless Meristo could be involved in a way that would not publicly associate him: they are politically savvy enough to understand the undercurrents of this competition and not want Meristo involved in case it all goes badly wrong. I cannot blame them.)

What I did not anticipate was how ravenous I would feel. In fact I don't feel it until Deniel appears in front of me with a cloth-wrapped box. As he unwraps it and the scent of his cooking wafts toward me, my stomach surges into growls.

"You are a perfect human," I tell him fervently.

He laughs, and I resolve to tell him again later when he might believe I mean it.

But as soon as we've inhaled food—the community has outdone itself again, providing unasked-for meals for all of us after they did us such favors with the match—we have to make our way to the hall for judgment.

I look at Ari before we enter, intending to tell them to stand up straight, to not show how tired they are.

But there's no need: this is a lesson they've internalized at some point. It's not the angry pride of before, but an easy confidence that makes me relax in turn.

Even if Saiyana is right, if I'm not meant to be a tea master here, I've helped at least this one person be more at ease with themself.

◎

Hanuva and Lino are already on the platform, waiting together across from the panel of judges, and Ari and I join them.

To my surprise, given our order, a judge says, "Miyara and Ari, let's start with you."

Perhaps I should have expected this: they will attempt to take advantage of our fatigue to catch us in a lapse of judgment.

I breathe steadily.

I must ensure they fail.

"You clearly guessed which way Hanuva and Lino would jump, and I think it's safe to say your shop was a reaction to theirs," the judge begins.

"With respect, I do not consider that unarguable," I say. "Everyone's actions are informed by the worlds we inhabit, our choices shaped by our surroundings. If our creation was a reaction, it is in the same way that all art is in conversation with the world it exists in."

"That's a valid point, but do you deny it was also intended as a deliberate juxtaposition against what you predicted from your colleagues?"

I nod in acquiescence.

"Where I was going with this," the judge continues, "is that, as you said, this is a fantastic example of the creativity and targeted purpose borne out of this competition. Without your colleagues' shop first, it would have been impactful on its own, but with the one following the other that's a message with a lot of bite. Tell us about how you formed the shop—the concept, your team, all of it."

Mindful that in this space we are a team, I glance at Ari to rhetorically ask, *May I?* They nod and gesture for me to go ahead.

So I do: I talk about our limited resources and our ties to the community; I talk about how this was an act of coming together and highlighting underappreciated skills and undervalued people; I talk about learning not just to keep, but to center individuality and difference while working as a cohesive whole.

After acknowledging our success at this endeavor, the judge says, "Forgive me, but this venture is pretty clearly your brain child, Miyara, in a contest that's supposed to be a team match. Can you talk to me about what Ari brought to the table?"

Ari tenses, and I lift my eyebrows deliberately, with a silent reminder to myself to use Ari's public pronoun for this gauntlet. "Ari's magic not only made the metaphor of our shop possible, he also demonstrated his vast expertise with tea throughout the contest."

"Yes, and Ari, we were delighted to see you take our critique to heart and take a more active, customer-centric role today, without sacrificing the magical element that's made you such an exciting candidate. We saw skills from you today we've been hoping to glimpse throughout this entire competition."

As the audience applauds, the judge turns back to me. "But my question, Miyara, is what did Ari bring to your *partnership*? The concept was clearly yours: what was Ari's?"

It is at this moment that, conversely, as Ari's tension is almost palpable, I realize the judge is, for once, on our side.

The judge knows I am better with people and playing for an audience, and so she directs the question to me: she's intentionally giving us the best opportunity to present ourselves well.

Something has changed.

"You noticed Ari talking to customers about the tea," I say. "While I leant my palette when it came to refining blends, much of my preparation was devoted to logistics. With access to the Lorwyn's—our witch brewmaster at Talmeri's—experience working with Cataclysm ingredients, Ari took the lead in producing the tea blends we served to all our customers today. It was his knowledge of tea, his innovation in experimentation, and his application of magecraft twists. After your comments in the last match, we wanted not only to expand your understanding of what Ari's capable of, but to center his ability with tea specifically. Ari, would you like to talk about how you approached the tea for this?"

With an inscrutable glance at me that tells me they fully expected me to seize this moment to lift myself up at their expense, Ari takes the opportunity I've handed them.

Maybe Ari is more comfortable with themself already, but some wounds take longer to heal.

I'm not interested in my star rising at the expense of theirs: I want to lift everyone or no one. And the latter is unacceptable.

And Ari has grown, because although it's not their focus, they do follow the example I set and references the help they received working with Lorwyn.

After discussing the qualities of the tea itself for some time, the judge turns back to me.

"We've talked about your concept already, but I don't want you to think, as we discuss the new skills we witnessed from Ari today, that we missed yours," the judge says. "In the first match of the finals you proved you could think strategically, but today what blew us all away was your awareness. I'm not sure everyone in the audience appreciates how hard it is to do what you did today, not just to keep track of everything happening around you, but to notice every person specifically. You gave every single customer of yours a unique tea crafted specifically for them without them often noticing what you'd done until Ari explained it. That was an incredible display, and every one of us on this bench is humbled to have witnessed it. If anyone here doubted you were a true tea master, you've blown any of their concerns away."

I doubt, I think, but only bow.

It's nice that someone is convinced.

"Now let's move on to Lino and Hanuva," the judge says, her tone shifting. "To recap, your shop was exactly what we've come to expect from you both: smooth, efficient, and competent. It perfectly showcased each of your abilities. And frankly, in comparison with what we saw from Miyara and Ari, it made it impossible to ignore that such a pristine façade is always covering something. Let's talk about that."

My heart thumps. Lino's scowl may practically be his usual expression, but Hanuva, I can tell, did not see this coming, and knows something is afoot.

"It is with profound disappointment and outrage that I must announce it has come to the attention of the tournament board that contestant Lino has been using our tournament to engage in espionage and seditious activity," the judge says grimly.

The audience, predictably, erupts.

"How dare you," Lino yells amid the din. "*Sedition*? This accusation is an outrage."

"At the conclusion of our judgment, you may take up your disagreement with Istal authorities," the judge informs him. "The tournament, however, is convinced."

"Unfounded accusations should have no place in your judgment of a contest of tea," Lino snaps, ornery through it all.

It is difficult for me to understand how he can be more upset at the focus being moved away from the quality of his tea than he is at being known to be a criminal.

"It is the tea tournament's long-held and profound belief that a person's character is part of the experience of their tea," the judge replies coolly. "If you aren't prepared to be judged and awarded by our standards, you may feel free to retire from competition at any time."

That silences Lino quickly, and though he's clearly furious, his eyes dart around the room—looking for escape or his watchers, I'm not sure.

It has no doubt just dawned on him, as the judge intended, that his visa permitting him to be in Istalam at all is under the auspices of the tournament's authority: without that sponsorship, and with the Istal government now looking into his activities as criminal, he'll shortly find himself in an Istal prison with no options. He already knows Velasar is prepared to drop him without hesitation. His best option is to cooperate fully with the authorities and hope he can make a deal, which he is canny enough to realize.

Still, he glares at me as if this is my fault.

Perhaps, ultimately, it is. But I can't help but appreciate Saiyana's deviousness: she has neutralized Lino's threat without panicking the people of Sayorsen. And the tournament has the opportunity to come out of this without looking like they supported his candidacy all along, a publicity move I can only imagine they seized with alacrity.

I wonder what favor it cost them.

"Now, Hanuva, let's talk about you," the judge says.

"You don't mean to suggest I had anything to do with Lino's activities?" Hanuva protests, abandoning her teammate without even an instant of hesitation.

"Do you mean to suggest, in front of all these witnesses, that you had no knowledge of what Lino was up to?" the judge returns. "Think very carefully about what you want to say here, Hanuva."

"There's no need," she says smoothly. "My focus is and has always been on the experience of tea. The choices Lino made while we weren't actively working together were none of my affair, and I paid no attention to them."

"I submit that you knew what Lino was about and actively covered it up when you found out, believing he was your ticket to victory," the judge says. "I submit you've spent your career learning how not to ruffle any feathers, and you thought you could get away with no consequences if you pretended well enough the problem didn't exist. You may save your protests for an Istal court as well, Hanuva: the tournament is satisfied with the evidence that has been presented to us, and we are perhaps less impressed with your character than with Lino's."

And for the first time I see Hanuva is honestly shocked speechless.

It never occurred to her she might be punished for playing the game *too* safely—or for believing the safe choice in the judges' eyes was maintaining the status quo at the cost of defending criminal behavior.

The audience is afire with shouts of speculation and accusation, and it takes the tournament staff—working alongside police, so perhaps Saiyana warned Entero what she was about after all—some time to restore a semblance of order as the judges sit impassively, and all of us on the stage hold very still.

"In our judgment, both tea shops today were well executed," the judge finally says. "But one was clearly superior, even if the other had not been built on the foundations of such critical character flaws. The tea tournament contestants who will be moving onto the finals are Miyara and Ari."

The crowd erupts once more, and I find myself glad that the tournament first spent such time demonstrating its appreciation of what Ari and I accomplished today, because no one will be thinking about that now except in juxtaposition to our competitors.

It is a victory, and yet standing on the stage, it is as though chasms have opened up between every one of us, and no one is able to move, as if a single twitch will take us off the edge of the precarious cliff we stand on.

Eventually, police storm the stage and tournament officials hustle the judges as well as Ari and me away, leaving Lino's close-lipped anger and Hanuva's devastated shock in our wake.

CHAPTER 22

THE TOURNAMENT OFFICIAL SURVEYS Ari and me narrowly. We've once again been sequestered in the same room where we previously met with Hanuva and Lino as well.

Their absence now is striking. It's not that the atmosphere among us was in any way congenial before; animosity practically hung in the air. But it was not so grim.

I wonder if the others felt the dwindling of their compatriots so starkly earlier in the contest, but with a look at Ari I think not. It's not only that it is down to two of us, and the room is almost empty. It's that the tournament has become something else, and we are caught up in it.

Abruptly Ari asks, "What are we waiting for? I have preparations to make."

Do they, already?

This is something else about the tea tournament I don't know, clearly, another aspect I've had no chance to research in the days leading to now. But Ari clearly does, which once again puts me at a disadvantage. They've been learning from me, but I fear the reverse is not sufficiently true, which does not speak well of me.

"I imagine they are keeping us here until they have sufficient control of both the crowd and the narrative," I murmur.

"We are waiting," the official says, "because I've decided to."

I look at him.

He glares right back, haughty as can be.

I continue looking, waiting patiently, pointedly, until his composure cracks.

"I suppose you won't be surprised to hear I didn't want it to be you," the official says, glancing between us. "Either of you."

Ari has come a long way in the last few days, because rather than sitting quietly and tensely, they snort derisively. Even the official is startled, but only for a moment.

"I can't say that it is, no," I say. "From a show-running perspective, this must put you in a difficult position."

My understanding startles him too, but he once again recovers quickly. "To put it mildly. No one expected either of you to win, and we've been building up Hanuva and Lino for a while now. Not only does the tournament's judgment appear suspect, we come into the finals without a clear narrative, which only compounds the questions about the tea tournament itself. It is, to put a fine point on it, a publicity disaster."

Ari asks, "Are you going to tell us why this is our problem?"

They've grown more comfortable with themself, but still have a distance to go toward understanding politics. This is the perfect opportunity for Ari to step in as the official's preferred candidate, but they're not making it easy for him.

"Watch yourself," the offical warns.

"No need," Ari says coolly. "Miyara's outmaneuvered you twice in a row, and you haven't exactly been subtle about how much you detest having her thrust into this. I'm your best bet to keep her from winning and destroying the tournament's credibility entirely."

Or perhaps Ari understands better than I've credited. They meet my eyes, and for the first time at one of these meetings, it is clear they are my equal, not someone in need of help.

I am glad of it, even if it means I have trained an opponent to defeat me.

If they can, I deserve it.

"Do you need our help to recover from the poor publicity?" I ask the official. I can't think why else he hasn't gotten to the point already, as little as he likes being here with us.

"We are going to do several specials on each of you in the coming days to craft that narrative," the official says, which is a *yes* without actually admitting to it—and that bothers me.

All he has to lose is his self-righteousness, and I find I am not inclined to grant it to him.

"So, that's a yes," Ari says.

"I imagine that would also serve as a distraction from inquiries about Hanuva and Lino," I say. "A neat idea."

The official narrows his eyes at me. "Would?" he echoes.

"As Ari pointed out, you are in a poor bargaining position," I say. "You cannot afford to lose us at this juncture, yet you remain unwilling to exercise basic courtesy. Because I gather these specials are not standard practice, they are therefore outside of our contracts, and you are not obliged our cooperation. So perhaps you might explain what precisely the tournament has in mind for us—for these specials, and for the match itself—and Ari and I will decide if we can accommodate you."

Incredulity and fury war for supremacy in the official's expression.

"I am not Hanuva," I say quietly. "I will not make your life easier at the expense of the interests of myself or others. And you may be glad of that, because you can be assured I will not leave you in the position she has."

While the official attempts to master himself, Ari begins, "The final match is always an individual performance. They make a big production out of it to maximize the spectacle."

In other words, Ari's area of expertise.

And they've had months to plan out their act.

"It's more than that," the official says, throwing himself into a chair in defeat. "The format is borrowed from pageant competitions, where, say, a dancer will choreograph in such a way that the movement or the music tells the story of whatever they're advocating. You prepare the tea in a way that reflects a cause you're passionate about.

"Ideally, this should be something you've woven into your previous matches so there's a common narrative thread, but we don't know what drives either of you. It should be what attracted your sponsors, so they should be able to help shape the spectacle with expensive displays while also bringing the tournament the advertising money that keeps us operational. Neither of you have any notable sponsors to speak of. You see the problem?"

I do, and it gives me greater appreciation for what Saiyana managed with the tea tournament on short notice: she convinced them to make a public decision that directly impacts their finances.

I exchange a look with Ari, who shakes their head.

"What now?" the official asks.

Evidently I'm to be the spokesperson between us. I can't say I disagree with their logic.

"We are not going to do the specials," I say.

"What do you want," the official says flatly.

I can only assume Ari has whatever they need already, as they've been planning this for some time. So I say, "Nothing. More importantly, you're missing the key point, which is that you don't need anything from us, either."

"Oh, this should be good," the official says, leaning back in his chair. "Do go on."

"By your own making, you have a unique opportunity to capitalize on what audiences always crave: true mystery," I say. "Specials are not in my interest, because my performance will benefit from a surprise impact. But you can craft your narrative around focusing the audience on the mystery of what to expect."

"The tea tournament does not want any more surprises," the official says.

"Then you have work to do," I say, "because if you pay attention I think you'll find the threads of both Ari's and my stories are, in fact, already woven in. It is your prerogative to tease them out, if you wish to. Will you message us the particular requirements for timing, venue, and so on?"

The official stares at me, but I can already see his mind chewing on what I've said. "You're really going to do this."

"We are," I say, and without another word I rise to precede him out the door.

Ari follows me, and we walk side by side for a moment in silence.

Until they say, "You know this is my last chance, right?"

My chest tightens.

"I've risked everything on this," Ari says. "I left my home. I alienated everyone I knew for their protection. I did whatever I had to to get here, to this stage, so I could make people see once and for all.

"I know your tea mastery is at stake, and I know you want to help the dragon people. But they, and you, have time. The world doesn't. The damage has gone untended too long, and we're running out of time to fix it. Will you help? Will you put all of us ahead of the few?"

I close my eyes.

Unlike the official, Ari is asking. They are being honest, and open, and treating me like a person. This is a cause that truly matters.

Still.

I stop and face them.

"I will help," I say, "and that is a promise. But I will not throw the tournament."

Ari's gaze searches mine.

And then theirs closes.

"So be it," Ari says. "Then we are enemies again, because I can't afford to lose."

They stalk off without another word, and I watch them go.

"Excuse me, Tea Master Miyara?"

From the garden one of Hanuva's girls, the same one that approached me here before, lurks, wringing her hands.

"Can I help you?" I ask, surprised. "Are all of you well?"

She doesn't mistake my meaning. "Oh, we'll be fine," she says. "Legally, at least. We're being questioned in rounds, but... I don't think anyone really expects us to know anything important."

"And do you?" I ask.

She looks startled. "No, of course not."

I refrain from saying that in this case, there is no 'of course' about it. In her role as mentor, Hanuva could very easily have pressured any of them into helping her cover for Lino by staying quiet.

"Then I'm not sure what you need," I say gently.

"It's just—it's all gone so wrong," she says. "I came here for a chance to change my future, and now it's all in shambles. What Grace Hanuva did was wrong, and I don't want to be associated—no. I want to make it *right*. And I know the other girls do, too. Most of them, at least. That is—" She squares her shoulders. "I was wondering if I could help *you*, in the final match of the tournament."

I am probably not much older than this girl, but in this instant I feel unbearably ancient.

It has less to do with her innocence regarding the likely dynamics between some of the other girls and Hanuva and more with her willingness to jump to a different perceived authority figure rather than plot her own course.

"Thank you," I say gravely. "I appreciate the offer, and more than that I appreciate the intent behind it. But I cannot accept."

"Is it because this is an individual match? I can help in other ways," she says. "Not just the tea. I can put you in touch with any of Hanuva's sponsors. Or if you need any equipment—"

"If I understand the terms of this challenge correctly, the final match is, fundamentally, a test of conviction," I say. "Specifically, mine. So I must win or lose on my own merits, which means I must already have everything I need."

Her gaze searches mine. "I think I see why Grace Hanuva found you difficult. She is very... opportunity-oriented."

"So am I," I say wryly. "I'm just—perhaps not more selective, but my criteria are different. It sounds like you've learned a lot from her."

Her expression twists. "For all the good it will do me now."

Perhaps not quite so innocent; she understands enough to know what Hanuva's fall will mean for her future.

"You can be selective, too," I say. "And it looks to me like you may already have everything you need to recover from her betrayal without me, on *your* own merits."

She blinks at me, perhaps considering what she's already revealed to me in just these few minutes: her character, initiative, and resources.

Or perhaps it's never occurred to her she had merits of her own, that weren't a reflection of Hanuva's.

I bow to her and continue on my path, leaving her to forge her own.

Ari was wrong, before. There is an older wrong, one that I'm not willing to compromise on.

Before we came for the Te Muraka, before we came for the Gaellani, Istalam turned on witches.

It has become a basic, endemic fear and hatred that permeates through everything, from our unwillingness and inability to deal with magical catastrophes to casual, unquestioned acts of awfulness in everyday life and written into our laws.

And it is long past time we root it out and all learn to hold out our hands—in apology and welcome.

I will keep my promise to Ari, but not at the expense of this.

Not at the expense of another promise.

Even my grandmother, with all her power, couldn't protect witches, and a tea master is not supposed to be partisan. So perhaps I am neither a princess nor a tea master, but what I am is a question that can wait for another day.

This has fallen to me, and I will see it done.

※

Not that, of course, I am telling Lorwyn what I've been about this whole time. She will only worry, or possibly try to lock me inside Talmeri's on the logic that I will be hurting myself by advocating for her. This is not the part I need her help with, anyway.

She's watching me putter with tea blends, but so far I haven't created anything particularly inspired. I can't afford for my showcase to be any less, though, and while I expected that pressure to be motivating, thus far it does not seem useful.

"The final match is in three days?" Lorwyn demands. "That's not much time to plan a spectacle that can rival the magecraft you know Ari's bringing."

"I suspect the goal is to show the audience who we really are under pressure," I say. "To force us to demonstrate what we're already capable of, the growth we've undergone in the tournament."

"Or maybe they're feeling vindictive about your refusal to accommodate them and moved the match up."

"Possible," I say, "but I'll be glad to be done with this in any case."

I'm using the tea tournament for my own purposes, but I can't deny it's been a distraction. From helping the Te Muraka acclimate or fixing the barrier; from my friends, my life. Though perhaps not from my work, in the figurative if not the monetary sense.

"You're frowning," Lorwyn says. "What else is wrong, aside from what you just did to that leaf?"

I put her tools down with a sigh. "I promised Ari I would help them."

"That sounds like you," Lorwyn remarks, "except you're usually more careful about making promises you're not sure you can deliver on. Which I assume is the problem."

"In the long-term, I'm confident I can help," I say. "With their cause. But they're right that the problem requires immediate action. And I'm worried."

"About Ari," Lorwyn says, because she knows me well.

"They've risked everything to this," I say quietly. "I might lose my tea mastery, but at this point I believe I could find some other way to support myself if I truly had to, if not a fulfilling one. Ari has committed more, and worked longer, for a cause I can't disagree with. I feel uncomfortable standing against them."

"So why are you?" Lorwyn asks. I look at her, and she shrugs one shoulder irritably. "Don't give me that. I know you have a reason."

"I do," I say. "It just seems... not wrong, but—insufficient."

"You know what, get out of here," Lorwyn says.

"What?"

She waves her hands at me. "You may be on a deadline, but after everything today Talmeri's is a disaster. I don't have time for this, and neither do you. Go have your existential crisis somewhere else."

"Thanks," I say dryly. "I'm glad I can count on you in my time of need."

Lorwyn snorts. "Come off it; I'm not the problem here. You feel like you haven't done enough, or aren't planning to reach high enough? You feel guilty about the situation with Ari? Do something about it. Of all people, you can. So get going."

I blink. "Maybe I should come to you with all my existential crises."

"Always happy to give you a kick in the right direction, or at least *a* direction," Lorwyn says blandly. "If you're still here in five minutes I'm making you taste test something you won't like."

I flash a grin, already gathering my things. "A warning? I knew you liked me."

When in doubt, I do what I always should: I head for the shrine, and once again I settle into the altar to earth.

The problem isn't really that I don't think I can help Ari. Arguably I already have: by involving Saiyana, Ostario, and Entero in the political situation here, I've secured the highest level of interest in solving this problem. It's not the same as public awareness of what's happening in Taresan, but it's actionable: for all Ari's growth, I don't think they know how to mobilize a populace into specific, concrete steps.

But that's not all Ari needs. Ari has given up everything, and while I don't consider myself at odds with them in spirit, it can't be denied I am going to prevent all their effort from culminating in victory by seizing it for myself.

A tournament can only have one winner.

So what am I doing to Ari if I usurp their role in this as well as their cause?

I am thinking of this like a trap for both of us, and that's where I need to change. Our roots may be tangled in each other, but that shouldn't be strangling; that should mean we can support each other to reach greater heights.

That's the key: I am going to win this tournament, and in doing so I am going to get Ari everything they need and free them to work on themselves, whatever that means.

There. That's that sorted.

Though it does of course mean that I *must* win.

My thoughts drift inevitably to logistics; not truly in the spirit of contemplation, but unsurprising.

I know *why* I need to win, but not *how*. I'm missing something that will make the connection between the two clear.

I review the basics: my performance will be a tea ceremony, of course. As a tea master it's my greatest asset and one I've yet to display in the tournament.

But tea ceremony is at its most powerful when performed for a person; it is powerful in specificity and in connection.

I cock my head to the side and go still.

Can I perform the tea ceremony for a group?

In particular, is it possible to have a true ceremony for a *crowd*?

Are my roots strong enough to reach out so many branches at once and connect truly?

There it is; that's the true crux.

My doubt is not really about my ability, but about myself.

My earlier thought that the question of who I am is for later was unequivocally false. It's a question for now and always.

If I do not know myself, I cannot be the source of steadiness and strength that other people can latch onto. If my trunk wavers, so do all the branches.

Who am I? I'm not a princess, and perhaps I'm not a tea master, either.

Or: perhaps I am both.

I smile suddenly as I recall what Thiano termed me weeks ago, before Deniel gifted me the bracelets I turn now to absently: *tea princess*.

It was a joke, but it was also Thiano, and so it occurs to me belatedly, or perhaps again but with new consideration, it may not have been too much a joke.

If there is no space for the kind of princess I would be nor tea master, then I must create the space for myself.

I dedicated myself to finding and walking my own path, and I mean to do so.

So I will use all my power, as a princess, as a tea master, as myself, to serve my people in the way I can.

This time, when I rise out of the earth, I think maybe I have finally come to the realization the spirits have been waiting on.

With that, I have a baby dragon to collect. I'm not due at the dragon-sitter's yet, but Yorani is part of this, too, and she belongs with me to see it all through together.

CHAPTER 23

YORANI RESTS TENTATIVELY ON my shoulder as I head for my meeting. I'm worried I've passed her off to so many other people she's begun to believe she doesn't belong with me, which hurts my heart. Even if I can anchor no one else in this world, I must be a solid presence for her.

Approaching the edge of the Cataclysm, I see Saiyana has beaten me here.

"I can't just come whenever you call," Saiyana says without preamble.

I messaged ahead to arrange this. For most people, the Cataclysm would seem like a suspicious place to meet, but with her investigation into the breach, Saiyana has every reason to be here. Given my public interest in the Cataclysm, as well as generally in issues that have nothing to do with tea, no observers will be surprised to see me here, either.

"I know," I say. "I figured if this was a bad time you'd say so."

"It's a bad time," Saiyana says. "And it's likely to be for the foreseeable future. Don't count on our being able to meet again anytime soon."

My eyes narrow as Yorani nestles into the crook of my neck, staring off into the barrier, or perhaps the Cataclysm beyond. Her ears are perked up, listening to us, but apparently she's not worried about this conversation. "Lino?"

Saiyana nods. "We didn't apprehend his accomplices," she says, and I suck in a breath. I'd assumed she would have them in hand. "We're looking—Entero's taking it as a personal challenge—but they're not amateurs. It's possible they fled once Lino's cover was blown."

"But it's also possible," I say, "they'll try to take Lino out of the equation to keep him from talking. And since they're not amateurs..."

"Yeah, we can count on seeing them again. Especially since they haven't finished whatever they were sent here to do."

That gives me pause, though Yorani remains unconcerned. I am never quite sure how much she understands of what is said around her. "Lino hasn't told you yet?"

My sister snorts. "Lino knows perfectly well his value to us decreases the more information he gives us. He has no loyalty to Velasar, but he's no fool. It's in his interests to stall so we stay invested in devoting resources to keeping him alive. As a priority, I mean; he's obviously a fantastic witness in his own right, but we need information first and foremost, and he knows that."

I blow out a breath of frustration. "Intelligent enough to have useful information and also be difficult."

Saiyana huffs a laugh. "Pretty much. But I am going to have to focus on that situation for the near future."

And she's gone to the trouble of explaining it to me. "Since I've somehow caught you in a sharing mood, I don't suppose you'd tell me what favor you extracted from the tea tournament for their opportunity to save face?"

My sister looks at me archly. "Guess."

"Agreement to allow you to use the tournament in the future to plant operatives like Velasar did," I say promptly.

Saiyana stares at me with such blandness I know I've pinpointed it exactly—and she didn't expect me to but is also unsurprised.

"Spirits, Miyara," she says.

All at once I am reminded she is here to bring me back to being a princess, and I warn, "I'm still not going back with you."

Saiyana tilts her head back, staring up at the Cataclysm's border as if she can find answers there. "I saw you in the tournament match," she says.

My throat tightens. "I wasn't sure if you were monitoring another part of the job."

"I was," Saiyana says, "but I was there. What you did there was unreal. I was wrong, before. You are a tea master."

I blink rapidly against the sudden tears that prick my eyes at those words from Saiyana, of all people, and reach up to pet Yorani to steady myself.

"You were also right," I say. "I'm not objective, and I fully intend to keep inserting myself into situations with a princess' awareness. I'm not sure what that means yet."

She glances down at me, eyebrows raised. Perhaps she didn't truly expect me to consider what she'd said before.

"I'm not giving up," she says.

"I didn't expect you to," I say, "at least not yet."

Saiyana nods. "You still have to win the tournament. But I won't interfere."

Now that I've proved it can be useful, and that I can be useful through it. That's something; in fact, that's more than I dared hope, at this juncture.

It's not enough. We're still at an impasse. But it is something.

"So I gather that's not what you wanted to talk to me about so urgently," my sister finally says. "Since I do have some pressing matters of international magical security to attend to..."

"I actually wanted to talk to you about the final match of the tea tournament."

"What, you want my sisterly advice?" She says it with a crooked smile, which makes me wish that were in fact what I want.

"No," I say. "Actually, I want your royal advice."

One princess to another.

Saiyana faces me, but her posture shifts—I'd expected her to tense, but the opposite happens: she relaxes.

She knows how to be a princess with me, after all.

"Okay," she says. "You've got my attention. Shoot."

"Three things, mainly," I say. "Are you familiar with the setup of the final match of the tea tournament?"

"Yes, as I have left the palace once or twice in my life," she drawls.

I sigh. Of course she would have known as a matter of course what I had not. "Yes, well. I'm planning on bringing witches into focus. Are there any ramifications you'd suggest I plan for?"

Without missing a beat she replies, "Ah, you mean, 'hi Saiyana, here's a tip that you should consider preparing for a riot'? Duly noted."

I frown. "Do you really think it will come to that?"

"I think it depends entirely on whether you want it to," Saiyana says. "You're the tea master. Do you think it *should* come to a riot?"

"I don't think that will help my case, no," I say dryly.

She shrugs. "Then see that it doesn't."

I search her gaze, wondering if my performance in the last match really impressed her so much. But then I realize, "You don't really think whatever I choose to do will have much effect."

"I'm not going to put anything past you," Saiyana says, "but honestly, no, I don't. This is a tea tournament, Miyara, not the royal council. I will be the first in line to sing your praises if you can manage to give me enough momentum to actually get anti-witch legislation reversed, but no, I don't expect a response that dramatic from a single tea ceremony. Which is what I assume you'll be doing?"

I nod. I can't say her logic is faulty in an abstract sense, but I think she has put too little faith in the power of people, and in me. She doesn't understand what I can do yet.

I also don't understand what I can do yet, so this is perhaps fair. But to hear this from someone who always believed I could do so much, it is not heartening.

In fact, it spurs a rare competitive instinct in me to prove her wrong.

"Speaking of the ceremony," I say, "that brings me to the second point. I'm going to perform here—"

"No. This is the site of an active investigation."

"You have everything you're going to get without new data, most of which will not involve favorable outcomes, and I'm going to provide you a piece," I counter. "Where I was going with this, is that I'm going to be using the special teapot, which means I'm probably going to produce a tea spirit in full view of an audience. Is *that* going to be a problem for you?"

Saiyana's eyes are bright as she chews on that, her gaze fixing on Yorani, who preens helpfully. "Tricky little Miyara, baiting me with magical novelties," she murmurs. "But bringing spirits into the mix in this climate is risky."

"You were just saying this is only a tea tournament," I say.

"The barrier has been breached, and you'll be right in front of it, doing what looks like unknown magic? False equivalence, Miyara."

"So you think it will cause difficulty," I say.

"It may," she says. "Can you be sure you'll produce a spirit? We can test now."

I shake my head. "It wouldn't be a useful comparison. I'm planning to perform tea ceremony for a crowd; that will have to affect the tea spirit created."

"*Can* you perform tea ceremony for a crowd?"

"We'll find out," I say blandly.

"Ha. I notice you didn't answer my first question."

"Yes, I'm sure," I say. "Every time I've used the teapot to perform the tea ceremony since I brought it into the Cataclysm, I've created a tea spirit."

Saiyana taps her fingers thoughtfully against her leg. "Is that the only difference, I wonder?"

I frown. "What else could it be?"

"I mean, technically, practically anything. But I'm thinking about how you're always rubbing those bracelets on your wrists, and that I keep noticing."

I'm about to point out that she always notices people's tics, but the way she phrases that aborts me in the motion of opening my mouth: *keep* noticing. She wouldn't normally allow her attention to be drawn to redundant information.

"I wasn't wearing them inside the Cataclysm when I met the Te Muraka," I say instead.

"But have you worn them for all the tea ceremonies since?" she presses.

I nod. "I haven't taken them off. They were a gift."

"I suppose I don't need to ask from whom. But where did Deniel get them?"

Thiano. "You think there's something magical about them?"

"I think it's worth looking into, in our copious spare time," Saiyana says. "And it's a line of inquiry likely to actually bear fruit, since you've blocked all potentially useful avenues concerning the teapot itself."

A valid point, and an alarming one. I wear these bracelets constantly. If they are magical, and I don't know what kind—

But I am also not taking them off, even for Saiyana's suspicions. Not yet.

"Miyara, bracelet questions aside, I am going to have to insist you practice the tea ceremony in front of the barrier in view of a monitoring mage before the performance," Saiyana says. "The magical situation is too unstable to let you try something big without knowing how something small affects it."

Beyond fair, especially since she hasn't vetoed my using the space in front of the barrier entirely. "All right. I'll arrange something with Ostario, then."

She crosses her arms. "You really don't want to perform tea ceremony for me, do you?"

"I do someday," I say, "but not now, no."

"Why not?" Saiyana demands.

"Call it a tea master's intuition," I say. "I could perform it now, but I think it will be more meaningful later. I'm not sure what I'm waiting for, just that we're not there yet."

I hadn't put that feeling into words previously, but now that I have I realize I believe every word. It's like the spirits themselves have tipped me off that there is something brewing for us on the horizon.

"I think I'll call it cowardice," Saiyana says, "but I won't force you to perform for me."

"Nor could you."

Her eyes flash. Patience at an end, she asks, "What's the third thing?"

"It's about Ostario—"

"No."

I roll my eyes. "It has nothing to do with you as a person. This is about your incarnation as an eminent mage in the council, and I need a favor."

She smiles. "How big of a favor? And what do I get out of it?"

"For you? Small, truly. And in exchange, I'll give you that tea ceremony before you leave town, whenever that is."

"Even if you're leaving with me?" Saiyana challenges.

"I won't be," I say firmly. "But yes, hypothetically, even then."

"Then let's hear it," she says.

"Well well," Thiano says. "Look who's decided she has time for me after all."

Yorani suddenly launches off my shoulder, straight at Thiano. He stumbles back a pace, but it's too little, too late: she rams into him head-first.

And then she coils, twining in midair, as Thiano automatically brings his arms up to hold her, staring in shock.

"Well well," I echo dryly. "If I needed confirmation I'd come to the right place, I suppose I have it."

"Do you always trust a newborn tea spirit to be your compass?" Thiano asks, his tone abruptly acid. "Are you raising her or is she raising you?"

"Some of both," I say. "If you're going to hold her, you should pet her, too."

He rolls his eyes—but nevertheless complies.

"I assume you're here because you've thought of another question for your shadow."

I almost startle, but he means Entero, not Elowyn. I think. I will behave as though I'm certain, because I do *not* want Thiano taking an interest in Elowyn.

At least, not until she's a little further in her development.

"I actually wanted to stop by because you said the gift for Deniel's sister would be ready by now," I say.

"Yes, well, you'd hardly be doing the one without the other."

"I do sometimes do things without ulterior motives, you know," I say. "This gift, for instance."

"Gift-giving is an action you take, and you wouldn't give it such consideration if you didn't mean for it to have an effect," Thiano says. "Your conversations are no more innocent than mine. Ask your question, and I'll answer or I won't."

I sigh, but it's with a smile. "You're exasperating. If you're going to be like that, I have two."

Thiano chuckles, using his petting hand to wave me onward until Yorani lifts her head to stare at him. He dutifully returns to his designated task.

"I'm sure you can guess what I might have inferred from our last meeting," I say carefully, because in a case like this he needs to have deniability from his government. But he knows perfectly well he as good as told me the Isle of Nakrab is involved in all this somehow.

"I have been in a conversation or two in my time," Thiano answers noncommittally.

Ha. "And yet, you still specifically suggested Entero should look into Kustio's smuggling operation," I say. "Which, given what you wouldn't say, I can only take to mean the Isle of Nakrab was not involved in it—and yet you knew."

Thiano rummages around behind a set of shelves with one hand. "I'm waiting for the question."

"Why didn't Kustio try to move the Te Muraka's enchanted objects through you?" I ask.

"He did try," Thiano says. "It did not work as he intended."

My mind races. There is so much he isn't saying, and I can interpret it too many ways. "How did it work?"

"Poorly," he says.

"For whom?"

Thiano flashes me a tired grin. "Clever girl. What's your second question?"

"You're not going to answer?" I press.

"I'm sure I will eventually," Thiano says. "But my role or lack thereof in Kustio's plans is not your immediate problem. And no, before you say it, it's not your shadow's, either. All things in their time."

"That is a very convenient answer," I say, "when it's me you're expecting to act in the present."

"Oh, counting on you isn't convenient at all," Thiano says, pausing to stare at me intently, "but I work with what I have. You have a more immediate problem between there and here and you know it. My curiosity is piqued."

"Oh, of course *your* curiosity gets to be assuaged."

"Humor an old man," he says.

I narrow my eyes back at him. "The Isle of Nakrab is notorious for not letting magic leave its shores. So Thiano, I have to wonder, what, exactly, are my bracelets made of?"

Whatever Thiano was expecting from me, it wasn't that. He freezes so utterly that Yorani thumps down onto the shelf in front of her with a squawk.

Yorani scrabbles into the air to puff smoke in his face before fluttering back to my shoulder to sulk. By the time the smoke has cleared, Thiano's expression is under control, and he's produced a cloth-wrapped package.

"Here it is," he says, untying the knots to reveal a box. "You want to take a look?"

"No need," I say, and his head shoots up, face turning suspicious. "I trust you, Thiano."

"You shouldn't," he says seriously. "You already have several good reasons."

Like the fact that he's now revealed he knew the Te Muraka were stranded in the Cataclysm and left them there.

But that's not the same as not doing anything about it, and I have to wonder exactly how poorly Kustio's attempts to smuggle Te Muraka goods went—and not just when he tried to move them through Thiano.

The Te Muraka magic should have been undetectable, yet somehow it was, ultimately, detected.

"Yorani and I will decide that for ourselves," I say. "But please avoid dropping her again in the future."

Thiano sketches a perfect court Istal bow, and this time it's me who has to struggle to maintain my expression. What *is* Thiano's background, that he can perform such a gesture without pause? "My apologies to the little lady."

Yorani puffs another whorl of smoke, apparently unimpressed, and Thiano laughs and begins to wrap up the box again.

"Wait," I say. "Please. Would you show me how to tie that? It's a Gaellani wrapping scarf, isn't it?"

He blinks at me slowly.

Then: "Get over here and watch carefully," he says.

I do, and we say nothing else until I leave. His hands are steady, and despite his usual brusque gruffness, he's patient and sure as he shows me how to give a gift.

Perhaps someday I will understand enough to give one to him on purpose.

I had hoped Deniel would be at his shop, but probably he's out on council business. A few moments after trying the door, I hear a thump, and a patter, and then the door swings open of its own accord.

I blink as Talsion drops down from hanging off the handle on the inside of the door to let us in. Perhaps I don't need a key after all, though perhaps it is also unwise to rely on a cat's convenience.

In any event, I have several hours to work in peace. By the time Deniel arrives home, I've made his kitchen into a mess Lorwyn would be proud of.

Every cup, pot, and utensil has been used. I have piles of ingredients—different tea leaves, Cataclysm ingredients, and actual food—arrayed across the counter, more small bowls containing combinations of them, and I'm so sheepish about the disaster he's come home to he can only laugh at my expression.

"I promise I'll clean everything up," I say, "though, ah, I imagine this may make it slightly challenging to make dinner."

"I'll help," Deniel says, amused. "If you're done?"

"Yes."

"...and you're not just saying that because I'm here?"

I smile and shake my head. "I don't have trouble working around you."

As soon as I've said this, I realize it's a lie: I've had trouble concentrating around Deniel more than once. Sometimes his presence is calming; sometimes it is something else.

"That's good," he says while I'm debating whether I should correct myself in the spirit of honesty. "And what about our friends?"

I nod my head over to the chair, where Yorani and Talsion have curled up together for a nap.

"Well that's rare," he says.

"I imagine they're saving their energy for as soon as we're ready to sleep," I say dryly, which makes him laugh.

"Shall I take over the dish-washing?" Deniel asks.

"I already believe you're a perfect human," I say. "You don't have to go to any more trouble."

Deniel looks at me like in exasperation. "You realize when you said that before I'd just finished watching you overwhelm everyone—and I do mean everyone, given what I'm hearing both at city council and among my customers—with that explosion of tea mastery? If anyone here is a perfect human, it's obviously you."

And that is also how Saiyana got the tea tournament to agree to her terms. I'm helping her in her princess work after all.

I blush, but it's mild; I know he's teasing me, but also that in this context he's still not hearing that I truly do mean the sentiment. So I lighten my tone and say, "Talsion and Yorani have excellent taste in humans, clearly. Thank you again for lunch."

I almost can't believe that was still this day.

"You're welcome," Deniel says. "And you can call this self-defense: I don't want to be in charge of your Cataclysm ingredients, and I'm not sure I can tell which they are."

I laugh and make space for him in the kitchen.

"So," he says, "why are you doing this here, instead of at the tea shop?"

"I felt ill-at-ease, preparing this in front of Lorwyn," I admit, and explain what I'm trying to do. "I could have brought all the ingredients to my apartment, I suppose, but I decided it was important for me to feel like myself, and comfortable in that, to make this blend." I shrug, self-conscious again. "I am more at ease in your home than in mine."

Deniel's hands twitch and his ears redden, but aside from that he only nods and asks, "Why is it important for you to feel at home with yourself now, when it hasn't been for other challenges?"

I consider that a moment, not immediately sure he's correct. I've visited the shrine to feel at peace with myself, though today that wasn't sufficient. But I have, after all, taken steps to make my living space feel like mine before—but not to any particular goal. Hmm.

I carefully sweep two Cataclysm ingredients into different piles, one to be washed away in water and the other to be burned, as I consider.

"I am confident in my current course, but less so in my ability to meet it," I finally say. "It seems presumptuous to think that I alone, with one performance, can begin accomplishing what even my grandmother couldn't. When I'm still so new to my place here, and its structure seems shakier than ever—can I reach others when I can't ground myself?"

"You are grounding yourself," Deniel counters. "You're reflecting carefully, making choices, and taking action. Ultimately that's all any of us can do."

"That's true," I concede. "But so much depends on this, and I'm not sure I can pull it off. Perhaps I'm overreaching. It is, after all, just a tea tournament."

Deniel pauses at that, glancing over at me—and his gaze snags on the gift I wrapped at Thiano's. "What's this?"

"Oh, that's for Elowyn," I say, and his stare is so intense I find myself rambling. "No occasion, just—it's a tea pet. Which isn't something she needs to practice tea, but I wanted to give her something that isn't about needs, but that might bring her some joy."

Deniel stares a moment longer.

Then he abruptly sets down the dishes and wipes his hands dry on a towel. "Are any of those Cataclysm ingredients dangerous to be left out for a few hours?" he asks.

"No," I say, confused. Not in their current state, anyway; I've learned a thing or two working at Talmeri's.

"Then there's someplace I'd like to take you." He smiles crookedly. "It'll get us dinner faster than if we cleaned, too."

My heart pounds; he's up to something. "Are you sure?" I ask. "I'm sure you're tired after your day—I still haven't heard how things went with Saiyana—"

"That can wait," Deniel says, taking my hands in his. "Are you sure you don't need to spend more time working on your blends? I know how important this competition is to you."

I'm about to say that he's wrong, I don't care about the competition, even though I know he means about my future as a tea master.

But the truth is, I've *made* it matter. I've forged meaning out of this ridiculous happenstance.

I'm not sure what the future holds for me as a tea master or as a former princess, but today, I am confident I'm walking a path true to myself.

"I'm sure," I say. "But where are we going?"

Deniel smiles, and it's gentle, but I can sense his excitement through his hands. "You'll see. Are you ready?"

I am.

For all of it.

CHAPTER 24

ALTHOUGH DENIEL ASSURES ME Talsion is too canny to eat anything he shouldn't, I do not have such confidence in Yorani, who has been perking up at our movement, regardless. So it is that Talsu gets to continue his nap uninterrupted, only moving to take advantage of the warm spot Yorani has vacated, and Yorani assumes her usual perch on my shoulder. In her still-waking state, she is calm and watchful as Deniel and I set out.

We don't have far to go, it turns out, and I hear the noise and see the lights before we get arrive.

I look at Deniel in confusion. "What's going on?"

He smiles. "I thought you might have missed it. Tonight is the sky lantern festival."

I blink at him. I've never been to a lantern festival, though I've seen artists' renderings of the tiny glowing dots filling the sky like a river of stars.

For that matter, although I know the basics, I've never been to a festival at all, which Deniel must know. He wants me to have this.

I link my arm with his, keeping stride. "Tell me about it."

"Traditionally it was a water lantern festival," Deniel says. "But since Istalam's rivers aren't quite as ubiquitous as the Gaellani homeland, we've adapted an older tradition. You write your hopes and dreams—or your fears—on a lantern, and then send it up into the sky. Either letting them go, or offering them to the spirits, as acknowledgement and commitment. Depends on your interpretation."

"Those are markedly different interpretations."

"Most people aren't here for spiritual reflection," he answers. "They want to see pretty lights in the sky."

"I am... intrigued and excited, but also tired and hungry," I say in the spirit of honesty. "I'm not sure I'm really in a position to partake in this experience, if it involves more than watching the sky. And not falling asleep standing upright."

"There will be food," Deniel assures me. "It's a good thing your match earlier was in a different courtyard, because folks have been setting up here for the last few days. I'd bring you another time, but—although it usually goes for two nights, I'm not sure if it will this year because of the tournament match."

Another interference.

And another reminder, that if I'm not victorious tomorrow, I won't have another chance to experience it.

I must do all I can in the time that I have.

So I ask Deniel what one does at a festival besides launch lanterns into the sky and hope they don't set trees on fire, and together we enter the transformed courtyard.

I stare around just like I did when Lorwyn first took me around town, and Deniel laughingly pulls me along with him.

There are stalls with children's games and prizes where we try our hands to equal lack of success; there are even more stalls of Gaellani street food, and Deniel introduces me to a kind of savory pancake covered in sauce I've never tried before.

"What, no festival dress?" Lorwyn's voice breaks into my rapture. I look up to see her and Entero, with Risteri and Sa Nikuran trailing behind.

"It was a last-minute plan," Deniel says. "I'll show her another time."

Deniel has clothes like we've seen others around us wearing? "I badly want to see that," I say out loud.

He smiles crookedly over his blush. "That can be arranged." As warmth suffuses me Deniel adds to Lorwyn, "I see you aren't, either. Your sisters didn't catch you this year?"

"Last-minute plan," she echoes with a drawl. "Your sister's the only one of us who came prepared. I helped her tie the sash provided she protects me from my sisters' wrath if they find out I came without them."

Deniel's eyebrows shoot up, and he looks over Lorwyn's shoulder to where Elowyn, glowing in a traditional Gaellani dress, is excitedly showing Tamak how to play one of the games Deniel and I just finished failing at. Tamak doesn't.

"Those odds don't seem in her favor," Deniel says.

"Not my problem," Lorwyn says.

"I think it is," he answers.

Entero interrupts. "Elowyn's sure they won't be here yet."

"Which she knows because...?"

Entero shrugs and doesn't elaborate, which I take to mean either he confirmed it as well or Elowyn obtained that information like she learns so much else—and he trusts her work.

I wave to Elowyn and Tamak, who begin making their way toward us.

"You should give her the gift now," Deniel says to me.

"But I didn't bring it," I protest, only to find him handing it to me.

"I thought we might see everyone here," he explains.

Everyone. Me, Deniel, Lorwyn, Risteri, Entero, Sa Nikuran, Elowyn, Tamak.

As they approach I see behind them Glynis tugging a protesting Ari into the festival. They argue briefly, and then Ari storms off. Glynis turns on her heel, scans the crowd, and then makes a beeline toward us, too.

My heart aches at Ari's rejection, but all the rest—Deniel is right. These are my people, my home. These are the important anchors I've wound my roots into so I can stretch my branches out and see how tall I can grow.

As if sensing my thoughts, Lorwyn says plaintively, "How did this happen? How did I manage to get away from my sisters and still end up surrounded with you people?"

Entero snorts, but although her question was rhetorical I realize there is a firm answer, and it's me.

They may not have come for me tonight, but I am the one who brought these people together, or enabled them to find each other.

I meet Deniel's eyes as I pull the gift from him, and he nods.

This is what he brought me here to remember. That just as myself, I can be part of joy, the center of connections that radiate outward.

When Elowyn arrives, I give her the gift with a bow. "Elowyn, I have something for you. But please, open it later?"

TEA SET AND MATCH

Tamak scowls, even though in her other hand Elowyn is already holding a cloth cat prize from the booth he just won for her.

Her eyes round, Elowyn nods silently, accepting the small package delicately.

"What's that for?" Risteri asks.

"No particular reason," I say, uncomfortable, but I don't want Elowyn to feel the kind of obligation I find myself beholden to so frequently. "I thought she might like it, and it was within my means."

"When do you start bringing home presents for me, then?" Risteri jokes.

Deniel says, "El, if you have any hands left, could you watch Yorani for a few minutes?"

Elowyn looks up sharply as I begin to protest. "No, Yorani should stay with me—"

Before I'm done, Yorani has been plucked off my shoulder by Glynis' quick fingers, and her eyes gleam at me in amusement. "We've got this, D. Go on before someone else finds it."

Deniel grins and sketches a bow, leaving me apparently the only one who doesn't understand what's going on.

Or perhaps just the Gaellani know—and Yorani, somehow—as I hear Risteri and the Te Muraka pipe up with questions as Deniel tugs me away and through the crowd, my heart pounding.

Where is he taking me?

It's not far. But Deniel snags a lantern for us and pulls me outside the hubbub of the festival—

Into a copse of trees, with a perfect view of the night sky. Already I can see the lanterns floating up, and up, and up.

Deniel hugs me from behind, and I think this moment can't get more perfect.

"I forgot to grab a pen," he whispers sheepishly.

I laugh, holding his arms tighter around me. "That's all right. I can focus my hopes and fears for the spirits in my heart."

Gently, Deniel extracts. "You should hold onto the lantern; it'll gather enough lift to take off soon."

Sure enough, the lantern he snagged is inflating—the festival vendor must have started the process without my noticing. I put my hands on it, feeling the lantern swell in time with the thrill coursing through me.

"Is this a popular lantern release spot?" I ask.

"Yes," Deniel says, "though it's also a popular spot for, ah, lovers, to be frank. Lots of promises exchanged, that sort of thing. Though that's not what I—I mean—" He sighs. "I'm doing this all wrong."

I can't stop smiling. "Not as far as I can tell."

He leans over the lantern and kisses me, and I almost lose my grip on the lantern.

I open my eyes when I feel a weight drop around my neck.

Looking down, I see a key silhouetted against the glow of the growing lantern, hanging from a cord around my neck.

The key to his home.

"I promised I'd tell you what I realized when your sister was being horrible at dinner," Deniel says. "I had no idea what to do, except it was the most natural thing in the world to stand by your side. To do all I could to be a support to you, whatever that meant. Which in that case largely meant sticking it in Saiyana's face, but more broadly—a lot has been changing for me, too. Maybe not as drastically as it has for you—I didn't leave my entire life behind—but, still, a lot. And in all that the one thing that does feel solid is my relationship with you. Whatever else happens, I know I want to be with you. Whatever that means."

"The lantern's ready, Miyara. You can let it go."

No.

I'm going to hold this moment in my heart forever.

I blink back tears, staring at him over the lantern, so full of emotion I can't move.

But he steps in and covers my hands with his, and our gazes lock.

And then I am lifting my arms, and guiding the lantern into the sky.

My hopes and dreams and fears, all jumbled together in this instant, a glowing package I release to the spirits, watching it float gently into the night to join the path the wind is taking all the lanterns on through the sky.

I clutch the key in my hands, tears streaming down my face. Apparently I didn't manage to blink them back after all.

Staring into Deniel's eyes, I think, I love you.

But what I say is, "What are your thoughts on sex?"

Deniel's eyebrows shoot up. "What?"

Oh, spirits. If only I'd thought of this conversation a moment ago to rid my fear of it into the lantern.

I stare down at the key. "I mean—we talked about my starting to stay over, and the last time—"

"Oh," Deniel says, understanding dawning abruptly, thank everything, and runs a hand through his hair. "I—to be honest, I don't think I'm ready," he says carefully.

"You're not just saying that to make me feel more at ease?" I ask.

His brow furrows. "Where is that coming from?"

I flush. "Saiyana, I suppose," I say. "I shouldn't have let that comment get to me, but I wasn't sure if I was the problem?"

"You're never a problem," Deniel says firmly, taking my hands in his. "And no, I'm not just saying that. We've been honest with each other from the start, and I hope that will always continue."

"So do I," I say softly.

He nods. "Then whatever pace works for both of us is right," Deniel says, "no matter what your sister or anyone else thinks."

"But you do want to?" I press, hoping we both don't erupt from embarrassment before I can see this through. "With me, at some point?"

Deniel kisses me softly and then says in a low voice, "Yes, Miyara."

"Even if it takes... months?"

"Even if it takes years," Deniel says. "In the spirit of honesty, I admit I'm hoping we're on more of a 'months' timeline, but I hope more than anything you'll feel comfortable telling me how you feel, whether you're ready or not. I'll be here, Miyara."

I stare at him, this perfect person, my root and strength and support no matter what height I reach for, and I've opened my mouth to say three fateful words when my bracelets blaze burning hot, searing my skin.

Reflex takes over. These aren't the same security bracers I wore as a princess, but I trained for years to react to that signal and dive over Deniel, knocking us both to the leafy dirt.

The trees that were behind us explode.

I look up and see no sign of what they were hit with: it's like a cannon ball of wind tore through them.

Deniel coughs, and I roll off him, facing the other way.

At Ignasa, who holds a glass and metal contraption I've never seen before. She steps through the trees after us, where we sent up a beacon for anyone who might be looking.

There are glowing metal lines on the weapon, glowing like my bracelets, and who knew they did that? And the lines are lengthening, like a power charge—

Like it's readying for a second shot.

"What was—" Deniel starts, before he sees Ignasa and her weapon, too.

Glass and metal is what the Te Muraka work with, and I am instantly sure this is one of the smuggled devices.

Which means it's undetectable by normal magical means. No wonder I didn't see it, then.

"We have to go," I say absently, numbly, my brain reeling through the implications.

Deniel has already scrambled to his feet and pulls me after him.

We run.

The action jolts me back to myself, and I do the most sensible thing I can think of:

I start screaming for help.

Whatever magic I might be able to work is not up to the task of what Ignasa is wielding behind us.

Deniel catches on and starts up too, and before we're even all the way back into the festival—a terrible destination, full of targets—why am I letting him pull me this way?—Entero erupts out of the trees.

And leaping above him, higher than any human could jump, is Sa Nikuran.

They land between Ignasa and us, and I gasp, "She has a weapon—it—"

"I know what it does," Sa Nikuran snarls, her eyes changing color, skin tone darkening.

"Get to Lorwyn," Entero says. "She needs you now."

Deniel starts to ask why, and this time it's me who pulls him along, leaving Ignasa to the dragons.

Lorwyn is frighteningly not difficult to find. While other people flee for cover, she stands in the center of lightning-like attacks that seem to come from all directions, sniping them with witch-fire before they can land.

"Glynis, I need those rocks in place now!" Lorwyn screams.

"What do you need?" I gasp, stumbling up with Deniel. He looks wildly around for Elowyn only to find her directly behind a crimson-eyed Tamak, Yorani sitting on her shoulder and hissing.

Lorwyn swears as another bolt snaps toward us, and it's Risteri who answers me. "She's fusing magecraft and witchcraft somehow to make a shield against whatever magic this is," Risteri says rapidly.

"Not just a shield," Lorwyn spits. "A web."

Before I can ask what that means, Risteri continues, "Glynis helped her work it out, and apparently it needs a specific kind of structure so she's off putting it in place while Lorwyn holds, but I don't understand, so—"

"I do," I say, understanding now why Entero thought Lorwyn needed me: to set this up faster.

Because with Glynis to bounce the theory off of, Lorwyn doesn't need that from me, either: she can already do this for herself.

But as I turn to back Glynis up, Yorani launches herself off Elowyn's shoulder and throws herself right in front of Lorwyn.

With a screech I've never heard from my tea spirit, she releases a jet of flame that crashes into an invisible force, splintering it into transparent shards that I can see bent reality through like glass mirrors.

The same force Ignasa tried to hit me with. But is it her again?

Over Yorani's scream I somehow make out Glynis calling and yell at Lorwyn, "NOW!"

Lorwyn erupts power, a spider web of glowing tendrils of magic unfurling from her and billowing outward. It catches whatever the attack is and wipes it away and continues moving.

And I don't watch any longer, because as soon as Lorwyn's attack passes the invisible stream Yorani was holding back through the force of her fire, the tiny dragon falls.

I dive to catch her before she hits the ground, cradling her spent form in my arms.

Sa Rangim's voice echoes in my head as I stare at Yorani through my tears as she shrinks in my arms, as I remember him telling me she would learn what I cared about from my actions.

I've demonstrated over and over that I believe in defending Lorwyn, and Yorani is my familiar, and so she did.

She has spent her own fire in defense of a friend.

"Got him," Lorwyn growls.

"That's Aleixo, the Velasari agent," Risteri says.

I'm still not looking, my eyes only for the dwindling form in my lap. I hug Yorani tighter, as if I can bodily protect her from going.

"So when you said web, you meant like a spider, drawing in the prey," Risteri says. "Miyara, he was attacking the entire festival until Lorwyn started fighting back, and then he focused on her—Miyara?"

Then Entero's voice: "Ignasa is neutralized."

"She will wake up, though," Sa Nikuran growls.

And then finally, it's Elowyn who sees. "Oh, Yorani, what's wrong?"

Everyone is silent as I sob.

Yorani is still there and has stopped shrinking, but she's small, so much smaller, she fits in the palm of my hand.

"I'm sorry, Miyara," Entero says, his distress making me squeeze my eyes tighter. "I thought Lorwyn could take care of things here—"

Lorwyn snaps, "I did."

"I know you did, that's not what I mean, I just—"

"I wasn't fast enough," Lorwyn says. "I know. I know, spirits take everything!"

Sa Nikuran's growl starts next to my ear but moves past rapidly.

Risteri shouts, "Stop that! You don't get to eat him!"

And she does stop, or so I can only assume by the lack of chomping sounds, but the rumble of thunder in Sa Nikuran's voice is enough for me to raise my tear-stained face. "Stop now," I say in a deadly voice.

The growling ceases.

"We don't have time for more destruction," I say. "Yorani needs us now."

My voice breaks on the last word.

Deniel hugs me from behind, and I take a shuddering breath.

I'm not giving up.

I'm not.

"Glynis," I say, and she appears in front of me as if by magic, but the only magic is her speed and attention. "Get Saiyana here, and get her fast."

TEA SET AND MATCH

Glynis vanishes.

Then before me in her place is Tamak, crouching down and meeting my eyes with a steady blaze of his own.

"Sa Rangim will know what to do if you do not," he says.

Faith in his leader, or does he know something I don't?

I don't know anything. It doesn't matter.

"Where can I find Sa Rangim?" I ask.

It's Sa Nikuran who answers, coming up behind Tamak and looking at him hard. "How fast do you need to get there?"

"I need to get there now," I snap. Deniel's arms fall away as I stand.

Sa Nikuran takes one look at the tiny curled spirit I hold in the palm of my hand and leaps into the air, even higher than I saw before.

"Then climb on," she says.

And there, in full view of the courtyard, in the middle of the air, she transforms into a dragon.

Another time, I will have questions.

Another time, there will be repercussions.

Another time, I might have handled everything differently.

But today, now, Sa Nikuran crouches down in the remains of the already devastated courtyard, the glitter of the festival shattered around us, and I gather Yorani carefully in my arms and climb on without another word.

Without another word, we launch into the sky with our hopes and fears clasped tight.

CHAPTER 25

SAYORSEN IS A LARGE CITY, but Sa Nikuran is a large dragon. It does not take long to cover a great deal of ground.

This is for the best, because if we went longer or higher, and were it not for the horns on her head for me to hold onto, I would have fallen for sure.

Another time, I can reflect on the feel of dragon scales beneath me, how they are both smooth and rough, hot like fire but somehow also cool like metal—or on potential improvements to the practical experience for passengers of dragon flight, or on what seeing a full-sized dragon will mean for the precarious political situation in Sayorsen.

I can reflect on the fact that without a second thought, I flew.

Another time, when I have room in my heart and mind for wonder. When Yorani does not lie nearly lifeless in my arms.

But as it is, all my faculties are devoted to holding onto Yorani with one arm, Sa Nikuran's horn with the other, and keeping my legs firmly locked around her neck.

Until that neck shimmers beneath me, and the horn vanishes.

I cannot see the ground; perhaps I *could*, but not with my attention focused on practical matters of coordination. I cannot see how close we are, or if Sa Rangim is there, or if something has attacked Sa Nikuran. All I know is that the dragon beneath me is vanishing.

I tuck Yorani into my arms, curl around her, and close my eyes, praying to the spirits to please protect her one small life with mine.

Then Sa Nikuran is gone, and I fall.

It is a common truism that in the moments before death, you will see what truly matters to you in your mind: a lasting image of what you have loved best. Our stories are rife with these flashes of insight, people realizing who they actually cared about all along with tranquil acceptance.

Perhaps it happens this way for some people, but it is not what I see. As the earth rushes up to meet me, I am consumed with anger.

That I didn't do more.

That my time has run out.

That it has come to this, literally falling to my death.

Everything seems to slow as resolve coalesces as well: if I am going to die, at least it will be having acted, and with conviction, for at least a few brief moments.

But by all the spirits, I do not want to die.

And with that final thought, my body makes contact.

But not with the ground.

I open my eyes to see that Sa Rangim has caught me.

Instants later I realize the slowing I felt was perhaps not the experience of my final moments, but magic to slow my descent.

"Sorry Miyara," Sa Nikuran says from behind me. "I didn't think I wouldn't be able to tell you more once we were in the air—"

"I assume your cause is urgent, to have transformed in the city," Sa Rangim cuts her off. "What has happened, Miyara?"

I unfurl my arms and lift the tiny Yorani up—but not too far, because I cannot bear to release her. "I think she's dying," I whisper, and my tears start anew. "Can you help?"

Sa Rangim's pupils flash through a series of movements—dilating and contracting, along with swift color changes. I don't know enough to interpret the meaning for sure, but in my heightened emotional state I think I know: shock and distress and anger and an immense well of sympathy.

"What happened?" he asks.

Sa Nikuran answers succinctly: "The Velasari agents used weapons we created. Yorani defended Lorwyn from a frontal assault before her magical defense was ready."

Sa Rangim frowns down at Yorani. "She should not have been able to do that."

"Nevertheless," Risteri says. "Miyara's bracelets may be connected. They blazed like stars while Yorani's fire was active against the assault."

Did they? I was so focused on Yorani I didn't notice.

Sa Rangim cuts a glance at Sa Nikuran. "And the source of the assault?"

"There were two weapons in use," she says. "Both now destroyed. I did not have leisure to check for others, but Tamak is on site."

"Tamak does not have the authority in Istal eyes to make his will a reality. Go back and see it taken care of—without your wings."

Sa Nikuran bows, turns on her heel, and leaves.

"Come in," Sa Rangim says, setting me on my feet. I wobble, my balance on solid ground unreliable.

Perhaps my body no longer believes there is solid reality underfoot, either.

As I sway, Sa Rangim reaches out a hand to steady me, and I latch on, leaning on him, letting him be my support.

"Can you help?" I ask again, because that seems to be all I can say.

"I can," Sa Rangim says, "and so can you. In fact, you must."

"I will."

"I have no doubt. But we should not lose more time than we must, either. Come in, Miyara, and let's get to work."

His words ground me. He has not said everything will be fine, but he has extended a hand in welcome and is willing to show me how to do the work necessary. The rest will come as I will.

Sa Rangim is not at home, exactly, but at the unofficial Te Muraka headquarters. It is a building ceded to the Te Muraka for their use—a place Kustio had driven Gaellani out of, but that is in fact in such poor condition that once the city officials became aware of it they could not expect anyone to live there again, not with Istalam watching to see how Sayorsen would redeem itself after Kustio. I helped Sa Rangim negotiate for city resources, and in exchange, making the building habitable is a project for the Te Muraka. It is not where they live, because it was not immediately ready for their use, but it is a place that is unequivocally theirs, when much is still in flux.

It has changed a great deal since I have been by, but I barely take it in. The hallway we pass through has been scrubbed raw, for one—I assume the rampant black mold must be gone, or Sa Rangim would not have invited me to enter. Beyond that, I am in no state to be interested in what they are doing with the place.

Until we come into a great room that has been likewise completely scrubbed—a room that had many more walls previously, and yet apparently the building no longer needs those supports to stand—and I see the beginnings of a rock circle that takes me back to our first meeting in the Cataclysm.

This may be the unofficial Te Muraka headquarters, but Sa Rangim is setting it up to be theirs in truth, legally and spiritually. I haven't even managed with my own apartment; I can't imagine the undertaking for space for an entire people.

But we cross through the space into a connected back room, and this one is *not* scrubbed.

It is rich, and warm, with dark wood and plush seats of soft fabrics and a fireplace. It is an explosion of color after the gray austerity that preceded it, and I blink rapidly.

"That is how many of us feel, coming from the Cataclysm to Sayorsen," Sa Rangim says wryly. "This room, for now, serves as a sort of practice for those who need more time to ease in."

"Not the brightness, but the stability of it," I say suddenly. Of course the Te Muraka would have learned not to trust the variation of the Cataclysm. As I have fretted about the strength of my roots, they have wondered if roots can exist at all. Something I should have realized, and something I should attend to.

"Just so," Sa Rangim says. "Sit, please. I see your kit has been left behind, so I will bring tea."

"But Yorani—"

"Yorani is a tea spirit, Miyara. The tea is for her. Stay close to the fire, and keep her as warm as you can."

I glance toward the fireplace, which flares to life before Sa Rangim leaves the room.

He is a dragon, with magic I do not understand. I should not forget.

But all I do is hold Yorani as close as I can, mindless of the world around us.

Sa Rangim returns in less than a minute with a tray full of tea utensils. He sets it down on the table between us and offers his hands to me.

Rather than take them, I only look at them, and so I see them warm with fire.

"Yorani is your familiar, Miyara. Closeness to you sustains her, but to keep her from dwindling it is your hands that will need to brew the tea. I am Te Muraka. I will hold her flame."

I shut my eyes tightly, forcing tears out the corners. I swallow.

When I open my eyes, I carefully place my heart in his hands in the form of one tiny tea spirit.

Sa Rangim bows.

Yorani does not stir.

I turn my attention to tea.

I sort out what I need quickly, setting aside the tools I won't use and which tea is appropriate, scarcely thinking. When I glance up with a question about heating the kettle, Sa Rangim asks, "What sort of tea?"

"The traditional black earth blend."

With a breath, he blows a gentle whorl of flame at the kettle. The flame engulfs the teapot, causing it to glow, but where my hand sits I feel only a faint tingling.

"The water is ready," Sa Rangim says, a mild strain in his voice.

I try not to think about what that means, and begin.

I perform the tea ceremony with almost no thought at all. Rather than deliberately crafting it, this ceremony erupts out of me like my soul has shed its barriers in the natural world. Yorani's need claws it out of me, but I hold onto the magic of the moment, drawing it out.

Sa Rangim senses when I am about to pour and lifts Yorani up. "Pour a serving over her."

I do, and although I expect the water to splash out of his hands, instead it's as though it seeps into Yorani's scales.

She stirs, and I suck in a breath.

"Good," Sa Rangim says. "Now, lift the lid of the teapot."

My hands shaking now, I hold it steady enough for Sa Rangim to slip her inside. His hands cover mine as he guides my hands to closing the lid and setting it back down.

Then he takes a deep breath. "I've lent her my own fire to compensate, and this will stabilize her. But you should perform the tea ceremony for her again using your own teapot to help her rebuild what she's lost. I know how distraught you were, for Sa Nikuran to carry you to me, but never leave it behind again. The magic in my fire is not a perfect substitute for the magic of the pot that birthed her."

I can scarcely track his words. "That's all? She'll be all right now?"

"*All?*" Sa Rangim huffs. "Miyara, I am confident that in a few minutes your adrenaline will crash, and you will be asleep for hours. I will be weakened for a time, too, after magic of this sort."

I frown. I think of the tea ceremony metaphorically as magic, but although it is the process that created Yorani I do not think of it as magic in truth. "What sort, exactly?"

"Life magic," Sa Rangim says simply. "It is a profound undertaking, and not one many people can hope to attempt safely. That is why Sa Nikuran brought you to me."

"But it was so simple," I say. "And I wasn't tired after Yorani's birth."

"Yorani was born out of the magic of the Cataclysm focused into form," Sa Rangim says. "Outside, it will take more out of you. Without your bracelets as a focus, I do not think it would have been possible at all."

I fixate on one part of his statement: "A focus?"

"For magic," he says. "Your will focuses it to you. And, apparently, for Yorani."

I stare, my thoughts racing between *focus* and *magic*. "But the tea ceremony..."

Isn't magic. Or is it? Not in any way I know, not like magecraft or witchcraft or what I've seen of Te Muraka craft. I know too little about Nakrabi magic, but if the tea ceremony is a kind of magic, it is figurative, metaphorical. It is for altering hearts and minds, but not in a physical, tangible way.

And yet, I formed a tea spirit with it. Not on my own—there was the Cataclysm, Sa Rangim, the teapot, the tea. But a tea ceremony doesn't just exist; it must be performed, which means there must be a person to perform it.

"I confess, Miyara, I am more than a little concerned that your tea guild does not appear to have explained its lore to you," Sa Rangim says. "Given the reaction when you first presented Yorani, they certainly know what she is. While I am glad to have been in a position to help you for a change, it should not have been needful."

"The tournament is a test for me," I say. "They will not contact me until it is done to ensure I am fully on my own, and that no one in the future can accuse me of depending on their aid. I win or lose on my own."

Sa Rangim just looks at me.

"I know," I say. "Believe me, I have understood what this is from the start." I gaze down at the teapot. "But this is not a cost I knew to consider, and it casts their betrayal in another light. With the breach, and the revelations about the Velasari agents... they had context to know this was a potential cost that I did not."

The anger I felt as I fell burgeons in my anew.

I cannot go back to the palace and accomplish my work there. I know this well.

But nor is the acceptance of a tea guild that would behave thusly sufficient. Not anymore.

"What will you do?" Sa Rangim asks.

I look up. "You're sure Yorani's all right in there?"

He nods gravely. "I can feel her, little one. She will rest for a little while before she is ready for a new pot, but she'll recover faster with you here."

Little one. It's usually what he calls Yorani. But in Sa Rangim I feel as though I've found a mentor, or perhaps the elder sibling relationship I never had with Iryasa or Reyata.

"Then with your permission, I will rest too," I say. As the words leave my mouth a wave of exhaustion sweeps over me, as if my body was only waiting for my acknowledgement. "So when it is time to act, we both are ready."

Sa Rangim nods approvingly. "I will bring you a blanket. And send someone to retrieve your tea kit. Rest, Miyara."

He's scarcely finished speaking before I am curling up on the floor, eyes drifting shut.

Late that night, I take a breath outside the door to Saiyana's headquarters in the city.

In the last few hours, many things have become clear to me.

Sa Rangim woke me to brew a new pot of tea for Yorani with my own teapot, and I was nearly overcome with relief when I lifted her into the new pot and found her awake and cranky about being moved out of one hot bath, even temporarily.

We both fell back asleep immediately.

The next time I awoke when Yorani nudged me with her nose. She'd regained a fraction of her former size and was ravenous for magic, which Sa Rangim was able to assist with.

In the meantime, he'd learned of another breach in the barrier, which was why Ostario wasn't on hand when the magic started flying: he had been single-handedly stabilizing it.

If he'd been on his own, too, I was willing to bet Saiyana had been likewise occupied with a distraction from the Velasari agents' primary goal: attacking me.

Which meant I had questions.

So I understood Yorani's urging. She was stable and recovering, and it was time for us to get to work.

I pet her where she sits on my shoulder, and she noses my ear.

I heft my tea kit. Time to go.

I knock in a long-ago learned pattern I have no business still using as a civilian.

There is a pause, and then Saiyana throws the door open.

"Who do you think you are," she snarls.

"The person who's going to solve your interrogation problem," I say coolly.

She tugs me bodily inside and slams the door behind me, throwing her wards back up.

It is the side of my sister I was braced for. If she thinks I will be surprised by her bile, that I would think she'd be as calm as our last conversation, then she will be the only one off-balance for this conversation.

They came for me, they came for my people, and they nearly killed Yorani.

It's time they understand that this was a mistake.

"You are not a princess anymore, as you are so fond of reminding me," Saiyana snaps. "You don't get to just waltz in here. You don't get to interrogate prisoners. You don't get to summon me across town when I'm busy thwarting an assassination attempt on *another* prisoner—"

I knew it. "Hired thugs I assume you had just enough difficulty with to keep you here? I called you to where the real threat was."

"You mean the barrier breach? No? Did you even know about that?"

"I do, and the cause of the breach wasn't there anymore either, because they were busy trying to kill me," I say. "Since I'm not a princess anymore, don't you think that's interesting?"

"What I think is *interesting* is that you have the gall to make demands of the Seneschal of Istalam while you disappear to *nap*. You think I should respect your choices, when you let yourself be distracted by this one creature and neglected your duty to people as a whole?"

"It's not my duty anymore," I say, calmly and clearly. "In fact it's yours, and *you weren't there. You* didn't stop it. And you should have."

"You dare—"

"How do *you* dare," I interrupt. "I serve individual people, and I believe that is service of the greater good. That is my choice. If you have a problem with that, if you're going to keep second guessing me or trying to make my work harder, then get out."

There's a beat of silence, in which Saiyana wrestles with her shock.

Torn between outrage and incredulity, she demands, "You think you can make *me* leave?"

"You've always said," I say quietly, "I could be capable of so much if I tried. With no royal resources at my disposal, I've uncovered a plot against the crown, discovered and rescued a new race in the greatest magical disaster in known history, become a tea master, and forged a spirit that hasn't been seen in centuries, all before you were even watching.

"Well, you've never seen me try against *you*. Do you truly wish to see what I would be capable of?"

Saiyana stares at me for another long, silent moment.

"Yes," she finally says, "but only because I am the most competitive person alive. This place really has been good for you."

"That's not an apology."

"I'm listening, and that's as good as you're going to get right now," she growls. "What did you have in mind?"

I exchange a look with Yorani, and she noses my cheek.

Turning back to Saiyana, I say, "You're going to let me walk into the room where you're holding Aleixo alone, and you're not going to interfere."

"And why," Saiyana says, "am I going to do that?"

"Because I'm going to perform the tea ceremony for you." I lift my kit.

"Now?" she asks, floored. "Miyara—"

"Now," I confirm, and bow. "It is my honor to serve you. Please be seated."

And with a last flabbergasted look, she is.

CHAPTER 26

SAIYANA'S OFFICE IS NOT a tea ceremony room. But it is a kind of setting that is familiar to her without being crushingly over-familiar to me, so it will do.

I find her kettle, sitting full of still, neglected water, and think, *This will do.*

"Here, I'll spell the water for you," Saiyana says, "since I'm sure you haven't practiced that in ages. Do you want a particular temperature?"

"No need," I say.

From my shoulder, Yorani lets out a breath of flame.

It circles the teapot like magic, then slowly fades. Yorani hops off my shoulder and snuggles in beside the kettle, next to the tea ceremony tray.

"...I see," Saiyana says.

No, she doesn't. Not yet.

But she will.

I bow, and begin.

In a way, performing a tea ceremony for a person I know well is a harder challenge than intuiting the needs of a stranger: the more I know, the more I feel compelled to encompass everything about their circumstance.

But in this case, I know precisely how to focus, and it begins in reverse, which is the crux of us: *made from earth, formed in water, released into open air.* I begin with me, for once, rather than her.

It is the surprise of power released into air, affecting the physical world, fire and allies and knowledge harnessed into action.

It is water, where we are formed, always there and never tended, left to fade into the background, but ready to be made, flowing into a hole, a needed shape, at a moment's notice.

And it is with the dark earth blend that I reach out to my sister with my branches, to show her my roots.

It is that she has treated me backward, starting with the model of strength she knows and putting me into it, rather than seeing me and drawing my strength out. She has always understood I could be powerful, but not *how*; not that there are ways different from hers.

But this is where my power lies: in connecting individuals. In seeing them, and drawing them out of the shadows where I grew, and hid, for so long. It is an implicit power, rather than explicit, impossible to comprehend for Saiyana, who deals in hard truths.

And yet: I can make her feel this.

I can walk into a room and command a princess' attention.

I can create substance out of where no one else sees value.

I can see into hearts and change minds without a word.

This is the power of tea, and ceremony, and it is mine.

Not greater than hers, but not lesser. Merely different.

And *mine*.

I will grow, and change, and I will still be her sister, a power to contend with as she always hoped, but I will do it on my own terms. Anything else would be a loss: for me, for her, for our duties and our people.

I see her love and her worry and her desire, I see who she is and how much she is capable of, and to that self I show her me: a pillar of flexible yet steady strength, and roots that will not be swayed by her.

Because I am not merely *enough*: I am strong, strengthening; and I will not let myself or anyone else be lost.

As I bring the tea ceremony to a close, Saiyana is struggling to control her expression.

"Drink," I say. *I know. It's fine.*

She does, and shudders.

I know she wants to reject that I have done anything real with only tea, but sitting here, in this moment, she can't deny the truth of me.

"I never knew—" she starts.

"I couldn't have told you, before," I say.

Saiyana takes a deep breath, visibly steadying herself.

"If I let you interrogate Aleixo alone," she says, "will you forgive me?"

For what she has tried to do, and done; for who she has been, for what she has said.

"This is work," I say, making my tone dry. "That was personal. So unless you actually apologize, no."

Saiyana laughs like a sob. "Spirits, you are tough these days," she says. "Fine, yes, Aleixo is all yours. Let's just... start with that."

I gather Yorani back and bow. "It is my honor to serve you."

The room Aleixo is being held in is sparse. Saiyana's headquarters are temporary and hardly designed for state prisoners, but she doesn't dare trust him elsewhere.

The room has been stripped of all magecraft except for what I recognize as my sister's own personal signature in the chamber pot behind a rapidly assembled curtain to keep his quarters hygienic and at least a touch humane, in the loose magic-suppressing cuffs around his wrists. There is a moderately uncomfortable wooden chair, which Aleixo sits in stubbornly, a discarded blanket folded neatly on the floor next to him. I sit across from him on a couch, a small table in between us.

Istalam's standards are also, I know, a very different treatment than a prisoner would receive in Velasar, and Aleixo does not trust it.

"Do you think I will be more cooperative than Ignasa?" Aleixo asks me idly.

"No, actually. I rather think the reverse, and I don't intend to speak with Ignasa at all."

While this would be true regardless, I have also learned that in the distraction Yorani's near-death presented, Ignasa, wily to the end, was not apprehended after all. Which means even more depends on the outcome of this conversation, and I will not falter.

I hold up a tea canister and rotate it slowly so he can inspect its lack of magecraft. I open the top and take a careful whiff, close it again, and lob it at him.

Aleixo lets it fall next to him without moving to catch it.

"I don't care if it's not poison," he says.

I shrug, walking around the table so I can pick it up; Aleixo doesn't move.

"It's a blend from Velasar," I say. "I thought you might like to ensure for yourself that I haven't adjusted it."

"I don't care," Aleixo repeats.

"I see that you do," I say as I return to the couch, his eyes narrowing behind me.

"You must realize I'm not going to fall for your tea master tricks," he sneers.

"Tricks," I repeat. "What a curious choice of words, coming from you."

He shrugs easily; too easily: a practiced response. "Then I would know to recognize them, wouldn't I?"

"I wonder," I say, holding the kettle up for Yorani to heat again. She does so, which is heartening, though she is still and watchful on my shoulder. Given her last experience with Aleixo, I thought she might reject anything to do with him.

"You may continue wondering," Aleixo says.

"May I always," I agree. Rather than performing a tea ceremony for Aleixo, I simply brew a pot of the Velasari tea: an unpretentious, stark blend with sharp spices that will taste to him like home.

If he drinks it.

"For someone who has no faith in my ability as a tea master to affect you, how interesting it is that you chose to attack me and my familiar," I say, petting Yorani.

Aleixo glances at her. "She's smaller."

"Yes," I say. "You attacked a true spirit, and hurt her deeply. She will recover, but through no grace of yours. You will have to account for yourself to the spirits. I hope you believe your cause just."

His face tightens, which tells me another useful thing: he does not. At least, not entirely.

"I'm not going to answer your questions," Aleixo says.

"Or drink my tea, or feel any remorse, or allow yourself to sit on a something as soft as a blanket in case it makes your spine less rigid," I remark. "Is that how General Braisa trained you?"

"Keep her name out of your mouth," Aleixo snaps.

"I've heard Princess Reyata speak of her before, and only with utmost respect," I say. "Given such recognition from her direct opposition on the fields of battle, please understand I can only regard her highly. But she is your former commander, is she not?"

"She will always command my loyalty," Aleixo tells me coldly. "Never expect different."

"I do not, in fact," I say. "On the contrary, it is what makes your behavior so confounding to me. Your government, and indeed Ignasa, are virulently anti-Istalam, but I know General Braisa is not. If I know that, I can only assume you must too. The general is a woman of honor, and yet you are a spy."

"Do you think spies are without honor?" Aleixo scoffs.

"There is gathering information to shore up your strength, and there is illicitly attacking your opponent from the shadows, using skills not your own," I say quietly. "I think General Braisa would be ashamed of what you have become involved in."

Aleixo looks away, and I sip my tea.

"There is truth in what you say," he says finally. "But I am not going to betray my people now."

I sigh. "We always come back to that, don't we? 'My people'. Who are they?"

"Don't twist my words," he warns. "You know exactly what I mean."

"Of course I do, but I don't think you understand mine," I say. "*My people*. Is it my friends, who you did your best to kill? Is it my community, whose livelihoods you devastated? Is it my neighbors, many of whom I've never met, but who share common experiences? Is it all of Sayorsen, or Istalam? The continent, or humanity?

"There are times when we have to choose, and this, Aleixo, is one of those for you. Are your people Ignasa and your current supervisors, whose goals you doubt? Are they the people of Velasar, who, if you are successful in destroying the barrier, will be devastated for the vainglory of your government? Are they your comrades from military service with General Braisa, whom you respect to this day? In whose interests are you silent?"

"Leave," Aleixo says.

"Oh, well, since you asked so nicely," I say, and stay exactly where I am, sipping again at my tea.

Aleixo breathes heavily, glaring at me.

"You really ought to have some of this," I say. "It'll likely be Istal everything for you from here on out."

"I'm not turning on my people," he grinds out.

"No, of course not," I say. "Only yourself, and in the scheme of things, what do you matter?" I let a note of my own scorn for such an ideology into my tone.

"I serve Velasar," Aleixo says, "in whatever capacity she requires."

I sigh. "You really have forgotten, haven't you? Why General Braisa will have your loyalty for all your days."

"I have forgotten nothing."

"Oh, then she made a habit of sacrificing individual soldiers for the greater good, did she? She treated you as interchangeable parts, rather than seeing your unique strengths and utilizing them accordingly? She did not absorb failures to protect her people who could not bear the consequences from them?"

Aleixo's scowl deepens with every word, and he finally demands, "What makes you so sure you know who the general is?"

"I am a tea master," I say, "and no one could command such loyalty as yours if she were not strong in the ways that matter. Which makes your choice to protect these people all the stranger."

"You've just pointed out General Braisa protected people who made mistakes," Aleixo says. "This is no different."

"Of course it's different. There is a distinction between people who make mistakes and people you believe are knowingly acting wrongly. More importantly, there is a distinction between protecting those with less power and sacrificing yourself for those who have more. Intentions matter, but so do actions; moreover, power dynamics matter, and you have misconstrued your place in those. Why do *your people* not protect *you*?"

"Because I don't need protection," Aleixo says. "I am not a liability like Lino. You are insinuating I have been led astray, as if I am too innocent to know what I am a part of. You are incorrect, and you will lose."

"Am I?" I ask. "You fired into the crowd at the festival, but your first shot didn't kill anyone. As soon as the witch began contesting you, you focused your attacks on her."

"A witch changes everything," Aleixo says. "Witches are the bane of this world."

"Yet it was a witch who protected the innocent people you would have murdered, so do spare me that nonsense," I say. "And whether she had witchcraft that could have countered you is a moot question: you did not try. You focused your attacks on the person who could fight back, and from that point on left the innocent people alone. Is that what you were tasked to do, Aleixo? No, don't give me the justification you'll give your superiors give the opportunity; we both know the answer."

"It's not a justification," Aleixo growls. "It—"

"Oh, do you want to talk to me after all, then?"

He snaps his mouth shut, and I shake my head.

"Careful, Aleixo," I say. "Perhaps you really should have some tea. It may help you focus on what matters."

"Why do you keep trying to make me drink this tea, if there's nothing special about it?" he snaps.

"Because you think it's meaningful not to drink it," I say, "when it is, in fact, simply tea."

"This, from the tea master?" he scoffs.

"Facts are facts," I say. "And the facts are these: that you are intentionally causing the barrier that keeps every single person on this continent alive to breach. The spirits will not grant us a second miracle. We will all die. Not just witches or Istals, but every single person on the continent, and Velasar will not be immune.

"You have been into the Cataclysm, and you understand, I hope, there is no amount of righteousness that could save you from it. Even if there were, if *you* don't possess such moral purity, and to be sure, you *don't*, then think how many of your countrymen you are killing, too."

"You don't know that," he says.

"I do," I say, "and so do you. Perhaps you didn't before you first entered the Cataclysm, but you know that now, too. The Cataclysm has nothing to do with ethics."

"Yes," Aleixo says, "it does."

"Really?" I ask. "Whose?"

He glances away. "Moral righteousness is not a mutable thing, tea master."

"Is that what the Nakrabi who gave you your destructive technology told you?"

Aleixo laughs shortly. "If you already know everything, why do you even need me?" He gestures at me vaguely. "You've already deployed defensive measures."

"You mean my bracelets," I say calmly. "Yes, their power is quite something, isn't it? And, of course, my familiar."

Aleixo's gaze sharpens on me. "You didn't know."

"There are many things I don't know," I say. "If I had all the answers, I wouldn't be here, attempting to rescue you."

"*Rescue* me?"

"From the mess you've made of your life," I say. "I'm sure it began innocently enough. A transfer, a promotion, a new way to serve Velasar in a way your skills are uniquely suited to. But you will destroy Velasar, and you will destroy yourself, and I am offering you a chance to avert your course while you can."

"Even if I agreed with you," Aleixo says, "it would be far too late for that."

"It is never too late," I say fiercely. "We can't always choose freely, but every choice we make matters. We can always turn the tide. We can always take a different path. And you may reject such wisdom as platitudes from me, but you know exactly whom I'm quoting, don't you?"

Aleixo's face shutters, because while General Braisa is not much given to speeches, she has a blunt eloquence that sticks with a person when she chooses to speak.

"What, exactly, are you offering?" he asks, scorn suffusing his voice—scorn for himself. "Asylum, a nicer cell? A seat on your private councils, perhaps?"

"A chance," I say. "What you make of it is for you. To make."

"Drink your tea, Aleixo."

His head bows, and his face isn't visible for a long moment.

When he looks up at me, the violent desperation and self-loathing I see in him is like a blow.

"This is why they sent you," he says, staring at me. "You, who have no standing in government, and who ought to have been just another victim."

"This is why I insisted on bringing myself here," I say, "because I will do whatever I must to protect *my* people."

I do not tell him whom I mean.

I only nod my chin toward his cup.

He picks it up, staring at it like it's the end of the world.

He closes his eyes, and sips.

"Spirits," he whispers, hoarse.

"I know," I say.

Aleixo glares at me. "You don't—" And then he subsides on a frustrated sigh. "I suppose you do."

"Tell me about the attack at the festival," I say.

"Not the breach?"

"We'll get there."

He sighs. "The weapons are dragon-made, which I assume you know by now. They should have been a stealth weapon that would enable us to do what we needed without being traced, and the ensuing consequences would be blamed on the Te Muraka. But I assume your counter here made them visible."

Yorani, who can bring the invisible into focus.

"Why?" I ask simply.

"Why attack you?" Aleixo snorts. "We're not amateurs, tea master. We know exactly who's making the investigation into us possible, hampering our movements."

My people.

"And we know your mechanism for stabilizing the Cataclysm—" He nods at my bracelets "—is actively preventing our success."

That is a statement that bears further examination, but not now.

"Success at," I prompt.

Aleixo looks ill as he regards me, and I meet his eyes with surety.

His echoes mine.

"Nakrabi technology, in exchange for the magic of the Cataclysm," he says. "That's Velasar's deal."

My heart pounds. "The magic?"

Aleixo nods. "They want to harness it for their own tech. Why, I don't know. But they've never been allowed to study it, so they're stealing it. We capture magic in their devices and transport it across the water, and then they send back new machines to fill up."

Many things begin to click into place.

Nakrabi farming technology, which kills the land itself—an effect the Isle of Nakrab won't feel. And when the machines break down, Taresal farmers must purchase new ones to remain competitive, and the cycle compounds.

But if Nakrabi tech has that effect here, and they want to use magic, perhaps to *power* it—

Then maybe they have run out of their own. Whereas here we have the greatest source of magic in the world, which they have no access to—

But through people like Kustio, black market deals that smuggle Te Muraka magic out of the Cataclysm and into the hands of bigots within Istalam, and Velasar, and onwards to catch the attention of the famously insular Isle of Nakrab. Velasar fixates on its target of Istalam so strongly they never realize, or perhaps simply decline to care, they've tapped the only currency Nakrab cares about.

And Thiano knew.

No: Thiano knows *more*.

"That's it?" Aleixo asks.

"Oh, no." I set my cup down and collecting Yorani. "If I might make a suggestion, you might consider offering your aid unraveling the former Lord Kustio's operation. I imagine you know many of his contacts?"

"Enough," Aleixo concedes. "Ignasa's still out there, though, isn't she? Her loyalties aren't like mine, and she won't give up on removing you as an obstacle to her job. I can help."

"Thank you," I say, "but that is something I can handle with my own resources."

Aleixo nods, staring down at his teacup. "I can't even do that right, huh," he whispers.

"You just made the choice to turn away from the path of destroying the world for the sake of a set of orders you don't believe in," I say. "Keep going that direction, and the rest will come."

Aleixo looks up at me again.

And bows, a formal Velasari obeisance.

I bow in return, and leave him there still prostrate.

Ignasa will continue her mission of destruction as an agent of Velasar and Nakrab. She won't stop.

But neither will I.

CHAPTER 27

I DON'T HAVE ANOTHER opportunity to sleep before the day of the third match of the tea tournament dawns. There are too many details to arrange. But ultimately, I only have so much time before I'm called to attend Ari's performance.

It is as spectacular as I could have imagined. Ari has created a three-dimensional theater with sparkling magical figures enacting a heart-rending story true to their past told through the perspective of a tea farmer of the destruction of the land and the long-reaching effects.

The tea Ari ultimately serves, according to the judges, is exquisite: it is made with all-natural ingredients local to Ari's home that they have cultivated through magecraft. No magical effects in this one, now that Ari has the audience's attention; they are, after all, a genius, and have learned about narrative symmetry and reaching out for emotions.

Ari hasn't, as I feared, made villains of witches or dragons in the performance. But their lack of inclusion in the hopeful resolution of Ari's story is a deliberate, telling erasure.

We are at odds after all.

But not, if I can help it, for long.

The crowd has already gathered at my chosen location for my part of the third match when the official calls for me to set up, apparently unable to believe I've prepared no more than this platform so the whole audience can see me equally.

I take Yorani on my shoulder, I take my tea kit, and I take the stage.

The official's voice is amplified for announcing as he asks, "You're sure you have nothing more to set up?"

"I have everything I need right here," I say. "I am ready to begin."

The crowd is buzzing as I unpack my kit, probably expecting magic. That's not what they'll be getting—at least not in the way they think.

The official begins, "It looks like Miyara is going to grace us with a tea ceremony! Miyara, will you tell us about this ritual?"

I shake my head. "It is for the audience to witness, and feel. Please, stand aside."

The official opens his mouth to object, to continue extending the lead-in, but he catches the warning in my eye—and for once, he heeds it.

"A mystery to the last," the official declares, vacating the stage. "Will Miyara present in defense of the dragons? Keep watching, and let's find out."

With Yorani on my shoulder, gazing out with me at the now curious audience, it's a reasonable leap. No doubt everyone expects me to stand for the Te Muraka, or perhaps the Gaellani.

Because no one ever stands for witches.

I'm going to change that.

I stand before my people, taking them in, and focusing; feeling their focus shift to me. I am at once grounded in my course and full to overflowing of the urge to reach out and take action.

I bow to them all, my heart pounding, the beat steady and driving, as roots should be.

The audience is quiet, waiting to see what I will say, what I will do.

I'm no longer a tea master living in obscurity.

I am a force.

"It is my honor to serve you," I say.

Here we go.

Yorani breathes a gentle flame onto the kettle I've brought, warming it. She's not going to watch this from a distance: she will be with me, on my shoulder the whole time, a part of this ceremony as much as I am.

I kneel, and we begin.

The people who've been in Sayorsen these past weeks are beginning to see that Te Muraka are in fact people, and to largely understand that Gaellani are people just like any other. There are exceptions, of course, people unwilling to face the source of their bad opinions, but exposing Kustio's plot has created a notable shift there, too.

The fear of the Te Muraka and what they will mean for Istalam is new, and can be reversed before it takes root. But the fear of Gaellani is deeper, going back to the fear of the Cataclysm, our collective trauma.

Which we as a society have made our witches bear.

That is the root, and I will root it out.

Into the stillness of my concentration, a light breaks, and I look up to meet it.

Across the clearing, in the middle of the audience, stands Ignasa.

With her is the same Nakrabi machine we saw in the Cataclysm so many days ago, and it is shining, a beam gathered at its core.

I see it coming, and know it is for me. But deep as I am falling into the ceremony, I remain kneeling, ready, open, and utterly unwilling to abandon my stand.

The bracelets on my wrists begin to glow, and so do Yorani's eyes.

From the corner of my eye I see magic I recognize as Saiyana's shoot at Ignasa's tech, attempting to circumvent what I know is coming. But it bounces off, reflecting as it does so a transparent, spherical shield around the Velasari agent.

Ignasa, evidently with more technological control these days, wastes not a second once the weapon is ready.

While my sister screams, Ignasa fires.

And a dark shadow blocks my view as Sa Rangim leaps from where he has been hidden, deflecting the beam with his own body.

"My apologies, Miyara, but I could not eat that one," Sa Rangim says. "That one is for eating."

It takes me a moment to parse his meaning: he couldn't simply destroy the beam, and nor could he inflict it on the audience before us.

So instead he has deflected it right into the barrier, where a hole begins to eat away like it's been struck with acid.

Breached.

Ignasa grins maniacally—

—right up until more Te Muraka emerge around us.

Perhaps she was depending on their being unwilling to risk further alienating their new neighbors with a display of force, or to be drawn back into the Cataclysm on behalf of their new and unreceptive neighbors.

If so, she was wrong.

The audience is clamoring but largely frozen, unsure where to turn.

"The Te Muraka stand for Miyara, a tea master in truth," Sa Rangim says, somehow directing his voice to both Ignasa and the audience. "She would not be in this position if she hadn't sacrificed her examination for us." He looks back at me. "And I want someday for all of my people to have the opportunity to strive and care as fiercely as Miyara does."

In that moment, it's as though all the pieces that have been coming together in my heart come together and crystallize, and I know, precisely, what my role is and should be.

And I stay right where I am, still moving, still commanding attention as magic begins to pour out of the Cataclysm through the hole Ignasa and her awful technology have breached in it.

The magic billows out, chaos finding form as it escapes into our world—in venomous plants, in conscious winds, in shape-changing monsters.

Saiyana charges past me over the stage to where Ostario is rapidly shielding, throwing her own structures into the mix as two of the strongest mages in Istalam attempt to hold back what no person or people have ever held back before.

Sa Rangim leaps again into the air, jaws snapping on a wind, and turns to me with glowing eyes.

"We will deal with the chaos that escapes the barrier," he tells me. "Focus."

"Us too!"

In front of the stage, Risteri has bagged a spiky critter, and a glance tells me Cataclysm guides around the clearing are doing the same.

"Everyone remain calm," an amplified voice comes.

Deniel. What? He was never part of my plan.

But he stands next to the ashen tournament official, where Saiyana had been set to coordinate if the crowd panicked.

"We will not evacuate," Deniel says firmly.

He is a city councilmember: a readily recognizable one, given the recent events in Sayorsen, and one who is, and has been, present.

When he speaks, the audience listens.

"We are here together," Deniel says, "and there is strength in that. Let the Te Muraka and the guides who know the Cataclysm best take care of you."

He looks across at me, meeting my eyes, and mine well with tears.

I expected nothing from him for this moment, but he has still managed to do exactly what I needed: to stand by me, to stay by my side, to support me when I can't shoulder the burden alone.

And in this case, to keep everyone else here, too.

"While I," Lorwyn says, emerging in front of Ignasa, "will take care of *you*."

"You can't stop me," Ignasa says, patting the machine, which is powering up once more. "Not now."

"Think your machine knows what to do with witchcraft?" Lorwyn taunts loudly. Boldly.

Around her, the audience *cheers*. She is a witch, but—no, *and*—she is *theirs*.

"I'll have a taste," Ignasa snarls, "and I'll swallow you."

The machine reaches full capacity.

"Let's do this," Lorwyn says.

Ignasa fires, once again aiming for me.

But this time, the beam bends around and meets a witchlight beam of Lorwyn's own.

"Did she say 'I'?" Glynis shouts from deep in the crowd. "She meant *we*."

"Witchcraft and magecraft together, you monster," Lorwyn snarls. "Try us."

They have it covered.

And we, Yorani and I, are not done.

I focus, sparing a motion to pet Yorani. With her beside me, I know exactly what we have to attempt. All that remains to be seen is whether we have grown strong enough together to make this work.

We never did test this in front of the barrier. Saiyana may have forgotten, or perhaps she decided to trust me. But although the second match of the tournament was in some sense practice for this, I have never performed the tea ceremony for a crowd before, not like this.

I'm dimly aware of Lorwyn feeding the harvesting machine focused magic, and her and Glynis' magecraft solution redirects its dreadful beam always towards Lorwyn, always making her the focus.

I'm dimly aware of Entero managing to break through Ignasa's shield and take her down. It doesn't stop the machine.

I'm dimly aware of Ari, exhausted and aloof Ari, stepping forward with all their knowledge and genius and stopping it personally.

I'm dimly aware that even as the Te Muraka and guides pluck Cataclysm creatures out of the very air we breathe, Saiyana and Ostario fight a losing battle: they can, just barely, and not for long, prevent the hole in the barrier from widening, but they cannot close it.

But that's fine.

That's why I'm here.

That's why we are *all* here.

Because I am performing this ceremony for the audience, and I reach out with the connection established at the start and tug their attention to me.

This tea ceremony is for all of us.

It is for Te Muraka and humans, sharing work.

It is for magecraft and witchcraft to come together.

It is for a witch to stand in the spotlight.

It is for the people the world neglects—those who live in the shadows and fringes, the refugees and the poor and the despised and the privileged—to come together, to support each other, to be valuable for being different and themselves.

With the tea ceremony, I weave us all together. Our roots are all in this land, now, and I draw on that, and the branches that reach out to each other and overlap and connect us all.

We are all Sayorsen. Witches are part of us, and there is space, and we will *make* that space.

We will reach out our hands in apology and welcome and commit to doing the work together.

With this tea ceremony, we each bear witness.

When I pour the tea, the cup overflows.

Out of the steam arises a spectral shape.

Then another.

And another.

The spirits keep coming, rushing out of the spout of the teapot, a spirit for every person in the audience, hundreds of them.

But this time, they don't fade away.

This time, glowing, they float right into the whole in the barrier.

And *then* they vanish—*into* the barrier. For each spirit that vanishes, a piece of the barrier is restored, grown back, the hole shrinking.

From my hand through my teapot comes a river of spirits shining like stars, flying into the night with our fears and hopes and being our dreams.

The breach in the barrier seals.

The world is still.

"I present, for your judgment, the dark earth blend, the traditional tea of roots," I say quietly. "With a spark of brightness in honor of my dear friend Lorwyn, a witch, made from an element of the most powerful chaos in our world."

In the end, I'm declared the champion of the tea tournament. The cause of witches has won the day.

But my work isn't done yet.

Surprising perhaps only the tea guild, I call them to a closed meeting with my sister.

In the same conference room where I was handed my future throughout this tournament, a piece in the game they'd laid out for me, now it is my turn to sit on the other side and tell them how things will be.

"Tea Master Miyara," a master I don't know—because aside from Karekin, I don't know any of them, and it is their fault—greets me. "It is our honor to make your acquaintance."

She has named me tea master, implicitly communicating that I have passed their test.

"Indeed," I say, and in not returning her the honor I begin my case.

She stiffens. "Are you a princess after all, then, to treat us with such disdain?"

Days ago, that hit would have landed.

Today, I say, "You should know precisely what I am. Or is tea guild lore not clear on what it means to produce tea spirits?"

Her eyes narrow. "What do you know of our lore?"

"Less than I ought to," I say. "Not enough to save my own tea spirit without outside intervention, and let me state clearly that I will never forgive you for allowing that danger to come to pass when you had every ability to prevent it."

The tea guild knowingly endangered Yorani by not educating me in her care, and I am going to shove that knowledge down their throats and lodge it there until I'm satisfied they will *never* repeat such an action.

"We—"

"Have no justification suitable," I interrupt. "And moreover, what I know about your *lore*, tea master, is what I have experienced myself *in communing with hundreds of spirits at once.*"

That shuts her up.

Saiyana watches from the sidelines, clearly enjoying the show, but knowing full well she has a part to play in it that I haven't yet revealed to her.

After exchanging glances with the other masters of the guild, the spokeswoman says, "We regret the hurt done to your tea spirit, and that lack of knowledge played a part in it. We would like to correct that now, and invite you to travel with members of the tea guild for a year, to accelerate that process."

"No," I say.

The guild's spokeswoman stills. "To refuse our education is to refuse your rank among us," she says.

"I refuse neither, only your terms," I say. "I am not leaving Sayorsen. To make amends, you will train me here."

"Amends? For your spirit's danger? Education—"

"—is only part of the guild's failures," I say. "It has become abundantly clear to me that the tea guild in its current form has failed across multiple axes. It has not, for instance, supported tea experts outside the guild, leading to wide distrust. You yourselves must believe the citizens don't have confidence in your judgment sufficiently to accept your standards for membership, or you would not have insisted on such a public trial for me.

"Furthermore, it is abundantly clear that the citizens of Sayorsen don't trust you enough to call when it is the precise skills of a tea master that are needed to address their problems. The tea guild has upheld the ideology of remaining separate from communities to maintain impartiality, but it's precisely that lack of connection that also inhibits your ability to solve problems. You can't resolve issues if no one will talk to you, not even due to lack of trust, but the deep-seated—and *earned*, as I judge by your behavior toward *me*—belief that authority only benefits the status quo. Or how else have you let the Gaellani's situation here continue for so long?"

"We can only come when called," the spokeswoman says.

"That's not good enough," I tell her.

And with that, I turn to my sister.

"If we don't make a different choice here, history will repeat itself all over again with the Te Muraka, and I won't have it," I say.

Saiyana eyes me narrowly. "So now you want to be a princess after all?"

"Absolutely not," I say. "The crown hasn't addressed the situation here with the Gaellani any more effectively than the tea guild."

"I'm working on it now."

"Correct me when I'm wrong," I say, and begin counting off on my fingers. "The Velasari have been found to be working to destabilize Istalam with Nakrabi technology that is likely also being used against Taresan, and this discovery will bring about far-ranging political repercussions."

"Correct."

"Changing a culture, as you said, takes time, and it is profoundly unlikely that a single act, even an act of magic on such a scale as what I produced today, will irrevocably change the tide of public opinion. Which means settling the Te Muraka, and changing the balance of power for the Gaellani, let alone witches, is going to take time."

"Correct," Saiyana says, but more slowly, because now she begins to see where I'm going with this.

"Not only do you specialize in crisis resolution, but specifically because of that, and your involvement in recent events, you are about to have an international mess on your personal plate and will be needed elsewhere. Leaving no one here qualified to manage the unique challenges and changes focused right here in Sayorsen."

Saiyana is silent.

"Correct?" I prod.

"You know it is." Saiyana sighs. "What do you have in mind?"

"You all have hopes and fears regarding whether I will be princess or tea master," I say. "So you will no doubt be pleased I have determined to be both."

Across the room, Tea Master Karekin declines to cover a smile.

These were the final pieces I needed: not just the practical understanding of what was happening with the barrier, and what I could do about it. But that Sayorsen is unique as a source of magic, which makes it the focus for machinations both domestic and international.

People will seek to steal what makes it unique, but we can restore it.

Because what I also realized is that I, too, am a focus and a source. I don't just need roots for myself; I am the tree trunk, branching out.

"Explain," Saiyana says. "You want to be, what, a tea master just for Sayorsen?"

"A tea master specifically for the *people* of Sayorsen," I say, "not the city."

"The people are the city," Saiyana says.

"And I want there to be no confusion that I am here to serve people, not institutions."

"You think the Sayorseni work with you?" Saiyana asks. "Tea masters are, as you yourself pointed out, known for keeping themselves removed."

"I will capitalize on that remove from the government, but not from the Sayorseni," I say. "And yes, they will talk to me, because they already do. They know I have put myself out for them at potential personal cost. I work, I run a business like they do, and I live in their neighborhoods. It matters."

Saiyana drums her fingers on the table. "The city council won't like an outsider."

"I trust you, dear sister, to make them accept it," I say sweetly.

Saiyana snorts. "You're a brat. Lay it out for me. What's the proposal?"

"Integrating the Te Muraka will take time, and we don't want a repetition of what happened to the Gaellani," I say. "And integration isn't a one-time crisis: it's an ongoing process, and I am suited to guiding the evolving situation."

"In a way I am not, you mean," Saiyana remarks, "on account of lacking patience and care for individual people."

"Because your strength is bringing your power to bear on or against people," I say. "Mine is bringing my power *for* them. I will be an advocate for communities outside the normal governmental structures, which have demonstrated they're not equipped to deal with Sayorsen's unique issues—the refugees, and simply the proximity to the Cataclysm—on their own, in their current forms. I will use my training in those structures to fight for the people the system has failed and serve as an independent counsel advising reform measures that will then set precedents you can use for all of Istalam, and beyond. Institutional change takes time, but Sayorsen needs it immediately. Let me leverage my power to impel it to progress faster."

Saiyana searches my face. "You're really doing this."

"I really am," I say softly. "I'm not going back to Miteran with you, Saiyana. I'm going to stay here." I turn to the tea guild. "As an independent tea master, whom you will nevertheless support. I claim the right. Will you dispute it?"

As the guardian of the first tea spirit seen in centuries.

As the victor and the betrayed party, of their ridiculous tournament test.

As the practitioner who successfully used their art to restore the barrier to the most dangerous phenomenon in our history.

"No," Tea Master Karekin says.

"Karekin," the spokeswoman snaps.

"No," he repeats, firmly. "We will not dispute your claim."

And she sighs, and after a moment, nods tightly, and waves him onward.

Karekin continues, "With your permission, Tea Master Miyara, I will stay in Sayorsen as the first of your tutors in what you should have learned from your aspirant mentor upon your attainment of mastery."

Of course, I hadn't had an aspirant mentor; I was self-taught. It is probably uncommon for an examiner, but Karekin has shown more attention to the circumstances of Sayorsen than anyone. I'm not sure any other master will be more on my side. "I accept."

He bows. "Then I look forward to formally inducting you into the tea guild. The tea guild has no objections to your proposal as outlined and concurs with your reasoning. Princess?"

Here, at last, is my true, final test:

Do I have the power to hold my place?

Do I have the power to make a place as I will it, and to induce those with power over my life—the tea guild *and* my sister, the seneschal of the realm—to accept *my* terms?

"Miyara has my support," Saiyana says, her throat thick. "In this and all things. By mutual agreement of the Istal government and the tea guild, Miyara is now officially the tea master for the people of Sayorsen. Let's get this on paper."

At last, I bow, trying not to cry.

Fought for and won, this is my home now; these are my people, and this is my place.

EPILOGUE

POLITICAL REPERCUSSIONS ARE COMING, but they are largely Saiyana's problem. Whereas somehow this strange group in front of me has become mine—and Ostario's.

Ostario is here at the shop to take his leave from Lorwyn, because she's his apprentice. But the lab is fuller than just us.

"I'm coming back," Ari tells a scowling Glynis. They're having trouble looking at me. "I'm not abandoning my home."

I look fondly at Yorani on my shoulder, thinking about how quickly being thrust into someone's life can morph into such an encompassing relationship.

Yorani is quieter than she was; still recovering, Sa Rangim thinks. I'll ask Tea Master Karekin if he concurs. Her mischief returns with every day, so I am content to make her tea and tend to her every whim, just to have her here with me again. Yorani, for once, seems to be antsy from such tireless attention. Her near-death scared me worse than her.

Ari flushes when Ostario's gentle hand lands on their shoulder. "Indeed not. Ari will be able to take advantage of the education they always should have had access to at the university. We know more about what precisely is happening to the land now, but not how, or how to reverse the problem, as Miyara's solution with the barrier is not currently scalable in that way."

"It also may not work on the earth," I point out, turning my attention away from Yorani for a moment. The barrier was restored by my actions during the tea tournament, but the barren patches remain.

"That doesn't mean you're coming back here," Glynis says. "That means you're going back to Taresan, when you're not in Miteran."

Without me, she doesn't add, but from the way Ari looks away, they understand.

Ostario answers, "Miyara has seen to it that, despite any tests to my credibility given the circumstances surrounding my rapid apprenticeship of Lorwyn, I'll be able to sponsor Ari at university as well."

That was most of what I'd spoken to Saiyana about days ago, and it's why Ari won't look me in the eyes now.

I don't know how to tell them everything is fine between us. The importance of any misunderstanding, disrespect, or competition have vanished for me. But I suppose the problem is perceived obligation, and I am perhaps the worst person to help Ari cope with *that* feeling.

I pet Yorani absently, reassuring myself tactilely that she's still there, even though I feel her with me in my heart. She noses my neck and then flicks my fingers with her tail—as clear of an 'I love you, but stop crowding me' as she can communicate, and I leave off.

"Ari will have to come back to Sayorsen as part of their research, since doing that research in Taresan would involve navigating far too many diplomatic and bureaucratic regulations," Ostario continues. "I will be supervising, so I can continue training Lorwyn. And that will give me the opportunity to train you, too, Glynis, if you'd like."

Glynis stares at him. "What?"

"You've shown a remarkable aptitude for magecraft, as well as interest," Ostario says. "You'll need training for the entrance exams, but I have no doubt you'll be able to follow Ari to university by next year, with me sponsoring you. If, that is, you wish to."

Glynis and Ari both stare at Ostario in shock.

Then Glynis whoops and launches herself at Ari, a one-armed hug they are totally flummoxed by but nevertheless causes them to grin foolishly.

"Did you do this?" Glynis demands, turning to face me.

"I hardly had to do anything," I say. "This was a pretty self-evident course to anyone who's been paying attention the last few weeks."

I learned later that Elowyn and Tamak were also involved in the setup of the spell in the final match—Elowyn by slipping through unseen, and Tamak by exuding an aura that encouraged people to get out of his way. It's possible I may have helped bring together a dangerous team.

I'm not sorry.

"Does this mean Glynis and I are going to be in lessons together?" Lorwyn asks Ostario, and I think he and I are both surprised by the poorly disguised note of hope in her voice.

But then, while Lorwyn is used to being alone with her magic, perhaps she doesn't wish to be. She is used to being surrounded with younger sisters, too, and she and Glynis have proven how well they work together.

"I think we will try it that way, yes," Ostario says, causing Glynis and Lorwyn to start playfully sniping at each other. Ostario turns to me and remarks dryly, "The longer I spend with you the more strays I seem to collect."

"They never should have been strays in the first place," I say. Our systems have failed, for all of them to have been abandoned without resources. Helping them individually won't change what's broken, but it's a start.

"True, and I wasn't complaining," Ostario says, watching them fondly. "I expect to acquire quite a reputation for unorthodox recruitment, which will no doubt garner more than my fair share of naysayers. I do look forward to being the most astonishingly successful mentor in history."

"I am glad you're taking this seriously." Although I'm teasing, I mean it.

He smiles crookedly and nods. "I've made it this far, after all, despite everything stacked against me," he says gravely. "I will do whatever I can to lift others up, too."

I bump my shoulder into him, and with a laugh he returns the gesture. In this, we have always understood each other, and it is perhaps why we get along so well.

And why I will be so delighted to have family ties between us if he and Saiyana manage to work their mutual attraction out.

"You don't know that you'll like Miteran," Ari is pointing out in front of us. "It's a bigger city than Sayorsen."

Glynis snorts. "*I* am a city girl, farm boy. I will do just fine there. And so will you." She glares at Ostario. "Won't they?"

At the stress on her last question, Ostario makes his expression serious. "People in cities do tend to be more progressive about attitudes toward gender," Ostario says. "I can't say they won't have any trouble, and there will certainly be other difficulties, but I will personally ensure they are safe to be whoever they are."

Lorwyn looks up at that, her instincts snagging on something.

But Ari, finally, looks at me—defiantly.

"I'm going to keep using 'they'," Ari says. "At least until I find a pronoun I like better. Ostario says that's normal."

It's not *quite* a question, but I nod anyway. "It is. You can always change your mind, and people will respect your choice. I'm glad you will have an environment where you can explore and choose whatever is best for you."

Ari's jaw works for a moment.

Glynis crosses her arms and waits.

"Thank you," Ari finally says.

"You are welcome," I say with utmost seriousness.

They nod, and before their flush finishes forming Ari has turned around and dragged Glynis with them.

But something about this conversation has made Lorwyn fixate on Ostario like a shark. "What if they want to change more than their gender?" Lorwyn asks him quietly.

"One thing at a time," Ostario says, meeting her gaze.

"That's it, though, isn't it," she presses. "Unlike magecraft, witchcraft changes the nature of physical reality, and I'm going to be a publicly trained witch. That's why you're bothering with me."

"I am bothering with you because everyone should have choices," Ostario says. "That includes you. And yes, Ari as well. I could change my own body. They should have the option as well."

"I can't be everywhere," Lorwyn protests. "Even if people ever decide to trust witches."

"I can't either," Ostario says. "And nor will many people choose to trust me, perhaps especially when it comes to witchcraft. But if I can help even one more person to be free and themself in this world, Lorwyn, then I will do so. What else is magic for?"

Ostario doesn't specify, but I know, and I think Lorwyn does too, that he's no longer talking about just Ari.

They hold each other's gaze for a long moment. Something passes between them, and I think it may be resolve.

Finally, Lorwyn wipes her hands across her eyes. "Miyara, let's take a walk. Ostario, if anything in my lab is destroyed before I get back, you'll regret it."

Ostario's eyes glint, and he ignores Ari and Glynis' enthusiastic emptying of Lorwyn's rock and stick magecraft stash onto the floor. "As if you'd be able to tell."

She casts a dirty look his way, and Ostario laughs.

"Yes, master," he says, sketching a dramatic bow as Lorwyn grabs my hand and drags me out the back and Yorani by extension.

We walk in silence until we pass into a familiar alley.

"I have to stop meeting people here," I remark.

She looks up, and around, and then scowls. "That is not where I meant to be walking."

I snicker, and we change course.

But being the first to break the silence is enough for Lorwyn to continue.

"We haven't talked," she says.

"I know," I say, because what she means is alone: after I met with Saiyana and the tea guild, Yorani and I both slept for almost a full day. I woke up to Lorwyn's glare and an anxious Risteri peppering her with questions about how to nurse a person back to health. There's been so much to catch up on—eating, first and foremost, but most time-consumingly checking in with my people after the events of the tea tournament—that I've hardly talked with anyone.

But for once, Lorwyn doesn't want to put a talk about feelings off, and I shouldn't get to.

"I'm sorry," I say. "I should have told you what I was planning, given how centrally it concerned you. I wasn't thinking of it as a manipulation, but it absolutely was, and I'm sorry."

Lorwyn lets out a breath. "I mean, I feel like I shouldn't encourage you here, but I absolutely would have freaked out if you'd told me."

"I know," I whisper. Which is why I hadn't, and why I should have.

"And I would have been wrong," Lorwyn says.

I glance at her, startled. "Ends don't justify means, though," I say cautiously.

She snorts. "Yeah, sure, but I trust your manipulative means."

"...that should probably concern us both."

"I don't trust that anyone actually cares about me," Lorwyn says, still facing ahead, rattling this off like it's a long-accepted fact of life. "I don't trust that anyone will actually work to help me. I don't trust that anyone will help if there isn't anything in it for them, and I definitely don't trust that anyone will actually want to. I would never have believed what you were planning wouldn't backfire, because I never would've believed you would—not that you would *do* it, I guess, but that you would mean it."

"That's a me problem. And you shouldn't have to lie to me because I have trust issues."

I'm more than a little shocked to hear this come out of her mouth, and that last makes me wince. "That's arguably why I especially shouldn't lie to you, even by omission."

"That's not what I'm saying," Lorwyn says.

"Are you saying you're not mad?"

"Not saying that either," she says dryly. "Though I'm so annoyed people who've avoided me for years are starting to come up to me in the market like I want to *talk* to them I probably should be madder than I am."

It's a start.

Not everything, not enough, but something to build on.

"Then what?"

"It's... I don't think I can explain what it felt like to stand in front of everyone and fight openly with witchcraft, knowing they wouldn't come after me—and that they even appreciated me, because of what you've done—"

"I feel I have to point out that in that moment you were useful to them," I interrupt softly, my throat tight.

"Oh, I know," Lorwyn says. "Believe me, I know. But in that moment, when I was visibly using witchcraft as offense, they also weren't afraid of me, which is more than I ever could have imagined."

"It's not enough."

"Will you let me get this out?" Lorwyn demands. "What I'm *trying* to say is that I didn't really think you meant it, when you said it would make it okay for me to be a witch."

"I didn't really expect you to," I say. "It wasn't your job to believe me; it was mine to do the work."

"Yeah, well, I still may not be up for whatever you decide is next on the list. But what I'm saying is I trust you," Lorwyn says. "And unlike with most people, I actually believe that, and I'm working on remembering. I'm saying you can lie to me if you think you need to. But that you probably don't need to."

I stare at her. That is an awareness of power that will stay with me. *No pressure.*

"That's moderately terrifying," I finally admit.

Lorwyn smiles slightly. "I know. That's why I figured I had to tell you."

I huff out a strangled laugh. "You're the worst."

"That's the other thing," Lorwyn says. "Just... don't put me on a pedestal, in your campaign, okay? I'm a person. I want to be able to be one, or else what's the point?"

My heart twists. She is such a better friend than I deserve. "Agreed. You brought me in from the rain, but you also made me drink beetlescale tea, and I'll remember."

"Good."

"There is one other thing," I say. "Risteri and I meant to talk to you together, but the way things keep going I'm not sure when that will happen."

"Talked about what?" Lorwyn asks suspiciously.

"Such trust," I murmur.

"Out with it."

"We want you to move in with us."

Lorwyn stops. Stares. "What?"

"We don't have a huge space, but Risteri says it would still be more room than you have with your sisters," I say. "And Sa Nikuran's been largely managing the restructure of the Te Muraka building and thinks she can move our walls around so there are three bedrooms without much trouble," I say. "Since I'm hardly there anyway and will be moving some things to Deniel's too, I won't need as much space, either.

That way you'll have space to focus, or sleep, or whatever—we thought this might work better than a permanent loan of our couch."

She's still staring. I rush on.

"I know it may seem impractical, since you can save money by living with your family and help them, but I think—and I know you know better than me, I swear—but I think in the long-term you can earn more and help them more by giving yourself space to grow. And in the short-term I'm confident we can get another sizable raise out of Talmeri for you, given recent events, which I'm working on already regardless: I'll be getting a stipend from the tea guild to defray her costs. So you should only move in if you want to, obviously."

Lorwyn stares some more.

I decide maybe staring means I should stop talking.

Finally, Lorwyn asks, "You've already done this much when you haven't even been awake a whole day yet?"

"I'm not sure how much I've *done*—"

"Miyara."

"Fine. Yes. So, will you?"

"I'll think about it," Lorwyn snaps. "*You're* the worst."

I can't say I'm surprised she doesn't know what to do with an offer like this. Risteri said she wouldn't have ever considered not living drowning in sisters. And she might not want to be so separate from her family, especially now, with so much changing. I can understand the need to want to hold onto stability.

But I want her to know Risteri and I can be roots for her, too.

"I should warn you that Entero already knows how to break in," I say.

Lorwyn shoots me a look that tells me she knows full well what I'm doing, but still says with a hint of amusement, "I will ward the place for free. Hey, Yorani, you ready?"

Yorani hops off my shoulder and onto Lorwyn's, and my heart clenches.

"What are you doing?" I ask.

"You two need a break," Lorwyn says. "I'll bring her with me to the festival."

"Being close will help her recover faster," I say. That's part of what it means for her to be my familiar.

"She is not going to waste away if you don't fuss over her for a few minutes," Lorwyn says. "She is being remarkably patient with you and understanding of your fear for her for a baby dragon only a few weeks old, but you need to let her fly on her own, too. I think she's demonstrated she knows enough about what matters to you. Don't you think?"

Yorani flutters back to me, chirping, and bonks me on the nose with her head.

I close my eyes, breathing deep.

Yorani's mischief is returning along with miniscule increments in size, but it's the understanding between us that has changed most. But right now, while Lorwyn is absolutely correct, I sense Yorani has another motive, and it's to make space for *both* of us.

We're different, but we'll always be together. Just as I see to her needs, she'll look out for mine, too.

"You know Deniel wants to meet before the festival, don't you?" I murmur to Yorani, whose tail twitches.

And my relationship with Deniel is between me and him, not me and him and Yorani—and Talsu.

Seeing me calm, Yorani hops back to Lorwyn's shoulder as she says, "It was never clear how much Yorani understood before, but either it's more now or she's decided to listen more. Either way you may want to start being careful what you say around her."

"Absolutely not," I say immediately. Then pause. "Except perhaps if I'm annoyed with a customer. They probably don't deserve what she can do to them."

Yorani huffs a little whorl of smoke, as if to dispute me.

Lorwyn snickers. "Go on. You can trust us."

I can, and I do.

After the first night of the festival was interrupted, and then the interruption, as it were, of the final match of the tea tournament, Sayorsen collectively decided to hold the lantern festival for one more night. It's expanded well beyond the Gaellani markets, too, with ethnically Istal

Sayorseni throwing themselves into the preparations. The only reason I even had a chance to notice was because of how hard it was for messengers to find my people given all the flurry of activity.

Deniel asked to meet me before the festival is fully in swing, before all our friends arrive, before goings-on carry us away. There have been so many interruptions for us, I think he doesn't want to risk any more delays between us. I can't say I disagree.

The festival is just beginning—energetic children and amused parents make up most of the people so far, and I smile as I wind my way between them, my heart filling.

"I think I will become a festival enthusiast, if this is the kind of happiness festivity brings into people's eyes," I comment, knowing exactly who has come up behind me from the shadows.

Thiano snorts. "You would. Just don't come trying to decorate my shop."

"I make no promises," I say serenely, matching my gait to his so we are walking together toward the grove where I am meeting Deniel. I look at him sidelong. "In fact, perhaps my demonstrable presence in your shop will help mitigate consequences for you somewhat. Because given what we now know of the Isle of Nakrab's involvement—with Velasar, and Kustio—this will no doubt have consequences for you."

"Oh, yes, absolutely," Thiano says, nodding easily. "There is nothing good in store for me after all this."

I stop, facing him. We are still in the middle of the mass of human happiness continuing to shift and move around us.

"Then why aren't you upset?" I ask.

"Because I'm playing a long game," Thiano says, staring at me. "And for the first time, I think there's a chance I might win."

His intent gaze leaves me no way to misunderstand what he thinks has changed for him.

This ought to be more pressure than what Lorwyn said earlier, but somehow, it isn't.

I hold up my wrists, as if showing off the bracelets. "I've grown quite comfortable wearing these," I say. "I don't suppose you'll tell me what they are?"

Thiano smiles enigmatically.

"Watch out!" a father cries as his child barrels into me. I catch the girl who's latched onto my leg and pass her gently back to her apologetic guardian.

When I look back, Thiano and all his enigmatic answers have gone.

※

"I brought markers for the lantern this time," Deniel says once I arrive in the grove.

"I thought this was a popular spot," I say. "Won't we be hogging it?"

"Not this early," Deniel says with a smile. "The competition for trysts will come later. Also, since it's still light out, I thought we'd be able to see what we were doing."

I settle in next to him, our arms brushing, and my heart rate accelerates like it always does when I'm with him like this. "Shall we do one together, then?"

He smiles at me, and I think my heart might explode.

"Yes," he answers softly.

Maybe someday I will stop blushing crimson with him, but it is not this day.

As the sun sets, we talk.

Deniel catches me up on how working with Saiyana has been going. "She was right about how much I would learn by watching her," he says. "Particularly about when she uses her knowledge, and how she uses her presence. The latter she says I'm picking up perfectly well from exposure to you already, but for the rest, she's going to arrange an apprenticeship with me through a law university back in Miteran. She'll be my tutor, and I'll be able to earn my degree remotely."

I gasp. "You're going to be able to get your degree? Deniel, that's amazing!"

"I know," he admits, sheepish. "I still don't entirely believe it yet. Saiyana says I will once she starts sending me paperwork. Not the homework, but the bureaucratic side of things."

I laugh and set my markers aside to hug him tightly to me.

A strain of lively music pops up from the festival, and Deniel pulls away, looking shy, and then offers me his hand. "Will you dance with me?"

I smile and bow over it. "Always."

I expect him to show me the rapid footwork I saw on our last visit, but instead he spins me slowly and then brings me in close.

At his—our—own pace, no matter the music.

"What have you been up to?" he asks. "Where's the little one?"

Moving together, I tell him, though once I've reached the part about inviting Lorwyn to move in with us I pause.

"What is it?" Deniel asks, one hand cupping my cheek.

He gazes into my eyes as we sway together to the music, and I gaze back.

"I love you," I say clearly.

Deniel's eyes widen, and a blush darkens his cheeks.

I see questions flitting through his eyes, doubts and hopes and finally, finally, he leans forward and kisses me sweetly.

I savor it, my heart hammering, pressing closer to him.

Deniel breaks away enough for us to breathe, leaning his forehead against mine.

"I love you too," he whispers, and it is perhaps even sweeter than his kiss.

Not because I had been worried about it, exactly, but hearing him say it is different, and it matters differently.

"I'm so happy I fear I'm going to burst," I whisper, and Deniel erupts in soft laughter.

"Then I will go with you," he says, "but let's at least wait until you're done with whatever you were saying."

I blink up at him.

Deniel smiles. "It's never just one thing with you."

I kiss him this time, this perfect person, laughing against his mouth.

This time, when we separate, I gasp, "I want to move in with you. I know it's sudden, and we were going to take things slow, but—"

"We can take some things slow and others quickly," Deniel says. "Our own pace is whatever we make it."

I peek up at him. "You don't mind, then? I didn't want to invite myself into your home, but—"

"I already invited you," Deniel says. "And I only didn't suggest this myself because I thought you might want to get used to the idea first. It hasn't been that long since you left the castle, and then you only just resettled with Risteri—"

"I didn't," I say seriously. "I only ever feel at home when I'm with you."

He smiles crookedly, and my heart flips over. "And I, you. I love you, Miyara. I'm ready if you are."

My smile outshines the emerging stars. "Then let's do it. My love."

We kiss, and we dance, in harmony with each other if not the world.

And soon our friends, my people, begin to arrive, invited into this space with us by Deniel. First Lorwyn and Yorani, then Risteri with Sa Nikuran and Sa Rangim followed closely by Entero, Elowyn, and Tamak; later Glynis and Ari, Saiyana and Ostario, and even Taseino and Meristo.

We release our lanterns into the sky together, and together we go to join the heart of this place, and by our existence together, change it.

THANK YOU

Thank you for reading!

I started posting Tea Princess Chronicles as a web serial in 2017, Kickstarted the whole series (and funded in an hour and a half!) to transform them into books in 2021, and now here we are. Whether you've been part of this journey for a while or are just joining in, thank you for being here.

If you enjoyed reading this book of the Tea Princess Chronicles, I hope you'll tell someone about it or leave a review!

For a FREE, newsletter-exclusive Tea Princess Chronicles short story, sign up for my newsletter at caseyblair.com! Subscribing will keep you in the loop on free fiction opportunities, sales, and new books.

Happy reading!
Casey

ABOUT THE AUTHOR

Casey Blair is a bestselling author of adventurous, feel-good fantasy novels with ambitious heroines and plenty of banter, including the completed cozy fantasy series Tea Princess Chronicles , the fantasy romance novella *The Sorceress Transcendent*, and the action anime-style novella *Consider the Dust*. Her own adventures have included teaching English in rural Japan, taking a train to Tibet, rappelling down waterfalls in Costa Rica, and practicing capoeira. She now lives in the Pacific Northwest and can be found dancing spontaneously, exploring forests around the world, or trapped under a cat.

For more information visit her website caseyblair.com or follow her on Instagram @CaseyLBlair.

ALSO BY

Tea Princess Chronicles

A Coup of Tea

Tea Set and Match

Royal Tea Service

Tales from a Magical Tea Shop: Stories of the Tea Princess Chronicles

Stand-Alone

The Sorceress Transcendent

Consider the Dust

Printed in the USA
CPSIA information can be obtained
at www.ICGtesting.com
LVHW031107250824
789209LV00004B/220

9 798985 110135